Collide

Shelly Crane

Collide - Shelly Crane

Editing services provided by Jennifer Nunez.
Printed in paperback September 2011 and available in Kindle and E-book format as of June 2011 through Amazon, Create Space and Barnes & Noble.

Printed in the United States

10 9 8 7 6 5 4 3 2 1

More information can be found at the author's website
http://shellycrane.blogspot.com

ISBN-13: 978-1463512545
ISBN-10: 1463512546

This book is dedicated
to my two boys who always keep me on my toes and my imagination flowing.
You are my inspiration for craziness and I love you!

PREFACE

The Black Ones. The Dark Ones. The Immortals. Lighters. They'd been called many things over the centuries, all of which were true.

The Keepers, ever watchful and ever evasively present, stood by and waited for the moment where they could no longer sit idle, for when they'd have to intervene once more. This wasn't the first time they'd fought for the humans, they always had, and it wasn't the first time they'd fought for earth. The Keepers just hoped that this wouldn't be the last time, that there would still be something left to protect and fight for.

The Keepers got ready to go, to make another appearance on earth, but this time, one Keeper in particular was overly anxious about this trip. Keepers weren't supposed to be anxious. He couldn't wait to see the person he'd guarded all these years in the flesh. He couldn't wait to finally meet the one he'd watched…even though he wasn't supposed to watch her…

Meet the Pattersons
Chapter 1

It was a busy Monday evening in foggy and wet Chicago. None of those things made for a good combination. The streets were packed, as were the sidewalks, with joggers and bikers, commuters making their way in all directions. The blinding sun over the ridge was irritating…

As was the smug little jerk in the seat next to me.

It irked me. I mean we're family and it shouldn't, but it did.

I fumbled with my sunglasses and dropped them from the visor onto the gear shift knob only to realize that they were now broken. Great! I squeezed my eyes shut for just a second in frustration. That just added to the fire already fueling my aggravation, but it still was not what irked me most.

Danny needed to learn some responsibility. He needed a car! What kind of man-boy didn't have a car these days? Why Mom and Dad thought that just because I lived near his job meant that I should be *obligated* to drive him around was beyond me, but I was never one to say no.

He was almost eighteen for goodness sake! When I was eighteen I had a job, a car, was living on my own and already in college, which I paid for all by myself. I was so done with all of it!

I put on my responsible big sister voice. "Danny, look. Believe it or not, I have a life. I'm not going to drive you around anymore and you have got to start taking some responsibility and buy yourself a car, among other things. You graduated high school! Make a plan for college or something. You can't just live with mom and dad forever, just because you think they'll let you," I said in a rush suddenly fearing I'd lose my nerve.

"Sure I can. That's the beauty of being the family baby. And no…you don't have a life," Danny looked at me so smugly, I could have punched that sickly sweet smile.

He knew he was telling the truth and it made me sick. I certainly wasn't allowed to behave this way when I lived at home. It wasn't fair and no, I didn't have a life, per say, not one worth mentioning, but I was doing better than him

7

even if my 'better' was the bottom of the food chain.

"Danny," I sighed, "don't you want a girlfriend someday? Don't you want to go to parties and have your own place away from your parents? And yes, I do have a life, that's what this," I spread my arms out wide for emphasis, "is called you know...a life."

Danny worked at 'The Coffee Place', which sold coffee in a drive through, and not good coffee I might add, with cheap Columbian blends and watered down flavored creamers. The only reason it was still even in business was because coffee was cool, coffee was hip. High school kids worked there and high school kids went there and hung out for hours on end, sitting at the outside booths under the little umbrellas, texting on their cell phones, reminding me of the carefree life I had not long ago.

Danny was not in high school anymore, but wanted to pretend that he still was.

"I'm not interested. I'm happy right where I am. Ambition isn't for all people," Danny said as he threw his wadded gum out the open car window.

"Daniel Lucas Patterson, that's the stupidest thing I've ever heard," I shot back running my hand through my curls in frustration. "Even if your ambition is to live with our parents forever, that's still an ambition, just not a good one. Don't be such a dork! You could do so much with your life. College doesn't have to take forever, like me, I've only gone for a few semesters but it's better than nothing. Besides, fine, don't go to college, but do something. Don't be one of those thirty year old guys who still lives with his parents and his mom folds his underwear." I paused and thought of another tactic. "College is really fun, you know. Just like high school, but cuter girls." I winked at him, hoping to appeal to his good humor.

He did not seem amused.

"You hated college and your life's not so great, Sherry. Quit being so high and mighty. You live in a crappy apartment, you don't have any money, you drive a piece of junk and you don't have a boyfriend anymore." He turned to look at me. "Matt wasn't so bad was he but you dumped him like everything else good. You are a glutton for punishment. You brought this all on yourself you know with your need for your *independence*," he said waving his hands in the air.

"Fine. Whatever. Just shut up, ok. But tell Mom and Dad I'm not your chauffeur anymore. Got it?"

"You tell them," Danny said as he got out and kicked closed my fragile and beaten door with his green Converses as he leapt for the curb by our parent's house, then stopped and turned around.

He still looked so young to me. Still my little Danny, though that physical description no longer applied since he had about a foot of height on me. His light brown curly, unruly, but styled that way hair and brown eyes were a family trait.

8

He was slim and it always puzzled me how because the kid could put away insane amounts of food and was incredibly lazy on top of that.

His Barista uniform was hilarious to me. Barista seemed like such a feminine term anyway, but the full on mocha apron with coffee steam swirls just added to my enjoyment.

I could see he had calmed down as he spoke.

"Look, I'm sorry ok. What's with the sporadic tantrums?" he said, leaning on the door with his palms.

I was suddenly very grateful to have such a perceptive pain in the butt for a sibling.

"I didn't get it," I barely whispered.

"What? I thought it was already decided?"

"Apparently not. They said my pictures were too...earnest," I scoffed. "I mean, whoever knew there was even such a thing, let alone it being a bad thing. I'm sorry if I was rough on you, I just know how hard it is, even with college let alone without it, trying to make it out here."

"Do Dad and Mom know?"

"No, I'm not telling them either until I find something else. I still have my job at the paper; I'm just looking for something different. Something catering more to my sense of propriety," I laughed. "It'd be nice to go home at night and not feel sleazy and useless and short a few brain cells. Sorry, ok? Truce?"

"Of course."

Danny leaned across the shut door to give me a hug. No matter how much we fought, we always forgave each other.

We were really close growing up. I was still in diapers myself when he was born, but I remember feeling like he was some precious thing that needed protecting. I was always telling my mom to 'be careful' and 'hold his head so it doesn't fall off'. She always laughed and followed my haphazard instructions. Even now, he still seemed like he needed my protection, from himself.

"Love ya, shorty. I'll tell Mom and Dad that you're busy and can't drive me anymore, ok."

"Thanks, brat. Love ya, too. See you Friday night right? Mom's birthday? What'd you get her?"

"A purple Bohemian scarf. You? Wait- the massage right? She *has* actually brought it up one time already this week."

"Really? Good. Yeah that's what she seems to like and I can't find anything I could ever give her that would make her happy other than that. Maybe I should've been a masseuse. That's holistic, she would have approved."

"You know you don't like it though. Just because you're good at something doesn't mean that's what you should be doing." He smiled at me angelically like he was making a point. "Dad's already got the piñata in the basement. It's the year of the Tiger. Man it's hideous. They are so wack."

We both laughed as he turned to walk away and into our parent's house.

As I watched him leave I pulled from the curb and drove up the hill, headed up to the ridge to overlook the city as I sometimes did when I needed to think. It was weird to some, but noise actually soothed me.

We've lived in the city our whole lives.

Looking out at the buildings and lights of a foggy Chicago, I needed to think tonight. My life was definitely not going as planned.

Thinking of the past made me feel...I don't know. The Pattersons: Mom, Margaret and Dad, Robert, were really into otherworldly things and practices.

Dad had always gotten mom a piñata for whatever the Chinese year was for her birthday, for good luck and union with the universe, and whatever. Mom was a feng shui designer and somehow made a decent living off of it. Dad was a dentist. Figure that one out, 'cause I never did.

Danny and I were always being lectured about the importance of things in and of this world, whatever they may be at the time: free speech, free will, free healthcare. I was more conservative than they were, but I let them have their fun and try to put their ideas of what the world should be to them in my brain.

And Matt, don't get me started on Matthew Borell. What did he think he was going to accomplish by stalking me? I thought this kind of stuff only happened to super models. I wasn't even the super model type! My short legs stopped right where they should and went no further. What was it that he saw in me that was so desirable?

I had always thought he was cute, gorgeous even, but never understood the opposite attraction. He hadn't always been like this, well not quite like this.

We used to have fun and he used to be somewhat nice. Although he was always possessive and demanding, I kind of liked that in the beginning, it was exciting. Then it got very old and even scary. I was too chicken to call the cops. He wouldn't have really hurt me was what I thought.

The next time he showed up on my doorstep in the middle of the night, I would definitely call the cops though. Yeah...

He wasn't particularly thrilled about the breakup or the fact that I refused to sleep with him. It wasn't love on either of our sides so I just couldn't do it.

So, he hit me.

He actually swung his hand back like some movie gangster and slapped me across the face.

I hadn't called the police that night either, which I regretted fiercely and I had to call in sick that next day. Thank goodness it was a Friday. I had the weekend for the bruises to dissipate and wouldn't have to tell anyone what had happened.

I didn't tell a soul, not even Danny.

I never spoke to Matt after that except to tell his answering machine to leave me alone, for good. We were together for all of five months, an eternity when I looked back. I thought I deserved such a man, because I couldn't do any better. No one had ever told me I was pretty.

Ever.

So it must be true that I was a plain Jane with a plain life to boot.

As I pulled out of my hidden spot behind the shrubs and the city sign, I paused and ran my hands through my dark wavy curls in frustration, twirling the ends between my fingers. My nervous tick. Some people bit their nails, some paced, I twirled.

Why did life have to be so hard and *so not* what we planned?

My boss at the paper - bless her - was evil incarnate. 'The Devil Wears Prada' had nothing on this lady, this she-beast. She acted like she was on some runway when she entered the lobby to the office, scarf blowing behind her like she was posing with a fan at some swanky photo shoot.

I could think of a few things to do with that scarf around her neck; tightening it being one of them.

My life at the Chicago Print wasn't dazzling in any light. I was one of the photographers and followed the journalists around to snap whatever story they deemed worthy, fiction or non-fiction. I wondered how many stories one paper could do on the local politicians getting busted yet again with prostitutes.

Prostitutes! Something I never dreamed my camera lens would ever see.

Most of my personal pictures were of the city, the night life, the lakes...people. That was my interest; real life not sleaze.

As for my personal life, my short ugly stint with Matt was over. That was the extent of my love life. Even though I had my small family, I felt completely alone. How could you be alone in a city of thousands? Ask me. It wasn't as hard as it sounded.

I sometimes felt like I was being watched though, even as a little girl I felt it. Like there was someone out there waiting for me or watching over me, maybe just seeing how I would turn out.

Mom thought I meant I was waiting for a boy. Maybe I was. She said 'the right boy will come along one day, when the stars align in your favor'.

She also told me that guardian spirits from Mother Nature watch us. They might even intervene if we needed badly enough. That was a nice idea. If that were true, my guardian was on an indefinite coffee break, apparently having more of a social life than me. Probably making eyes at someone else's guardian at the water cooler, causing problems.

For some reason, pulling away from the ridge, the lights, the noise, felt wrong, like it could be the last time. I didn't get into all that stuff like my mom; fortune tellers and scientology and fate, so I didn't really believe in premonitions or gut feelings, but I *was* always able to detect lies accurately.

Pulling up to the highway I felt a chill and the hair on my neck and arms stood up, making me stop again. The stars were particularly bright that night as I laid my head back on the headrest to settle myself, for one final last moment of peace before heading back to my nonexistent life. Then I realized something was missing.

"Where is the moon?"

Make Yourself At Home
One year later...
Chapter 2

The news said they weren't everywhere yet, mostly big cities, but logically wouldn't that be so, considering large cities held more people. Ratio to ratio it was probably the same everywhere.

I wasn't too keen on travel myself since all cell phone, national television and wireless broadcasting services had gone down a year ago. Land lines, local television networks and radio stations were all that was left.

Those poor people didn't know how to act without their precious technology and Danny was *still* sleeping on the couch.

My couch.

These things, these dark beings had begun to arrive, per the so called sightings that no one could actually produce evidence for. A prank? Aliens? A cult? Gothic angels? The questions were endless and the answers few. People disappeared, dying and then being seen again later. They looked human, but with black eyes and hair and acting strange, as the stories that poured in kept saying.

Wild and domestic dogs and animals were running off and killing themselves, running into traffic, jumping through electric fences and off cliffs and drowning in the rivers and pools. It was like they could sense something was wrong and couldn't face it alive.

The moon hadn't shone in a year and it apparently had something to do with *them*. It took a while to see the connection. No one realized that something was even happening until people started disappearing.

The weather was awfully strange, too. Cold when it shouldn't be, among other things, hail, freezing rain, snow in the summer. The government tried to assure us to continue to live our lives normally while they conjured up a response and course of action to the happenings.

No one knew or had said whether or not to fear the beings. No one wanted to be the one to have started a panic. There were mixed reactions as to what the beings might want since in a year, there had been no contact or message to indicate what they were doing here.

The paper I worked for was an alien gossip mill since then. The she-beast had me out photographing every fool in the street claiming to have seen one of the visitors or phantoms, but for the most part, people were living their lives...normally.

I glanced up into my bathroom mirror to see a pitiful sight. The only feature I would've labeled as nice was my long brown, curly hair, but the rest of me left something to be desired; boring brown eyes and five foot zero inches. Yeah, that's right, I was a toddler. I was healthy and petite, curvy yet slim.

As I looked in the mirror at my naked, wet, pale bathed body through the steam from my shower I was somewhat overwhelmed. If I saw me on the street I would think 'fragile' or 'too much coffee as a teen stunted her growth'. That was not really what I was going for. I was nineteen but to me I didn't look a day over sixteen.

I dragged my clothes on, slicking on a smidge of makeup. I wasn't sure what I'd classify my style as. I wasn't really trendy, not preppy, not grunge. Cute, I guess. That's what you get for having to shop in the Junior's department most of the time.

Most of my clothes were jeans or skirts with comfy plain V-neck t-shirts and layered tanks. My staples were silver hoop earrings, the necklace I wore every single day and coral toe nail polish. Probably pretty boring to others, but to me it was my comfort zone.

I swept my curls into a loose and low hanging shoulder ponytail and mentally prepared myself for yet another day in the life of me.

"Got anything to eat, sis?" Danny was already in the kitchen behind me when he asked me, startling me with his ninja quietness.

"Yeah, lunchmeat and sandwich bread. That's about it until I get back to the store."

He had been staying with me since our parents went off the deep end.

A whole clan of individuals had begun a club of sorts where they got together every day to meet at the ridge with signs pointed to the sky that said 'Welcome To Our Planet' and 'Make Yourself At Home' or 'Take Me With You', convinced that the beings were aliens trying to make contact with us, but were too scared of us beastly humans with our guns and Mohawks and pop stars and Republicans.

It was happening everywhere, every big city in the world had stories of invaders pouring out daily and every big city had a clan of idiots ready to welcome them with uneducated naïve open arms.

"Could you make me one, too? I have got to go into the office in a few minutes. Are you going to be ok here?" I asked, frantically looking for my keys.

"Yes and yes. I'm eighteen years old now, you know."

"I know that, but I'm still scared. Things are getting worse, more people are claiming to have seen them and I know it's probably a hoax, but I can't help it. This has been going on for months that we know about, who knows how long before that. Something is happening and despite what the Lefters say, it's not global warming. Something is happening. I don't think the world will ever be the same again. It's just going to keep getting worse, not better."

"You don't know that. We have no idea what's going on. I've never even seen one. Have you? No. Only hearsay. No one even has any pictures of them. I think it's just some kinda phenomenon blown way out of proportion."

"The moon missing is a phenomenon?" I countered, turning to face him akimbo.

"Yes. If the moon was really gone wouldn't it affect us? The tides? Why hasn't the earth skipped off into orbit because we were pulled off our rotational spin? Why hasn't anything they predicted happened yet? It's freaky, I'll grant you that. But aliens? Come on college girl, you can do better than that."

"I never said that's what I thought it was. I don't know. I'm trying hard not to have an opinion."

"Whatever. I'm hitching a ride with Jamie to work today. She's going to wear that button up shirt, not quite buttoned up all the way. I can feel it."

Danny's eyes glazed over like some idiot ogling cheerleaders at halftime as he spoke. I'd seen Jamie and yes, that was exactly what she'd be wearing.

"Swine. I'm out of here. Be careful and please come straight home after work unless you call me and leave a message at home, ok?"

"Yep. You, too. Wait, here's your sandwich! You owe me a load of laundry for it."

I rolled my eyes and grabbed it, hugged him swiftly, thankful for his good sense lately. Not in girls of course, but the street smarts anyway. We always called if we were late; we always looked out for each other and always hugged before leaving. We'd already been abandoned by our parents, literally. They called one year ago and told me they were sending Danny to live with me and we'd hear from them soon. Just like that.

Pain in the butt, yes. Brother I love and would kill for, yes.

When the news first started reporting on the visitors Matt had called or came by everyday, sometimes more than once, whining and crying about how he couldn't die knowing how he'd hurt me, he needed me, wanted me, I needed him.

As soon as the door was shut in his face though, the fist banging and cursing followed.

Danny had manned up once and went out there to defend my honor against some of the obscenities coming out of the foul mouth attached to the violent man who claimed he loved me. The only deterrent for Matt was the baseball bat in Danny's hands and the fact that he practically fell backwards down the stairs in his drunken stupor, leaving him embarrassed and disoriented. Any other time, Matt wouldn't have backed down and I was afraid of what would have happened to Danny.

Matt wasn't exactly little. He wasn't overweight, but he worked out incessantly. His eyes were deep brown and his hair black, short and a little wavy. He was tan and pretty gorgeous by anyone's standards which, as shallow as it sounded, was one reason I agreed to go out with a guy I didn't know anything about in the first place.

Sadly enough for a greeting story, we met at the grocery store...officially. He was way ahead of me in school, like five years ahead, but he never knew me and I never spoke to him. So for our first real meeting, Matt asked me out on our first date over the fresh vegetables. His pick up line was 'So you come here often?' and then he smiled crookedly letting me know it was lame and he was partially joking.

Back then, I thought it had been adorable. That night he took me to see the new Rocky movie, then to the local all night diner for an omelet. We talked about school and work. He was a personal trainer and he bragged about his clientele, though I'd never really heard of any of them. Some were the Ultimate Fighting Championship competitors, bouncers from Chicago's Vision night club and such. He was nice, talkative and well mannered. He didn't even try to kiss me at my door that night.

The next date though, it changed. He was a little bit more open with his opinions and even commented on how I shouldn't wear 'that skirt' anymore, because he thought it was a little too pleated and did nothing for my figure. Yeah...

When he dropped me off that night, there was a very demanding kiss. One where you're pressed against the door and just kind of hang on and wait to breathe. It wasn't my first kiss, but my first kiss like *that*. I was so wrapped up in the novelty of some big handsome guy vying for my affection that I couldn't do anything but let it all happen.

He called me 'girly', like every other word was 'girly'. What grown woman wanted to be called that by a grown man? Maybe it only upset me because it was coming from him and it wasn't really a term of endearment but more of a derogatory nickname.

Every since he hit me I had been avoiding him like the plague, but he was resilient and had lots of tricks.

It should boost my ego I guess, especially since he started stalking me.

16

Nothing like a stalker to tell people that you're desirable, however, it had the adverse affect. I felt worthless, unworthy of someone who could actually feel anything for me. Only buffoons wanted me as a mate, primal instinct to possess and control and scare, beating their chest and sometimes beating on me.

Also, the virgin thing had been a little much for him. That was the first time he laughed at me. Really laughed *at me*. He told me I was 'the silliest girl he'd ever met' and that he'd wait for me to warm up to the idea but he wouldn't wait forever and he meant it.

The night he hit me was the night he'd tried to force himself on me and I had to bite his ear to stop him and then run for it.

Arriving home tonight, there was no indication if Danny was home or not as he still had no car to be in the driveway. With the assumption that he was inside asleep I stepped out of the car and checked the mail. The B on my apartment mailbox was broken, making it look like an R. How I still got my mail was beyond comprehension and my laughable landlord could care less.

I headed up the wooden creaky steps to the upstairs apartment. The door was unlocked, surprising me as we always locked it. As I entered cautiously, I saw Danny asleep on the sofa and let out of sigh of relief. Idiot! He knew to lock the door. He could've been killed five times before he'd known someone was in here with him.

I turned on the television and almost sat on Danny's feet. Breaking News was playing, as always. It was beginning to be the boy who cried wolf around here.

Every day was news of the visitors or whatever was going on in the world that no one still seemed to actually see with their own eyes. This had to be the biggest hoax / exaggeration gone wild I'd ever seen. There probably wasn't anything going on at all, some trick with the upper atmosphere that obscured the moons view or something and people just panicked and started putting pieces together than didn't fit.

Was H.G Wells reading 'War of the Worlds' aloud somewhere? Maybe people were disappearing because they wanted to. Maybe they were scared or saw an opportunity. Whatever the reason, watching the news was pointless, yet there I found myself tuning in as I did every night like some mindless follower.

"The new visitor sighting today came from downtown. A woman, whose name we won't release for fear of her safety, claimed she was driving home when her car spun out of control and her husband's side of the car was slammed into a telephone pole. She also claimed there was a visitor in the road and that's why she had to swerve and lost control on the car, to miss him.

"She stated her husband's body was mangled and bleeding and that there was no way he could've survived. Once she was out of the car and trying to flag someone down, her husband climbed out of the window, without a scratch, and walked away from the scene, not speaking a word to her.

"No one has reported seeing a man on the highway near the accident and after a look at the car from officials, they say there is no way this man could have survived that crash. The pole came clean through the passenger side of the vehicle..."

They showed what appeared to be an elderly woman whose face was blotted out as the reporter asked her the dumbest question ever.

"Ma'am, how do you feel about what's happened here tonight?"

"Well...my husband didn't even speak to me. He just walked away, didn't even look at me. He didn't ask me if I was okay, he just didn't care..." the woman answered in barely a whisper and then let it drift off as she turned to hide her face from the camera.

Wow. Things were getting stranger and stranger.

The knock on the door startled me.

As I pushed Danny's feet off my lap and marveled at how that kid could sleep through anything, I pulled the door open, but kept the chain latched. Matt.

Dang it.

What I wouldn't have given for a peep hole. "What, Matt? Do you know what time it is?"

"It's only 8:30, Sherry. You haven't turned into a grandma on me already have you?"

"What do you want, Matt?" I said crossing my arms over my chest and looking out beyond him into the parking lot.

"I saw one of those things, a visitor. I wanted to give you the scoop. You can write a story about it."

"No thanks. I'm not a journalist, I'm a photographer."

I started to close the door, but he wedged his foot inside.

Was that alcohol I smelled? Again?

"I know that! I just thought you might want to talk to me about it. Talk to someone who's seen one for real."

His slurring wasn't as bad as usual.

"Nope, I really don't. Can you move your foot please?"

"Come on, Sherry, don't be like that! I just want to talk. I miss you, girly." He paused and gave me the pout lip for some serious dramatic effect. "Let me in. I want to talk, please?"

"You're drunk Matt and-"

"I'm not drunk!" he yelled, pounding his fist on the door jam. "Let me in! I just want to talk, that's all. Don't be a-."

"Shh! You're going to wake my neighbors. I'm not letting you in when you're like this, just leave."

"Sherry, baby, come on. You know you miss me. Nobody treats you like I do. We were good together weren't we, girly?" He tried to grab my arm through the crack, almost falling in the process.

Why was he using that conniving voice on me instead of brute force? He must have been more drunk than I thought.

"We are not good together. You hit."

"You bite," he growled.

"You tried to force yourself on me!"

"You owed me after six months of dating!" he spouted and banged the doorjamb with his fist to drive home his point. "It's not my fault I snapped when you went all Mike Tyson on me!"

"Five months of dating," I corrected. "I didn't draw blood anyway and no, I didn't owe you anything, especially not that."

"You're not religious, Sherry, ok, you're just a tease. You just wanted to toy with me and jerk me around just like you're doing right now with this whole hard-to-get act."

"Matt, if that's true then why do you want to be with me? Hmm? If I'm such an evil tease then why? Leave and be rid of me!"

Once again I tried to shut the door, in vain.

"You still owe me. You know how many dinners I shelled out for? How many movies tickets I bought? I could've been out with tons of other girls, but I picked you. I don't think I'm asking too much in return here."

"I'm not a hooker, Matt! I don't get paid or give payment as sex and I'm not a tease. I never led you on to think that's what was going to happen. I chose to stay a virgin and I'm sure as heck not gonna give that up to someone like you! I deserve something better than that and you do, too. You deserve someone who wants to put out every chance you get so leave and start your search for such a girl."

My blood was boiling. If I knew I could've slammed the door on his foot and had it closed shut, excusing the pain I would cause him as a casualty of war, I would have done it. Instead I was stuck in a banter of stupid and drunk.

"I didn't say you were a hooker, don't be so dramatic. Just let me in. Please, girly, please...please?" he crooned and begged sweetly.

"No, Matt. Leave or I'll call the police for real this time."

"Go ahead! I'm sure Barney would love to watch this!"

Barney, the one standing in the picture beside Matt while he wore his 'I'm

With Stupid' t-shirt under his gown at their high school graduation. He was no better than Matt and somehow had managed to finagle himself onto the police force and they both used that to their advantage at every turn.

"Danny is here."

I was reaching then, goose bumps running themselves down my arms, betraying me, making me shiver in front of him so he could see me afraid. Matt drunk was much more persistent than Matt not drunk. He wouldn't leave on his own. Crap.

"Ha! I'm five years that boys senior and I'm bigger, not to mention better looking. Go ahead! Wake him up! Danny! Daaanny!"

"Idiot! Shh!"

"Hey! Watch it! Don't talk to me like that. Do I need to break down the door, Sherry, or are you done playing games?"

Think quick. Think.

"Ok. Ok. You know what, Matt, you're right I guess. I do kinda miss you, too. I just didn't want to say you were right. I'm sorry. Back up and I'll open the chain."

"You're not tricking me are you?" He eyed me but I could see the relief on his face.

"Matt, you know I can't lie. You said so yourself."

"Alright, that's my girl. You won't regret this. You know I love you, girly, and I'm gonna make it all up to you."

I saw his foot move back and waited until it was all the way out because I only had one shot at it. As soon as I saw it was free, I slammed the door and pulled the deadbolt home.

The banging and cursing and idiot speak and empty cycles of apologies went on for almost two hours. Why was he so persistent? What the heck did I have that other girls didn't that he couldn't resist?

I was short and awkward. I'd seen plenty of better bodies. My hair was brown, mud brown no less. My boring brown eyes didn't scream starlet, they whispered movie extra. I was a nobody. What was it with him and what was with Danny? I hadn't been able to get a wink in since I got home and he was still snoring.

I was surprised the neighbors hadn't called the cops themselves making the situation worse. It wouldn't be the first time I'd encountered Barney in cop mode. An idiot with a nightstick, a gun and a donut gut with no brain. I'm not cop bashing, this guy ate donuts long before he was a police officer.

All of a sudden the noise stopped and I couldn't help but wonder what he was up to. As I pressed my ear to the door and tried to peek out the gap in the door jamb I fully expected him to jump out and scare me, laughing, but I saw no one.

I wouldn't test my theory by opening the door, and though I was certain he had given up, I knew I wouldn't get a wink of sleep tonight.

I'm on the ridge. The moon is back and the city is buzzing with life beneath me. I have a letter from 'Travel Journal' in my hand but I'm afraid to open it. I also have a crappy cup of Coffee Place coffee in my cup holder. Danny's jacket slung across the backseat where he forgot it, where he always forgets it.

My cell buzzes. I check it, a text from Matt saying he'll be late picking me up for dinner and a movie tonight. Then I realize, I'm dreaming. I'm rewinding my life back to the way it was before the bad news, the hit, the visitors or beings or phantoms.

I try to wake myself up but I glance up and all I can see is a dark shadow figure walking on the road as I turn my head to survey the area.

He is a silhouette under the street lamps. I can't tell if I know him or not but somehow I feel like he's familiar. Like I shouldn't be afraid. I say hello and wait for an answer but receive none.

He's still walking, though it seems like he's not making much progress for someone that isn't that far off. Again I say hello and he stops. He points up to the sky. As I take my gaze from him slowly and reluctantly I see what he's pointing to. I gasp as I see the red moon slowly eclipsing over and is no longer visible, making the stars shine brighter than ever.

It's so dark, I can't see anything around me. Pitch black now. I hate dark. No sound. Utter silence and darkness except for my suddenly quick breaths.

Fumbling quickly for my keys to turn on the car lights, I gasp as I hear the stranger's voice right next to my ear and feel his extremely warm breath on my neck.

"Wake up, Sherry."

Bright lights. Was I still dreaming? No, I had somehow positioned myself in such a way that the one stream of light coming in between the curtains was right on my face. Something else was in my face…feet. Gross, Danny!

I must've fallen asleep not too long ago on the floor with my head laid back on the couch. Danny was still snoring.

Ingrate.

I wondered if I should have woken him up and warned him about Matt. He might decide to come back.

"Danny. Danny." Shaking him slightly doesn't cut it but punching his arm does the trick. "Danny, I'm headed to work. Listen, Matt was here last night, drunk. He might come back tonight so, be careful and don't open the door for him ok?"

"Why didn't you wake me up? I would've handled him, like before." He rubbed his eyes with his palms and blinked, but I could still tell he was upset.

"Before he wasn't as drunk as last night and it was daylight. I don't want you trying to go up against him to defend me, do you hear me? If you got hurt because of me..."

"That's what brothers are for."

"I thought brothers were for mooching and sleeping all day." With a smile I headed out but not before saying, "Be careful. Do not open that door! I mean it."

The ride in my car was bumpy though the roads were smooth. When I was a kid I always wanted a rabbit, but not this kind. I wanted the furry cute kind that was forbidden in our house because 'animals are living creatures with minds and souls of their own, not our prisoners or playthings'.

If Mom only knew about the poor innocent turkey slices in my brown bag lunch today, she'd disown me.

I missed my parents, though the deep end of the crazy pool was getting kind of full these days. Who knew when they would give up and come back to society?

So, instead I had the Rabbit. My white '79 VW Rabbit with a few dents and dings that just gave it personality. As much as I loved to complain about it I also loved to defend it. For whatever reason I loved this car. I wouldn't trade it and I'd drive it until its last leg fell off.

The previous owner wasn't as in love with it as I was. They tried to fix it up, but ended up just messing stuff up and then leaving it half done. For instance, I probably had the only Rabbit in America with a bench front seat, of course, that meant I didn't have an emergency break either.

I couldn't restore it myself; I just figured one day I'd be able to get someone to do it for me. Unfortunately, that cost money. Money that a job at 'Travel Journal' would have provided.

Was it really wrong to almost hope that something would happen just so I can stop photographing bogus claims?

Of course, that was terrible. I couldn't be alone in this though, right? It had been almost a year since the strange things started happening and for me that was a year too long to do the same story. Maybe I could talk Medusa into letting me cover something else today, quickly looking away before she turned me to stone.

Medusa's refusal and following reel of cackling laughter sent a shot of fire though my already sleep deprived headache. Her waving me off like I didn't matter as she turned didn't help either.

The office was beginning to be what I always dreaded it would become. A place where I didn't want to go but was stuck because no other offers were open to me. I apparently wasn't as good at my job as I thought I was or at least wanted to be. I was the youngest photographer at the paper though, that had to count for something.

At least Danny was happy at The Coffee Place. I surely couldn't have made that statement without lying.

Funny how you can go through a whole day and speak to no one. Other than my boss and Danny that morning I literally spoke to no one. Again, in a city this size, being alone really was a skill.

Following Madison wasn't the worse thing I could've have been stuck doing. She wasn't a talker either and we could sit in silence comfortably, but as soon as she needed it, her 75 watt smile would turn on and she would be in story mode, asking all the right questions and making all the right facial expressions in response.

The older gentleman posed for his picture with his dead cat in a brown shoe box, covered in a huge green bow. That huge pointless bow on a cat casket freaked me out almost as much the dead cat inside it.

He told us that one of the visitors had looked at his cat and the cat had fallen over dead right there on the sidewalk. He tried to get the government to test it for alien residue, but the FBI had refused and he was perplexed as to why.

He thought if he went to the media, they would take his claim seriously. Unfortunately, he picked the wrong paper for it to be credible. Poor guy. How were people getting so enthralled in this stuff?

After picking up some fast food dinner, a couple of burgers, I pulled into my driveway, looking around first for Matt. Seeing nothing I stepped out of the car and locked my door, putting the top up. I walked over to the mailbox juggling my purse, the food, my jacket, my camera and keys. I cut the end of my finger on the rusty broken letter on the mailbox, the envelope on top showing a bloody fingerprint on it and the mail added to the juggling act.

I was preoccupied with that and didn't think to look back around, though I couldn't have out run Matt even if I wanted to.

And then there he was, standing not ten feet from me, in between my locked car and the supposed to be locked house. He said nothing at first, just stared silently.

I tried not to gasp, but I felt my breathing pick up involuntarily. I tightened my hands to stop the shake so he wouldn't see, but I could feel them start to tremble. I silently cursed myself for not reporting him to the cops already.

He wasn't drunk this time, I could see his eyes were clear. Why was he staring at me like that? Should I run? Should I even try and give him the satisfaction of chasing me? No. I froze.

"Matt?" I barely whispered out his name, but I knew he could hear me.

He furrowed his brow at me, looking confused as I said his name. Then he looked horrified. Then...he finally spoke. "Sherry, don't run. Don't be afraid."

A New Kind Of Fright
Chapter 3

"Matt, what are you doing here?" I said as soft and pleading as possible. "I told you last night that I don't want you here. Please, just...leave me alone. Are you trying to scare me? Do you want me to be afraid of you?"

I tried to use my sweet innocent voice, hopefully pleading with something humane still left in him.

"Sherry, listen, please. I know you're scared of me and I know this sounds crazy, but I need you to open your mind and just listen to me for a minute, ok? I need you to come with me."

"Um...it's late," I stalled. "I'd really rather just go inside. I had a long day and don't really feel that good."

I stepped he stepped.

"Sherry, please, just trust me."

"Are you kidding?" I squealed. "What do you want, Matt?"

"I need you and Danny to come with me. Right now. You're in danger."

"There is no way I'm going anywhere with you. You're not drunk are you?"

I thought not but something was definitely wrong with him.

"Please, Sherry," he pleaded, "we don't have time for this. Just come with me. I'll let you drive."

"Oh, that helps," I said sarcastically, but regretted it for fear of angering him.

He paused. He paused and stared so long I thought he wouldn't say anything else and then...

"You don't have to fear me. I'm not...Matt."

"Matt! Stop it! It's not funny!" I yelled as I mentally catalogued everything in my purse, searching for something to use as a weapon but was coming up with nothing.

"I'm not trying to be funny, Sherry, just listen. The strange things going on in your world..." he started as I began to inch backwards towards the stairs.

He saw and made the same small advances towards me.

"What? What are you saying?"

"Matt...died, Sherry. I know this is odd and unsettling for you and I'll explain everything later, but we don't have time. I'm here to help you and we need to leave, right now."

I couldn't handle it anymore. Matt's freakish behavior could only be a distraction for something bigger that I was not ready to deal with.

I turned and pushed my legs to their full speed, dropping the mail and everything else, but he was already right there in front of me. Impossible! He reached for my wrist and turned me so fast my head swam and my vision blurred.

He grabbed me, covering my mouth with his insanely warm palm, and pushed my back against the wall by the stairway, holding me there. His body pressed against mine to keep me still. All I could hear were my gasping breaths muffled through his hand.

I closed my eyes shut tight and tried to brace myself for the desecration of my body, but exactly how do you do that?

Nothing.

I opened my eyes cautiously. He was just standing there, staring at me, holding my hands above my head with one hand and his other was still over my mouth, gently. I thought about trying to bite him, but the last time I bit him, it didn't end so well for me.

He just stood there, for at least a minute. Not a word. Just looking into my eyes, breathing heavy with confusion, like I'd never seen him do before. Looking unsure of himself. Not at all like Matt.

Finally he licked his lips and spoke.

"Sherry, I'm going to uncover your mouth. Please don't scream. I'm not going to hurt you, I promise, that's not what I'm here for. I just need you to listen to me. It's very important and we don't have time for this. Can I uncover your mouth?"

Sure, but would I scream? Probably, but as his hand slipped slowly from my mouth and up my arm to my hands with the other, I didn't make a peep. I just stared with frightful anticipation of his next move.

His eyes flicked back and forth from my features. My mouth, my eyes, my hair. He was definitely upping his game of trickery.

"I'm not Matt, ok, I need you to understand that. After everything going on, the moon and the visitors, I'm sure you can comprehend this. I'm not Matt. Matt died in a car crash about five hours ago in Orland Park. He was drunk and was out there by himself in his truck. I know your world has noticed the strange events taking place. I am a part of that and I'm on your side, but...they're coming. I need you to believe me and to get Danny. We have to go. Now."

Wow, Matt was really reaching. Did he think I was so spooked by all this that I would believe this cockamamie story? Last night his story was that he saw one. Tonight it's that he *is* one? What did I ever see in him?

I tried to squirm, move a leg, pull my arms down, something, but he was holding me so tightly, surprisingly not hurtful, but I still couldn't budge. He didn't seem upset by my squirming, just held me tight and watched me closely.

"Matt - I mean, whoever you are - let me go, and then we'll talk, ok? I'll go inside to get Danny and I'll be right back and then we can go. Ok?" I lied, badly.

I couldn't lie and everyone who knew me knew it, including Matt.

He must have heard the lie, too, because all of a sudden his left hand slipped under the hem of my shirt, rubbing and searching my belly and back, like he was looking for something...specific.

Then my skirt, same thing, checking my inner and outer thighs and behind my knees. It was all I could do not to knee him somewhere painful but he was still pressing against me as much as his searching would allow.

"They haven't gotten to you yet have they? I don't feel anything. Whew. Ok," he rushed the words out in a breath of relief, it seemed, as he looked around.

He was talking to himself more than me so I just stayed quiet, trying to process and think of what kind of angle Matt could be using. Why the charade? He could overpower me in a second. Why the game and why was his breathing so out of control?

"Sherry, I can see that you still don't believe me so, I'm sorry about this, but I can't waste any more time. I never meant to come here as Matt, that was a huge mistake. I hope you'll forgive me for that someday."

He barely finished his sentence before he poked something in my arm. I could feel the prick, but had no time to react. I couldn't stay awake and in only seconds it was black as night. My eyes closed against their will, though I was still conscience, but couldn't see or move. My arms and legs went limp as I started to slump to the ground.

What? Why would Matt do that? Was he kidnapping me?

I could feel him catch me up before I fell and throw me over his shoulder, bend, quite easily actually, and grabbed my keys from the ground, walking me to the car. He unlocked it and put the top back down, impressively with one hand.

The cold, scratchy and torn leather of the Rabbit was biting against my legs as he placed me gently in the back seat. Then he left me there. Silent minutes passed in the dark, alone.

My skirt was bunched up passed the comfortable point of my thighs, but I couldn't reach to pull it down. Suddenly I heard voices and I panicked, but soon recognized them. Danny and Matt were coming and I felt them climbing in.

"What happened?" Danny almost yelled as he took his jacket off to throw over my legs.

I tried to speak, but couldn't. Then I realized he was not talking to me.

"She fainted, but she's ok," Matt said, with a clear voice, only a faint indication of the lie that he was telling.

"What happened? She really saw one?" Danny said sounding really worried.

I felt him pushing my hair back to see my face better.

"Yes, it was waiting for her when she got home but I scared it off," Matt lied some more.

"What did it want?"

"I don't know but don't worry. I'm taking you guys somewhere safe. Look, I'm sorry if I've been...not so nice lately. I'm really sorry. Just trust me when I say that I love your sister and I won't let anything happen to her...or you. Ok?"

Jeez. He really sounded sincere. I couldn't hear a lie at all. He has never said he loved me like that before. Not without a condescending 'baby' or 'girly' at the end. Maybe those stupid one act acting lessons at the community college paid off for him after all.

Danny didn't say another word, just climbed in and started the car. I could tell he was the one driving by the horrid grinding of the gears and the all too fast take off, spinning the gravel rocks in our driveway.

I still kept testing myself, so sure that I would come out of it soon and awaken to reveal this fraud for what it was.

Where was he taking us anyway?

I stayed still and listened to Matt's instructions of where to go. They didn't say much else. Danny asked Matt why he had been harassing me. Matt explained that he had a drinking problem, but was getting help. Lies. Matt *did* have a drinking problem, but he wasn't getting help. He would never admit he had a problem.

I felt it as we pulled to a stop. I almost fell into the floor board with the momentum, but swung back just in time.

"Where are we?" Danny, finally, started getting inquisitive. Only an hour too late!

"A little place I found. We'll be safe here. Nobody knows about this place."

"A warehouse? What are we going to do there? I mean, we don't have food or anything."

"I'll handle that. First let's get her inside before he figures it out and comes for her again."

"Can he track her or something?"

"Um, yes," Matt lied.

"Ok. Let me-" Danny said and I felt him tug at my arm.

"No, I'll get her. I'm faster with the weight. You grab the duffel bag from the trunk if you don't mind," Matt said as he gently lifted me from the back seat under my back and knees, cradling me to his chest.

Wow, he was warm. Really warm. Maybe he was running a fever. Maybe he was in some fever induced delusion.

He was probably carrying me to my death in some Silence of the Lambs craziness! He was not the man I thought he was.

They weren't talking anymore as we walked, and I could smell dust, oil and mold as Matt carried me through the warehouse. We stopped.

"Does it work?" I heard Danny ask.

"Yes. I put these things here in front to hide it. We'll be safe."

"Wow. Thorough, Matt. Thorough," Danny said approvingly.

He told Danny that he was Matt? Ugh. Why the charade with me and not Danny? Didn't think he'd believe it I guess.

I can feel us moving down, like an elevator. It was squealing and screeching and hot in there, it seemed to go on forever.

"What kind of place is this? Who has an elevator that goes down in a warehouse?" Danny asked.

"The kind of people who want to hide things. We can turn off the elevator once we're at the bottom so no one else can come down after us."

"Nice. Thanks man, you saved her. I owe you."

"No problem."

No problem? Was I ever going to wake up?

Who knew how many floors the elevator went down before we jolted to a stop. A lot or that elevator was slower than molasses. I assumed Danny went to look around because Matt carried me silently to one of the rooms. I felt him maneuver us through the doorway.

A big comfy chair was under me, one that smelled like antiseptic. He set me down in it and took my face in between his hands. I wanted to gasp at his touch and closeness but my body refused.

"I know you can still hear me in there. I'm sorry I had to do that to you, but I had to get you and Danny to safety. It'll still be a while until you wake up. Listen, I know how this sounds and looks and I can explain everything to you both when you wake up, but I'm not Matt. Matt is dead and I'm sorry to be the one to tell you that. I'm not here to hurt you or Danny. We're underground in a warehouse with only one way in and one way out. The elevator and I have the key. I promise you, I'm not going to hurt you. I'm here to help.

"We are going to be here together for a while so it would be nice if you'd get use to the idea... Sherry," he breathed my name with such a sweet tone. I could feel his breath on my face. He was closer. "I can't believe I'm actually here, actually touching you." His thumb rubbed back and forth over my cheek. "You don't know how long I've... Just try to get some sleep. We'll go over everything together later. By the way, my name is Merrick. I'll be around when you wake up."

He let his hands slide away from my face slowly, almost reluctantly, and then I heard him shuffle from the room. What was all that? Why was he touching me like that?

I was more confused than ever.

Could it be real? Did this have something to do with the visitors or the moon? No. This isn't the...twilight zone. I can't decide whether to believe this or not. I'm thinking not and he wants me to sleep? Really? Matt already caused me one sleepless night and now this.

Dang it! I must've fallen asleep. Wait. My arms, they're moving but why aren't my eyes opening? I pulled my wobbly hands up to my face and pried my eyelid open with my shaking fingers.

The room had a cot and a bed? Looked like a hospital or something? What the... I could feel my eyes start to flutter, back under my command. I could see flashes of light blinking in front of them.

I didn't feel right, but I felt somewhat back to normal. I couldn't hear anything but the humming of appliances. Where was Danny? Where was Matt? I got up slowly, fighting to get my bearings and peeked out the room into the hall. This place was huge, rooms and halls all down the way.

I entered the hall, peeking first. I couldn't hide in there forever. Wait. Danny!

"Danny!" I yelled, knowing that it would alert Matt but not caring at the moment.

I could see Danny in the room next to mine, but his door was locked and he was lying on the bed.

Matt turned the corner cautiously. I recoiled into the wall, hitting my funny bone on the door knob, letting out a little gasp and rubbing the sore spot. Matt inched towards me, his hands up in front of him as if in surrender.

"Sherry, come on. Let's go talk. I'll answer any questions you have, just please, don't do this. I don't want you to hurt yourself."

"Stop it! Like you really care about me. You kidnapped me!"

"Sherry, don't. Please."

"Why did you lock my brother up in there then?" I asked, still inching back along the wall.

"Because...I knew you'd wake up and I wouldn't be able to fend you both off without hurting someone. So I put him in there, because he's bigger. I'd rather worry about you than him."

I was too scared to be offended by that right then, so I let it slide that time.

"What do you want, Matt? Why did you do this?"

"I told you, I'm not Matt. My name is Merrick. I'm a Keeper," He seemed to be getting a little exasperated, but he was telling the truth.

"A Keeper? Hmm...and what exactly is that?" I snapped, crossing my arms over my chest and waited for the slue of lies to spill out.

"A guardian. I've been watching you, well Danny, every since he was born. I'm his guardian, a Keeper, and he is a Special. My charge."

All true.

"A Special?"

"Yes. Someone destined to do an act or something of importance towards the greater good of mankind, thus needs to be protected until that act can be carried out in the way that was preordained. That's why I'm here."

Was he reading a script? I could tell he at least thought he was telling the truth but I wasn't giving in that easy.

"Matt- I mean Merrick, why would I believe you? You drugged me, you kidnapped me, and took me and my brother somewhere, where only you have the key."

Suddenly there were thoughts in my head, thoughts not my own, words I wasn't speaking and his lips weren't moving, but his eyes were glued to mine. Pleading.

Sherry, please, I know you can tell if I'm lying. I don't want to frighten you but you leave me no choice. I'm a Keeper and my name is Merrick and you are safe with me. Please. Come sit down and listen. I'll tell you everything.

My mouth dropped open. My breaths quickened, but I couldn't feel it in my numb shocked lungs. It didn't sound like Matt, it was another voice altogether but it was coming from the being across from me. I didn't break eye contact with him, I couldn't. He did it again.

Danny is fine. I gave him the same thing I gave you. I just didn't want him to jump me before I could explain everything to you. Will you let me? So you'll understand what's going on. You will have to help me explain it to him. Please? Come sit with me. I won't touch you, I promise.

I couldn't not go. My body moved without my permission. It wasn't him doing it. It was pure fright and intrigue. If he could go in my mind, what else could he do to me?

I walked slowly and carefully towards him, hugging the wall like I was balancing on a ledge. I sat in the white club chair he motioned to in the little vestibule at the end of the hall and continued to stare at him, drawing my legs up under me for some semblance of personal comfort. He began, not waiting for me to come out of the shock.

"As I said," he began, and sat in the identical chair on the other side of the

31

side table, "I'm a Keeper. We are not from your world. We watch over you humans, the ones who are deemed as Specials. We have a forty eight hour time window. We see that far into the future so we can intervene if needed to make sure the Special is safe until the task has been fulfilled."

"What task?" I interrupted, but it just popped out.

"We don't know until it happens. We just know to guard them until it does. There are others out there, we call then Lighters. They try to interfere from time to time with the Specials. Now they are here to mess with everyone. They are your black eye and hair persons that you have been reporting on. They remain undetected because they cannot be photographed or filmed by your media. I'm not sure why. They are the Keeper's opposites. They come to Earth and claim bodies so they can take the lives of Specials before their time, to keep them from fulfilling the task. We are a balance, well, we were, but they have broken the rules and we can no longer stand by and watch them destroy you. They are planning a mass destruction of the Specials which would mean a slow spiraling end of the human race. They can only enter the atmosphere after taking someone....a dead person. If they stay, the world is out of balance. That's why your moon is gone. It's still there, but the light has gone out because the Lighters are all here. They've been turning people against each other, looking for Specials to invade or kill, tricking people into thinking that they are here to save you from us. The only way to tell a Lighter from a Keeper is the symbol behind our ear, and they have the dark hair and eyes and when you break a Lighter's skin, you can see the light that's on the inside."

He reached over slowly, pulling his ear lobe back so I could see the black tattoo looking symbol behind his ear. It looked like a circle with some lines across it.

"How did you get in my head?" I asked, having no idea why that was the first question I chose to ask.

"I can speak to you without talking with my mouth. All Keepers can, but we can't hear your thoughts."

That was my next question.

"Your eyes..." I started and drifted off, not really understanding what I was seeing. "Matt's eyes were brown."

"Yes. We bring our own eyes with us into the body."

Hmm. Strange looking at Matt- I mean Merrick's face with different color eyes.

"Why do you care about what happens to us?" I asked.

"We have always been there. Always cared. Ever since you were created, it's just who we are. Your God who created you created us as well, just as He did everything else. You have heard us referred to as aliens, guardian angels, ghosts, phantoms. We call ourselves Keepers."

32

"So Danny is a Special? Am I?"

"No."

"But you said you've watched me and couldn't believe...you were actually here with me." I should have been shy about bringing it up like that but after what he just told me, I could probably say anything right then.

"Danny is my Special," he lowered his eyes and looked at the floor, looking ashamed and I had no idea why but I had a strange sensation to comfort him, "my charge. You were just there a lot being his sister. Because you were so protective of him, I couldn't help but watch you, too, sometimes."

What a horrible liar he was, the world's worst. Why would he lie about that? He looked like he wanted to say more but stayed silent. His eyes roamed my face affectionately, making me squirm under his gaze and I decided to press on.

"So, any other super powers? Anything else I should know about?"

"Yes, there is much more to know. The reason I had to come to get you was because Danny was in danger. A Lighter was coming for him."

My breathing hitched. He had said everything but that to warn me before throwing me into that reality but I was too caught up in everything else to pay attention.

"What do we do?"

"We're safe for now. They can only track Specials through someone who sees them. They are opposite of us. We place thoughts in others, they take them. They can read minds and see where the Special is if a person has seen them. It's a long process of going through every person they pass looking for one face in a mind. So, whenever we go out for food and such, Danny will have to stay here and you will have to concentrate very hard on not thinking about him."

"Why do I have to go? Why can't you go by yourself?"

"Soon your world will change. People will start to recognize and look for us, the Keepers. They will classify us as evil, coming to destroy your world and will try to destroy us. The Lighters will turn you against us and as long as I'm in this body, I die when it dies." He stood up and started to pace in front of me. "I can only leave the body, when the task has been fulfilled. I had to come early, because of the Lighter. Danny isn't supposed to...we have a long time to look out for him. Soon, we will probably have to move, and then there will be more Keepers with Specials in hiding. Things are going to get bad for us and the others. We'll be having some company here soon ourselves."

"Wait. I thought you said you can only see into the future forty eight hours? How can you know all this?"

He looked at me wearily, letting me figure it out for myself. Letting it sink in.

"Oh, no. That soon?" I clutched my throat, suddenly unable to breath.

"It's already begun. All the Keepers have come that could. We can only come to Earth when someone dies, just like the Lighters. We take the body of a person of the same gender that they are no longer using. We use to only use the ones that no one knew had been killed. Car wrecks, overdoses, where they were alone and never take the body of someone that the Special knew. But since all the Lighters are here we had to come as quickly as we could." He stopped and looked right in my eyes. "I'm sorry about Matt, and I'm sorry about this body." He bent down to squat right in front of me and then continued his fervent apology. Even though I was freaked and confused his eyes were open and honest and very green. I felt my heart flutter at his closeness and chided myself for it.

"Matt was miles away from here and I just chose the first body close enough to get to you and far enough not to be someone you knew. I didn't even know it was Matt's body until you said that name to me in your driveway. I'm sorry about that and I hope it won't be a problem. The Lighters have taken or corrupted most of the authorities in Chicago. They can put a spell on people, so to speak. It's not really a spell, they just have a way of making you believe them if you listen long enough. By tomorrow morning, Keepers will be front page on every newspaper and channel as most wanted. We will be blamed for your troubles here and they will begin to hunt us and anyone with us."

I couldn't move. I believed him, more than I've ever believed anyone. Was he a Lighter? Is that how I believed so easily? No. He explained everything rationally and thoroughly with no lies.

Danny would be a hard sell. We'd have to keep him locked up until we could make him understand. He might go nuts on Merrick for doing this. He wouldn't think first, he'd just start swinging, in his protective mode. Little hot head.

Merrick offered me his hand to help me up from the chair but I ignored it not knowing what else to do in my shock and not wanting to know what his touch would feel like now that it's him and not Matt. I wasn't that upset about Matt, which made me feel some guilt because I didn't want the guy dead, but he wasn't exactly on my list of favorite people.

I didn't know this Merrick guy either. I wasn't scared though, just cautious, and though I was not one to ever refuse a gesture of politeness, I just couldn't make myself take his hand. He kidnapped me, whether it was for my own good or not.

I could hear Danny moving around in the other room, trying to speak. I let out a long steady calming sigh as I stood. This big, long, crazy story wasn't going to be fun to tell him, but it would be better coming from me.

I tapped on the glass with my fingernail to get his attention. He jerked his head and ran over to me at the window. I could hear him just fine through the thin glass between us. He was not happy to say the least so I started to talk quick, but the look on Danny's face was strange. He backed away in awe, shaking his head and plopped himself onto the bed again, staring at Merrick. I glanced over at him, too.

"The mind thing?" I asked moving a bit towards Merrick.

"It's the best way to...cut through the red tape," he answered.

We both finished our half hour long plea for Danny to believe and understand, which he did. After the mind trick it was hard not to, but Danny was mainly concerned for my safety...on the other side of the glass. Merrick opened the door to let him out and Danny hugged me as if he hadn't seen me in years.

"Are you ok? He didn't hurt you, did he?" he asked loudly, glancing back to glare at Merrick.

Always my tough guy.

"No. No, he didn't hurt me," I said looking at Merrick, too.

"Don't mess with her, you hear me? I don't care what's going on with everything else. We may be stuck together but just...stay away from her."

It was strange how it looked like Merrick was actually fighting a smile.

"I would never hurt her, or you, but alright, Danny. I understand," Merrick replied steadily.

"I can't believe I went along with that story you came up with. I should've known better."

"Yes, you should have," I replied flatly.

"You...you were awake, well aware...in the car, weren't you? You could hear that whole time?" Danny said with comprehension setting in.

"Mmhmm," I answered tersely.

"What was that stuff you gave me?" He turned to look at Merrick. "I heard you guys out there mumbling the whole time but I couldn't get up."

"It's a drug. When we come here, sometimes we have some explaining to do. When we arrive, we are in the body of someone else and have to leave their family to help our Special. They don't understand that the person has died. Sometimes it's necessary to put people out for their own good so they don't hurt themselves or us," Merrick explained.

He was looking at me, subtly apologizing for doing just that to me not a few hours ago, and once again my heart fluttered at being on the receiving end of such an honest look. I shook it away.

"Makes sense I guess," Danny muttered, rubbing his hand over his face. "Ok. Well. Wow. Whew. What a day, huh?" Danny was a talker when he was nervous.

The whole "He's a Special thing" would go straight to his head. All this time, I told him he needed a purpose, a goal, an ambition. He had a bigger one than I could've ever imagined.

"So. What now?" I asked.

Stuck in the ground with a Special and a kidnapping Keeper, no clothes or anything else personal and my stomach growling, every girl's dream.

"Well, I have food for tonight in the bag I brought. Sherry and I will have to go out tomorrow and get some supplies and we'll be getting some company tomorrow as well."

"Can you still see the future?" I asked, praying the answer was yes.

What a useful tool that could be.

"No, not once we take a body. Then we are basically human, except for the mind projection and the symbol behind the ear, there's no way to tell. Not that I know of anyway. We usually aren't in a body very long so...we're kind of in uncharted waters."

"Hmmm. Ok. Well, can we eat now, maybe? I'm pretty hungry," I said looking at my watch, 1:30 a.m.

I'd been 'asleep' for a few hours then.

"Sure, let's head into the kitchen, and then I'll show you two around the place."

We followed him down the wide, white hall with the rooms on it and to the right, there was a grand kitchen area. All silver and chrome, with two entrance way doors on either side of the room. Industrial ovens, stoves and a refrigerator. Even a huge double door freezer.

If you were going to hideout, this was the way to do it I guess. He pointed towards the bathroom and showers as we passed. There were no shower curtains, doors or stalls.

Hmmm. That would be interesting.

There was a lab area and even a room with a basketball goal and court in it. Upon asking, he told me this was a facility used for scientists and geneticists. They stayed here for months at a time when they worked on fertility drugs. They were afraid of activists trying to thwart their efforts, so they hid in this warehouse with their families while they worked and did their internships.

The cans of tuna he brought, with no crackers or bread weren't appetizing, but to an empty stomach and no breakfast in sight, it hit the spot. Stale water in the pipes, but clean water nonetheless, and thankfully it wasn't sulfur water. I just tried to make a good situation out of something crummy. At least Danny was safe.

"There will be ten Keepers coming tomorrow with their charges," he told us as we walked past another hallway of rooms.

"How long can we stay down here? I mean, won't the Lighters just keep looking? How long do we have until Danny's supposed to do...whatever it is he's going to do?"

"I don't know specific dates, Sherry. I don't know when he'll need to do something or where, it'll just happen. As far as staying down here, I don't know that either but you're right, we won't be able to stay here forever. Don't worry, I'll do whatever I have to do to keep you safe."

The way he was still looking at me was very strange. He wasn't looking at Danny that way. It was almost like a man looking at someone he...desires or admires. So I asked.

"Do you have Matt's thoughts and memories?"

"No. Everything of Matt is gone but his body."

"Hmmm." Well, that solved nothing.

"Alright, we got a big day tomorrow. Things might get tense with all of us getting crammed into this small space."

"You mean things *will* get tense right? You've seen it?" I suggested.

"Yes." He actually smiled, and it was amazingly gorgeous. He was pleased that I was listening to his story I guess. "Things will get tense. A few of the other Specials and family members aren't thrilled about this. Some still don't believe ,and some are angry and want to fight back, want to fight us, the Keepers."

"So you can't see past tomorrow right? That's your forty eight hours?"

"Right. After tomorrow night we are all walking blind, but just my coming here can alter the course of things. Anything we do can change the way things happen."

We all exchanged loaded heavy glances. I sighed and fidgeted with my necklace.

"Ok then. I'll guess I'll go pick a room and get some sleep? Good night...Merrick," I said nodding to him and turning.

"Um, Sherry," he said catching my sleeve. His fingers brushed my skin sending a zing through me. I jolted slightly, looking at him sharply and he released it. "I think it would be best if we all stayed in the rooms next to each other. Either you and Danny can share a room or Danny and I can, but someone will have to. There's only fifteen rooms so..."

"Ah, I guess I'll share with ya, sis. No snoring though," Danny said pointing, clearly back to his old self and the shock gone.

Wouldn't be long until the ego reared its ugly head.

"Fine, and I do not snore." I punched his arm and then turned back to Merrick. "Night Ma- Merrick. Sorry, uh...You do sleep, right?" I asked as I twirled a curl in between my fingers, unable to stop my nervousness.

Merrick watched me do it, like he had watched it a hundred times, reminiscent. His eyes were dark and watching but they still have kindness in them, a familiarity, but not Matt's. The dark brown eyes I was used to seeing on that face were deep green now, all Merrick.

"Yes. As far as you're concerned, I'm human."

"Ok. G'night."

As we turned the corner I couldn't stop myself from one last look and there it was again! That look he'd been giving me all night. Like he was in some kind of trance. Tomorrow I would find out what that whole 'you don't know how long' business was all about.

Merrick - Explaining To Do
Chapter 4

I sat down on the surprisingly soft and comfortable bed. The white sheets were clean and smelled like bleach.

Smell.

I actually could smell the bleach. I chuckled under my breath at how every experience on Earth was so different. I'd never really paid attention to smell when I was here before. I guess I didn't have to worry about it anymore. I would always have smell. It wasn't like I could go home, not like I would.

I couldn't believe it. I was actually lying in a bed, on Earth, next to the room where Sherry and Danny were sleeping, safely. I was actually here again, but for them this time. I never thought I'd get the chance to be with them.

I slipped out of bed and walked the short distance to the next room to check on them, again. My charges. Danny was snoring and drooling on his pillow, sprawled out on his stomach and limbs spread wide.

Normal.

My conscience was already starting to buzz with just the thought of leaving him here alone tomorrow.

Sherry was lying on her side with one leg stuck out and curled around the covers, her hand under her cheek and her hair fanned out on her shoulders. Normal for her, too.

I guessed the beds were comfortable enough for them. Me, having never slept on a bed, I had no idea what it should feel like, but it felt pleasant enough.

I watched their little mannerisms, Sherry's sighing softly and shifting slowly, almost dreamlike, rubbing her neck in her sleep. Danny talks and snores, rattling the walls as people say but doesn't move. They probably wouldn't be comfortable with me watching them like that, but it was just habit for me. Comforting.

I'd always watched them, even in their sleep. They have been my only priority for many years.

Sherry was even more gorgeous in person, and her scent...is amazing. Again with the smell. It lingered in the air even after she was gone from the room. Carrying her was almost unbearable. Light as a feather and yet, my knees wanted to collapse from actually being able to hold her, touch her.

And why? Why did I have to come here as Matt? What the heck was Matt

39

doing way out there? She would have nothing to do with me, not even as friends. How could she with this face? He was so brutal to her, berating and belittling her. She could never see past it, not like it mattered. She could never love me, let alone like me.

I was not a human.

And Danny. I couldn't believe he fell for that act, and with Matt's face no less. How naïve and gullible was he? Even if the Lighters hadn't pulled this stunt I would've been down here soon enough to save his lazy behind. Sherry was right. She thinks she was too hard on him, but he needed guidance that his parents definitely didn't give him.

They were both so wonderfully normal and real to me.

It still amazed me, even after all that time, how different people were in person than when you watched them. It was like a dream, a haze, a cloud. Color, but a copy. Not real, but here. Everything was alive.

Smells, facial expressions, the fluidity of movement, the way they banter and flash smiles at each other, the way she protects him and the way he loves and reveres her. It was all so real and colorful, loud and wonderful. I was glad Danny has had Sherry all these years.

It definitely takes some getting used to, the humans and their bodies. I couldn't believe how tired I was. My eyelids were forcing themselves down over my eyes, though I was still looking and seeing and being aware. And hungry, my stomach making those noises that command me to obey or else.

These bodies betray them with their senses. Like the way Sherry looks at me and I freeze, my limbs shaky and stiff, this heart pounding against my ribs. I knew she could tell, she had to. If I knew how to be embarrassed, I was sure I would be. The body would show me soon enough.

Tomorrow, we'd gather the supplies we needed. Please let everything go smoothly. I knew Sherry wasn't thrilled about going out alone with me. I didn't blame her. I had to gain control of myself around her. It was just after watching her for so long and to have her there...right in front of me...

But...I was going to be a good man. I was going to be noble and gallant. I had to be. I'd keep my distance and just enjoy my time with them here. I couldn't let her know how I felt. I'd hate it if she felt uncomfortable around me, more than she did already. I had to control myself, control the body's reactions.

Something had changed with the Lighters. Something that they thought would help them get away with it. Gah, this is bad! How could I tell Danny and Sherry that their world was...over? Centuries and centuries. Why now?

As I looked at the human face in the mirror of the bathroom, rubbing the hairs growing on my chin, I couldn't help but not recognize myself. The face looked nothing like my true self. I was utterly devastated to be stuck with the face of someone who could degrade a woman like he had Sherry.

I thought about how I'd have to start shaving, brushing my teeth, taking showers. I poked under my eyes, that were lined with gray semi-circles from fatigue. I ran my hands through my new black hair. The face was young. I had no idea how old Matt was, looked to be early twenties. He kept himself healthy and worked out a lot. I could tell that from the body. My t-shirt was tighter than I'd like and uncomfortable around the arm bands. I guessed human girls like that sort of thing. And this stupid tattoo, a bull of all things. I was stuck with a bull on my chest. Of all the galaxies and planets I knew of, Earth was by far the most puzzling.

Earth. Never spent more than a day on Earth before in one stretch. I never saw the end coming. I had a feeling we wouldn't be returning to our home, that there was no going back to the way it was for the humans. Maybe that was just me, being selfish. If I didn't finish my task, then I couldn't leave. And I wouldn't have to find a reason to stay.

I couldn't leave. Danny and Sherry were my...family. They may not have felt that way, in fact I knew they didn't but I couldn't let them go. I'd never felt that. Never had a need to feel it but I couldn't leave, she was too close. Even if I could never have her for myself, she was everywhere here.

I was stuck and there would be no going home for me.

A New Way To Be Human
Chapter 5

There was no sun to wake me in the morning. No windows, no birds' songs or honking horns. Only the fluorescent lights that were on a timer as I heard them click and buzz to life. I opened my eyes, squinting against the harsh light. My watch said 6:30.

6:30 a.m.? Ugh. And no coffee.

I hated to admit to myself that I was one of *those people*. Those coffee people. But I liked- not needed- but liked my coffee in the morning. That was why I was so bitter about Danny's coffee job. I could work there and drink the heck out of some coffee. But no. Danny, who didn't even drink coffee, worked there. No, the coffee wasn't good, but at six thirty in the morning, I'd take coffee in any form.

Letting my eyes adjust, I lay there quietly, looking at the white ceiling tiles in my small white room. A big perfectly square one with popcorn plaster above my bed. The bed was pretty comfy, firm but soft enough. The room was nice enough, dreary white, but nice. A whole basement of nothing but hospital white and sterile chrome. Lovely.

Danny, still snoring passed the lights and clicking sounds, hadn't moved an inch from where he fell asleep last night. There was a bed and a cot in the room. Danny graciously took the cot. No matter how unruly he was, he was still a gentleman about some things. Shaking him, I said his name and he moaned and groaned, sucking the drool up from his lip and mumbling something about mom leaving him alone for a few more minutes.

I rolled my eyes. Walking into the hall, I dearly wished we had grabbed some clothes in our hurried escape. I should've known that Merrick would have that covered, too. Outside my room, on the floor in the hall, were two stacks of clothing. One for me. As I examined them, I realized they were sweat pants and a t-shirt. Universal grey. Great.

I grabbed them up and went to jump in the shower, assuming Merrick would be in the kitchen, though I didn't know why I thought that.

As I walked in I saw the steam but it was too late to turn before getting a peek of Merrick's/Matt's, backside. All those months we dated I never saw anything but his chest. Gosh, it was nice. What! Turn around you fool!

I blushed what I'm sure was an extreme color of rouge and tried to turn and

42

run but once again he was there before I can escape. Not humanly possible. He had the towel around his waist and already in front of me, blocking the way out.

"It's ok. It's all yours," Merrick said towel drying his hair, not looking a bit bashful.

It was awfully hard to not look at him. I did mention how gorgeous Matt was right and that I'd never seen anything but his chest at the pool?

I averted my eyes to the wall behind him in a desperate attempt to regain some coherency. Then focused on Matt's tattoo, right above his right breast. A black and gray horned bull. I'd always thought it fit him and his attitude, but I guess it didn't belong to Matt anymore.

"I'm so sorry. I should've...knocked," I said, licking my suddenly dry lips.

"It's all right. I thought I had more time before you got up. I'm sure you've seen it all before anyway...wait. I'm sorry. I shouldn't have said that," he said, running his hand through his wet hair.

I assumed he meant he saw me in the future walk in on him and he was trying to hurry to avoid this.

"No. It's ok. And no, I haven't seen it before actually. Matt and I weren't...like that," I said, feeling myself blush again and wondered why I thought I had to explain myself.

He seemed to ponder this thought, and then moved on.

"I meant, about his death. I shouldn't have spoken so callously about him."

"No. Really. Matt was a...I mean, I'm not glad he's dead, but in all honesty, I'm surprised something like that hadn't happened already with as much as he drank. And he was a jerk. He was...very cruel to me."

"I know."

"You know?" I asked, raising a questioning eyebrow.

"Yes. I...I told you I watched Danny, sometimes I saw you, too. I saw that he wasn't nice."

Lies.

"Why are you lying? I have a gift. I can tell when people are lying to me and I know you know that already. Course I'm a horrible liar myself but...what is it that you keep trying to hide from me?" I said, inching a bit closer, looking into his extra green eyes.

As I asked him, I had completely forgotten he was standing there in nothing but a towel from the waist down, dripping and steam all around us. Avert eyes Sherry.

"I'm not lying," he lied coolly.

"Yes, you are," I insisted, taking another brave inch closer.

He looked down at me as if he was wrestling with himself. His eyes went from hard to soft, confused to more confused. He looked like I felt.

"Merrick?" I waited, but he took a deep breath and still didn't say anything. "Fine. Don't tell me now but one day soon, I'll get it out of you... So what's the plan for today?"

It was not at all odd for him that he was having this conversation in a towel? I mean, he wasn't human, he probably didn't even get shy or worry about modesty right?

"As soon as you get ready, we need to head out for supplies. The others will be here after lunch. They will have supplies for themselves as well. We'll be down here, I hope, for at least a month before having to leave again. We'll see how that goes-"

"A month? Whew. That's quite a stint," I mused.

"It's probably short compared to what some of the other stints may be. I told you. I came early, and I have no idea how early. Our time is not the same as yours. It may be years before-"

"Years! Merrick, you're telling me that we could be stuck down here for years? What about my job? What about.. our parents? What about-"

"Sherry," he interrupted, as he tilted his head and spoke softly and sympathetically. "Were you listening yesterday? The world you knew is no more. Your collected, logical, gadget filled world is over. The world of the Lighters has begun. They will not stop until every Special is gone or taken and they can be the majority over the humans. They are here to take over your world, Sherry," he said and pronounced each word individually and with emphasis.

"I was listening. I just think... what do these Lighters gain from the Specials being gone, not fulfilling the task?"

"They want to live your life. They want to take over your world, to live here, but there are billions of you and thousands of them. They knew they couldn't just come and take it from you. And they are like us. They can only come to earth when someone dies, to take their body. The only thing is that the ones that are already here are persuading people who aren't ready to die yet to be reckless. I told you, they are very suggestive. It's compulsion. People are listening and are dying and carrying out their deeds. Soon, every Lighter will be here and it will be near impossible to stop them. Listen. Take a shower and we'll talk more later in the car. We've got to get going."

As I watched him leave, I realized something for the first time since I met this so called guardian. If he was right, this was the end of the world. Days end. What could that mean? What would happen to Danny after he fulfilled his task? What would happen to Matt, still be dead once Merrick leaves his body? Of course. That was stupid. Merrick would go home then I guessed. Wherever that was.

The water was really hot down there. Even though Merrick just took a shower the water was still deliciously scalding and the pressure was wonderful. The water in my apartment wasn't even that hot. It felt great on my frazzled nerves.

I wondered if we could work out a way for a door to be put on that particular room. I wouldn't have been so cool about it had Merrick walked in on me. Course, he probably would have announced his arrival, or knocked. I was so spacey sometimes. He probably thought I was rude. Poor little prodigy's sister. I laughed out loud and heard the echo at the thought of Danny as some prodigy.

Danny wasn't too happy about being left behind, but held tight. He had his Nintendo DS in his pocket. It wouldn't be long until the battery was dead but Danny would probably sleep most of the time anyway and I could pick him up some batteries. We'd be back as quickly as we could. After Merrick's pep talk, I was pretty anxious about being out in public.

I wondered how we were going to pay for all the stuff we needed? I hoped he wasn't expecting my meager wages to sustain us.

Once he put the key in and turned it, the elevator creaked to life, the doors shuddering open. We stepped inside and I got ready for the long ride to the top. I was 'asleep' before and didn't realize the elevator lights were blown and it was pitch black in here.

Silence is a killer. I felt the need to say something and that was as good a time as any.

"Merrick, what did you mean yesterday, that you've waited? That you couldn't believe you were here...with me?"

Saying it out loud was suddenly terribly embarrassing and my cheeks flushed and burned hot. Thank goodness for the darkness.

"Sherry, I'd...I'd rather not do this right now, if that's ok. Let's focus on getting to town and back safely."

"So you're blowing me off again and still lying. Ok, fine, we'll focus," I said and snorted a humorless laugh.

"I'm not...Sherry, I'm sorry, ok. I can't imagine how weird this must be for you and I'm sorry if I made it worse with my...gibberish. It'd been a long day."

"It didn't sound like gibberish or lies to me. You did tell me you would answer all my questions didn't you?"

Silence in the small space, ignoring me. Fine. Awkward silence it would be. Instead he asked me a question after a moment.

"Is it weird for you, confusing? With me in Matt's body?"

I thought for a minute and went over the things I'd realized. The eyes were different, the body language, in fact everything was different.

45

"Not as much as you'd think I guess. Matt didn't talk or walk, really do anything like you do. Your eyes are green and his were brown. Even your facial expressions and tone of voice are so different. He never talked to me or looked at me the way you do, or anybody for that matter. He was...a character. Can you walk egotistically?" I gave a small laugh, shaking my head at my own stupidity. Thankfully he couldn't see my face. "That's sounds dumb, but that's how I saw him...you're not like that at all."

"Hmm."

"Hmm? What? No insightful wisdom this time?" I jested.

"I'm just wondering what you ever saw in him to begin with."

"Wow. That's...direct," I mumbled. "Um, I don't know. He was just the first guy to show interest I guess."

"Hmm."

As the elevator slowly and graciously opened, relief swept over me as did the warm sunlight, blinding me. What a strange conversation and thankfully it was over. He hurried ahead of me, probably just as eager to go and get back as I was.

"You drive," Merrick commanded, tossing the keys to me.

"Ok. Seeing as how it's my car, I won't object," I said as I climbed in the driver's side.

The top was already down. They'd left it down last night before heading down under. Men should know better than that, you would think.

"Remember to be careful, ok? Don't speed. We'll have to be on our guard at all times," he said in a firm tone.

"Ok, sir. I will, sir." I gave a soldier salute which, in turn, I received a raised brow and slightly amused smirk.

I cranked the car and turned on the radio, then grabbed my emergency hair band out of the glove box and pulled my hair back, shaking it back and running my fingers through it before grabbing it to pull it into a loose bunch. It was particularly unruly this morning what with no hairbrush or styling products.

I saw in my peripheral that I was getting the look again. What was with him? I mean, hey, if he thought I was cute, I was all for that, but that's not what this was.

This was a...something else.

Like I was the last piece of candy in the bowl sitting on the boss' desk, taunting him day after day- because you can't take the boss' last piece of candy. I would figure this out but first, shopping.

"So, can you drive? I'm assuming you didn't drive last night."

"I can but...driving a manual is new to me."

"Really? Hmmm. I think I'll let you drive home then. You really should know how to drive the getaway car," I teased as I put the car in first gear and started down the road.

"Mmmm...I don't know."

"It'll be ok. I'll teach you. It's easy," I said as I glanced over and flashed him a reassuring smile.

"Ok. Whatever you say."

He returned my smile, but it wasn't reassuring. He looked ill.

They had driven us all the way to Gary, Indiana last night. 'Music Man' town. How my grandma would love to be here, under different circumstances of course. She loved old musicals and forced me to watch them. I say forced, but in honesty I loved them too, but I wasn't about to let the old lady know that.

We were going to the city, far enough away that no one would recognize our faces. Somehow I could tell if he was speaking to me with his mouth, or with his mind. His mind voice sounded softer, huskier; a different voice altogether. Maybe that was what his real voice sounded like.

Did the clothes fit alright?

"Yeah. They're fine. Definitely the latest fashion." I smiled to show him I was joking.

We can get you something else, anything you need. Do you have your Costco card with you? I should have asked you that before we left.

"Yes," I said out loud. Kinda not fair he get's to be lazy with the chatter. In fact I'd tell him that. "How come you get to the do that and not me?"

I could see the smile in his profile. A real smile, not the fake baby-you-know-you're-the-one-for-me smile I had always received from Matt. I didn't remember Matt laughing at anything I had ever said.

"Sorry. It's habit."

"So Costco then? Is that it?" I said as I readjusted the seat back to my short legged setting.

"Should be. We can get some clothes and toiletries as well as food there. This car is going to be stacked up pretty high. We might need to buy some of those things...the cords..."

I knew exactly what he was thinking about, but it was hilarious watching him struggle, waving his hand in the air, trying to force it out. His expression turned into a five year old, frustrated over figuring out the answer when the teacher called on you.

"Bungee. Bungee cords," I saved him.

"Yes. Those."

I couldn't help but laugh out loud. It was easy to forget he wasn't human. If he only knew things from earth from watching Danny, no wonder he didn't know about bungee cords. Wait a minute. I wondered.

"Is Danny the only Special you've ever had?"

"No. He's my seventeenth."

"Really. Out of that many, of course Danny is the problem child."

"Not exactly. I was the Keeper for Orville Wright. That was a problem child." He chuckled. "It took me three trips to Earth to keep him from breaking his neck before he could finish his task."

"Wow! Really? That's kind of neat actually. I bet he was a really nice guy. Adventurous and a pain in the butt, but nice. Guys were gentlemen back then."

"Not everyone was a gentleman, but yes, he was and it was fun. As fun as it can be watching someone everyday, all day."

I caught his tone.

"That's sounds miserable, actually." I didn't want to get started on the negative so I changed the subject. "So what are you like? I mean, if you don't mind me asking. What do you look like?"

"I look pretty human. Very pale and blonde, we all are. Skin is almost translucent, albino."

"So, what, you just sit in office up there and watch us on the TV or something?" I said, not sure if he got jokes or not.

"Ha ha," he said smiling, and the breath left my body at how genuine and gorgeous he looked with that real smile on. I smiled back, happy to see he had *some* humor. "No, it's not that elaborate. I can't really describe it. We aren't really anywhere, we just...are. No needs, no discomfort. Coming back to Earth is always a shock, but it gets easier every time."

"How many times have you been here?"

This was the most he'd talked, though I had only known him a day, I was going to keep him going. He looked amused. I guessed he wasn't upset at my questions, not these anyway.

"Ten."

"Three with Orville," I reminded him I was listening.

"Yes. Three with Orville." He smiled at my remembering.

Wow, that was a good smile.

"Do they usually know who you are? What you are. Do you tell them or..."

"No. Not unless it's an extreme situation and we have no choice. We just do what we can. A stranger's kind word or advice, a helping hand with something heavy, a question about directions that leads to something else. We don't know until the time comes what the Special is meant to do nor what we are meant to do for them."

I couldn't think of anything relevant to say after that. He was so selfless. This was *his* life? Making sure others fulfilled theirs? How old was he? Could he really be happy like that? He seemed to be. What a useless life I'd led, and look at him. This guy made me look like Dahmer.

He looked over at me just in time to see my tortured expression.

"Are you all right? Did I say something wrong?" he said as he twisted in his seat a little to look at me better.

"Nothing. You might want to put your seatbelt on." I laughed a humorless laugh under my breath to cover.

"What is it, Sherry?" he ignored my suggestion and probed further.

"Are you happy? Living this way?" I looked over to see his eyes. I wanted the truth to my question.

"I am what I am. Why fight what you can't change?"

"I guess so..." I said as we pulled into the half empty parking lot.

It had taken longer than I thought because I had driven so slow, lost in thought and conversation with Merrick. I wondered if Merrick had already seen all this, our conversation and everything in his glimpse of the future.

We got out and I pulled on Danny's thin blue corduroy jacket that was left in the back seat last night. It shouldn't be cold in June.

The sleeve caught outside in as I tried to force my arm through, quite comically and unsuccessfully. Merrick grabbed my arm to help me and reached in the sleeve, grabbing my fingers instead and readjusting to grab the fabric out gently.

I watched his face with great interest. When our hands touched he looked up into my eyes, then jolted his gaze away. The look. He refused to meet my gaze again as we started toward the doors, but instead he briefed me on the rules we discussed earlier.

"Remember, no thinking of Danny or the warehouse. No thinking about anything you wouldn't want one of them to see. Let's get in and out as quickly as possible."

"Okay. Understood."

I flashed my card and the door attendant flashed a smile. We snagged a squeaky shopping cart and he pushed as I grabbed. Then I pushed while he grabbed. I thought we were getting too much, but when you started to add how much three people eat in a month, I guess it did add up pretty quick.

How the Rabbit would hold all this was beyond me? Beyond. Then I remembered a pretty important question still left unanswered.

"Uh, Merrick. How are we going to pay for all this? I'm sorry, but I definitely don't have the cash."

"I've got it under control. Now, do you want to go and get some... personal items? For yourself? I'll keep going and meet you in the toilet paper aisle in fifteen minutes, all right?" he said looking a little uncomfortable.

"Oh, I've only dreamed of a guy saying that to me..."

He looked at me puzzled, going over in his head, no doubt, what he could've said to have prompted my dreaming. I pursed my lips to keep from laughing.

"It's a joke, Merrick. A joke."

"Oh. Sorry."

"No, I'm sorry. It apparently wasn't that funny," I said as I chuckled and walked over to the 'personal items' section.

After grabbing a few things I made my way over to the clothes section of the warehouse for a five pack of underwear and then two pairs of jeans and two tank tops. I mean, if he's paying.

I grabbed a pack of socks as well, and a new under wire bra. A girl couldn't live on one bra alone. I was set. Where was Merrick...oh yeah, toilet paper. I chuckled to myself as I made my way down the aisles.

I heard my name being called behind me and swung around thinking I somehow missed the toilet paper aisle, but no. It was Racine, Matt's flamboyant gorgeous older sister. Oh, no. What in the world was she doing there? I'd have to keep away from the toilet paper aisle.

I ran to her as I usually did or she'd think something was up. Crap. I wondered if Merrick saw this too in his future glimpse. Racine and I had been friends since grade school. Surely this would be ok, we didn't have to worry about her.

"Racine! Hey! What in the world are you doing way out here?"

"I'd ask you the same thing. And Lord, what *are* you wearing?" She gave me a cursory glance and then covered her heart with her hand like she was in pain as she went on. "Honey, did you hear about Matt? They found his truck at Orland Park. Burned. He crashed into something, but escaped somehow. Haven't seen a trace of him. Mom and Dad are out looking with a search party. I'm just here stocking up on supplies for our trip to Georgia. The news said those things, the Keepers or Seepers, or whatever, were crawling closer to town and we should evacuate and run like heck if we see one. I heard on the radio that Georgia and New Mexico are safe, they aren't there yet."

"How can you tell if it's one or not?" I asked, trying to probe and see what the news was saying about them.

"They have a mark behind their ear, but other than that, you can't tell them from anyone else. Little deceiving suckers," she said in her usual southern belle accent which I've always found weird because they're originally from a prominent subdivision of Detroit.

"What do *they* want?"

"Well, the news said they want to trick us onto their side. They want the world but the good guys have come now and told us all about them and their shady plans. They've already taken the moon, that's what happened to it. Isn't that awful? They're trying to flood the earth by messing with the tides."

"Yeah, it is." I didn't contradict her that that would have happened along time ago if that were true. "But maybe we shouldn't believe everything we hear on TV though right? I mean, have you seen these so called good guys? Did they come on camera and say these things?"

"Oh, no, they are strictly anonymous. They don't want to take any credit or focus for this. They want us to concentrate on savings ourselves from these things."

"Ok, well, I've got to go, but it was so good to see..."I couldn't finish because her eyes bulged and her mouth dropped open. I knew exactly what she saw before I even turned around.

Merrick - well Matt - standing there with our loaded down cart, alive and well and out with me. I squinted my eyes to tell him to stop, but he had already noticed her face and realized a mistake had been made, though not knowing which one.

Sherry, what do I do?

I shifted me eyes toward her so he'd come our way.

"Matt, honey, look who I ran into. Your *sister*, Racine. They found your truck; someone crashed it and left it in Orland Park. Pretty crazy, huh?" I said before I turned back to Racine, waiting for the blow.

"Sherry! Why didn't you tell me Matt was with you?"

"I'm sorry. You got to talking about those...things, the Keepers, and I got sidetracked. He's fine though, see," I spouted, waving my hand over him.

"What are y'all doing? I thought you broke up with him, Sherry. What? Are y'all on a getaway or something together?"

That was more of an accusation than a question. She never saw her brother for what he was and thought me 'ungrateful' to let such a handsome catch get away. I had better lay it on thick if she was going to believe me. I reached over to grab Matt's arm and laid my head on his shoulder. I felt Merrick tense a little under my touch.

I knew I was about to lie. Racine was always so unfocused I doubted she'd notice. She kind of seemed to have only two cylinders out of six running most of the time. I could pull this off. I could lie.

"Now, Racine, you know me. I'm so back and forth, but I can never let him get away for too long." I glanced up at him and smiled. "We just decided to head up here and get away from things for a while and spend some time, alone."

She totally bought it. "Ah! That's so sweet! I'm so glad you finally came to your senses, girl. Well, little brother, you're never this quiet. Get your butt over here and give your big sister a hug!"

Think. Think.

"Oh, me first! I mean we have been separated for a whole ten minutes," I said lamely, hoping she took it as loveydoveyness.

I reached my arms up around his neck and hugged him, up on my tiptoes, while I whispered in his ear. He put his shaking hands on my waist while he listened. I pulled his cheek down to touch mine.

"He always picks her up and twirls her when they hug. Be cocky and enthusiastic," I whispered against his ear and pulled back to give him a reassuring smile.

I let go and stepped back, he seemed to be breathing heavier. He was just nervous, fearful of a scene in the middle of the store. I placed my hand on his back, rubbing to soothe him, but that seemed to make it worse. His eyes glazed over and he shivered, but quickly recovered.

"Ah, you two are so sweet. Now get over here!"

He smiled and scooted forward, picking her up and twirling her around a couple times before letting out a very convincing and enthusiastic "Miss me?"

"You know I did! Why you trying to give everyone a heart attack? Geez Louise! I guess we can call off the search party!"

And there was that Racine cackle.

"Racine, I'm sorry, but I'm very eager to get back to our, uh, getaway. Can we call you later?" I wrapped my arms around Merrick's waist for emphasis and again, his breath caught in response, but he stiffly put his arm around me.

His eyes were shifting like he didn't know where to look. I was confused. I thought him being a Keeper would give him some kind of idea of how to handle himself under pressure. He was freaking out.

"Oh, of course, honey! You two have fun now! Matt, you sly devil you. Call mom or she'll just have a cow, you know she will! Bye, lovebirds!"

Just like that she trotted away, her lime green heels dyed to perfectly match her Capri pants clacked on the concrete floor. I blew out an exaggerated breath of relief, but Merrick didn't look like me, he looked sick or something.

"Merrick?" I whispered leaning in, still not completely comfortable with people we know in the same vicinity.

He said nothing, but turned his head to me and looked down into my eyes.

"Merrick? Are you ok?" I asked and I could feel my concerned face was on

The scrunched forehead, pulled up eyebrows and tight lips.

"I'm fine." He shook his head a little to clear it. "I just wasn't expecting that, I didn't see it coming. We changed something, I didn't see this." He swallowed. "You took too long, so I came looking for you. I was worried."

"Yeah, sorry. If I could've warned you I would have. Why wouldn't you have seen that in the future?"

"I told you, you can change things if you know about them ahead of time. In what I saw, she would have been here but we missed her. Something happened that changed it. I don't remember you putting on the jacket in the vision I saw but...it could be anything. Even a few seconds of change can alter a lot."

"I drove too slow. I usually don't drive that slowly, but we were talking and having fun..."

He looked right into my eyes. "We'll never know what changed it for sure, but it doesn't matter. We handled it. It's over."

"You did great. Really great," I said, trying to assure him.

He just nodded. I advised him we probably needed to make a medicine cabinet stop. We grabbed cold medicine, aspirin, everything you can think of. Then got to the clothes department again and got him and Danny a few things. I didn't know what all that was going to cost, nor the way to get out of there with it.

We headed to the cashier and Merrick put on a serious, concentrating face. He didn't look at the cashier, just stared at the conveyer line as our stuff passed by. I looked between him and her as we put our items on the belt. She seemed dazed, eyes shifting wearily. That's when I realized what he was doing.

He was talking to her in his mind. Who knew what he was telling her but she seemed to be buying it as she started scanning items. He handed me the receipt and we walked away, just like that. Merrick was turning out to be a 'just like that' kind of guy.

As we loaded down my poor defenseless Rabbit, who squeaked and moaned in protest, we didn't speak much. Then when we were finished, I had to fill the passenger seat with stuff too, so I scooted in the driver's side first and slid over to the barely existent middle seat.

Merrick was a little reluctant to get in. I figured it was because he didn't want the driving lesson. After I gave him a bewildered look, he sighed and slid in, too. Our arms and legs brushed against each other inevitably.

It was comfortable for me, it was cold, freezing even, and the top was down and he was so very warm. He didn't seem to share my sentiment however and it kind of annoyed me.

Was he so repulsed by humans not to want to even touch them? Or was it just me? That was why he was so weird in the store and I was making it worse with my incessant need to comfort. Mother Hen Syndrome. I always did the same thing with Danny.

The absolute most uncomfortable part was his being able to reach the gear shift, located in between my knees, so in an effort to thwart the weirdness, I decided to start the driving lesson to get on the road home even faster.

"Ok, now just press the clutch on the left and then slowly let off as you ease the gas on the right a little, while it's in first gear, here." I pointed for each instruction as I spoke.

I put my cold hand on his to shift into first and it felt like warm stone.

"Relax," I breathed and he blew out a long breath.

He started the car and sludged it into gear as it sputtered and coughed, but went a little bit, and then slammed to a stop as he stalled out.

I tried not to laugh, but I couldn't help myself and a giggle slipped out of the palm covering my mouth. He looked over at me in frustration, helplessly turning off the key and rubbing his hands over his face.

"Merrick, no one gets it on the first time, ok? Just relax and try again," I tried to encourage him in a soothing voice, holding back my laughter.

Thank goodness we were on the less empty side of the parking lot, with plenty of room and less people. He tried again and made it a bit farther this time before stalling. I laughed again, but he didn't seem very amused with his sour face and pursed lips like he was eating lemons instead of driving.

"Lighten up, Merrick! It's ok. Don't you remember my dad teaching Danny and me? It took quite a few tries. Try again. You'll get it this time. You're doing really well. I believe you can do this, ok. Just have fun with it."

After a few more failed attempts and a little neck lash he got it going and with no red lights to halt us, we headed out of the parking lot and down the road.

He made a very pungent point not to touch my legs as he shifted, which made me even more sour. I wasn't sure why it bothered me so much. I repulsed everyone except Matt. I wasn't a guy's girl. Why wouldn't I repulse aliens, too? However, this fact didn't exactly cheer me up so I sat, shivering in my anger stew.

I twirled my hair in one hand and fidgeted with my necklace in the other. He could feel me shaking and could probably faintly hear my teeth chatter over the roar of the wind as well as he turned to look at me. His body was trying to press against the door as far as it would go. I gave him a quick glance and then went back to shivering and staring at the road.

"Are you cold? I'm sorry. There's not room to put the top down," Merrick said glancing over at me a few more times with concern.

"I'm f-fine," I stammered not looking from the road.

"Are you ok? You seem...agitated," he observed, glancing over at me again, trying to meet my eyes.

"Well, I'm just sorry you're so uncomfortable with my sitting here," I spouted quickly, refusing to look at him.

"I'm not."

"Liarrr."

"Sherry," he breathed and I did look then and I saw the hesitation on his face. "I'm not human, ok. I've seen things, but not actually done them. It's hard for me to..."

"I d-don't understand what you're saying."

"I know. Would you feel better if you leaned under my arm? I hate to see you so cold."

"No, not if you don't want me to."

He pulled his shifting arm up and around my shoulders. I wanted to fight it but oh the warmth! I moaned loudly and embarrassingly, but couldn't care too much. I pressed my head against his chest and turned slightly to him pressing in a little more. Still teeth chattering but much better.

Again, I felt his intake of a deep breath and felt the goose bumps rising on his arm, but I couldn't see his face and I didn't dare leave the warmth to look. After a few minutes he spoke again.

"Better?" he asked, trying to sound at ease with the fact that we were touching.

"Yes, you can let go now."

He did not let go, in fact I felt his grip tighten and pull me closer. It was strange to me how Matt had never embraced me this way, just holding me without expecting anything in return.

This body was perfect, a foot and some taller than me, not hard to do though. Toned tan muscle everywhere with strong arms that used to scare me but now, I felt...safe in them.

I could feel the muscle contours of his arm and chest as I melted into his side as he was very warm for it to be so cold out. The rest of the ride was loud, wind whipping but way more comfortable than before. I fought sleep in the middle of the day, though it looked more like twilight. Weird weather was getting even stranger.

Before we got fully out of town, I felt my stomach growl.

"Can we stop and get something to eat before we head back? It's been a long drive and I'm starving."

Somehow he understood my stammers the first time over the roaring wind and I felt us slow down, jerkily as we pulled in somewhere. Looking up I saw a local burger dive with a clear drive thru lane. He down shifted but didn't stall. I was pretty proud.

"What'll it be folks?" the high-pitched chipper voice asked through the speaker in the shape of a painted chipped hamburger with all the fixings.

I wanted to laugh, but was too hungry.

"I'll have a cheeseburger- extra mayo and onion rings and...a raspberry tea," I said loudly, then looked at Merrick. "What are you having?"

"Make that two." He leaned towards the ordering board for her to hear.

"Nine dollars and two cents, the first and only window, please and thank you," her shrill voice rang out like a song chorus.

Was she trying to be funny? It must be one of those funny places with humor in every commercial and slogan. The owner in the commercials with costumes on and his nieces sitting at a table in the background, looking like they are at Disneyland instead of chewing on a greasy burger.

When we reached the window I held up my hand in protest to Merrick and grabbed my wallet from the glove box.

"I've got this one. You've charmed freebies out of enough ladies today I think." He just looked at me, cocking his head so I reiterated my point. "Joke, Merrick. Joke. You've got to lighten up."

I chuckled and then reached across him to give my card to the cashier. He shifted in such a way as if trying to push himself through the back of the seat to avoid me.

"What is it?" I asked, and he didn't say anything just looked even more uncomfortable. "I'm sorry I touched you, ok?"

He didn't speak so my assumption stayed right where it was.

Repulsed.

I let him grab the card from her. We drove away with our dinner and I scarfed it, as ladylike as I could, what with being wedged between an alien and a huge box of paper towels with a gear shift between my knees. That surely didn't help his driving either.

Merrick finished in record time, even commented on how good it was. I thought to myself that he had probably never had a burger before. I wasn't able to finish my monster of a burger so I slouched back as far as I could and tried to find a comfortable place to shiver, but his arm was already in the air above my head, waiting for me to tuck myself under.

"Oh, thank you," I said, trying to sound super grateful even though I was still peeved.

I didn't understand why I repulsed him so much, but didn't feel the need to fight about it right that second. I could have sworn I felt him smell my hair when I pressed into his side. Probably not.

It grew darker and darker as we reached our hideout. My watch said one p.m., but it looked more like seven. You'd think in a world of technology they'd invent a car that unloaded itself, but not yet. Therefore, the fifteen trips it'd take to unload this beast would just be that much more exercise. Merrick had already started.

"We'd better hurry. Wind's picking up and I want the elevator clear for when people start arriving. The first one will be here in about half an hour," he said as he walked a box away from the car.

We hauled and carried until my little car was empty again. Merrick pulled it into the loading dock on the side and pulled the warehouse door down halfway. I guess this was where we'd park so people wouldn't be suspicious of a bunch of cars lying around.

The small, loaded-down elevator was tight, but we got it all in somehow and packed ourselves in with it before pressing the button.

I had to stand so close to him that I could feel his unsteady breaths on the back of my neck, his deep inhaling. Why did he always freak out? I wasn't t even touching him, trying really hard not to in fact. Jeez, get a grip. I wouldn't act this way even if I was stuck with a Nazi! Well, maybe a Nazi. But I'm not a Nazi! Why was he so...weird? I blew out an exasperated breath, too loud I realized.

"Are you ok?" he asked.

"Yep. Fine, fine." Pissed, pissed was more like it.

"Thanks for your help today. I think we did well. Should last us a while."

"Welcome," I bit out.

"Sherry?"

"Why does this dang elevator take so long?"

"Because we're so far dow-"

"That wasn't an actual question, Merrick!" I cut him off, snapping. I hated that I did that, it wasn't like me, but I couldn't take it anymore. "It was rhetorical. I'm just ready to get out of here and unload all this crap."

"Ok. I'm sorry."

"You're really driving me crazy, you know that." I turned to him, though it was still pitch black and I knew he couldn't see me. "You flinch and jerk away if I even think about laying a hand on you, which sometimes just can't be avoided. I can't recall anything I've done to make you be so upset with me. Then you're constantly asking *me* what's wrong. *Me*? What's wrong with *you*?"

"I'm sorry. I told you, things are just intense for me. I'm not used to this human...stuff."

"I get it, Merrick, ok. I do. I can't imagine what it would be like to be you right now, but if you're going to be here with us, you have got to lighten up. Just because I touch your arm doesn't mean acid's going to shoot out of my human fleshy skin, ok. I'll try to keep my distance so you'll be more comfortable." I turned back around just as the elevator stopped.

"That's not what I think. Sherry, I don't-"

The doors opened and I bee-lined for the bathroom, already holding two bulks of toilet paper. The amount of rejection was enough to last for quite a while. I really wasn't interested in his reasoning. Repulsion was repulsion right?

Seeking Roommate
Chapter 6

The first people to arrive from the elevator doors, as Merrick escorted them in, was a young couple introduced as Lillian and Michael. Michael's Keepers name was Mitchell and being only the second Keeper I'd ever seen, he looked normal enough. So he was right, there really was no way to tell by just looking at them. He was a little bit older with brown hair and eyes, extremely polite and even shook my hand with no problems and didn't hyperventilate.

Lillian was so sweet. Extreme blue eyes and a fluff of blonde hair and pale creamy skin that looked like it never saw the sun. She brought a plate full of brownies and blondies with her. Only the sweetest of the sweet would bring brownies to the apocalypse. I loved her already.

The second group was Polly, the Special and Piper, the Keeper. Polly was loud. Really loud. She couldn't have been more than eighteen. Piper, who was so far the youngest Keeper, seemed a little... oh, I don't know…prickly, especially for a Keeper.

Then there was Susan, the wife, Frank, the Special, and Kathy, the Keeper. Susan seemed scared out of her wits, very opinionated and talkatively nervous. Frank only seemed insulted to be under the guardianship of a woman. His comment about Kathy 'wearing the pants and him wearing the skirt in their relationship' would have been funny, except for his tone, and was met with silence.

Next was Margo, the mom, Celeste, the Special, and Kay, the Keeper. She was just like every other Keeper, quiet, reserved, waiting, watching, polite, but with a shock of shoulder length wavy red hair. Celeste was a tall, sweet faced doll of yellow blonde and legs. Add her green eyes and it made her impossibly gorgeous even though she was so young. I smelled trouble before she was even introduced and then I could see it.

Danny's eyes bulged from his head. Where was Celeste's Keeper? Why didn't she *Keep* her away from him? He would certainly break her heart and then I'd feel bad for not intervening. Just because they were the only ones in the same age group that were single didn't mean they had to play house.

Then there was a good looking pair of what seemed to be 'good old boys'. Bobby the Special and Jeff the Keeper. Bobby was good looking, but a little round, stocky. Jeff was good looking as well from the short glance I got of him; his skin was the color of barely creamed coffee.

Bobby was wearing work boots and jeans with a polo shirt, a huge green duffel bag thrown over his shoulder. He met eyes with me first thing stepping off the elevator and I couldn't help but smile back at his wide grin and cockiness. He cocked his head and winked at me before moving to the side to let his Keeper off the elevator.

And last off the elevator was Sam and his Keeper Lavonne. She was gorgeous, but not her fault, the body was gorgeous. She was probably gorgeous on the inside, too, and as selfless as Merrick was.

These weren't all the ones who came, but the ones I could remember names for and focus on. So many came at one time.

As I stood on the wall with Danny and waited for Merrick's prediction to come true, it literally unfolded right in front of our eyes.

Not there an hour yet and already bickering over who will have what room had started, loudly. Someone else was starting in on one of the Keepers about how dare they drag them down here with all these other people and not have better accommodations than this. That was Polly. The rest ran together in slurs and blurs and a few curses, I couldn't even make it out anymore.

I saw Lillian standing right next to Merrick. She even reached over to touch his arm to steady herself when she leaned to ask him something and he never flinched, not even a wince, as he leaned in to listen over the babble.

I had enough for today. Things to be put up in the kitchen were calling my name so I tried really hard not to roll my eyes as I turned to leave, but darn it, they wouldn't listen. As I turned I heard Susan yelling my name, wrong I might add.

"Shirley! Do you have something to add here? Don't you think that a couple of aged people should have the room closest to the bathroom before someone else should?" she called me out and glared at me, daring me to contradict her in front of everyone and darn it.

I'd had enough.

"Susan is it? I think...I think that we're all stuck down here together and the last thing we need to be doing right now is fighting over rooms to sleep in, bathrooms and accommodations," I said looking directly at her, then I opened my visual range to include everyone suddenly feeling a wind of inspiration. "Do you all realize what is happening outside? Have your Keepers told you as mine has? Because for the life of me, if I knew that they had, then there would be no way we'd be having this conversation right now."

The huddled Keepers seemed just as interested that I'd spoken up as the rest of them. Shocked even. The adrenaline pumping and lack of sugar and coffee put me on a roll and I couldn't stop.

"The world as we know it is ending. Don't you see? I've seen it and heard with my own ears. We're not fighting each other. We're fighting... extinction. I don't know about you, but I'm not spending what could possibly be my last few days on this Earth bickering over something as trivial as a bathroom. We should be grateful that we even have that much. We have no idea how bad it's going to get for us before this is over and there is no room to be petty with each other. And in fact...I'm sorry, Merrick." I looked over and up into his dark green eyes, already looking in mine. "About the elevator. I was wrong. I shouldn't...hmm...I shouldn't be so sensitive. I'm sorry... I'm going to organize the kitchen."

As I turned on my heels and walked out, I could feel at least twenty sets of eyes on me. Not something I'd felt before, but that was it. No screaming, no yelling ensued, no one followed after me to refute my outburst as allegations. Quiet shuffling was all I could hear. So no one wanted to hear another rant from the disgruntled help, huh?

I started stacking the soup cans on the shelf above me, already the guilt and shame setting in, when Merrick came in behind me. I knew it was him before I turned around. He was pretty predictable about some things already.

He didn't speak a word, just started helping to put things away, glancing my way quickly every so often. Did he think that was helping, coming to assist me in silence? I was trying to keep my boiling blood under control. How could someone I barely knew anger me so much?

It wasn't Matt's face, it was Merrick. He was hopelessly in my wrath. Apparently so was everyone else. I couldn't stand it when people were mad at me.

That wasn't me. I didn't want to be known as the crazy lecture lady, not a very good first impression at all. I sighed, feeling sorry for myself and felt Merrick glance over again, but I ignored him.

At some point I stopped working and twirled a piece of hair, staring at the same box of rice before Merrick interrupted my thoughts with my name in my mind. My glued eyes pried away slowly and I looked up to his across the counter.

"You did good back there. That's what they needed to hear. Don't beat yourself up about it," he said firmly, like he knew exactly what I was doing.

"Didn't you know I was going to do that, Mister Future Seer?"

"No. You stunned quite a few of us actually. You changed it, because you knew about it beforehand. I told you they were going to fight and so, you were prepared."

"Yeah, well, I think I was a little harsh. I feel bad. I'm not someone who yells at people. I shouldn't have done that."

"It was exactly what you should've done. They don't want to listen to the Keepers right now because we're different, but you are just like them. You've had just a little more time to adjust than them. They aren't mad at you either."

"I thought you couldn't read my mind."

"I can't, but I can read your face." He chuckled slightly. "And don't worry about earlier," he said suddenly serious. "You don't ever have to apologize to me." I couldn't look away from those eyes. He was so very serious. Intense. He wasn't looking away either, for once. Was he trying to prove he meant what he said? I felt like I was trapped in his gaze, my breath seemed to be pulled out of me. Somehow, after a few sluggish seconds, I nodded and snapped myself out of it and turned to start on the soggy frozen foods, left on the counter too long.

I tried to put things on the bottom so Merrick didn't feel the need to come assist me. I felt him watching me, dissecting my every movement with his eyes, but I refused to look back at him and get swept away again. He stared at me for a long moment before returning to his work.

I wanted to believe it was just curiosity, seeing what made us tick. Us humans. How and why we react the way we do up close but the way he looks at me... No. He wasn't human and didn't even have those kinds of feelings. His eyes being so open just tricked me with their depth, making me see something that wasn't really there. He was just curious.

I took a couple deep breaths to settle myself. What's with those eyes? Matt never looked at me that way, in fact, I barely even remembered that face on Matt at all. And why, if Merrick loathed me so much, did he still take the time to come and try to make me feel better? Must be some Keeper thing. It definitely wasn't a human thing.

The Keepers had a meeting to set up some kind of schedule for showers, meals, etc. They decided that females should have night showers while males had morning. Of course there were complaints but not many and no yelling out in the open like before.

There were six showers and toilet stalls so that would work. One more bathroom down the hall was parted, female and male already. Thank goodness, but that one only had two toilet stalls. Grateful for a stall at all at this point.

The place was a gold mine for people looking to hide out for while. I didn't really see where there was much room to complain.

Everyone seemed to be in agreement for showers and supper was a whatever-you-wanted-to-fix-for-yourself kind of thing. We had too many mixed foods to make huge meals for everyone.

Most of the people were already in their rooms unpacking. Some put sheets up over the huge windows on each wall of the rooms. Good idea.

As I walked to check up on Danny, in our room, I saw Susan come out of the bathroom, which was located directly next to her room. She just looked at me and then turned, not looking back before shutting the door. I giggled a frustrated laugh as I started walking again. Some people.

As I made my way around the corner, I almost bumped into Bobby. He grabbed me with both hands in an overstated motion to catch me as if I would fall. He apologized, his gaze never leaving my face and he didn't release me.

"Hey there. Where's the fire, beautiful?" he asked with the biggest grin.

"Ha ha. Sorry. I wasn't paying attention. I'm a little rattled, I guess."

"Yep. Understandable." He put his arm over my shoulders and I found myself smiling up at him like a frigging idiot. "We haven't been properly introduced. I'm Bobby."

"Sherry."

"Well, Sherry, I know we just met and all, but...I want you to know you can come talk to me any time you want to or need to. We'll get through all this. You'll see."

"Thanks, Bobby. I really appreciate it," I said, just as Merrick rounded the corner.

I immediately pulled away from Bobby and gave us at least a two foot buffer zone. I had no idea why I did that. Who cared if Merrick saw Bobby hugging me? Merrick stopped for just a second, looking surprised, but then composed himself and made the corner not looking at either of us.

Bobby had been making a point to touch, look, stare, or speak to me at every opportunity since that afternoon. *Every* opportunity, which I liked at first but it was amazing how quickly it started to get old. There was no TV, no couches, nowhere to escape down there. We were all just kind of in each other's space so I tried not to blame him too much, chalking it up to boredom, but it was more than that.

I was cooking some lunch in the kitchen when Bobby came in looking fiercely confident. He came up to me while I stirred my pot and brushed his shoulder against mine.

"Hey there."

"Hey," I answered trying to sound normal.

"What are you cooking in here?"

"Clam chowder."

"Hmm... You know clams are considered an aphrodisiac."

He said it so calmly and easily that I thought he must be serious so I replied just as calmly. "I thought it was oysters, not clams."

He laughed loudly throwing his arm over me and squeezing my shoulder. "Girl, I was just joking. What kind of guy do you think I am?" Then he winked at me and grinned.

I was completely and utterly lost so I chuckled a bit, hoping to cover. "So, what do you do?" I asked to change the subject.

"Construction. HVAC."

"Oh. Hmm. Well, do you like it? Or did you, rather?"

"Yep. It kept the ol' guns a blazing." He grinned and lifted his arm not around me and flexed his bicep, making the muscles jump up and down.

Oh, boy. My view of Bobby was quickly going down in a blaze of flames.

At lunch the next day he grabbed my hand in the kitchen like we were a couple already while I waited for the soup to boil. I finally was able to pry myself from his grip and practically ran to my room with him calling after me that he'd see me later. As cute as the guy was, he was a little grabby and had seemed to already have claimed me in some way. Hmmm. I didn't like that.

I did mine and Danny's laundry, cleaned my room, again, cleaned the bathroom. I was so incredibly bored already and it was only week one.

By the time I got to the kitchen that night, it was full of bustling and, to me, looked like unintentional and intentional shoving. Oh boy. This was what happened when civilized people got shoved into confined spaces together. Civility went out the window, if there ever really was any. I decided to wait until later, not craving more conflict.

Maybe everybody was just having a hard time adjusting. It was quite a blow, finding out our loved ones were in danger and being hunted by something we couldn't even really defend ourselves against, just hide from.

The basketball room was empty so I settled myself on the floor and laid down on the freezing hard linoleum, more tired than I realized. If I closed my eyes I would miss dinner, and so would Danny, because all he knew how to do is microwave soup. I saw Merrick walk by through the glass, but he didn't stop. He seemed startled to see me in there alone, lying on the floor but kept on going.

The haunting silence was all around me. I wished I could have my ridge for a minute, some of the noise, the lights, the old feeling of calm I got from it.

Then a gust of wind caused me to look up and see Danny standing in the door. "What are you doing in here, shorty? It's eating time."

"Yeah, I'm just letting the trough empty out a little bit."

"You know, I can't believe you did that. That's not like you," he said as he came to lay down beside me and I knew what he was referring to; my earlier outburst. He'd been sleeping all day since then and hadn't had a chance to rake me over the coals about it yet.

"I know. I feel terrible."

"They all need to grow up a little if you ask me."

"I'm sure they *won't* ask you. And look who's talking Mister I slept all day...

64

I shouldn't have done that."

"No! I mean it was great! They needed to hear that. They're scared and they need someone to tell them how it is. We can't have a panic and melt down every time some one gets upset or their feelings hurt."

"You sound like someone else I know."

"What's with Merrick?"

"You noticed that too, huh?"

"Yeah. He's...anxious."

"More like disgusted. I bet he couldn't wait to take a shower this morning and wash my human stink off."

"What are you talking about?" He rolled over on his side facing me, putting his head on his elbow, so I did the same.

"He just freaks... I had to lean against him in the car and I thought he was going to have a coronary. He doesn't like human contact apparently."

"What did he say?"

"Nothing, just that being in a human body is different and intense for him. Whatever that means."

"I'm sure it is different, but, Sherry, I don't think he didn't *want* you touching him."

I saw where he was going with this. "Danny, that's sweet, but you didn't see his face. I promise you that my touching him was not something he enjoyed."

He chuckled like he knew a secret.

"Well, I've seen his face since he's been back. He couldn't keep his eyes off you while you were ranting out there and just now in the hall...he just looks so...strangely confused."

"Yeah, it is strange. And he was staring at me because everyone was. I was a complete freak out there. I feel bad for him I guess, but he's going to have to get over whatever it is if we are stuck down here together, you know?"

"I think he likes you. I think that's what he meant by 'intense' for him. I mean, think about it. He's only seen human contact. He's never touched a human, let alone a woman, let alone the woman he's watched for years," he dragged out the last few words for dramatic emphasis.

"He hasn't watched *me*, it was you."

"Yeah, but did you hear him earlier, he said 'we are supposed to only watch our charge'. *Supposed to*. I think he watched you and I think he likes you."

"Danny, that's so ludicrous. Besides, I'm Plain Jane not Megan Fox. Aliens don't come all the way here to fall in love with Plain Jane. Jerks do."

"Well, I guess that's my fault...and Mom and Dad's, too wrapped up in our own crap to tell you how great you are. You are pretty, you know. You're a-"

"Oh, shut up, Danny!" I said, playfully pushing his shoulder.

"I'm serious."

"If that were true then how come the only *thing* I ever attracted was Matt?"

"Matt told everyone, and I mean everyone, about you and him. His work, my work, your work, and he said you guys were getting married and threatened anyone who even talked to you."

"What? Danny, please. He couldn't keep every guy in Chicago from asking me out."

"True, but almost every guy you came into contact with did with him also. Where did you go besides work without Matt? I'm telling you, people were scared of him. He wasn't exactly a small dude and he was a total crazy man when it came to you. I'm sorry I joshed you for dumping him. I didn't know what was going on until much later. You should've told me what was happening."

I didn't want to tell Danny what was really going on with Matt. He would freak. He could never find out what Matt did so I skipped the whole last part of his statement.

"You're not lying... What? Why would he do that? All this time, I thought..."

"It's ok, sis. He's not coming back, but Merrick seems...nice."

"Danny, don't you dare! I think you're misinterpreting what Merrick is thinking. He's not even human. I doubt he can even have those feelings. I promise you that wasn't a face of "Ooh, baby, I want you", ok? You have no way of knowing."

"You're right...except I heard him say it in his sleep last night," he said, smiling smugly.

"What? You're lying. You sleep through anything."

"Am I lying? I got up to go to the bathroom and overheard him say some stuff."

"What stuff?"

"Just 'Sherry. I can't believe I'm here.' That was it, but it doesn't sound like he hates you to me."

"That's what he said to me when I was under the drug. What does that mean?"

"It means alien boy's got it bad."

"Shh! Danny! Ugh," I whispered loudly and pushed him as he fell backwards laughing. "You ready to eat, brat?"

"Yeah, I heated up some soup in the microwave, but it's probably cold by now."

I couldn't keep myself from bursting into laughter.

The next couple of days were spent assigning chores and getting to know each other. I tried to avoid Merrick most of the time, to make it easier on him. My favorite person still by far was Lillian, brownie girl. Michael and Mitchell, the husband and Keeper, seemed to be hitting it off rather well. They talked a lot. Lillian and I were on bed sheet duty and I was on night dish duty with Merrick as well this week.

Our first assignment would be tomorrow after dinner. I swallowed hard thinking about how he would handle this. I mean, heaven forbid our fingers touched as I handed him a plate. He'd drop it in disgust and feel the need to start apologizing again.

I usually wound up eating later than everyone else because I liked cooking when I wasn't fighting someone else for the frying pan. Merrick and I had tried to get a variety of items, but there wasn't much room, so we have tons of eggs, pasta and soup. Merrick had snuck in a huge box of blueberry cereal bars, when I wasn't looking.

I wondered if that was a coincidence or if it was because he somehow knew they were my favorite. With Danny's bantering in my mind, I was starting to second guess my own thinking.

Later on I sauntered into the quiet kitchen and got the pan ready, putting in the butter and whisking the eggs, placing in a few tablespoons of water instead of milk, old family trick.

I reached up to the spice rack, but couldn't reach the seasoning salt. I tried once more, pushing myself up on my tip toes, using the counter as leverage and barely touched the edge of the rack when a hand from behind grabbed it for me and I turned, startled.

Merrick was so close to me, but quickly stepped back, holding out the spice bottle for me.

"Thanks," I said taking it from him, wondering why I felt like I needed to catch my breath. I also wanted to bury the hatchet so I made him an offer of nicety. "Hungry? Want some eggs?"

"Sure," he said without hesitating.

"I have to warn you, I don't cook them the way most people do."

"I know how you eat your eggs, Sherry," he said matter-of-factly walking across to the counter to face me, leaning on it with his elbows.

"Yeah...that's right. So, you're ok with it then?"

"Whatever you do is fine," he spoke so soft, so meaningful.

I squinted my eyes, scrutinizing him, trying to find another meaning, but he just stood there, looking handsome and innocent.

"So, I guess you haven't seen me much the past few years, huh, except when I'm driving Danny to and from work." I had to get to the bottom of this, so I probed, conversationally.

"Mmmm. Some...but yeah, not much."

Lie. Hmmm. Could Danny be right? That doesn't make any sense though. Why would he watch me if he hates me? I continued to stir the eggs and watch him from the corner of my eye. He was watching me, too. It was best to not call him on his lies, he never cleared them up anyway.

"Since you've only been here a few times, have you ever even had scrambled eggs before?"

"Nope. Never."

I reached up to grab plates, praying I could reach, I hate having to constantly be in need of assistance, but I reached them and divvied up the portions.

"Bon appetite," I joked, handing him his plate. "Hope you like them. They are my second favorite food."

I watched him as we stood at the counter and ate opposite each other. He took his first bite and his face looked pleasantly surprised.

"This is really good, Sherry. Thanks."

"You're welcome." I took another bite. "Are you ok? You aren't your normal...chipper self," I said grabbing two glasses and pouring milk into them.

"Just tired. It's hard to get used to being here, in this body."

"You keep saying that. What do you mean? Earth?"

"We don't have needs where I'm from. These bodies seem like they constantly need something. Food, drink, rest...companionship." He clears his throat. "It's a little hard to adjust."

"I'm sorry I was so hard on you before. You could've just explained it to me."

"I told you, don't apologize to me...and I didn't really know how to explain it then," he said softly and I noticed he was looking at my lips.

"You seem to be doing a pretty good job to me." I smiled at him, still feeling strange about his indifference to me.

Drama, drama. This couldn't be the final ending for him to just come here and not like me right off the bat. I couldn't allow it.

"Thanks. And thanks for the eggs. I didn't mean to bother you. I'll leave you alone now."

"If you know so much about the way I eat my eggs," I started so he wouldn't leave yet, "you must also know I don't like to be alone in a silent, dark lonely kitchen. Silence is my nemesis." I chuckled.

"Yes, I know. I just don't know what to do. I don't know what you want me to do, Sherry. I'm very confused right now."

"We're all confused. This is pretty strange stuff, even for you, right? I can see... It's ok, if you want to talk, you know. I may not understand all of it, and I may not be the one you want to talk to, but I'm a good listener."

"I know." He smiled and chuckled a little before walking out of the kitchen into the dark hall.

Well that conversation cleared absolutely nothing up. It may have even made it worse for my understanding. I felt like banging my head on the wall.

As soon as he was out of sight I threw my hands up in the air in frustration. Why was I letting him drive me so crazy? So what if he didn't like me? Maybe he felt like I got in the way of his watching Danny, being so bossy and protective of him all those years.

I had to stop this and follow my own advice. We were stuck down here together, but before I could think about getting over it, in walked Bobby, which didn't bother me, but I wasn't really in a courting mood.

Liar, Liar, Pants On Fire
Chapter 7

"Hey, you make me some, too, girly?" he said and I flinched slightly at the 'girly', but he had a wide grin in place.

"No, sorry, didn't know you were interested in any."

"Oh, I'm always interested," he drawled and winked.

"Well, sorry. Goodnight."

"Now wait a minute." He grabbed the sleeve of my shirt, not hard, but enough to make me stop in my tracks. "How come every time I'm coming you're going, huh? I just want to talk to you."

"I know, Bobby, but I also know what you want to talk about. I'm just not...interested right now, ok. We all have enough going on right now than to be trying to date someone. I'm sorry, I just-"

"You seem to be plenty happy with Merrick," he spat out angrily, taking me by complete surprise.

"What are you talking about?" I rebutted in my most surely shocked voice. What was with this guy? "Merrick is just...my brother's Keeper. He talks to me because he has to. What's wrong with you?" I spoke softly trying to soften the blow of my words. "I don't even know you, Bobby. We just met."

"Nope. Sorry, not buying it, and you cooked him eggs and not me so, I think you know what's going on here."

I'm sure I wasn't hiding the utter disbelief on my face but I couldn't help it. I tried to shake off his hand on my sleeve, but he tightened his fist.

"For one thing, he was in the kitchen with me already, I was being polite. For two, cooking eggs for someone doesn't constitute courtship, and for three, it's none of your business who I cook eggs for. Merrick is nice and he's my...friend, and you and I are barely acquainted."

"Uhuh. Well I say he likes you. And you like it that he likes you."

"Maybe I do, and stop calling me girly. It's not your concern, Bobby. My last boyfriend treated me like he owned me, and I'm not about to get involved like that again." I felt his grip tighten on my sleeve. "Please stop, you're hurting me."

"Fine," he said, dragging me by my arm a little closer. "You go date your alien, fine by me, just don't lead me on anymore," he said through his gritted teeth, making me recoil, but not getting far.

Then I saw Merrick standing in the doorframe, arms crossed and face tight but blank. "Bobby, I think you should let her go, now."

Stunned, Bobby turned to look at him, but didn't let go of my arm. "Frankly, this is none of your business, Keeper."

"Actually, she is my business. Go," Merrick commanded firmly and my heart skidded at his words.

I am his business? Did he really think that or was he just saying that so Bobby would leave. Why! Why was I developing a crush on this guy, this guardian? I had to stop this letting my heart beat go nuts whenever he spoke.

Bobby released me so forcefully I had to catch myself on the counter. Then he stalked out, turning on his heels, but not before turning to look at me once more. He didn't even look angry. He looked like this wasn't over, a challenge now that he had competition. Oh, great.

"Are you ok?" Merrick asked, not coming any closer.

I breathed slow and long, my hands shaking. Why did everyone think they could manhandle me?

"Yes. He didn't do anything really, he's just persistent," I said embarrassed and straightened imaginary wrinkles in my clothes.

"Well, maybe you should head to bed. If you're all right I'll go-"

I cut him off before he could finish. I knew he was going to leave and I wanted him to stay for a minute. I needed to settle down.

"Why do guys do that? Why do they think they have to act like they own us? Does Danny act like that to his girlfriends?"

"No, Danny's a good kid. No, all men don't treat women that way. Tell me if Bobby keeps messing with you. I'll... Well, I'll talk to his Keeper about it."

"Why do guys have to be jerks with me? I don't really get it. What did I do to make them think that I'd like that?"

"I don't think...I don't think you see yourself very well, Sherry. You're nice and...pretty. Men like that. One day you'll meet someone not like Bobby, a nice guy, as you put it." He smiled a little, surprising me.

It seemed as if he was trying to actually joke with me.

"A nice guy. Hmmm. Tell me when you find one that likes lame cooking and muddy brown out of control hair and a lack of style," I said self consciously, twirling a piece of hair.

"There are plenty." He looked down at the floor as he spoke.

"Thanks, Merrick. Did you hear...what Bobby said?"

"Uh, no, not really. I just got here at the last second," Merrick lied.

"Ok. Well, thanks. Goodnight," I said, but didn't call him on his lie.

He knew by now I could tell if he was lying but he still chose to lie anyway. He must have a reason.

"Goodnight, Sherry."

I touched his arm as I walked out and said my thank you again, quickly. I just felt the need to reiterate the thank you. He sucked in a slow, quiet breath, keeping his arms crossed but didn't completely freak as our eyes locked for a mere millisecond. I closed my eyes and laughed under my breath at myself as I walked away.

I shouldn't have done that.

Danny's theory still carried no merit for me. Merrick couldn't like me and hadn't been watching me without Danny in the picture. I would just try to keep my distance, try to make it easier on him and definitely not touch him or brush against him in any way.

However, the next day as I rounded the corner to the kitchen, I saw Susan hugging him and crying, her gray wavy head on his shoulder. He didn't seem tense at all. In fact, he was even hugging her back, rubbing her shoulder to comfort her. I wasn't upset about Susan, though she was the closest thing to an 'enemy' I would have in this place. I was upset because he wasn't hyperventilating, no shaking, no recoiling. It *was just me* he hated then! Gah!

He looked at me and I could only imagine my face, twisted in confusion. I turned to stomp off and start lunch. I decided to make lunch for all three of us. Danny, me, and Merrick. I couldn't let this go. What had I done to him?

Somehow, I had to make this better. People could not stay mad at me, especially for something I had no control over, being human. That was the only explanation I had and it made no sense at all.

I saw him walk in shortly after and stop in the walkway, propping his hands up in the door frame. I fought it, but the corners of my mouth twitched with frustration. I only glanced his way and of course, he was staring at me. Probably trying to decide what the heck was wrong with me. I must seem crazy to him. I heard it then in my head, his voice.

Sherry. She felt bad and wants to apologize to you. She started crying and...hugged me. I'm sorry, I know you were angry with her. I'm not taking sides.

"I'm not angry with her. I don't care about that," I all but shouted.

The others in the kitchen looked at me, and I realized to them I was having a conversation with myself. I shook my head. One more thing for these people to be disgusted about. Not only was I bossy, but loony, too. He tried again.

Sherry...

"It's fine," I mouthed this time, knowing he could at least read that on my lips.

I am so confused. I don't know what you want me to do.

That was the last thing he said wordlessly before turning and leaving, shaking his head. I wanted to crawl under the table. Why was I such a spaz?

I managed to pull myself together long enough to finish the pasta I started. I felt like a masochist, but I couldn't help myself for going after him. No matter what his reaction might be, I had to know why. People can't be mad at me.

I took a bowl to Danny, who pretty much confined himself to our room, unless Celeste was seen wondering around. I took a bowl to Merrick then, who I found in my hiding spot, the basketball court.

"Peace offering," I said, extending the bowl to him, careful not to let our fingers touch on the side of the bowl.

"Thanks." He took it, but didn't look up to my face.

"I don't care that you were hugging Susan. Why would I? And I'm not angry with her. When you put different people together, they are going to clash a little. I just don't understand why..." I sucked in a breath and bit my lip, deciding how to word it.

"Yes?"

"Why don't you flinch or get so...bothered when anyone else touches you but me? Why am I so...so...bothersome? Repulsive? Please tell me so I can stop doing it and we can just be normal with each other."

His twisted expression was somewhat of a shock to me. I fully expected him to stare at the wall as usual when something was brought up that he wasn't interested in answering. He put his bowl aside and got up on his knees, scooting closer to me on the floor, catching me off guard.

"Sherry, is that what you've thought of me this whole time? That I was repulsed by you? I'd say more the opposite. I told you I can't control these new human feelings. I've never touched a woman before."

"But you had no trouble touching Susan or Lillian," I countered softly.

His eyes never left my gaze as I spoke. He was struggling again.

"I don't... Sherry, I just like you. You're so close to my charge and I feel connected to you, too. I'm sorry if I made you feel uncomfortable."

Lies, lies, lies.

"I told you I'm a human lie detector."

"Can we just leave it at that? Please. I don't want you to be angry with me

73

and I don't want to hurt you."

He hated me. He knew he couldn't lie to me, but he couldn't very well tell me the truth; that he hated me.

"Merrick, I'm not a grudge holder, ok. It's very hard to be mad at you, believe me. I've been trying for days now." I gave him a crooked smile.

The look on his face was pained and desperate. I instinctively scooted to him until we were almost touching. I wanted to comfort him, somehow, but being afraid to touch him hindered that effort. He finally looked up at me, resolution on his face, the decision to fill me in completely had been made.

He reached for me.

I couldn't stop the confused look on my face or my sudden intake of air. Just before his hand reached my face, there was a gust of wind and a voice. We both turned to see the Keeper, Piper, standing in the doorway, looking highly peeved.

"Merrick, I need you. Now," she snapped.

Without a word, Merrick grabbed his bowl and left. My lungs were the ones having problems then. It wasn't Matt's body causing confusion, Merrick just knew how to look into my soul. He didn't look at me, he looked into me.

I composed myself after a few breaths and ate my cold pasta and stayed for a while, wondering what in the heck had just happened.

Dish duty later with Merrick would be awkward to say the least. Of course, it was going to be torture cause I couldn't let things go. He was going to let me know the reason, let me down easy. What could it be? My bad smell? My hair too curly? I'm too opinionated, though that wouldn't affect him touching me. Rough skin? Agh! Wretched boys! Did I mention I hated drama?

The sound of Polly's screams were like nails on a chalkboard that afternoon. I mean, she had waited a full eight seconds since the power had gone out to let out this wail of terror.

Eight seconds. Count them. That's a long time. Merrick assured us that the generator was temporarily out of power from the storm, and needed to recharge. I certainly didn't have candles or a flashlight in my pocket so I just stopped where I was and sat down in the hall on the hard, freezing cold tile.

Being in a completely pitch black and silent enclosed space was unsettling. I could hear shuffling and whispering. I wanted to ask them why they were whispering. The darkness didn't make the noise sound any different.

The little boy, Calvin, was crying and I thought his mother would comfort him, but I kept hearing him. I could still hear Polly, too, whimpering, and Piper reassuring her.

The footsteps I heard were a little quick for someone to be walking that couldn't see where they are going.

"Hey, who's that running around?" I asked as I pulled my legs in closer so as not to trip whoever it was.

"It's Merrick," he answered, startling me with his closeness.

"So what's the deal? Night vision?"

"Yes, actually."

"Should've known," I said with a chuckle.

Everyone could hear our conversation and I heard some of the other murmurs as well.

"We just see things on a different plane than you, that's all."

"Why don't you guys share some of that power? I'd take the mind talking thing any day."

"Being a human lie detector comes in pretty handy, I'd say?"

Was he flirting with me? Keepers knew how to flirt? No. I tried not to make a face, knowing then that he could see me in the dark and I thought back to the elevator when I got in his face thinking he couldn't see me when I was yelling at him.

Sigh.

"Yes, but it's just...intuition," I answered. "It's not a super power."

"Do you know anyone who can shoot fire from their fingertips?" a small, yet carrying, voice careened through the hallways.

Everyone chuckled at Calvin's question, as we heard him yell it from his room. He had apparently been listening and it seemed to calm him down as he was no longer crying.

"Nope. Sorry," Merrick answered loudly for him to hear.

"That would totally be my power, if I could pick one. Totally," Calvin yelled back.

The humming of fluorescents and sighs of relief could be heard as the lights flickered back to life. Blinking I realized Merrick was sitting almost right next to me. Or was he? When my eyes adjusted and I looked, he was gone completely.

A few days later, Lillian and I folded sheets for thirty minutes straight. The amount of sheets a group of people can use in a few days time was ridiculous but I followed orders like a good little soldier.

Bobby had come in to the laundry area to find the broom and decided to give us a hand. He kinda sorta apologized about the other night, so I wordlessly let him stay.

Lillian was far from interested in sheets because boy was she proud of Michael. He was chosen in her eyes. She continued her story, started earlier about how they met, that they'd been married a little shy of a year, their jobs before this all happened. How she dreamed of having kids that looked liked him one day, two

75

boys and one girl.

It really was sweet to watch and listen to but it was hard to concentrate with Bobby accidentally 'bumping' into me every few minutes. It's not like it was a close space.

He even asked if he could get one of my massages he'd heard so much about. In other words, he overheard Danny mention it to someone and ran with this wild line. He was handsome but just not for me. For some reason, I couldn't seem to care if Bobby was upset with me or not and I wasn't usually like that.

I thought I had made myself clear the other night. He hadn't even tried to explain himself and his odd possessive behavior nor said how and why he thought Merrick was interested in me more than just his charge's sister. His apology was "Sorry about the other night. I was tired." That was it. End of apology and on with the annoying pick up lines.

I subtly tried to leave them both behind as I turned to leave, stating a thanks for their help and that I'd see them later. I was apparently not very good at the brush-off technique because he continued to follow me down the hall back to the kitchen. When we arrived, Merrick was there. He did a subtle double take and went back to his stirring.

"So. It was fun doing laundry with you. Maybe tomorrow you can need my help again?" Bobby said and laughed whole heartedly and loudly at his own joke.

Oooh, mistake Bobby.

"Sheets are done for a few days I'm afraid, but thanks anyway."

"Well, you can help me sweep tomorrow if you want. I wouldn't stop ya."

"Ok, we'll see. I need to get to making Danny and I some supper, so..."

"Need some help, girly?" he said looking between me and Merrick.

"Nope." I was beginning to see a lot of Matt's traits in him and if I heard girly one more time... "I got it. Thanks anyway. See ya."

There were only a few ways to nicely tell someone to get lost and I was running out of them quickly. Waiting to see if he'd actually leave was an eternity, but he did turn and walk out the door, slowly, with a waggle of his fingers.

I grabbed myself a cup of crappy coffee, no one could make coffee right in this place, with no creamer to boot.

I walked over, pulling myself up on the counter next to where Merrick was standing and stirring, but not too close. We were alone in the kitchen and my curiosity of Piper's interruption in the basketball court had been milling.

"So, you in trouble for something?" I started the interrogation.

"Hmm?" he asked, only glancing at me from under his lashes then back to his bowl.

"Piper? She looked unhappy the other day."

"Oh, that. No. She's just worried about me."

Worried? Why? Huh. What is that? Was that jealousy I felt? That buzzing in my stomach? I'd never felt jealous before. Wow. Why would I be jealous of her? I didn't know her and I didn't even like him that way...right?

I decided to prod further and ignored that little internal revelation.

"Worried?" I asked, but my voice comes out a little strained.

"We can hear each other's thoughts, unless we're trying really hard to not let them in. She's just trying to watch out for me. She's worried that I might...be a little too attached to you because you're not my charge."

I laughed out loud, but he didn't. He stopped stirring and looked up at me curiously.

"Well, did you tell her that you loathe me? That ought to clear things right up," I said still laughing because I couldn't stop.

It was just hilarious to me that I had been trying so hard to get him to like me and not be upset with me, with no results, and now, more than one person thought Merrick had some kind of crush on me. Like he was even capable of such a thing and I was letting my mind run wild with it, trying to conjure up feelings for him myself. Absurd.

"Why do you think that?" he asked softly, looking tired and drained.

"Well, per our conversation earlier, we established that touching other humans isn't a problem for you, it's just me. In fact you go out of your way to not touch or really come near me much at all it seems. You only talk to me if you feel I need comfort, like after I make a fool of myself yelling at everyone, but that's just the Keeper in you, I think. And then you said you liked me before, but that was a lie. I told you, you can't lie to me." I shook my finger at him, but his face was anything but amused.

"I was lying," he confessed.

"It's ok, Merrick. I get it. I'm sorry, I just...I just can't handle it when people are upset with me and I can't fix it somehow. I'll stay out of your way, ok."

As I hopped down from the counter and turned to leave he grabbed my wrist and my skin immediately begins to tingle.

"You're so blind," he breathed shaking his head.

"I'm sorry?"

He steadied himself, took a deep breath and then let me have it, all the while, keeping my wrist in his overly warm, shaky, gentle grasp.

"I did lie. I don't like you, Sherry. I...I love you." I heard my breath falter, but he continued. "I can't touch you because it drives this body insane." He was barely speaking, breathing the words as he leaned closer to me. "My skin... tingles and I can barely breathe, which you've noticed. I can't explain it. I know you'll probably hate me now when I tell you this, but I couldn't help it. Sherry, I watched you, too. The first time I saw you was when you were little, when Danny was

77

born," he smiled while remembering "you were so protective of him. I enjoyed it, I thought you were my little helper, but over the years, I never stopped watching. I split my attention in half and took my full focus away from my charge, your brother. I felt so protective of you. Somewhere along the way it stopped being just protective. As you got older and I saw the person you were, the kind of woman you were, it became something else. I fell in love with you and kept watching and protecting you even when you were on your own. After I came here, when I saw you in your driveway..." He shook his head, his eyes closed. "I'm so sorry. I know what you must think of me, but all this time as a guardian I've never broken the rules, never gotten involved when I shouldn't. I know it doesn't matter, I'm not human, but I...just can't let you sit there and think that I hate you when the opposite is true."

It was all true, not a lie in the mix, which meant he did love me.

I couldn't move or speak. Shock overtook me, as did those smoldering green eyes. He reached out and cautiously, gauging to see if I'd flinch, he ran his free fingers down the inside of my elbow to my wrist. The goose bumps came and he looked at me for indication, good or bad? I had none to give him.

I was the one confused now. How could this perfect, selfless being love *me*, especially if he watched me over the years with my worthless life and pointless existence? I was short and awkward in my own skin. My lousy apartment with no real friends to fill it. My stupid job. My weirdo parents who didn't even love us enough to stay with us. My horrible judgment I pounded into my brother's head.

How did I always gauge every situation so wrong?

I realized I was panting. He looked worried, but I couldn't stop. The hot tears spilled over and I wanted to run so he wouldn't see, but then I guessed he'd seen it before, hadn't he? He'd seen it all.

The tears overtook me and a low sob broke loose. I pulled my wrist free and ran to my room, too embarrassed to face him after I'd thought so many horrible things about him, but he somehow was there again, already in my room waiting for me. He reached for my arm, but retracted it before he touched me.

I'm sorry. I'm so sorry, Sherry. I shouldn't have said anything. I didn't want to hurt you, that's the last thing I ever wanted to do. Please don't cry because of me.

Wrong. All wrong.

"I don't hate you," I squeaked. It was all I could get to come out.

He thought I was mad because he watched me against my will, without my permission, without his call's permission. But no, it was because I was embarrassed for being lame and not doing something more with my life. To have something for him to see that was worth something and not just embarrassment. For some reason, I *needed* him to comfort me again, even after this, I was surprised that I wanted him to.

I'm sorry. Forgive me, Sherry. Just forget I said anything, all right? I'll never bring it up again and I'll stay away from you as much as I can. I promise. I'm so sorry.

He started to leave, maneuvering around me. I reached for his shirt in one swift movement, pulling my face into his chest. He seemed surprised, but not as reluctant as usual, as he let me and even wrapped his warm, strong arms around my shoulders. He continued out loud.

"I never watched when I shouldn't have. When Matt and you...your showers, among lots of other things, I always tuned out. I know I don't deserve it, but...please forgive me, Sherry. I never wanted to hurt you."

I felt one of his hands slip to the small of my back and to my utter embarrassment, my heart rate picked up and I felt a little sigh release from my lips. I tried fervently to tamp down on that and focus on what he said.

"There was no Matt and me. That was the reason he got so upset with me that night and he tried to...he hit me when I wouldn't..." I sniffed and looked up at his face, realizing. "But you tuned out and didn't see that, did you?"

His enraged face suggested that he had not and if he had, it would have been a trip here to stop Matt. He suppressed his anger and looked back at me as I spoke again, his green eyes so close in our embrace and I focused on them as I explained to him the truth.

"I'm not mad at you, I'm mad at myself. I have nothing to show for my life. For all these years; school, college, work, family, friends, I just caused problems and...I did nothing worth anything and now, it could all be over. It just sucks having someone see the entirely lame failure your life is."

"That's not true," he said with conviction and I felt his arm tighten around my waist. "I saw a lot of things worth something. Why do you think I fell in love with you?" I gasped slightly and looked up to his face as he continued. "The flowers you always sent your lonely old neighbor at the apartments on holidays, anonymously. The way you always straightened your boss' desk when she was gone, even though she was terrible to you. You let your parents push their ideas on you and were respectful, never complained. You always made sure that Danny knew what was important, and you hugged each other and loved each other. You may not know this, but Danny had a really hard time, for a while. You were the only thing he looked forward to, driving him to and from work so you could talk."

This brought a whole new round of tears and hysteria, remembering my rant

79

with myself over being Danny's chauffeur. More tears spilled over my already red and burning eyelids.

He looked even more concerned and guilty as his hands moved towards my face. I slightly gasped at the warmth when they actually reached it this time, cradling my face on both sides. He wiped the tears from my cheeks with his warm thumbs.

It was strange; these didn't feel like Matt's hands. The calluses were the same, the size was the same, but the movement, the warmth...the reason behind it, made all the difference. Both of our breathing was out of control at this point, but he didn't stop this time. I could feel tingling in my cheeks doing nothing to slow my breaths or heart beat. Little sparks. He spoke again.

"Please don't cry anymore. I can't take it," he breathed hoarsely.

"I'm sorry."

"Don't apologize to me, Sherry."

"I'm sorry for saying sorry," I joked and try to laugh, but his hands on me distracted me beyond thinking.

"It's not important whether you're angry with me or not. What's important is that you stop thinking that you're worthless. I want you to be mad, what I did was wrong, but *you* have done so many right things. You're still doing them, look at Susan. She was so moved by what you said and the way you spoke to everyone with such...conviction. No one here is mad at you, Sherry."

"Are you sure you can't read my mind?"

"No, I wish I could. Right now more than ever," he chuckled to himself as he spoke.

He swallowed and moved one of his hands to rub my necklace charm in between fingers, then moved it up to rub the ends my hair laying across my shoulder, his fingertips brushed the side of my neck tentatively. He looked fascinated by his exploring. His other hand was still on my wet cheek, his eyes fixed on my lips again.

Then Danny burst through the door, knocking me into Merrick's already close body, forcing him to catch me from toppling us both over. Danny was more surprised than we were, judging by his dropped jaw and wide eyes. We straightened up quickly, and Merrick immediately turned to leave, stopping at the door.

"See you later, Sherry," was his grand departure.

"Bye," was mine.

Danny grinned from ear to ear, more from I-told-you-so than genuine happiness for me, I thought. I was still reeling from the past half hour of crammed emotions and shocking revelations, as I wiped my eyes with the sleeve of the hideous sweat shirt that was folded on the end of my bed. I stood still for a few minutes, eyes closed, settling myself, letting my breathing and heart rate slow.

I was in no mood to have playful banter with Danny, and he could tell, because he settled into his cot and closed his eyes as I walked out without a word.

If I thought doing dishes with him was going to be weird before, it would definitely be weird now, but I hadn't eaten supper either, so ditching dishes wouldn't solve that one. It sounded pretty quiet as I tiptoed into the hall and crept towards the kitchen. When I looked, the dishes were done. There was no way Merrick had time to do them. I was startled by the voice behind me.

Merrick - No Touchy
Chapter 8

Oh! I actually touched her. She was so soft. Softer than I'd ever imagined possible. I just reached out and grabbed that sweet teary face. Tears she was crying because of me.

What a jerk I was, but she said she wasn't mad, didn't hate me, and she was telling the truth. I had no idea what to do. She was driving me every kind of human crazy. I wanted to just give in to my senses, but I also had a job to do. I wanted to ignore her, but I knew I never could, and if I was honest, I didn't want to. I wanted to kiss her but how could I after what I've done? I wouldn't even know what to do anyway. What would it be like to kiss her? Her lips were fascinating.

And she smelled so good. So, that was what vanilla smelled like. And her hair, curling around my fingers...

What was I thinking? She must've thought I was crazy. Worse than crazy. She didn't flinch away though, didn't move. Her breathing even seemed to quicken like mine. Ah! Don't get your hopes up, you were such an idiot.

And Bobby. As much as I don't like him what could I offer her that he couldn't and more? He was a jerk, but any human would be better for her. Right?

I shouldn't have told her all of that. Things were just going to be weird between us. She did hug me though, but no, she was crying and just wanted comfort, just like Susan did that day. Humans act that way. These bodies were constantly in need of something. Comfort and compassion being a couple of them. Don't read anything into it, fool.

Driving back here from the store with her was unbearable. I could smell her the whole time and her hair was brushing my arm, her face against my arm and chest. Embarrassing, her having to teach me to drive and then me freaking out about it like that, but I couldn't seem to keep this body's reactions under control.

She actually thought I was repulsed by her. How could she ever think that? Of course, she had no idea how gorgeous she was. Gorgeous and cute, tiny. I just wanted to snatch her up and keep her behind me at all times, protected. My conscience didn't buzz for her because she wasn't my charge, but my heart did.

I walked slowly to the laundry room to check on my clothes that I had put in the dryer earlier. It was hard to get these minds to focus on more than one thing at a time; remembering to get your clothes later, remembering what time is lunch and dinner, remembering what day it is for chores.

After I had a quick lesson on the washing machines knobs from Jeff, who had been shown by Bobby, folding clothes was pretty self explanatory but not everything was. Take cooking, for instance.

I had to ask Lillian to show me how to turn on the oven and then which pans to use, and such. I had to read the instructions on every box and can on how to prepare it.

I tried to mentally prepare myself for the awkwardness of doing the dishes with Sherry after that whole scene, after making a human fool of myself. I saw Susan finishing up the dishes in the kitchen.

"Hey. That's my job," I said smiling.

Human humor was strange to actually perform instead of listen to. I wasn't sure if I was pulling it off correctly or not.

"Hey. I thought it was Sherry's. Just trying to make amends, ya know."

"It was supposed to be both of ours. She's not angry at you, Susan. It was me. All me. I'm not...making this transition very pleasant for her I'm afraid," I admitted pulling a soda can out of the fridge.

Soda was one thing I had definitely grown to enjoy.

"Well then, stop it. She's very bright and brave and you can tell she cares about people. We just got off on the wrong foot, that's all."

"Yes, she does care. She's very...sweet." I couldn't help but smile as I thought back on things from Sherry's past that she'd done.

"Uhuh. I see..." Susan dragged her words out and I wasn't sure what that meant, but it didn't sound reassuring as she lifted her eyebrow at me.

"I'm just saying she's...you know...one of those people that...really...try to...care about people." I shook my head in frustration, unable to think of words to describe her accurately. "Anyway, she's not mad at you, ok. She told me so herself. She's not one to hold a grudge. So, I guess I'll see you tomorrow. I'm turning in for the night. Thanks for doing the dishes for us," I said as I turned to leave.

"Uhuh. You have a good night, Merrick."

"You, too."

I wandered into the hall, back towards my room, which just so happened to hold Jeff across the hall from me. I saw him standing in his door frame and looking pensive, and then I felt the tell-tell fuzziness of him digging into my brain once again with his.

You can stop that anytime, Jeffrey.

83

I tried to keep the bite from my tone, barely managing.

Can I? I thought you wanted our help, brother?

"Not like that I don't. I want your support. Brother."

Jeff pushed off the doorframe and followed me into my room on my heels, shutting the door behind him with force. "Well, I think you need my help more than ever."

"I'm fine."

"Are you? I'm sure this Sherry is a sweet girl. In fact, I know she is from seeing her in your memories, but that's just it, Merrick. She's a girl, a mundane human, and you're not. How can I convince you how many levels of wrong this is?"

"You don't have to convince me of anything. I know. I had to make her aware of my feelings. She was upset because- well, you know why. I can't deal with this, too. I'm just trying to get through the day right now and keep my charges alive."

"Charges? You mean charge right? As in one charge, as in Danny."

"You know what? You have no idea what I'm going through so just back off, Jeff." I all but gritted my teeth, but he didn't seem to notice.

"I know I don't but I can see what you feel and I can't believe what I'm seeing. You would actually stay here with her if she accepted you. You say you don't plan to actually do it but if she gave you the slightest hope, you'll stay. I know you will."

"You're probably right, but I'll never get that chance so stop worrying. Stay out of my head and tell the others to as well."

I pulled off my t-shirt and flung it on the chair along with my jeans. It didn't occur to me that it might not be proper human etiquette, to undress down to boxers in front of another person, but I wasn't feeling proper at the moment.

"What about Piper?" he asked, looking at me closely.

"What about her?" I asked quietly as I sat on the edge of my bed.

"You know what about her. She chose you, Merrick. That's rare. You're lucky. Most female Keepers don't choose at all, you know this." He spread his palms, making my jaw twitch with my need for him to leave. "It's a great honor for her to make such a leap of faith on you instead of waiting for you to do it and you are turning her down for something you can never have."

"I have no personal interest in Piper."

"This isn't about her body is it?" he asked me incredulously. "Because you know that won't matter once we go home."

"No, I don't care how old her body is. This is about her. Actually it's not about her, it's about me."

"Merrick, come on!" he said throwing his hands up in frustration.

"She's..." I tried to think of a word that wouldn't be a lie, but came up with nothing, "great and I know it's an honor, but I've made up my mind. I won't settle. It's my life, especially now that I'm literally alive to live it. God gave me free will and I intend to use it. I mean it, Jeff. Stay out of my head and let me worry about myself. You and I are the same age, you know that."

"Yes, I do and you would think that after living thousands of years, you'd be a little smarter."

"I appreciate what you're trying to do, but I promise you that I don't need or want your help on this. Goodnight, Jeffrey," I said and pulled the covers over my head as I lay down. "Turn out the light, would you, on your way out?"

I heard him sigh and the click of the light switch before I was plunged into darkness. I lay there thinking about what he said and knowing he was right but not caring. Who would I hurt but myself if I stayed here and kept watching Sherry, even if I couldn't have her?

I hoped Sherry went to bed when she saw the dishes done. Maybe I should've checked on her... No. She was fine. I just worried about Bobby messing with her. He was persistent, I'd give him that. I would check on her in a little bit.

I wondered if I could watch Sherry fall in love with someone else. I wondered how noble I'd be to let her live her life. I knew I could, if that's what she wanted, but...

I wondered if I should explain to Piper again that it isn't anything personal with her. I just couldn't be content with someone when I was completely in love with someone else.

No, I don't think so. They didn't understand. The first conversation along those lines didn't go so well anyway. She was the strangest Keeper I'd ever met.

Friend or Foe?
Chapter 9

"I did the dishes. Peace offering?"
Susan was standing behind me, startling me as I entered the kitchen.
"Susan, I'm not angry with you, please don't think that. I'm just rounding out a very stressful few days. I'm sorry."
"I understand that. I talked to Merrick, your Keeper, well your brother's Keeper. He explained that he'd been kinda driving you crazy, and it was his fault. You know Sherry, I think that boy, well that...guardian, likes you." She spoke slowly and sounded like she thought it would be something new to me, like she was exposing some revelation.
All I could do was chuckle and avert my eyes innocently, what else could I do? Tell her he was in love with me? She chuckled, too, a little.
"I'm sorry," I reiterated.
"Me, too."
She turned to go back to her room and I stayed in the kitchen for some quiet but not completely silent dinner, with the humming appliances to keep me company. I wished someone would come in with me but then I changed my mind when someone did.
Bobby came waltzing in reminding me of Matt and all his arrogance.
"Hey there, girly."
"Hey," I muttered under my breath.
"Late dinner?"
"Yep. I like it quiet so..." Lies, but I didn't think he could tell.
"Me, too."
Not taking the hint yet again, he plopped himself up on the countertop across from me. He was slightly pudgy, but not in an off putting way, just stocky. His hair was very light brown and straight, perfectly brushed, as in he brushed his hair to meet me here. Great. I was determined to take my bowl of macaroni and cheese and head to my room but he stopped me with his leg outstretched.
"Where you going?"
"I told ya, I like quiet. I'm heading to my room to eat my dinner. It's been a very long day. I'm tired."

"Why don't you come hang out in my room? We can talk, while you eat?" He waggled his eyebrows, flashing a smile.

"No thanks. I'll just-"

"Ah, come on," he interrupted still smiling.

"Bobby," a new voice called his name. His Keeper, Jeff, a stout, muscular, obscenely good looking black man with a deep and pelting voice. Very Darius from Hootie and the Blowfish "Come on, leave her alone. It's late."

Bobby left without another word which surprised the heck out of me.

"Sorry about him. We haven't been formally introduced yet. I'm Jeffrey. Jeff," he said as he extended his hand.

"Sherry." I smiled and took his rough hand thinking the previous owner to that body must have been in construction, too.

"Ah...so, you're Sherry," he drawled like he didn't know, backing himself up to lean on the fridge, propping one foot behind him.

"Hmm. So you can read his mind all the time, or just when he lets you?"

I knew exactly what he was referring to and it didn't quite seem fair to me, thoughts should be private.

"Only when we try." He looked slightly amused at my directness. "I'm sorry, Sherry. We just saw him struggling and thought if we knew what it was, we could help. We never would have guessed what it was though. He tried to hide it from us, if that helps?"

"Ok. So why is Piper so upset about it? What's it to her?"

"Well, what worried us most was his want to stay here. You see we can live perfectly human and natural for as long as the body does but when the body dies, he dies. His thought was that he wanted to stay in his human body...for you."

That shocked me. Why would Merrick give up his life for me? It's not like we'd ever live to see that day anyway, but it shook me up none the less.

"Ok, so my question, why does Piper care? You explained it rationally and calmly and she didn't look either of those when she snatched him away the other day."

He rubbed his chin in contemplation before answering, which reassured me. At least I know he was thinking about it and not just placating me.

"When we are done with our job, when we wish to be through with being a Keeper, we retire so to speak. We don't have mates like you do. It's not physical for us, but most of us find our so called 'mate' at that point and we just spend the rest of our days together. Piper is upset because she feels that, that kind of contentment is more valuable than what you could give him here."

"So Piper wants to give him that...that kind of love."

"Well, not right this second, Keepers don't work that way. One day maybe and it's not really love, we just have an understanding, enjoy each others company.

It's just such a wonderful thing for us, to live in peace together. It's hard to see your side versus ours. I mean, here you fight and hurt each other, leave each other, among other things. And sex is so common; it's not anything special to anyone anymore. It's something for fun and just seems to cause even more problems."

"Not to me it isn't, but we don't even know if we are going to make it through all this, so can we back up a step? Why are we talking like this is something that is actually going to happen? I don't have expectations for Merrick. I just found out a few hours ago that he loved me *instead* of loathed me. Though, I didn't know then that he had the option to stay," I heard myself barely breathe those last words as they sunk in.

"It's not really an option. It's a decision. An indefinite one."

"Jeff, I'm not going to try to talk him into staying with me, ok. I don't even understand to begin with. I mean, why would he want me when he can have what you're talking about?"

I figured there was no reason to be coy. He had been in Merrick's head and seen it all so there was no reason to pretend any different.

"Love does funny things."

"Yes, but do you love in the same way as I do? Can you?"

"We have free will, just like everyone else. We choose how to live our lives, when we want to be done with a chapter we start a new one."

"Hmm... That doesn't exactly answer my question, but ok. I guess that's all I'm going to get?" I lifted my eyebrows, but he stayed silent. I nodded knowingly. "Thanks for helping with Bobby...and trying to explain everything to me. I think I'm going to turn in."

"Ok."

"Nice talking to you, Jeff."

"You, too, Sherry... He does love you, you know." He sprung that on me as I crossed the doorway. "Like what you're talking about. I can't understand or define it myself, but he does."

I took a deep breath and I knew the truth. "I know. I can't be lied to," I stated and shrugged.

He eyed me curiously, but smiled as I walked out with my cold again pasta. There should be a sign posted in the kitchen, 'No Hot Meals'.

They must have figured out how to turn the light timers off because they didn't wake me in the morning. Thankfully. I was beaten, emotionally beaten and exhausted. The restless sleep last night did nothing to help that fact.

I couldn't stop thinking about how quickly my feelings for Merrick had taken off. It was not because of his professing his love for me either. I mean, Bobby and Matt did that and I couldn't make myself even like them anymore. It was just hard to believe that someone like him would care for me. How had he watched me and still wanted to be with me, seeing all my embarrassing mannerisms and...ugh, the list could go on for days of things I'd rather Merrick had not seen.

It had been three weeks down there and as Merrick said, supplies were running low. Today, they would make a decision as to who would head out for supplies on the next trip. Merrick had bought a little hand held radio on our first trip and listened daily to see what was going on with the world.

Things were getting worse, but not as quick as we thought. Not knowing how much longer we could stay here, we all decided that since I had the Costco card and we already knew basically what to do, that Merrick, Jeff and I would take Bobby's van to the store and stock up for a couple more weeks at least.

Merrick seemed a little reluctant for me to go this time, going on about how it wasn't necessary to put me in danger, but Jeff conceded that they needed me for my membership card. Nice. Hopefully, we'd have no problems in the big, busy store and could get in and out quickly. We'd leave in a couple days, early.

I placed my curtain sheets up over our window but this place was still devoid of any real privacy. The walls and windows were so thin you can hear pretty much anything that was said in the rooms, even with the doors closed if you were close enough.

I was finishing up putting on the last of my purse size vanilla lotion on my legs in my room, just having gotten out of the shower. I didn't think to close the door for that, but when Merrick and Bobby walked by and saw me in my shorts and tank top, lotioning my leg propped against the bed side, I quickly wished I had closed that dang door as I felt the blush come up my face and neck.

Merrick did the usual, quick intake of breath, weird face, turn away to be a gentleman. Bobby, on the other hand, gawked shamelessly, tilting his head and even stopping to stare and smiled villainously, winking.

As I quickly tried to straighten up and close my door, I saw Merrick pushing Bobby's back forward, telling him to move along I guess. Bobby took it as playful man behavior but I knew better.

Merrick didn't even understand that kind of stuff, not really. He was pushing him to tell him to leave or he'd *make* him leave. I kind of felt weird about it, but in a good way. I'd never really had someone defend me before Merrick, besides Danny, and brothers didn't really count.

Bobby had been *not* taking hints left and right these past couple weeks, but Merrick and I sat or lay down and talked in the basketball court sometimes or in the club chairs in the hall. Not touching too much since that day in my room, but talking was good, and sitting close was getting to be more comfortable for both of us. Or uncomfortable, as I was becoming more aware of the spark. The tingle of electricity that shot through my skin without my permission every time Merrick laid a finger on me.

That first day after our embarrassing confession encounter in my room was sure to be awkward to say the least. It was in the kitchen at breakfast, after everyone else was through. I was attempting to reach a cereal bar from the shelf, silently cursing the person who had moved them way up there, when a hand came to my rescue from behind me.

I turned and he was smiling crookedly and sheepishly, holding out the bar for me to take. I purposely let our fingers touch when I took it to see his reaction. Other than a hint of amusement in his eyes, he stayed perfectly calm.

"Thanks," I told him. "You always seem to be saving me in the kitchen." I laughed a short snort of a laugh.

"No problem. That's what Keepers are for."

"I'm seeing that." I smiled. "I seriously think we need to invest in a stool. I mean, it's degrading to have to ask for assistance every time I want breakfast, don't you think?"

He laughed and I laughed. It seemed comfortable, not half as awkward as I had imagined it all would be.

"I'll see what I can do."

"Thanks. You want some coffee?" I asked him, grabbing two mugs from the hooks.

"Uh...sure. I'll try a cup." He smiled, making it hard to breathe, let alone remember how to pour coffee. "I've never had it before."

"Well, don't judge all coffee off of this coffee. It's not as good as it can be, trust me. I made great coffee at home, but we have limited resources here."

He thanked me, taking the mug and took a hesitant sip, sucking in a breath as it burned his lip. I felt bad for not warning him, but fought back a laugh at the same time at his face when he finally got a sip down.

"Well?" I asked.

"It's...good."

Lie. I laughed out loud because his face was priceless. He hated it, completely hated it.

"You won't hurt my feelings, Merrick. I didn't even make it. I told you it wasn't that good down here."

"Well, it's odd tasting."

"You hate it."

"No..."

"Merrick, you can't lie to me," I reminded him.

90

"Alright, I hate it."

I laughed again as he still continued to force himself to sip it and make the most hilarious faces of disgust.

"You don't have to drink it, Merrick! Really! Put the coffee down!" I pounded my palms down in the air for emphasis.

"Oh, thank you," he groaned, pouring it down the sink and rinsing the cup. "You really like that?"

"Well, most of the time. It's mostly just addiction at this point, I'm sure."

I chuckled as I drank my horrible coffee and we ate our cereal bars at the counter. He lifted to sit beside me on the counter so I lifted myself up as well.

"So, how can you be addicted to coffee? Or were you just joking again?" he asked with a little smile playing at the corners of his mouth.

I laughed as I explained my coffee situation to him. He smiled and listened intensely. Easy breezy conversation flowed like that from pretty much then on for which I would be eternally grateful for.

Merrick was making points to touch me more here and there, slowly easing into a routine of it. Helping me up off the floor with his hand outstretched for me or opening the door and guiding me in with his hand on my back, barely. Being my helper in the kitchen for meal time and dishes and grabbing the things I couldn't reach, brushing our fingers when he handed me things.

He even tucked a stray curl of hair behind my ear once in the middle of one of our conversations, like it was totally normal, sending goose bumps down my neck and arms. I'd never had anyone do that to me before. Seen it in the movies, though, the girls going all glaze eyed when some guy ran his hands through her hair and I never got the whole thrill about it, until it was done to me. It was amazing and worth every movie fetish made about it. It was intimate and sweet.

I wondered if he noticed that I noticed what he was doing. Testing me.

Over these past days, he has told me all about his other charges and his three trips to Earth for Orville. Danny had even liked that one.

Danny joked that I was spending more time with his guardian than he was, which was true. Other people noticed as well. Celeste asked me once what is was like to kiss an alien. I could only laugh. Hard.

Jeff and I spoke some. I liked it because he didn't feel any attachment for me, so he didn't spare my feelings on anything. He was always straight up and truthful, about their work, about the Lighters, about Merrick's thoughts. Though I felt some guilt, he had watched my life like a television program for 20 years, so I deserved a little insight, too.

Calvin, one of the younger boys that I didn't remember from the first meeting had begun to blossom. He had brown hair and big brown eyes, always wearing funny t-shirts. He ran through the halls and tried to play with Celeste, the unfortunate next to youngest member of our clan and not happy about it. Or maybe it was Celeste's doll like qualities that attracted him. She tried to spend every extra second of her time in our room with Danny.

Danny didn't mind.

She managed to grab a few play dates with Calvin, out of pity. He took to me as well. He caught me humming, possibly singing quietly in the wash room one day. He begged me relentlessly to sing to him since then. I didn't understand it. Why would someone want to hear someone sing to them other than their mother? Lillian filled me in and said his mom, Lana, was deaf. How had I missed that in the beginning? We didn't see her much but as horrible as I felt about not knowing that his mom was deaf, I wasn't a very good singer and had no intentions of making a debut. On purpose.

"Please, Sherry! Sing anything you want. Please."

A seven year old's pleas were hard to deny, but I stood my ground.

"Calvin, I'm sorry. I'm not a good singer. Why don't you go ask Celeste?"

"She won't either," he said sulking, kicking his sneakers on the floor, making scuff marks.

"Maybe one of the guys will play basketball with you? I bet Merrick or Ryan would if you'd ask."

Ryan, a young surfer looking guy, was Calvin's Keeper but Calvin seemed almost scared of him. I'd seen Ryan try to make an effort, help him in the kitchen, but Calvin always rejected him. Who knew what these people saw and heard before they came here? I certainly couldn't imagine being his age and dealing with things like this.

"No. It's ok. I'll just go see what my mom's up to."

As I watched him sulk and walk away, he reminded me so much of Danny when he was little. Kid had no one here and a mom that no one knew how to talk to. Poor guy.

The next day I took it upon myself to organize a game of basketball to lift Calvin's spirits. I went hunting for Danny and found him.

And Celeste.

Kissing in the foyer by the elevator, off in a darker corner.

Not just kissing as he had his arms wrapped tightly around her waist, bending her back a little and her hands were in his hair. I heard her small groan, almost a whimper, and I couldn't quiet the gasp that escaped and they quickly parted and looked at me, mouths gaped open.

Torn between scolding him and running away I decided to proceed with my original plan with hands on hips and chin raised.

"Uh...I was coming to see if ya'll wanted to play some basketball. Calvin's been a little restless lately, so I wanted to help him blow off some steam and feel better," I said, trying to keep my eyes on them but finding it impossible, eyes drifting to the ceiling, floor tiles, my shoes.

"I'm game," Danny said, then cleared his throat. "Celeste, you want to play too?"

"Sure," she said cheerily, but refused to meet my gaze as she followed Danny out into the hallway.

How the heck were they kissing already? I mean, Merrick was in love with me and I'd only even hugged him once and never kissed him. It didn't seem fair. I wanted to kiss him, but he was taking it all very slow.

I called out to Danny to get a couple others to play as I went to grab water bottles for everyone and to escort Calvin personally to his game.

When I entered his room he was wearing a "More Cowbell" t-shirt and I felt a swell of pride that he would know anything about one of my favorite Saturday Night Live episodes at his young age. He was ecstatic and bouncing on his heels as we made our way down the hall.

When we got there Ryan, his Keeper, and Merrick had joined Danny and Celeste and were warming up inside the basketball room.

I met Merrick's eyes from across the room and we each did one of those slowly growing wide smiles. I felt my cheeks tinge with pink.

"Hey, Calvin!" Ryan shouted, but then realized how the room had great acoustics and lowered the volume. "Are you ready to show us how to play some ball?"

"I believe the correct term is 'school' Ryan. And yes, we are ready. We've got Calvin," Celeste teased, taking a defensive stance, her hands on her knees.

"Oh! Are you gonna take that from a girl, Ryan?" Calvin chimed in and it made me smile to see him so easily thrust into the camaraderie.

Not to mention the fact that he actually spoke directly to his Keeper.

"Am I not supposed to?" Ryan said looking genuinely puzzled, which made everyone laugh, except Merrick, who was just as clueless.

After a brief explanation on how guys don't "take smack, especially from girls" from Calvin, and a quick run through of how to play, we started a game of three on three. The Keepers and I, against the Specials.

Calvin was pretty impressive to be a shorty, like me. Celeste was busy trying to look cute, throwing her leg back when she tossed the ball and then glancing at Danny, but still managed to get some in.

Merrick and Ryan seemed to thoroughly enjoy themselves, though they were terrible at dribbling, shooting, pretty much all of it. They laughed and got into it. We pushed each other playfully and smack talked. It was hilarious.

Once, I tripped over my undone shoe lace and started to fall backwards, but Merrick somehow was there to grab me from behind under my arms. I turned and thanked him. He wiped at a piece of sweaty hair stuck to my face and was hit in the head with the ball by Calvin during the distraction. Calvin doubled over laughing. Merrick laughed, too, and then bent down to tie my shoe for me, which I thought was just about the sweetest thing ever.

"Aho! Check it! That's game!" Danny yelled loudly as he scored the winning shot.

Final score. 21 - 7 Specials. Ouch.

I mock punched Merrick and Ryan both in the arm and scolded them for letting us lose to a bunch of kids, but quickly had to explain that it was a joke, and they did eventually laugh.

"Hey, don't make fun of me. I'm new to all things sports related. None of my charges were ever really interested in sports before Danny," Merrick explained as we all made our way out to the hall.

The others left, but Merrick and I lingered in the doorframe.

"Really? Well, I wouldn't really call Danny *into sports*. I don't think couch lounging is considered one."

He chuckled. "No. Probably not, but you guys played a lot of basketball and Frisbee together. And he did play t-ball once. And football his freshman year."

"Wow," I muttered, completely astounded at the nonchalantness of it all.

"What?" he asked settling in across from me, leaning on the doorjamb with his hands in his pockets.

"It's just so strange, you knowing everything about us."

His eyes immediately looked down at the floor guiltily and he started rubbing the back of his neck as if uncomfortable. "I'm sorry."

"No," I hurried to say and touched his cheek to bring his face back up. He didn't flinch, but took a deep breath as I slowly let my hand fall back to my side. "That's not what I meant at all. I meant strange *good*, not strange bad."

He tilted his head and looked in my eyes for a long moment.

"You are spectacular," he murmured in a low voice, seemingly more to himself than to me.

"No, I'm not."

"Yeah, you are." He stepped a little closer. And then another step. My breath caught. We were mere inches apart. He closed his eyes for a second and opened them slowly. He smiled bashfully. "Sorry," he muttered and tried to step back, but I grabbed his shirt with my free hand to stop him.

"I don't want you to be sorry." I decided to be bold. "You can invade my space anytime."

What? Not that bold! Holy cow. I felt my cheeks flush, and I smiled trying to make a joke out of it, but eventually just looked away.

"I love that, you know." He caressed my cheek with the backs of his fingers and I looked back up to him. "Even your face doesn't let you lie. I always know that what I see is what I get with you. You aren't hiding things. You are completely honest and good to the core."

I had no idea what to say to that. "Um..."

"I didn't mean to embarrass you."

"You didn't. I'm just not good at this," I admitted, feeling even more blush creeping up.

"At what?"

"At...you know...anything." I laughed. "I have no idea how to handle these situations."

"What situations are these?" he asked, his eyes following every move my face made making it impossible to look away or escape the depth of those penetrating and honest eyes.

"Well, you know, uh, dating situations."

"Are we dating? Is that what this is?"

I looked at him and he was completely serious. He had no idea about any of this any more than I did. With Matt he was so sure of himself and he dominated everything in our relationship, I didn't have to think or act or make decisions. He did it all for me. He never even asked me if I wanted to be exclusive. It was implied by him and I didn't think to disagree. Now, I didn't know how to proceed.

"Um, I don't know. I have no idea what this is. Dating doesn't sound like it covers it to me," I confessed softly.

"Do you like it?" he asked just as softly. "Do you like what's going on with us?"

"I like it a lot." As I spoke he grabbed my hand, which I'd forgotten was still touching him, and pulled it gently from his shirt, bringing it down beside us and lacing his fingers with mine. "Do you?"

"This is more than I ever hoped for." He watched our hands as he spoke and laced and unlaced our fingers over and over. "I have no idea what I'm doing, but I love spending time with you," he confessed and smiled wistfully.

"You're doing everything right," I assured him. "I don't want you to feel like you have to try to be something you're not."

"And I don't want you to feel pressured." He straightened his back and looked suddenly serious. "Just because I...have certain feelings for you doesn't mean that you have to return them."

"I know that. I like you. You're not like any guy I've ever met."

"Well, I'm *not* like any guy you've met," he said wistfully and managed a small chuckle.

"And I'm happy about that."

I smiled and looked at him until he smiled, too. I pulled my hands free and put my arms around his neck. His arms hugged me tightly and even lifted my toes from the floor a little. His hair tickled my arms and for some reason the smell of his soap and sweat on the skin of his neck was doing funny things to my senses. How had I dated someone for five months and never gotten goose bumps or butterflies, and never thought that was weird?

Our body's grooves fit together all the way up and I couldn't stop the thought of some girly notion about us being made for each other. It made me smile wider thinking about it and then I felt his breath in my hair, the tingles and goose bumps cascaded down my spine along with his warm hands.

When he placed me on my feet again he looked at me for a moment before smiling crookedly like he could read all my thoughts. He pulled his hands from my hips, reaching for my hand once more, and tugged me to follow him.

"Hungry?" he asked grinning and I couldn't help but feel a little smug for putting that goofy, gorgeous grin on his face.

"Starved."

"Maybe I can cook something for you this time."

"What can you cook?"

"Canned soup?" he mused.

"You're as bad as Danny," I laughed and nudged him with my shoulder to ensure that he knew I was joking. "I'll handle the snack this time. But you owe me, mister."

"Anything," he answered firmly and my heart skidded once again, because he was completely telling the truth.

As the same annoying cackle filled the stale air, I couldn't help but think that Polly and Piper were the strangest people I had met so far. They both had an Amazon women stature going and not only was Polly loud and dramatic - did I mention I hate drama - but they also insisted on being the center of everything.

Polly was tall for a teenager. Really tall and Zena looking. Black hair down passed her shoulder blades, that matched her shiny, black, knee-high leather boots and a very curvy body. Piper, whose tall body looked to be about fifteen or sixteen, had black hair, too. Short, straight and flat with sharp, slanted bangs, very slim, but curvy and her green eyes were anything but inviting.

These days even Piper, a Keeper no less, was getting on my nerves for a reason that didn't have to do with Merrick for a change. I guess she made herself honorary house mother and Polly was Mrs. Underground USA. It was like they were made to be Keeper and Special together.

The amount of orders and chore changes and food disagreements that came out of those two teenage mouths was astonishing. Not to mention the fact that Polly was a vegetarian, which I have no problem with, but how would we know to pack more vegan foods for an alien invasion and why was it all of a sudden our fault?

Her latest disagreement was about there not being any Crystal Light and the water was too stale to drink straight from the pipes.

The end of the world as we knew it. The old 'can't we all just get along?' saying wouldn't stop playing in my head. Celeste said it best one night after a particularly heinous kitchen meeting.

"Those two are dangerously persnickety."

I couldn't have said it better myself.

That night started normal enough. I had planned to hit the sack early since we were getting an early start for the store trip the next morning. Danny wasn't on his cot yet so he must have been out wandering the halls with Celeste. Where was Margo with all this going on? Shouldn't her mother care, like me? I want Danny to be happy, I do, but I just felt like they were only taking to each other because there was no one else.

Celeste was gorgeous, and Danny, though he's my brother, was handsome. Eeew. Under normal circumstances they would've been attracted to each other anyway. I guess maybe I should ease up.

There was a commotion that drew me from my white sterile room before I could lay down for the night. I exited thinking it was someone fighting over the last cereal bar but it was Celeste, lying on the floor, not breathing. A few faceless people were standing over her, her mother nor any of the Keepers being one of them.

Danny's face was sheet white as he kneeled beside her, looking clueless and helpless. I ran over, wondering why no one had started CPR yet. Shock? How long had she been out? What happened?

I grabbed her neck, tilting it up, and pushing Danny, him falling back on the floor in the process, to reach her. Someone screamed and that sent everyone out of their rooms to see what was going on. I blocked them out and focused.

I blew into her bluish mouth, holding her nose and turning to listen. Then I pushed down on her chest four hard quick times and I blew in her mouth again and listened. I kept repeating the process.

I glanced up quickly to see Kay looking stricken and pale as I kneeled over her charge. She was wringing her hands and leaning in to watch me.

I also heard Polly whimpering and no doubt in my mind her untimely screech of a scream was the one that summoned all the extra bodies that were now my audience. I heard her as I tried to concentrate.

"Are you sure you're doing it right? It doesn't seem to be working. Maybe you should let someone else take over, Sherry. Maybe you don't know how to do it," she whined as she wrung her hands and swayed side to side like she has some kinda emotional investment in Celeste and should care more than the rest of us. "She's going to die."

I'd had enough.

"Just shut up, Polly!" I heard my voice along with a couple others echoing the same or similar sentiment, glad I wasn't the only one needing her to pipe down.

I heard other whimpers and gasps behind me but I didn't turn too see. I was surprised I even remembered how to do it. Babysitting as a teen required taking a safety class, CPR included. This was the first time I'd ever had to use it and now I was wondering if *was* doing it right because, well, she was still not breathing.

After the seventh time of compressions she coughed back to life and a piece of something green fell out of her mouth to the floor. I leaned back on my heels with relief.

Danny was right there, saying her name and holding her hand. Had I not been watching them close enough? They looked more serious than I thought. Or maybe he was just being generally concerned. Although, being locked in passionate embraces in the hallway could constitute as serious.

Her lips were still blue, but her color was coming back in her cheeks from white to peachy. Eyes still red and teary.

Margo rounded the corner with a wide look of grief and terror at the scene. It appeared Susan had run and gotten her for which I was grateful. Margo grabbed Celeste up from the floor by her wrists and hugged her, running her hand down Celeste's hair, crying so hard, sobbing, while Celeste explained that she was all right.

When I tried to get up was when I realized the crowd around us.

Merrick, who wasn't among the crowd before, helped me up by lifting my arm at the elbow, but then he slid his hand down my arm to grab my hand, and didn't let go. I didn't look up at his face behind me; I just knew it was him by his familiar warmth and tingle.

We all stood there for a minute and waited for Celeste and Margo to catch their breath.

"I'm sorry," Celeste breathed and whimpered. "I was running and my candy..."

"It's ok now. It's over," Danny assured her, petting her hair though she was still in her mother's arms. "Sherry gave her CPR. She saved her life."

Jeez, Danny. A simple 'She's alive!' would have sufficed. He was looking at Margo, wanting her to know that I had been the one. He could have let her mother think that he had been the one. I was perfectly fine with that.

"Oh, Sherry!" Celeste screamed, leaping her tall body from her mother and throwing her arms around my neck, pushing me backwards. Merrick steadied me with his free hand on my back. "Sherry, I owe you my life! I can't believe you did that!"

"It's fine, Celeste, really. Let's not make a big deal out of this, ok?" Did I know Celeste was the type to not let things go? Yes. Yes, I did.

"Are you kidding?! We are so going to be besties! I'll be like your indentured servant. Anything you need, just ask. I can't believe this, Sherry!"

"Celeste, please. Anyone would have done that, ok? We can be...besties, whatever that is. That'll be plenty payment for me."

Margo eyed me with tears still streaming. She reached over and threw her arms around Celeste, whose arms were still around me. They were squeezing so tight and I looked around for someone to think it was as strange as I did and help but everyone just smiled at me.

Susan even had tears in her eyes. Gah! I couldn't even help someone without being thrust into some spotlight-o-drama that was never intended for me.

As Margo and Celeste backed away slowly, Kay who had been standing silently this whole time, wrapped her arm around Celeste's shoulder and whispered something in her ear, then looked up to me. "Thank you, Sherry."

I nodded. It looked as though they'd all regrouped and were calm but everyone still stared at me, smiling and the unwelcome silence and attention was everywhere.

I could feel my cheeks coloring, as that embarrassing, betraying deep color of red spread across my face and down my neck. I flicked my gaze back and forth, looking for an out. That was the response Celeste was looking for and once again leapt at me for another embrace. Celeste had almost a foot on me, so every time she jumped with a thank you, I got a chest full on my face.

This time, she knocked me slam into Merrick who still stood behind me, him having to catch us from falling backward. Even though Merrick's hand grabbed my hip in the process, I was begging inside for this to be over.

"Ok, ok," I breathed.

Thankfully Calvin came bolting down the hall to save me. "Celeste? Celeste! Are you ok?"

Without looking to see that sweet reunion I turned to flee from my prying onlookers. I realized after all that, Merrick was still holding my hand and was now being towed by me.

As I made a break away from Celeste and towards my room, I didn't remember him gasping or acting funny when he grabbed my hand nor when we fell into him. Of course it was loud out there what with the shrillest thank you's I had ever received.

I pulled him into my room and shut the door, leaning against it, him in front of me.

"Ah! That was terrible. Who knew saving someone was so much work? The *thank you* was worse then the actual saving," I laughed, breathlessly.

He smiled, amused, but wouldn't stop staring.

"What?" I said, finally catching my breath somewhat.

"You're just...amazing. Is there anything you can't do?"

"Reach the spice rack?" I said with a bashful grin.

He chuckled and lifted his hand still intertwined with mine and brought it up to trace my jaw line with his fingers. And there went my calm breaths as I felt a spark of something, electricity. I took my free hand, bringing it up to his forearm, and leaned in just a little. He tensed a tad, but didn't seem to hyperventilate. Or was he just getting use to me? I decided to ask him.

"Are you ok with this? Am I losing my touch?" I asked and laughed a short breathy laugh as I moved my palm up and down his forearm slowly.

"Under control." He chuckled and swallowed. "That feels...amazing," he said, eyes closed like he was savoring it, his fingers still moving up and down my jaw.

"What brought all this on? The control?" I said, but my voice squeaked.

"I just try to focus, think of you and not lose my heart in my throat, seems to be working. Practice, I guess." He chuckled. "What brought all *this* on?" Same question, different meaning, as he looked up to see my response.

"I don't know," I spouted, wetting my lips in nervousness. His eyes jump to the movement and then back to my eyes. "I've just begun to realize some things."

I thought back to the times before, the times I thought it was rejection when it was anything but. It hurt me to think that, but why? Because I wanted to touch him and I wanted him to like it? I thought back to how my heart fluttered when he looked at me. How he was so fascinated when he was lacing our fingers earlier, and how much I loved that look on his face.

A kiss would be too much right now. Though a kiss may always be too much for him. What were we doing exactly? He can't stay and I probably wouldn't make it through all this for it to matter.

A little rap on the door made me turn, releasing all hands. Calvin.

"Sherry, my mom is asleep and I'm really scared. I can't believe Celeste almost died and you saved her! Could you...maybe, please come and sit with me for a minute?" he said through his sniffles he was trying to hide.

Turning to give Merrick one quick glance, to which he nodded, I left to follow the boy, pulling me by my arm. His Spiderman pajamas reminded me yet again of little Danny. Danny used to love for me to sing to him, too. I had a feeling that I'd have to pull a song out of somewhere tonight.

Everyone was in their rooms and his mom couldn't hear me. I could just sing quietly. The words to Frank Sinatra's 'Fly me to the Moon' flew out of me like I had never stopped singing them.

Fly me to the moon, Let me play among the stars,
let me see what spring is like on Jupiter and Mars.
In other words, hold my hand. In other words, baby, kiss me.
Fill my heart with song and let me sing for evermore.
You are all I long for, all I worship and adore.
In other words, please be true. In other words, I love you.

Once I saw the kid was out, I patted his back and pulled the blanket up to his neck before creeping out. I turned to come down the hall and see a happy face, not the one I wanted to see, but a happy one nonetheless. Then I realized the reason Bobby was grinning so big was because he had listened to me. Hmm. Not good, Bobby.

"I can't believe you were listening, Bobby," I whispered.

"You sure can sing pretty, girly."

"Thanks," I grumbled, ignoring the girly remark for tonight.

I walked…and he was following.

"Bobby, look, I'm really tired and I just want to go to bed, please. I'm going to head back to my room, alone, ok." His face said he didn't like that. "Bobby, look. Just because I'm one of the only woman here, single and in your age range, doesn't mean that we have to be...together. Ok."

"Yes, it does. That's exactly what it means. It helps a lot that you're cute, but either way I would want to be with you. Once this is all over, we'll have to repopulate the earth."

The internal debate in me to laugh or cry with pity is waging. While that was going on I jumped at an opportunity to clear the air.

"Bobby, no, we won't and I wouldn't. Besides I'm already in love with someone else. Ok. So can we just be friends?"

I startled at my own words. It just popped out and it hadn't sounded like a lie to me. Love him? Merrick?

"You're in love with that thing. Merrick? He's not even human. Gah, I hate him," he growled the words.

"I never said I was in love with Merrick, though if I were, it shouldn't matter to you. I think being human is a soul that lives in a body. That's what he is."

"That body isn't his."

"Bobby, Matt was dead already."

"So they say. Maybe those Lighters were right. Maybe they are just

101

murderers."

I froze, trying to hide the panic in my eyes at that word and his inflection. "Lighters? Did Jeff tell you about them?" I prayed that he said 'yes', but I had a feeling he wouldn't.

"A Lighter. He said his name was Ian, he came to see me the day before my Keeper got there. He told me a bunch of stuff about them and it's all been true. Sherry, he's brain washed you." He grabbed my hands. "Let me take you out of here. We'll go to the Lighters and they can protect us. They know why the moon is gone, they know everything."

"Yes, they do because it's their fault it's gone. They are using trickery for trickery, Bobby, don't fall into their trap."

"Ok. You're right. I don't know what I was thinking. Goodnight," he said as he turned and walked away.

That was way too easy, but I was too tired to worry about it.

The next morning, I heard Bobby and Jeff arguing near the elevator. He wanted to come with us. As a rule, Specials hadn't been allowed outside or to leave because their... well, special. Bobby was red faced like I'd never seen him before and from the look of things, they've been at it for a while.

"You can't use my van if I can't come. I'm a grown man and you're not going to tell me to sit here and wait for you like some helpless woman," he yelled along with some other obscenities which made sweet Lillian gasp, placing her hand over her mouth and turn to go into the kitchen.

"Fine, Bobby. Fine. You can come this time, but once it gets bad, you will stay where I put you. This is the only way to keep you safe. Got it?" Jeff stated before punching the button to open the elevator doors.

"Whatever," Bobby sneered before hopping on and grabbing a corner, his arms crossed over his chest.

As we stood in the black elevator, making our slow ascent, I felt someone's hand threading their fingers with mine. I tensed thinking Bobby was the dumbest brick in the foundation, but then I heard *him* in my mind, and I realized I should have known it was him. I knew what his warmth felt like.

It's ok. It's me. Unless you don't want me to...

I squeezed his hand to reassure him, as these one sided conversations usually went, I didn't speak. I wished he could read my mind sometimes. Like now.

I would tell him all about Bobby's strange confession to me last night, since I hadn't been alone with him all morning to do so. As the doors screeched open and the light blinded me I was awestruck at the sun.

A month since we'd seen the sun and it never looked so good. Cliché, but true.

I refused to release Merrick's hand as we make our exit. He didn't seem to mind as we walked over to the van and he looked down at me and smiled. Maybe Bobby would see all it and get a clue.

I drove, it was daytime so I was fine with that. All the men insisted we'd be less likely to be pulled over with a young lady driving than a couple of guys.

Merrick filled us in on the happenings, per his handheld radio. They were checking for symbols already, but only on problematic cases, such as traffic stops, ect. He assured us that it would be fine.

I kept my foot light on the pedal, staying at least two miles per hour under the limit. Having people's lives in my hands instead of breathing life into them wasn't as much fun. If anything were to happen...

As we drove I thought about my life, flashbacks from when Danny was born. Trying to process how many embarrassing memories Merrick must have seen of mine over the years. Prom night red-punch-spilled-on-white-dress-by-date disaster. Slipping on the slide at the public pool in front of no less than fifty people, all laughing, at a ninth grade pool party. Getting caught picking my nose in third grade by the teacher and her calling me out in front of the class on it. Martin Spikes telling me no to a date I asked him on because he said I looked like an eighth grader, I was in the eleventh however, and it was the one time I'd talked myself up to ask someone. I never did it again.

That sent my thoughts to what possibly could Danny do that would make a difference in the world. It had to be big; the world was in danger of ending. No small gesture would do now. I was already beginning to beam with pride for him, still not knowing when or what his big act could be but proud none the less.

Our parents were gone and I doubted we'd ever see them again. It saddened me but also frustrated and upset me. They had a choice and they chose, and it wasn't us, it was an empty field on the ridge and aliens. What a shame looking back now, knowing the truth.

They were followers. They had no idea what they were welcoming into our world, but they followed their friends and politicians in the 'peace and love' route and look where we were now.

I almost missed my exit and Jeff asked if I'm ok. I nodded, not even looking his way. Merrick and Bobby sat in the middle back seat, not a word between them. I wondered if Merrick knew that Bobby hated him. I guess not. How could he? Bobby had no right though. He actually thought I had already considered his little proposal in my head and was on board with saving the planet...with our babies. Geesh.

Once we reached the store, I parked in our usual spot off to the side. Merrick took the list from his shirt pocket before we headed in and tore it in half suggesting we split up to save time. My heart leapt but then fell when Bobby grabbed my arm, claiming me as his partner. Merrick gave a suspicious glance to that arm but I sent a small smile to tell him it was ok. I wasn't in the mood for any arguments.

Are you sure? Don't let him bully you. It's alright if you don't want to go with him.

There was no point in talking about it there. I just shrugged and smiled and took our list as Bobby grabbed a cart. Merrick looked disappointed and I hated to have put that look on his face, but I was so tired of conflict.

Remember to be careful. Don't talk to anyone and let's hurry, ok? Please be careful. Stay on your guard, no thinking of Danny or other Specials, ok?

I nodded and glanced back at him quickly, sending him a little smile which he returned to me and shook his head. As we walked away from our Keepers, Bobby began to lecture me once again on the Lighters and how they were right, how I should come along and join him. That was when it hit me. "Are you leaving, Bobby?"

"Yep. I'm not telling Jeff. I'm just going. That's why I wanted to wait til we were out and could be alone today. Now you can leave with me and Merrick won't be able to stop you."

"You think I told you no because Merrick is controlling me?"

"What other reason is there?" he asked skeptically.

"Uh, well, I believe them."

"Come on, Sherry. You can't believe them."

"Bobby, listen. Just come talk to Merrick, let him explain-"

"I've heard it all and I'm done. The Lighters are the ones who are going to save us from all this and you'll wish you had listened to me. They have a plan in place already. They are going to win this thing. I'm leaving, now. I wish you would've changed your mind. We could've been really good together. "

Was I hearing things? He sounded like he was ready to drink the Kool-Aid. What was going on?

"I don't, and I do believe them. I've always been able to tell the difference of lies for truth. They are telling the truth. Bobby, please don't do this. Don't leave. Stay."

"I'm leaving. In fact, I'm leaving right now and I'm going to have to turn all

104

your little friends over to them. They are just a band of rebels that must be taken care of. If not, this kind of hatred and untruth will spread everywhere."

Bobby was sounding like some kind of robot now, programmed responses. As I turned to go I felt him grab my arm with excessive force. He was angry at me for not wanting to come with him.

"Ow! Bobby! Let go."

"I can't. You know what...you have to come with me. You're important. I need you and the sooner you get away from them, the sooner you'll realize I'm right. You won't be affected by them anymore."

"Ow! Stop it! Let go!"

I could feel the fiery pulse under his grasp.

"I ought to just drag you out of here by your hair, ya know. You don't know what you're doing. Can't you see I care about you?" he said getting right in my face.

"Yes...I see that, ok," I answered softly, "but I can also see the truth. I'm not in danger and neither are you, yet. Please stay and let us talk about this."

"NO!" he yelled, and started to pull me from my cart, not even stopping to see the prying eyes watching our little encounter.

No one came to my aid either, just stared. I was suddenly very disappointed in the males of the human race. I yanked my arm free quickly and turned to run but he grabbed my shirt and turned me, holding me to him to keep me from leaving. I imagined this would look like an embrace to someone looking now. He tried to kiss me and I squirmed to evade his lips.

"Sherry! Snap out of it! I know if I can just make you see the truth that you'll come with me."

"I would say the same to you! Let me go, now!"

He let me go but pushed me at the same time in frustration and I tripped backwards to the floor. In one swift movement I rolled and got up to keep going, running full speed. I had the van keys still in my pocket.

I ran barely slowing down as I reached the aisle end. Everyone and everything seemed slow motion and I bumped into a lady as I crossed the aisles.

"Oh! Excuse me. Sorry," I yelled back across my shoulder.

Looking, looking, where could they be? Aisle after aisle as I descended down towards the food court, nothing. Wait. I saw him. Them.

Oh, no. What would happen to Jeff now that his Special was gone?

As I approached they were in the middle of shopping cart traffic jam, waiting their turn to enter the aisle. Jeff saw me running, tells Merrick in his mind, his head jerking up quickly to search for me. Once I reached them, I grabbed Merrick's arm.

"There you are! I've been looking all over for you two. I'm done. Got everything I needed. Ready?"

I saw the worry in his eyes as he glanced quickly at Jeff. I hoped he could just trust me and he must because we were moving, him towing me away from our cart by my hand, Jeff following.

Once in the van, I fiddled with my shaking hands and the keys, trying to get the van started. I blurted out the whole story of last night and just now, all of Bobby's bizarre behavior as I drove.

"He asked you to leave with him?" Jeff asked and I saw Merrick watching my face in the mirror as I answered.

"Yes."

"What did he say?"

"Does it matter?"

"Yes. He's already been in contact with the Lighters. He may have slipped up and said something."

"He said I was under Merrick's control and he thought getting me away would break the spell." I heard Merrick grunt unhappily but kept going. "He said, he cared about me and I didn't know what I was doing. That we needed to...repopulate the earth and I was important." A quick glance at them and I saw something wasn't right.

"Was that it?"

"Pretty much. I was trying to get away, he may have said more."

"Trying?" Merrick asked.

"He grabbed me and held me there so I couldn't run while he tried to talk me into it."

"Keep driving," Jeff said as he began looking at my arms, pulling up my shirt to look at my back and stomach. Searching for something.

"Jeff, that's not necessary," Merrick barked.

"We've got to make sure, Merrick! You know how they work."

"Jeff?" I questioned trying to stay on the road.

"Just checking something. It's fine. Just keep driving."

"What's going to happen to you now, Jeff?"

Seeing is Believing
Chapter 10

"Well, I don't know. This is all new to me as I've never had a Special refuse a task, or leave my protection before," Jeff said blankly as he leaned back over to his seat, satisfied with his search.

I looked at Merrick, he looked at me.

"We gotta get out, now. We may be too late already. He said he was 'turning us in', whatever that means," I said, worry setting into my voice.

"Yes. We have to leave the warehouse," Merrick agreed looking straight forward.

It would take a while to return and grab our belongings and explain to everyone and then get back out.

"Where will we go?" I asked, not sure if they'd even have an answer.

"We'll have to split up," Merrick said.

"Yes. We will and we aren't going to find another place like the warehouse. We're going to have to run. There are a lot of us out there, we just have to find them," Jeff agreed.

"Split up?" I asked, my voice cracking.

"Yeah. I'll take Kay and Ryan, and you, Jeff, Piper, Kathy and Lavonne can take Mitchell and the others. That'll keep the ones who have gotten close to each other together. We can't be out searching around with a group our size. It'll draw too much attention and be hard to find a place to fit everyone."

They weren't talking to me anymore but trying to work out a plan with each other. I drifted in and out of recognition. I heard key words, 'rendezvous point', 'hotel', 'supplies'. I finally saw the warehouse in the wavy horizon, like a mirage. Nothing looked out of the ordinary.

We hopped out and cautiously ran looking around for signs of trouble as we stepped in the elevator. If only we had a way to reach them by phone, they could be getting ready now.

Merrick, reached out and grabbed my hand in the dark, swinging me around, pulling me to him with a hand on the small of my back. I was startled, but didn't stop him. In fact, I felt guilty. Even though we might all be meeting our doom very soon, my heart skipped and my skin tingled where Merrick touched me, even in this soothing, desperate embrace.

Did he hurt you? I could just... I'm so sorry I didn't go with you.

I just shook my head, no. I didn't want to speak, but I knew he could see me in the dark.

There was a tingling electricity everywhere as he leaned his forehead against mine. His breath on my face was intoxicating and as his arm squeezed around my waist I was bombarded with one thought:

How did I not see this before? This was what he was feeling with me and I thought he thought I had the plague.

My hands were on the sides of his gray pocket t-shirt, gripping it in my fist. He picked up the charm around my neck and twiddled it between his fingers, like I often have. Where his fingers touched my collar began to tingle with more intensity than the rest.

I've worn this necklace every day for five years and no one ever asked me what it meant, or who gave it to me. Of course, Merrick knew.

My dad gave me the small silver heart within a heart. Perfect for a daughter's birthday. The only perfect and normal gift I ever got from my parents. That was why I loved it so much.

It's wasn't a book on the ancient arts of chi tea remedies. No wooden bracelets to ward off evil spirits with its Mother Nature essence. No ornately framed pictures of the goddess of fertility. Just a normal gift.

I wanted to kiss him as he rubbed my necklace, though I wasn't sure how he would react. Plus the fact that we had an audience. It was loud and dark, but still, an audience that can see in the dark nonetheless.

We'd never kissed, and he never tried the whole month we'd been down this hole. He didn't touch me all the time either. I thought he was testing me, seeing how far I wanted to go. That was what it seemed to me and right then, it seemed desperate, like he was saying a preemptive goodbye. Like we might not make it.

But I want to kiss him. For some reason, the impending death hanging over us, the way his fingers were gliding across my collar bone. Something. I just needed to kiss him.

I worked up the nerve and leaned just a little, but before we touched, we jolted to the bottom. I bit my bottom lip in frustration.

He waited to release me. Jeff bolted out quickly with work to do, not fazed by us as he saw us touching and talking often, as most of them did those days. They didn't really understand. Some didn't condone it either, but gave us space.

Danny was thrilled by the new development. His exact words were, "What better guy for my sister to have than a frigging guardian angel?"

Slowly and reluctantly, Merrick let me go and we walked swiftly to gather

Danny, Celeste, Calvin and the rest of our half of the gang.

I packed some of the food, what little was left, after my clothes. Not too much, we may have to run, literally run, and we didn't need to be loaded down.
Calvin signed to his mom as Merrick explained and they were ready to go more quickly than anyone. As we headed out we told the last group, Mitchell's group, that we'd send the elevator back down for them.
I hugged Lillian and Susan, both upset and crying, scared. I tried really hard not to and mostly succeed but only because Merrick was urging us along.
Mitchell turned to Merrick.
"Brother, watch over them. Guard you in all your ways."
"And you in yours, brother," Merrick said as they hugged and patted each others backs and then he jumped on the elevator with us.
I had a sinking feeling I'd never see them again. Lillian waved and clutched Michael's arm as the door slid closed. Calvin talked and asked questions nonstop the entire ride up to ground level. He must be scared. I squeezed his shoulder to comfort him.
As the doors opened Merrick grabbed my waist and extended an arm around to block the others. He held me back and peeked out, listening and looking before releasing me.
We unloaded out of the box and he sent the elevator back down as promised. Calvin held my hand, I felt kind of bad. Didn't he want to hold his mother's hand?
Danny, Merrick and I took my car and Kay drove the rest of them in Bobby's van. He wouldn't be needing it. Celeste wanted so badly to ride with us but her Keeper, and mother wouldn't allow that one. I understood that, but Danny was a little miffed.
We have no idea where we were going. Merrick drove and seemed to be scoping out the land as we moved along the back roads. His shifting had really improved, he only stalled once and I punched Danny's arm for laughing. I thought I overheard him say something about camping. Ugh. Better get used to roughing it again.
I fully expected an ambush or a raid of some kind, but there was no flashing lights, no sirens, and no spotlights from helicopters. If Bobby told them and they knew of a group our size why not jump on it? I voiced those concerns to Merrick but he had no answer.
It was freezing again so without asking or waiting for an invitation I pulled up Merrick's arm and placed myself under. I heard a chuckle from the back seat but Merrick just tightened his grip on me and kissed my forehead, which was the only kiss I'd ever received from him.
It felt wonderful, warm and protective, leaving a tingle behind. I couldn't

help but smile into Merrick's arm.

We must have driven for quite a while because, I woke up with my head on Merrick's lap.

It was dark and we were still driving. I pulled myself back upright into the seat and it was even colder than before. I peeked back and Danny was conked in the backseat, leaning on our luggage and boxes piled in the other seat.

"Feel better?" Merrick asked me, his eyes never leaving the road, but I could tell he was tired.

"Yeah, I guess. Sorry. I was more tired than I thought. Bobby's pleas for me to run away with him kept me up last night." I laughed half heartedly.

"You've been out for a while. We stopped and filled up the gas tanks. We're just going to drive until we find somewhere we think we can all stop safely for the night. I also grabbed a bag of food while I was there. Hungry?" he said, looking over at me quickly.

"Yeah. Did you eat?"

"Yeah," he said through a yawn.

"Let me drive. I know you've got to be exhausted."

"I'm fine."

"Liar."

He smiled and chuckled groggily. I stood up on my knees in the seat and motioned for him to scoot over. "You don't like to drive in the dark, Sherry."

Merrick knowing everything about me was kinda nice actually. "I'll be ok."

"I'll wake Danny."

"It takes forever to wake him up, you know that. You can't keep going forever without any rest and I've got mine so...but I appreciate you thinking about me."

After a wary look, he slid over and I got behind him, taking the pedal from his foot, then the steering wheel.

"There. Now get some sleep," I said, patting his knee.

I was elated when he obeyed without a fuss, laying his head in my lap as I had done with him.

Keep driving down this road and wake me if anything seems strange or out of place, all right? Watch the speed limit. Kay will stay right behind you. Eat something...and thank you. I know you hate this, but you're sweet to do it for me anyway.

"It's no problem."

He rubbed my knee for a minute and then I felt his hand fall as he fell asleep. Blowing out a sigh, I reached across him to the floorboard for the snack bag. He got the blueberry cereal bars. I ate two of them, seeing as how I hadn't eaten anything all day with all the commotion. There was bottled water, too, which I grabbed and down half the bottle with one pull.

I turned the radio on to help the freezing wind keep me awake. Reception was horrible off the main interstates. I finally settled on a semi-fuzzy rock station and the slogan they said every five minutes was 'Get your fill, with Gill. The late night slamming, jamming, singer bringer'.

I would've laughed, but my sleeping crew wouldn't have heard me so I kept it to myself. Funny, how Gill probably thought that was pretty clever but the tunes were nice and loud, perfect for my current circumstances, and I even sang along. They were asleep and the rip roaring wind was loud enough to cover my howling.

Driving in the dark was not my strong suit. I drove too slowly, and got antsy when oncoming traffic appeared.

Kay probably was pretty annoyed with me, back behind us, but I couldn't help it. I'd always been a day time or well-lit-highway kinda girl. My dad used to laugh at me. He called me a city girl who halted the car as soon as the city street lamps stopped.

I let Merrick sleep for about an hour and a half, and then I saw it. There was an old, abandoned, rundown motel set back off the highway. There was no electricity to it and it was dark, only lit by my oncoming headlights with bushes and grass overgrown.

I pulled in and woke Merrick. Kay pulled in behind me and killed her lights.

"Merrick? Merrick? What about this place? For the night at least," I asked as I shook his shoulder lightly.

"Where are we?" Merrick was incredibly cute groggy.

"The last sign I saw about twenty minutes back was Potomac. It didn't seem like much of a busy place, but there is probably a grocery store or something."

"Hmmm." He rubbed his hands in his hair. "How long have I been out?"

"Almost two hours. You need more than that."

"I feel a lot better... Ok, some better," he recanted seeing my face, reading the lies spilling out.

"What do you think?"

"I think I looked for hours, not finding anything, and you take over and find the perfect place," he said looking at me proudly.

I rolled my eyes at his silly banter as he grabbed my arm, pulling me towards his seat as he opened his door to get out. He lifted me up in an embrace that took my feet from the ground. The urge to kiss him came back to me tenfold, with his face buried in my hair and neck.

111

"You did good. I adore you, you know that? Thanks for letting me sleep," he whispered in my ear as he set me to the ground. "Stay here."

Jeff came to meet Merrick, no doubt having an internal conversation, and they walked cautiously to check the door and see if anyone else is here, though it didn't look like it.

Danny woke up and looked around, for Celeste I was sure. When he saw Merrick and Jeff, I decided to fill him in. He nodded his head in agreement. This was the perfect place, for tonight. It was falling apart and ragged. You could tell no one had been there in a very long time. The exact opposite of a motel I would have chosen a year ago. Funny.

Jeff came out with cobwebs in his hair from the door frame and waved us the all clear.

I left my headlights on for everyone to begin to unload our cargo. It took a few seconds to get the sticky trunk latch but eventually I got it open. I saw Celeste bend down to brush off her pants by the van.

That was the last thing I remembered before a horrible pain in my head and then I hit the hard, dusty ground.

I felt achy and incoherent, my eye hurt and I squinted to see but everything was blurry and moving in gray and dark colors. I reached up to inspect my eye and jolted at the pain that shot through my cheek. I also touched something wet. Blood. I blinked to focus and I must not have been out long because I saw them running towards us, Merrick and Jeff. The rest were behind them, horror all over their faces.

The creature, gangily hovering over me, must have thought I was alone. I couldn't believe what was in front of my eyes.

Celeste and I had been the only ones left outside that I had seen, and I didn't see her or Danny now. Ah, please let her be ok.

I tried to focus on it, but it was black like the night and moved swiftly making it impossible to focus directly on it. The only light to see with was the dim headlights still blaring from the Rabbit.

I looked quickly to find Merrick. He was standing by Jeff in front of everyone else. Should it have surprised me that they were *not* surprised to see this creature?

The looks on Merrick and Jeff's faces were not like the others, fear and disbelief. No. Their faces were full of anger and resentment, like seeing a loathed enemy after a long hiatus. Then the creature turned his hideous face, or whatever it was, at me. Staring me down, daring me to make a move.

It resembled nothing of a face but had eyes there, completely huge white yellow glowing eyes but no mouth, no nose, and no ears that I could tell. It screeched or yelled at me and I flinched back and covered my ears at the high pitch. He took the last step that was between us and touched me with his freezing cold skin.

He took one of his clubby, clawed looking feet and began pushing and rolling me in the dirt, away from my rescuers who were making steady inches toward us. Then he jumped into a loud screech and as I examined it closer, I realized it had wings instead of arms, but still dark black hands. I screamed.

I tried to roll over and get up to run, but it knocked me back down hard and placed a claw on my chest to hold me to the ground. My ribs burned and strained under the weight and breathing was impossible. I heard an angry grunt from someone behind me but couldn't turn to see.

The thing grabbed for me when Jeff made a move towards us with a crowbar outstretched for a hit. It was all a blur. Jeff swung it around thinking he made contact but the creature threw his head back, unnaturally bending backwards, just in time. Jeff jumped over us and landed on the other side in a crouch. The creature's claw scraped my shoulder in an attempt to lift me away, but I slipped back to the ground and yelped more from the pain of his scratch than from slamming to the dirt. The pain was something I didn't recognize, burning,. blinding pain.

When I surveyed the damage, I could feel the deep gashes, skin and meat in long strips, felt to the bone. I could hear myself grunting in pain and shuddered.

Merrick and Jeff made another move for it, one on each side. Then, it did lift me, a few feet off the ground. I saw Merrick jump for us and just as he made contact, the beast screeched loudly and dropped me in the dirt again hard. I rolled with the momentum.

Merrick knocked the creature away from me, but now lay on the ground grunting and writhing. I looked to see Jeff with this intense look on his face as he eyed the creature as it began to screech louder and fell twisting to the ground like Merrick.

I couldn't look away from Merrick as he slowly tried to get up, my scared eyes watching him as his face was mangled and twisted in pain. I met his eyes, but couldn't hold his gaze because the pain was overtaking me.

My shoulder ached worse than my eye ever thought about, both now covered in sand and grit and blood. My shoulder tingled like needle pricks along with the burning and I couldn't stop the tears from coming. Pain and fright took hold of me as I watched the gruesome scene unfold with the nameless beast.

It thrashed on the ground, and the screeching was piercing the night and my ear drums like a knife. Merrick stood above it limply and eyed it while Jeff ran to the tree near our cars. He grabbed a branch and snapped it, twisting it off.

Running, he stabbed it through the beast's midsection on the ground. There was a brilliant blinding burst of light and then a rush of cold air and it burned up in a quick puff of smoke and bright orange fire...and then there was nothing.

The sudden quiet continued too long, or maybe it seemed longer than it was. As I saw Merrick running to me, he did seem to be moving in slow motion. I felt him pick up my upper body and say my name in my mind, everything muffled. Then I saw blackness. Blackness and darkness. I didn't hear them yell or smell the burning anymore. I couldn't feel pain, anything, for just a moment. Peace.

Then the peace was ripped from me with a gush of cold water on my face, pulling me into consciousness. I gasped and flailed as Merrick grabbed my face and steadied me with his soothing voice, but the face didn't match. If it was over and the trouble was passed, why did his face still look so scared and twisted?

"Sherry, listen. We don't have time." He stopped and looked at Jeff, who didn't look much better. "We have to... burn you. That thing, the creature is called a Marker. He marks the ones who are with Specials so the Lighters can find them. We have to burn the mark he left on you. The poison is slowly seeping into your blood and you'll go into a coma. I'm sorry but we can't wait any longer," Merrick voice cracked and he cleared his throat.

As I tried to focus and listen, I saw there was a crowd around me. My eyes started to burn and my arm was completely covered in excruciating pin point prickles making me gasp and groan against my will.

Danny came to hold my hand and arm as Ryan placed his hands on my shins. I became instantly coherent and understanding of what they were doing. Burn me? They had to burn the gashes. Oh no! They had to burn me and hold me down so they can do it.

Merrick held my shoulders and face, leaving Jeff room to work and Kay was yelling at the others to leave the room as she placed herself over my stomach with all her weight. I looked up at Merrick and he refused to meet my gaze.

Oh, this was so not going to be good.

Jeff returned with the fire stoker from the blazing fireplace in the corner and its end was burning with a red glow. I looked at him but he also refused to look at my face as he closed the space between us.

I closed my eyes and screamed even before he brought it to my skin and when he did touch me I couldn't imagine a greater pain. He rolled it over the skin and then back up to do another layer. Then returned back up to get inside the grooves of the scratches. The smell was God awful and the sound was worse. I was surprised I could hear the singeing of the flesh over my screams.

I could feel myself thrashing, I felt as though I should be on the floor already but when I forced my eyes open, I saw that they were holding my petite frame almost perfectly still on some makeshift table in a poorly lit room.

I met Danny's gaze for a second and he grimaced like I'd never seen him. I yelled Merrick's name and he did look, finally. He bent down and put his forehead to mine.

I tried with all my might to stop screaming and stop fighting them, pull myself together. This wasn't torture in the traditional sense. I was aware enough to remember the words he said. This was killing them as it was killing me.

I fought the urge and it worked, some. I squeezed my eyes so tightly shut, and it hurt but I forced myself to focus. I told my arms and legs to be still, that it'd be over soon. It'd all be over soon.

The moments were hours it seemed but that couldn't be right because I felt as though I'd been holding my breath. The violent shaking of my body with the effort to be still was painful.

And then it suddenly stopped and I exhaled. A cold chill ran over me. No, cold water. I slowly opened my eyes again and met the eyes of the others. I heard whimpering. It was me.

Jeff, my torturer, was breathing heavy and apologizing profusely out loud and in my mind, doubled over, his hands on his knees to steady himself. I could hear Kay also but it was so hard to focus.

Soaking wet and throbbing all over, the hands and bodies slowly came off my body except for Merrick. He couldn't seem to pry himself from me.

I heard Danny saying my name but it was hard to make myself respond. Everything was muffled and my eyes started to flutter. He snapped in front of my face and then I heard him more clearly.

"Danny," I squeaked.

"Sherry, I'm so sorry. We had to do it to save you. We had to. You would've died. We had to."

Danny never cried before in front of me, let alone for me. The tears in his eyes were real, I felt them fall to my good arm. I immediately felt the need to comfort him, pulling my free hand up, I placed it on his cheek and he cried harder, hiding his face in my palm and his together. Then he leaned closer.

"Ah, man, I thought I lost you, little sister," he whispered.

Jeff got my attention and Merrick lifted his face from mine.

"Sorry, Sherry. I have to check to make sure that was the only spot he scratched you. Do you feel that weird sensation anywhere else?" Jeff said, his raspy voice sullen.

"No. Only my eye hurts," I said but then gasped.

I realized they have to burn my eye, too. A look I can imagine looked like pure horror raced across my face. Jeff saw this and immediately intervened.

"No! No! We don't have to burn your eye, Sherry. That wasn't a scratch. It's just where he hit you into the car when he attacked."

115

He slowly began to examine my legs and arms, pulling up my shirt slightly to examine my stomach, I heard him grunt unhappily and when I looked I saw a few bruises forming on my ribs and stomach from being kicked around and dropped. The strained voice that released the next question didn't sound like my own.

"What happened? What's a Marker?"

Merrick gripped my hand and sat on the pool table beside me where they had laid me out. I saw a big, red, blister looking rash on his arm. A quick glance around the room proved it to be a game room or bar of some sort in the motel.

"Markers search for people traveling with Specials. I told you about them reading minds, and how it's such a tedious process. The Markers mark you by scratching you and you slowly fog into a coma from the poison, giving the Lighters your location and time to get there while we tend to you.

"Markers are Lighters who choose to become....hounds so to speak. Searchers, seekers. Markers are pure evil, mindless creatures. The only way to remove the mark and stop the poison is to burn the skin, quickly... I'm so sorry, sweetheart," Merrick winced as he spoke the word 'burn'.

I felt like a complete idiot for wanting to smile at his term of endearment for me, despite the situation. As if the situation wasn't bad enough and screwed up enough already.

"Where's Celeste?" I asked suddenly remembering.

"It knocked her against the van and she hit her head pretty hard. Danny grabbed her and brought her inside right after that but she's ok and awake in the other room with everyone else."

I nodded my head in understanding. The pain was starting to rise higher and higher into my thoughts and I knew I wouldn't be able to contain it much longer.

I tried hard to suppress it and not make their misery that much more for them having to do this to me, by bursting into painful tears and sobs. Talking wasn't helping. I started to shake, the tears rolled down my face. Merrick gripped my cold hand tighter and glanced over, silently telling Jeff something, who brought more cold water to pour on my shoulder and then pulled out a needle. I turned away from it and shook my head vigorously.

"Sherry, the poison isn't active anymore in your system but it makes for a very painful recovery. I can't just let you lay there and scream. I won't. I know how much you're hurting and I have to stitch you up, too. The only thing I can give you will put you out for a few days. It'll give you a chance to heal some and not be in as much pain when you wake up. We don't have much medicine with us," Jeff explains.

"No! Please, don't." I didn't know why but I felt scared of being in the dark after what happened, even though I'd be asleep, I felt like I'd be stuck there and something might happen. A nightmare. I couldn't be put in the dark. "It doesn't hurt that bad. I don't want to sleep. I'm scared. Please don't. I don't want to be in the dark. Please," I hysterically begged Merrick, pleading, looking into his eyes. "Don't let him."

But he just stared his painful stare back into mine and held my arm down as Jeff eased the needle into the inside of my elbow, against my will.

I'm sorry. I have to...

After I heard Merrick, he reached over to kiss my forehead before I drifted out in the darkness.

Merrick - Waiting Game
Chapter 11

I couldn't believe this happened. How was it even possible? A Marker? Not for so long, why now? Why here? Why her?

Jeff couldn't explain it either and the rest of them were scared, very scared. How was I supposed to be a Keeper, do my job, watch Danny, watch Sherry, watch them all with blows coming at us every turn?

Jeff was worried. It was a good thing they couldn't hear us talk to each other. They couldn't handle it, the truth. It made liars out of us when we tried to calm them with soothing words, the 'It will be ok's.

It wouldn't.

The ones who were here to protect them were almost as freaked and as clueless as they were. I couldn't help but wonder what else was coming. Who else could be lurking, waiting to pounce. Was this a doomed cause from the start?

No. I wouldn't think like that. For once, I was thankful that this body's human brain no longer existed.

The Keepers met nightly in Sherry's room since I refused to leave her side, amid their grumbles they were also supportive, in a way. Talking and discussing things helped some. Discussing Sherry, discussing Specials, discussing Markers and other unpleasant things that could be popping up.

The humans just moped around, in their rooms or convened in the kitchen. They were stressed and scared. Danny was distraught with guilt and worry. He thought he should have been there, he didn't see Sherry on the ground when he saw Celeste and he left her out there. By the time we got out to her, the Marker has dragged or carried her almost twenty five feet away from her car. It wasn't Danny's fault though. I'd told him that.

"How is she doing? Any change?" I heard Jeff behind me.

"Same. Fever, shaking, nightmares," I answered him without turning, too much blatant pain in my red tired achy eyes, begging to close and sleep and he didn't understand any of it.

I should have known as I felt the fuzziness and heard his voice in my head, that he would be listening to my thoughts.

Brother. You don't have to hide from me and you're not doing a very good job of blocking me out lately anyway.

I just don't want to make you uncomfortable.

I told you before, I don't understand this, but it's not for me to understand. I can't explain it but I certainly can't deny it. You love her. Like a human loves. And she loves you, I'm not so blind not to see that either.

Impossible.

Sorry Brother, it's true. You can fight it, but I know you don't want to. Isn't that what you wanted?

I don't know what I wanted. I just... I just couldn't not be with her. Even if she doesn't love me and it never goes further than this, I have to be here. I have to be near her, making sure she's safe, happy. Watching is not enough anymore, it never was.

Well then, be content. You are human now and can be still if you choose. She does love you, I've seen it. I hate to see you struggle so but I hate to see you give up so much in return.

You can't understand. It pales in comparison to her. Being able to physically see her safe. When she looks at me, touches me...

Ok, ok. I don't need to know everything.

No, it's not like that. You would know if it was. Too many things to concentrate on, I can't keep you out anymore, or anyone else for that matter.

Yeah, I've noticed. I'm sorry. We just worry about you.

I know but I'm...happy. It's such a strange sensation, so different from being content. Content is fine, I've lived my life that way, but happy is...warm sun on your face.

I can imagine, though I'm afraid I'll never know. Have you told her where we come from?

I've tried, but it's impossible for their minds to wrap around. She's fascinated, very good imagination but she just can't make it match up.

You'll miss it.

I'd miss her more.

Ok. I'll let you get back to...whatever you're doing. Human pining...or worrying is a better word I guess. Now that emotion I know. I've had enough worry in my mouth since we've been here to last a century. Get some sleep, brother. She'll be ok.

I know. Thank you, Jeffrey.

Jeff left silently, closing the door behind him and I was alone again with her. Even as she breathed heavy in pain, she was still so beautiful. She said my name twice already just today. I couldn't leave and miss it if she said it again or better yet, woke up.

My heart, this heart, skipped so violently hearing my given name on those lips. Almost every time I come to earth, I never get to use my name. No point when I won't stick around long enough.

All my trips to earth I've never had these utterly useless emotions...but they weren't useless. My heartbeats sped up when she touched me and my breaths quickened and I twitched, but it was because it felt too good, too much to handle.

It couldn't feel like this when the rest of them touch each other, it just couldn't. How do they function, contain themselves? It seemed she had started to respond to my touches as well. That was more than I expected.

I thought maybe she might find it enjoyable enough to let me hold her hand every now and then, maybe get a hug from her but she has started reacting like me.

Giddy...

Drunk...

In love...

I wondered if there was any way Jeff could be right. But how? How could she love me?

Third day, almost 1:00 in the afternoon, I was starting to get worried. She should be waking up soon. I couldn't keep telling Danny she'd be fine if I started to doubt it myself. Poor kid had been in here almost as much as me. My conscience had been buzzing lately for him. It knew I wasn't focused on Danny. I tried. I check on him, call him quite a lot in his mind but I couldn't leave her. He was changing too, becoming a man. He was quite taken with Celeste and she with him.

He was distracted a lot. Sometimes I wish I could read his thoughts too, so I could help him somehow. Waiting here is so much harder than watching. I felt helpless, waiting on his task to come full circle to us but now, with everything, would there even be a task? What could he do now? Even if it was over, I was not going anywhere. I couldn't leave the fragile girl under my hands.

4:00 p.m. Still nothing. They had been in and out all day, one by one, in groups asking about her. I hoped she knew how much everyone loved her here. She couldn't leave, they needed her. I needed her, but they needed her spirit.

Even though she's small, cute and fragile, and would kill me for saying that, she was such a leader and grounder for them.

I always wondered why Danny was the Special and not her but she shines everyday, he will have to wait his turn.

I saw her stirring. I brushed her cheek with the backs of my fingers and she moaned and leaned into it. Sounds like appreciation, not pain. Maybe she was coming around.

She kicked her leg out of the covers, wrapping it around the white sheets and rolled to her side. This was how she always slept and it was comforting to see it now. She leaned closer to me, unintentionally, and grabbed onto the edge of the pillow with her slim pale fingers.

Look at those lips. How I'd longed for those lips and there they were, inches from mine. How easily I could kiss her right now. Steal kisses.

These bodies hold too much power. People like Matt are prime examples of what bodily power in the wrong hands can do.

I couldn't believe this body was used to try to force her...and then he hit her! Slapped her. Look at her! How could you ever harm that face?

What a selfish... I guess I was, too. Claiming her as my own when I have no right to her. What a gorgeous creature, and she didn't even know it.

Wait. She was waking!

Sherry, can you hear me? Wake up, sweetheart.

"Sherry? Open your eyes. Come on. Wake up, Sherry."

Location, Location, Location
Chapter 12

Darkness.
Coldness.
Nothingness.
Silence.
Those are a few of my least favorite things. It was everywhere and nowhere. I couldn't move, I couldn't breath, couldn't hear or feel my breaths. I felt like I was being followed, watched, but there was nothing - wait. A light? A sliver of light like through the crack of a door. It opened further and someone was standing there, his black finger came up to beckon me to him.

How do I go? If I could, would I? I tried to speak but nothing. He appeared angry now, making wider motions for me to come but I couldn't. I tried to scream as I saw him make a swift advance my way, but he snapped his fingers in my face in frustration, and then I was gone and surrounded by light.

The lake. All else was forgotten for a moment as I recognized something. There was nothing but this tree.

This tree has always been my favorite. The one our parents took us to for picnics on special occasions. We ignored the whole, 'the tree is alive and deserves our respect' speech. I loved the tree for other reasons. A weeping willow. My favorite tree.

I loved running through its curtains when I was little and now that I was older, I loved it for its memories and soothing shade. Danny was more the sun type and was busying himself with the girls playing volleyball in the adjoining court.

You couldn't help but laugh at his skills, or lack thereof. It was hilarious the way boys threw out lines and useless facts to impress girls. I didn't personally know any girls that it actually worked on.

Of course, I didn't personally know many girls.

Mom and Dad were bickering, as the normal. I tuned them out completely these days. You were supposed to worry about the world, but not to the point of self destruction.

My mom was the worst activist I'd ever met. Worked so hard to saves lives, save the planet, save the animals, save humanity but she wasn't enjoying any of that and certainly wasn't trying to save her marriage.

She was miserable and trying to fill a void with all that other stuff, which in turn made Dad miserable, which in turn made us miserable. Just one normal family function would be nice.

Mom, apparently having enough on her mind, stomped off to the eco-friendly Porto-potty. Dad turned while I took my last bite of organic cream cheese icing cake and set my plate down, licking my fork clean.

He handed me a little blue box, smiling, he must have seen how surprised I was.

"Open it, pumpkin."

I lifted the lid slowly, trying to stifle the excitement on my face.

It couldn't actually be jewelry because that would be a normal gift. It was probably a pebble from the Nile River or some trinket supposed to bring me a worthy husband, but as the lid fell back and I examined the sweet charm, I realized this was not a pebble.

This was a real gift.

The silver heart within a heart charm and silver chain were sitting there, waiting for me to pick it up and put it on. How had dad talked mom into such a thing? Silver bobbles were pointless and wasteful, doing nothing for the environment or our spiritual welfare.

"Dad! Thank you. It's so perfect," I said and felt my eyes filling with tears.

"You're more than welcome, pumpkin."

He took it from me, motioned for me to turn around and I lifted my hair as he fastened it, then sat back to look at me. He looked pleased.

Mom was making her way back to the pallet and I rubbed the charm in between my fingers, almost protectively.

I quickly leaned up to kiss Dad's cheek knowing the moment would surely pass the second mom stepped foot on our pallet. He smiled back at me, not looking at her yet.

As I watched and waited for her wrath she began to wave. Not just her hands, her whole body, then the background began to shake. The grasses green bled into the waters blue and my dad smiled at me one last time before he, too, began to quake and bleed color and fade away.

"Bye, pumpkin."

I tried to reach for him but he was already gone.

A sweet voice was on the air, a familiar voice, calling me in my head. I wanted it so badly as I recognized it. As much as I wanted my dad in that moment, I pushed myself towards consciousness, towards the voice.

I jerked and rolled as I opened my eyes to see a white tile ceiling above me.

All too soon I realized the vision was a dream, a memory of my birthday. As soon as I could manage, I tried to swallow so I could speak, but the dryness and cobweb veins wouldn't let any sound escape.

I coughed and Merrick was immediately hovering into my line of vision. I blinked, trying to focus. Where was my Merrick? This Merrick, like the last Merrick in my memory, was guilt stricken and worrisome, tight lines around his mouth and eyes making him appear older and sullen.

"Sherry? Oh, thank God. Hey. Hey, are you feeling all right?" His thumb rubbed my forehead with his fingers in my hair while he spoke so close.

"I'm...I." I couldn't get any words to form so I whispered. "I'm ok. I'm thirsty."

He scrambled for a bottle of water he had there waiting for me and helped me sit up with his arm around my back. He placed the straw in my mouth for me and I gulped.

It seemed to just go down with no wetness at all. Eventually my mouth feels more like a sponge, as it should and I downed the entire bottle. I sucked in a few breaths to steady myself.

"Do you feel ok? I've been so worried about you," Merrick said, still there, holding me up.

"Better. Did all that stuff really happen?" I asked but I was already flinching as I reached up to grab my now bandaged shoulder.

Merrick grabbed my hand trying to stop me, but it was too late. He kept my hand in his.

"Yeah. How do you feel?"

"Just...give me a minute. How long have I been out?"

"Three days."

"Three days?" How was that possible? "Danny? Celeste?"

"Everyone's fine. Worried about you, but fine. Jeff gave you the last of the medicine we had. I'm so sorry we had to do that to you. You...remember everything?"

"Oh, yes. I remember." Closing my eyes, trying to stop that vision. "What are we doing? I mean...can we stay here? Did that thing come back?"

"We've been here with no problems and the thing is dead. Jeff and Danny went and got some food and supplies two days ago, and you some pain medicine, to last us a while.

"You let Danny go without you?" I asked shocked.

"Yes. I didn't want to leave you, in case you woke up. Jeff doesn't have a charge anymore so, I knew he'd watch out for him. Danny wouldn't have it any other way though. You know him, especially when it comes to you. When he found out we didn't have any medicine with us for you he practically drove off with Jeff

125

barely jumping in to make the ride."

I nodded, understanding. I felt definitely light headed and sore, and starving. I tried to swing my legs over the edge of the bed but they wouldn't go willingly.

"Sherry, wait. Take it easy, let me help."

Merrick placed his hands on my waist to steady my balance. I looked up at his close face. I couldn't imagine the mess I must have looked. Three days. No shower, no food, no water, nothing.

He helped me up and held me as I almost buckled under my own weight. He flashed me that *I'm sorry* face again and pulled me in for an easy feet off the floor hug.

"I am so glad that you're all right," he whispered.

"Merrick, don't. I'm such a mess."

Hunger and pain was making me irritable, but I wouldn't direct any of that anger at him. I tried to smile as he pulled back so he knew I was kinda teasing.

"You're a beautiful mess."

He just said I was beautiful. I allowed myself to dwell on that for a split second.

He set me down and reached up to touch my healing eye and cheek wound that I had forgotten all about. I inspected for myself and it was almost healed, it felt like scratches under my frail fingertips. I noticed the huge red rash on Merrick's arm and looked up at him questioningly.

"It's nothing," he leaned in and whispered against my cheek.

I couldn't tell if it was his close proximity or the lack of nutrients, but I felt weak. I wanted to take a shower, but I couldn't break his gaze. He looked past my eyes, into me, and whispered in my mind.

I'm so sorry. I thought I lost you forever. It was my fault, I'm a Keeper, I should have protected you. I knew better. I should never have let you out of my sight.

"Merrick, I'm ok and I'm not your charge, remember?"

But you are. I don't care what I'm supposed to do anymore. I won't let anything happen to you...anything more, I should say. You are everything that's important to me now.

"We are all in this together, now. It wasn't your fault I got attacked and I know you had to do what you did and I know why. I remember, it's ok. Please don't do this," I said and lifted my, what felt like, fifty pound hands to his upper arms. "Three days I've been in the dark, alone." I missed the guilt free, easily enticed Merrick. "Please just...let it go, just be you."

I was barely able to hold myself up, leaning almost entirely on him for support, but I refused to wait any longer. I licked my lips, reached up on my tip toes, pulling on his arms and very lightly touched his lips to mine.

This wasn't a passionate kiss. This was a grateful I-forgive-you-but-you-don't-need-my-forgiveness kiss.

Our lips touched, barely grazed, for just a few seconds and I could already barely breathe. I leaned my forehead on his chin and tried to catch my breath. I didn't even get to witness his reaction because I was so out of it.

He picked me up in his arms, as if I weighed nothing, careful of my shoulder and carried me to the kitchen. Kitchenette. A half everything. Half stove, half sink, half refrigerator. He sat me down on the bench at the table and went to make me a sandwich.

I looked around at the dark motel décor. All the windows had thick dark curtains drawn to let in enough light to see to get around. I saw candles and flashlights on the counter. There were about twelve cases of soda on the floor by the walkway.

Leave it to Danny to do the shopping.

I figured while Merrick has his back to me I should try to fix me hair somewhat, it was the only thing I could do. Pulling my hair from the rubber band was excruciating. The muscles in my arm felt like stone, unwilling to give and move. Using my other arm, I eventually managed it.

Putting it back up neater would be that much harder so I sighed in frustration and left my hair more disheveled and messy than when I started.

I ate quickly as I was starving, Merrick sat right next to me, watching me closely, and by the time I was ready to ask for an escort to the shower, before anyone else could see me, I was suddenly surrounded by a swarm of eager bodies from the hall.

Danny grabbed me in a hug under my arms and I could barely keep myself from toppling over.

"Sorry, sis. Still groggy? You never did do good with drugs."

"Yeah, I've slept for three days and I can barely keep my eyes open," I said and noticed my voice was still raspy from too little use.

Celeste was there, too, hugging me. She didn't say much, but it was hard with Danny there to get a word in.

Jeff even walked through the crowd to hug me, which surprised the heck out of me, and Merrick too, from his surprised face. I hadn't seen Jeff touch any of us let alone hug anyone.

"I'm glad you're all right. I'm sorry for what I had to do to you," Jeff

127

whispered in my ear and then quickly exited the room.

After a few more pleasantries, I couldn't muster one more ounce of it. As politely as I could, I asked if Celeste or Margo could help me with a shower. Celeste jumped at the opportunity to help. As she put her arm under mine we all saw Calvin running down the hall.

He jumped up and put his arms around me and it was all I could do to keep from screaming as his arm scraped across my shoulder.

Apparently my face didn't hide my pain well and he was berated by Celeste quickly.

"I'm sorry, Sherry! I forgot," he said with a quick enthusiastic apology.

"It's ok," I breathed. "Calvin, I've missed you."

I blew out a sigh trying to cover my deep, painful breaths. No one bought it and I was soon handed a couple of pills and a glass of water, then carted off by Celeste at the insistences of several others. Merrick threw me a sympathetic glance. He knew I hated being made a fuss over and he had apparently seen this recovery before. This must be what Jeff meant by 'the poison makes for a painful recovery'. No way just a gash would hurt like this hurt, taking my breath away.

The water pressure was bad. The place did have power, somehow, but no water pressure. At least Celeste's bathroom didn't. The shower, though much needed was torture on my shoulder and face and I hurried though it.

Once I stepped out, Celeste helped me towel dry and dress in some pajamas, some of her hip sleep pants and matching camisole.

"You have such a cute body, Sherry. I wish I was short and cute. It sucks being taller than most of the boys my age," she sweetly babbled on and on, for my benefit I assumed, taking my mind off the pain. She giggled. "I guess I don't have to worry about that anymore, do I?"

It was night time already as she sat me down on the bed to brush my hair for me. She braided a long, low ponytail and continued to tell me all about my wonderful brother. How he had saved her from the beast and had no idea that I had been hurt. Once the 'he is so sweet's started, I tuned out for a bit, throwing in a few mechanical nods.

With the mention of Merrick's name, my attention was brought back around. She said he never left my side, not once. In fact he slept nights in the chair next to my bed. He would sponge off my face and shoulder and bandage it daily. He was constantly peeking in the hall, looking out the window at Danny, asking people passing by in the hall to make sure he was ok, calling Danny in his mind. I could feel the warmth spreading out in my heart.

Jeff, Ryan and Kay came in quite a bit to check on me, too. Everyone felt so guilty for having to do what they did to me. Celeste told me she could hear the commotion and my screams in the next room.

I had a few questions about all this. For Merrick. Why hadn't he told us about this before and was this as weird as it was going to get?

Celeste walked me to my room, continuing to try to fill me in on the last three days. We took up a few of the rooms in one hallway, all right beside each other.

I caught a glimpse of myself in the hall mirror. It could be worse. My eye and cheek didn't look as bad as I had imagined, just a little pink and purple, but healing. Celeste had made a very pretty braid of my normally unruly hair and it rested over my shoulder.

Danny caught me in the hall, just before his door. He hugged me again. This time lifting me and holding tight for a long while. I let him, though his grip is tight on my sore body. I know he felt just as bad if not more so than Merrick and the rest.

I was so proud of him all of a sudden. When Celeste spoke of him earlier, I didn't catch it before, but she wasn't saying he was some crush that she had. She was saying he was becoming a man. A man that took charge in a situation and took care of her and others. He did what had to be done with me as well. I was beginning to see the Special in him. Maybe his time was coming sooner than we think.

As I pushed open my room door Merrick was inside. I turned to say my thanks to Celeste but she was gone already. Giving us privacy. Hmmm.

I turned to Merrick to see a new face, a happy one with a relieved smile. I smiled, too.

"See. Now that's more like it," I said, closing the door.

"I was just getting your things put away in here. New sheets and blankets," he told me, placing the pillows back on the bed.

"Thanks."

"Tired?"

"Surprisingly so. You?"

"Very." He chuckled, as if for some inside joke with himself.

"I heard from Celeste what you did. I guess I didn't make such a good pit stop choice after all, huh? Thank you. That was very sweet of you to look after me," I said stealing Celeste's description, but it fit Merrick just as well. "I have a lot of...questions but can we talk about everything tomorrow, maybe?"

I watched his happy expression change to unhappy, to disappointed, to trying to look not unhappy and disappointed. I figured I knew why, so I saved him before he could start to feel too bad.

"Merrick, would you mind staying with me? I really...don't want to be alone."

The happy face was back.

"Um, sure. If that's what you want."

"It is."

I grabbed his hand leading him to the bed before he could suggest another arrangement. I switched off the lamp before crawling in and waiting in the dark to feel him climb in beside me. I felt nothing.

"Merrick?"

"Are you sure you're comfortable with this? I can sleep in the chair again, it's no problem."

"Merrick, I know you, I know you would never do anything I didn't want to. I just don't want to be alone, at all. Please...unless *you're* uncomfortable?"

We weren't back to this were we? But I felt the mattress depress as he climbed in under the covers. He opened his arm up for me to fold myself into and I laid my head on his chest and took a deep breath, his arm lightly around me. He was so incredibly warm as always and smelled like soap and shaving cream.

"One question," I said baiting him.

"Ok."

"Why didn't you ever mention those creatures before? Or the fact that you're faster than everyone else?"

"That's two by the way," he laughed softly, "and you noticed that, huh?" He sighed. "I didn't want to scare you or worry you anymore than you already were. Things were weird enough as it was. Those creatures, the Markers, are supposed to be extinct. We haven't come into contact with one in many, many years. And I move just a tad faster, marginal." He laughed a quick breathy laugh.

"Anything else I should know about?"

"I missed you like crazy," he whispered, tightening his arms on me.

"I missed you, too, kind of. It was actually a pretty quick three days for me."

"Not for me." He chuckled a humorless laugh.

"Sorry."

"Don't apologize," he chided.

"You didn't have to do that, stay with me, but I'm glad you did...I had a dream...about my fourteenth birthday. Remember it?"

"Yes. The day your dad gave you that necklace. You looked happy that day. Mostly."

"It was the clearest dream I've ever had. I'll never understand our parents. We'll probably never see them again. But I feel guilty because I should feel worse about it. But they chose, and it wasn't us. I had all but forgotten how much they use to bicker back then. I always wondered if the reason for the fight that day was the necklace."

"It was."

I couldn't believe how much I loved talking to him about my life. I didn't have to tell a whole storyline to get to a point. He knew exactly what I was referring to and he liked it. He liked to reminisce about *my* life and I liked that he liked it. I liked it a lot. I liked him a lot.

I felt him chuckle beside me.

I'm glad you wanted me to stay with you. I was trying to think of ways to convince you to let me at least sleep in the chair tonight. I feel like I need to be here.

"Well, I'm glad, too. I want you here. I feel safer with you here."

"Good. I want you to feel safe. I was worried you'd be traumatized after what happened, but I should've known better. You're so strong and level-headed. You don't let much get you down."

For some reason, I blushed at his praise.

"Thanks. Though I don't feel that way about myself."

"Well, I could sit here all night and tell you all the ways you are those things, but I'm already fighting to stay awake."

"Oh. I'm sorry. Of course, I'll shut up," I said, feeling guilty as he had already said once how tired he was, because of looking after me.

"I would love to go back and forth with you about how you're as great as I think you are, this body is just tired, that's all."

I felt him chuckle again and I managed a giggle that hurt an awful lot, but tried to not let him know.

"All right. Whatever you say. Goodnight, Merrick. Thank you."

"You're welcome, sweetheart."

My heart swelled. I smiled and shifted so I was laying more comfortably on him and his hand came up to rest on my lower hip, lower than it ever had before. I felt myself tense, he noticed.

"I'm sorry, I wasn't trying to overstep-"

He immediately removed his hand and began to move away from me altogether, but I stopped him.

"Of course you weren't. It's fine. Better than fine."

He remained still. I fiddled for his hand in the dark and found it, replacing it on my hip and snuggling in closer. He moved it higher and I sighed. I grabbed it again and pushed it lower.

The last thing I want is for you to conform to whatever idea I set for us as what is passable behavior if you're not comfortable. I want you to say so, not just do it or let it be done so my feelings won't be hurt. I won't take your decisions away, so many people before me have done that. I just want you to be happy even if that doesn't include me at all.

"I know that. That's one of my favorite things about you," I said with certainty. "I did choose. Right now, everything is right where I want it."

I patted the hand on my hip and sighed happily before hearing his long breath release.

"You're sure?"

"I promise. You aren't making me do anything I don't want to. I adore you too, ya know," I repeated his earlier comments to him.

He laughed softly in my ear. "I don't think anything could make me happier than hearing you say that," he whispered into my hair and I smiled as I let sleep take me.

The next day I woke and Merrick was gone. Well, not gone but away from me, in the chair. Most of the day was spent pretty much lying around. I was so, so tired. So drained, so achy still. Merrick stayed with me a lot but I slept a lot, too. I tried to relay how grateful I was to him for taking care of me with little touches of reassurance.

Then at nightfall, I was still incredible tired but had been thinking about some things.

After pulling him down with me when he checked on me, I laid on his chest, a repeat of last night, and I pondered how I felt about all this. How I would feel if I knew I'd never see him again? How would I feel if he stayed with me forever? Where did I think this was going, what with the invasion and all?

All the things that Merrick has done for me. He was everything I ever thought I'd wanted in a guy but didn't know to look for it. I was so in like with him but another thought hit me. A painful thought.

I sat up to face him in the darkness on my knees. He sat up too, wordlessly, sensing my distress.

"Sherry?"

"What happens, Merrick? What happens when Danny's task is done. When the Lighters leave and everything's normal again."

"If that happens, we...would go home."

I reached up with my good arm to touch his face and he covered my hand with his. I let out a strained sigh. I told Jeff that I wouldn't ask Merrick to stay, but that was a lie. I wanted nothing more and that was precisely what I was going to do.

"You are home. I don't want you to go," I breathed against his cheek as I leaned in and wrapped my good arm around his neck.

He pulled his arms around my waist.

"I don't want to go. And none of us will until we're done here."

"Please...don't. I don't want to fall-" I was going to say 'fall in love and then have you leave me' but that seemed a bit too soon and crazy. "Don't leave," I whispered into his neck.

He lifted one hand up to my chin and tilted my face up with his thumb though I couldn't see him, he could see me, then he took that thumb and ran it over my bottom lip. I could practically feel his anticipation, his hesitancy, but also his wonder.

We hovered there for a few seconds, feeling the heat of each others lips so close but not touching. My heart rate couldn't have been more erratic.

"I'm not going anywhere, Sherry. No matter what happens. I can't leave now." He took a deep breath and then repeated firmly, "I can't."

Then I could take no more. Weeks had built up to this and I knew after that whole decisions speech yesterday he'd never make the first move. So I made the choice.

I closed the distance and pressed my lips to his warm ones. I felt him let out a breath of pent up longing against mine. I ran my hand through his short dark hair. His hand on my chin moved up to hold my jaw and cheek. I felt his grip on my waist tighten, but my sore body didn't protest this time. He was very careful of my shoulder and as we kissed, there was nothing but electricity. My skin tingled everywhere he touched me and everywhere he didn't.

His lips were hesitant and shy at first, but soon relaxed and explored, parting with mine at my urging. It didn't take him very long to get the hang of it and he began to urge me on instead. I could taste mint, toothpaste. I felt his thumb grazing the bare skin of my waist just under the hem of my shirt. If I had opened my eyes there would have been no doubt that there were static sparks in the air.

It was like something in us collided.

Then his fingers dug into the flesh of my waist deliciously and desperately, and when his tongue brushed mine...

I forgot that this is all new to him. For someone who had never done it, he was awfully good at following my direction. He was awfully good at this kissing thing. I was no expert, having only ever kissed a few frogs but never like this. The few boys I'd kissed had never made me feel this way. So precious and looked after, so wanted. It felt like so much more than just kissing.

This was exquisite.

I tried not to be too aggressive, taking it easy on him, but I couldn't help myself as his lips were rubbing mine, my mind stopped and my body took over.

When I caught his lower lip between mine, he groaned and pulled away slightly, both of us gasping loudly.

"Sherry," he could barely breathe, let alone speak. "You're making this very difficult for me."

At first I was horrified, but then he laughed roughly so I laughed, too, getting his meaning. "Sorry."

"Don't be sorry for *that*." He laughed breathlessly and then moved both hands up to my face. "I am so glad that you're well enough to do that."

"Merrick, I-" He stopped me with a thumb on my lips, and the electricity started again. I felt my eyelids flutter with passion.

"Let's get some sleep," he said gruffly and I could tell it was just as hard for him to stop as it was for me. "We can talk all day long tomorrow, I promise, but I want you to rest if you still feel like you can. You're a long way from recovered."

"Ok," I conceded, but I pulled him back by his shirt collar to my lips for the lightest touch of his lips, shocking myself at my boldness.

Short and sweet.

We lay back down and he settled his arms around me, cradled me from behind. I could feel the rise and fall of his chest, his wonderfully warm breath on my neck.

"Goodnight," I said, trying to tell my body to calm down and find the closing of my eyes, sleep was calling me again.

"Goodnight, Sherry."

He wrapped his arms around me tighter, knowing the warmth would end the struggle with my eyelids. In no time, I was out like a light.

I awoke to something warm on my face. I blinked and realized Merrick was still right here with me and I had turned toward him sometime in my sleep. He kissed the very tip of my forehead lightly. I couldn't help the huge grin spreading across my face.

"Did you sleep comfortably enough?" he asked, a grateful grin on his face. He looked like he almost thought I wouldn't be happy to see him there with me.

"Yes! I slept great." My eyebrows tightened just a bit at my embarrassing enthusiasm, but he didn't seem to notice.

"Feeling any better today?"

"I feel ok. Not quite as achy and stiff."

"Hungry?"

"Mmmhuh," I mumbled and nodded, but I didn't move from his chest.

Too comfortable and warm, he'd have to pry me off, and soon he did. Picking me up effortlessly and setting me on the floor, he checked under my shoulder bandage, carefully unwrapping and rewrapping.

He then turned my face to see my cheek and eye. I watched his face as he worked. I'd never met anyone so genuinely concerned for me before.

"Looks a lot better. I don't even think this one will scar," he said as he brushes my cheek with his finger making me shiver.

"That'd be nice." I smiled and stretched slowly, feeling the muscles complain but it was a good hurt. "What's there to eat in this joint?"

He grabbed my hand and led me down the hall and through the front office to the small kitchen, already packed with my new little family. Everyone greeted us warmly, but no attack hugs this time, and Danny had my cup of coffee for me, with creamer.

"I heard you coming, shorty," Danny said smiling.

"See, brat, this is why I love you."

I gratefully took the cup from him, and the peck on my good cheek, and as I smelled the aroma, I think that it had been too long. Coffee and I should get together more often.

Merrick directed me to a seat on the end and since the table was full he stood behind me. Coffee and a blueberry cereal bar. As far as I was concerned, this was heaven, and then I felt Merrick's hand on my neck, massaging gently.

No. Now *this* was heaven.

Merrick kept his promise and he let me ask a hundred questions without getting impatient with me, though I wasn't exactly sure what questions *to* ask. Jeff even joined in along with a few others to ask and listen and answer.

We sat out by the pool. Well the waterless hole where the pool water should be, under the shade of huge palm trees. Still unseasonably cool, Merrick had grabbed the blanket off my bed for me, knowing my proneness to the cold. He sat partially under the blanket as well, on the same large Adirondack lounger as me and held my hand underneath, his heat spreading through me, doing far more to warm me than the blanket did. I couldn't have been more comfortable, but serious questions were beginning to come up and everyone needed to know the answers. Everyone needed to be prepared.

"Will the moon come back?" someone asked.

"Not unless they all decide to go home, which isn't likely," Merrick answered.

"What made them this way?"

"Everyone has a choice, just like you. People, aliens, angels, all creatures. Everyone has a choice in their own evilness or their goodness."

"What do you look like?"

"Like you but...pale."

A few chuckles erupted.

"What's the purpose for trying to get us to turn on each other? What will that accomplish?"

"They want your world, your land, your homes, your bodies. If you turn on each other, and hunt each other, you'll eventually die out and they will get what they want that much faster. We don't look at time the same as you, because we're immortal, until we take these bodies. They'll wait. As long as they have to."

"Can they be killed?"

"Only by running them through completely, Markers and Lighters, that and burning them. That's the only way to kill them."

"Why can you only take bodies of the dead?"

"It wouldn't be right to take lives to come here and if we come here not in human form, we can't stay as long and we don't look exactly like you. You would be able to tell that something was off."

"What's your favorite color?" That was definitely Calvin, my favorite 10 year old.

"Mud brown," Merrick said looking at me smiling, knowing our inside joke about how I described myself, as he must have heard me say that a thousand times.

"Blue. Sky blue," Jeff answered laughing.

"Hmm. Never thought about it before. What's yours Calvin?" Ryan asked.

"Yellow."

"Mine's yellow, too," Ryan said smiling, still trying to make an effort with his charge.

"Will more of those things come? Beasts like that one that attacked Sherry?" Margo asked, getting everyone back on track.

I flinched at the memory and Merrick squeezed my hand. Jeff answered this time.

"The Markers, we don't know. We thought there weren't anymore of them so...it's possible there could be, yes, but don't worry. They only come out at night, for camouflage, and we'll make sure to always be in by then."

"What happened to you when you touched it, Merrick?"

I froze. What did they mean what happened? Then I remembered Merrick's writhing body on the ground, his face twisted in pain after he jumped on it to keep it from taking me away. I looked over at him but he just stared down at the empty pool. Jeff answered for him.

"We can't touch their skin, and they can't touch ours. A lot of the times we black out if we do but if nothing else, it leaves a mark on us, kind of like a burn, that's permanent. It is excruciatingly...painful for us."

Jeff looked over, suddenly realizing why Merrick had been so quiet about explaining it. My face at the memory of it felt tight and pulled together. I reached under the blanket, pulling his arm out and pushing up his short sleeve. I ran my finger over the huge red mark, taking up almost his whole arm.

"This is from the Marker? When you jumped on it...for me." I nodded in understanding and also, not understanding. I had no idea the things Merrick would do for me. "Does it hurt?" I asked, my voice breaking, tears threatening.

"Not anymore," Merrick muttered under his breath, like it didn't matter.

"It doesn't hurt for very long after, but the mark where our skin touched theirs will always be there and they'll have a matching one," Jeff said, looking at me, trying to soothe my fear of Merrick being in pain because of me.

Merrick glanced down at me. I caught his gaze and he flashed me a weak smile. He reached and slid his fingertips down my cheek.

"I'm fine. Don't worry about me," he whispered.

I saw everyone watching us out of the corner of my eye, but I asked anyway and pretended that I didn't see them.

"You knew it would be like that for you, you knew it would hurt like that, and you still did it."

He pressed his forehead to mine.

Anything. I would do anything to keep you safe.

My breath caught in my throat. It was true. I found comfort and upset in that thought. I continued to run my fingers over his red arm and bent down to put my head on his shoulder as he rubbed my leg, right above my knee, to comfort me.

"How long can we stay here?" The questions started again and I was grateful for it.

"Well," Jeff answered, "we all need to make sure our curtains are always pulled to at night. We won't attract any attention, see how long that gets us."

I wasn't the only one not wanting to be alone. Calvin had been shadowing me all night. I felt sorry for Calvin's mother, not being able to speak to anyone except him. None of us knew any sign language, but me. I knew the alphabet but finishing a sentence took longer than just writing it down.

Most everyone has gone to bed. Merrick, Danny, Celeste and I were up lounging in the large purple high back chairs in the sitting room, talking. It was late.

Danny found an old radio in the corner of the office and plugged it up to the intercom system. He was nifty like that. Right then, The Strokes 'What Ever Happened' played in the background from the ceiling speakers from the local radio station.

"So anyway," Celeste continued on her story about how Kay found her. "I was just walking out of school from cheer practice and she walks right up to me and says 'Come with me if you want to live.' I laughed so hard at her I almost peed my pants. I mean who says that? It was pretty clear she wasn't from this planet. Everyone knows who the Terminator is."

"So you were a cheerleader?" Danny asked and leaned on his elbows closer to her from his seat.

"Yep. And dance squad and gymnastics." I saw Danny's eyes bug at the word gymnastics. "I only got a couple years into it though so I wasn't very good at it, but I can still do a full split."

I heard Danny make a choked noise and decided to save him the embarrassment of making a fool of himself with any further comments.

"Calvin, come on out." I could see his silhouette behind the fake palm by the entrance way. He came and jumped in my lap. I winced just a bit at the jolt in my shoulder. "What's the matter, little man?" But he was anything but little. He was almost as tall as I was.

"Scared," he admitted softly.

"You don't have to be, ya know. There's lots of people here. Nothing's gonna happen to you. Want me to come tuck you in?"

He nodded his head up and down and took my hand as I walked him down to his room. I cast one glance over my shoulder to Merrick to see if he was watching and of course he was. I smiled and he smiled, too, before I turned the corner into Calvin's room. His mother was sound asleep, thinking he was, too.

"You sing to me again, Sherry?"

"Mmmm..." I considered when I really wanted to say no.

"Pleeeeease."

Oh, that pleading face!

"Ok, what do you want to hear?"

"I don't know anything. I never listened to songs before."

"What? Really? Ok. Hmm, I think a little Carpenters is in order."

As he settled in under his blanket and I turned out the lamp, I began to sing softly, probably more like whisper singing, still a twig of self-consciousness there, but I pulled through it, for Calvin.

Why do birds suddenly appear
Every time, you are near
Just like me, they long to be
Close to you

Why do stars fall down from the sky
Every time you walk by
Just like me, they long to be
Close to you

On the day that you were born
the angels got together
and decide to create a dream come true.
So they sprinkled moon dust in your hair
and golden starlight in your eyes of blue.

Calvin wasn't a snorer, but I could tell he was out by his soft slow breathing. Poor guy. I couldn't have imagined seeing a Marker when I was his age and being able to sleep at night. Afterwards, I tucked him in, dragged his legs back onto the bed and eased them under the blanket.

I crept out slowly and pulled the door to. I glanced up and saw that Merrick was waiting for me in the hall, leaning against the wall with his hands in his jean pockets. Smiling and looking every bit of gorgeous and protective...and sneaky.

"That's nice, what you're doing for the kid. I really miss hearing you sing," he said, coming to hug me gently around my ribs, clasping his hands together behind my back.

"Well, I'm sure you've heard me sing over the years to Danny many times so it doesn't matter if you heard that or not." I grinned at him with a mock scowl, thinking what a hypocrite I was because I had gotten so mad at Bobby for doing the same thing, but then sobered. "Calvin is so scared of the Markers, of all of it. It'd be hard not to be at that age. I'm pretty scared, too, actually."

"You don't have to be. I'm not going to let anything else happen to you."

"I hate to admit that I'm scared. It's just strange knowing how much everything has changed. There are things out there I never even knew existed. That's why I don't want to be alone."

I tried to keep his gaze while I confessed my silly fears, but he got the strangest look on his face.

"So, does that mean that I'm invited to stay with you again tonight?" he asked, so shyly, like he didn't already know the answer.

Then I realized...maybe he didn't.

"Every night," I said as I grabbed his arm.

His look of relief was funny as I towed him to my- our room. I didn't wait for him to make the next move, I knew he was being cautious with me, so I

139

reached up on my toes for a kiss. He reacted immediately, hugging me closely to him while he closed the door behind us easily with his foot.

Get Down Tonight
Chapter 13

Merrick and I were taking things slow, which was ok, great even. I'd only really ever been in one real relationship and it didn't turn out so well. Funny, that relationship was with this same body. It was strange that I wasn't confused at all, I guess I should've been but not once did I want to say Matt instead of Merrick, except for the first time, not even from habit. Merrick was so entirely different that, to me, that body was someone completely different altogether.

Over the next two weeks, Merrick stayed with me every night. We kissed some and cuddled lots and talked like crazy, but that was the extent of it. I was just so content and slept better than I ever had in his overly warm arms.

Under normal circumstances, I never would have allowed such a thing, sleeping with a man, even with nothing else going on, but this wasn't a man. And these circumstances were far from normal.

I think being attacked by a Marker should give me some slack on my rules of conduct, especially since Merrick and I both felt like he was my protector. Though I didn't want to admit it.

He wasn't supposed to be mine, but I let him take the role anyway, never feeling safer than now, knowing I was completely taken care of. He didn't follow me but kind of shadowed me everywhere I went. It was hard to explain, but it was sweet. Not like a stalker, it was just a complete need to see me safe with his own eyes. After all, he had watched me everyday for years. Old habits die hard. I could understand that.

Sometimes I didn't even realize he was there, but he couldn't let me out of his sight for very long. If I didn't let him stay with me at night, he'd probably wind up sleeping on the floor outside my door. Worrying himself into a tizzy.

I thought about the future too, a lot. Could things ever go back to the way they were? Could we defeat the Lighters and send them packing, get our moon back and start our lives again? Would I go back to the paper? Would Danny, the Special, having done his task go back to being a barista at the Coffee Place?

What about Merrick? What about us? Could I actually ask him to stay if I

141

knew that would mean his eventual death as a human?

Walking through one night on my way from the kitchen I noticed there was a beaten old black piano in the foyer, right near the chairs. I guessed maybe someone used to play for the guest back when it was a motel. I sat down on the bench and tapped a few chords out. The thing had clearly not been used in forever and sounded terribly out of tune and uncared for. I blew on the keys. Dust flew up into my face making me blink to clear my eyes and then I sneezed.

"Bless you."

I turned to see Merrick leaning against the wall. "Thanks."

I turned back to the piano and played the first Ben Folds Five song that came to my head, 'Narcolepsy'. I saw from the corner of my eye as Merrick sat down on the bench beside me. He watched my fingers with fascination, his eyes dancing from my fingers to my face.

"You've always been good at that," he finally said.

"Have you ever seen anyone else play?"

"No."

"Then I'm sorry to ruin it for you, but I'm not really that good." I laughed. "I'm too out of practice. I haven't played in years. I couldn't afford a piano at my place and Mom made me quit lessons when I was sixteen to get a job."

"I know, but you're still the best thing I've ever seen."

I smiled at him and nodded in acknowledgment. "You want to try?" I asked him.

"Nah, I just like watching you."

"Come on," I said with a mixture of whiny and seductive tones.

I felt that bold bone more than ever lately. I'd never been bold, I'd never been blunt, but with Merrick... I don't know if it was because he wasn't from here or if it was just because I felt so comfortable with him but whatever it was, I felt like a completely different girl around him.

I wanted to flirt, I wanted to tease, I wanted to giggle and be silly. It was like I almost wanted to shock him.

"Here." I stood up in front of the bench and motioned for him to come. "You can sit behind me and I'll show you."

He didn't put up much of a fight after that and I had to stifle a giggle. He scooted over behind me and I sat in between his legs on the very edge of the front of the bench.

"Do you have enough room?" he asked, his voice deep.

"Mmhmm," I answered and felt his hands tentative on my hips as he blew out a long breath into my hair. "Now, bring your arms over mine and place your fingers on top of mine on the keys."

He pulled my hair away from my shoulder, over to one side. He placed a small kiss on the back of my neck making me shiver then he put his chin on my shoulder. I turned to look at him and his nose brushed my cheek. He slid his hands up my arms until his hands rested on mine. I turned back to the piano, breathless, and again played 'Narcolepsy', but slower.

I pushed the keys and his fingers followed the motion of mine. We sat there like that until the words would come. I hummed them. I knew he'd heard me sing but I just felt weird doing it then.

So there we sat, him was pressed against my back, me feeling every contour of him. His arms were around me with me sitting between his legs and breathing with him, our chests rising and falling together. Then the song ended.

He didn't move, neither did I.

"So," I said after a few seconds that felt like loaded minutes. "How was that? Did you like it?"

His hands left mine to caress up and down my arms. I turned to look at him over my shoulder. He didn't say anything and his heart beat frantically against my back. One of his hands came up to my cheek. His eyes were full of passion and love, so loud he may as well have been screaming it. He searched my face for something, resistance maybe, but he clearly didn't find any as his green eyes flashed with something I couldn't decipher, then he licked his lips and leaned in, closing the scant inch between us.

He took my mouth gently, but I heard a small grunt escape him and he immediately began pressing harder, insisting on it. His thumb swept across my cheekbone sweetly as his other hand found its way back to my hip and squeezed affectionately.

I understood the significance of this. This was his first time for him to take the lead. Every other time we'd kissed or done anything really, even ate dinner, it had been at my insistence or prompting. This was all him and he was showing me with his lips and hands that he wanted me and could take the reins to show me, and I let him. It was amazing to be led by someone because they loved you and wanted to show you instead of wanting to just dominate you.

My hand wound up bunched in his shirt sleeve, feeling his skin taut and warm and as we kissed, though it was a slightly awkward position, there was nothing else. My lips tingled deliciously and my heart pounded heavily...and then Danny ruined it.

"Sherry, I know you won't complain, but I wanted to ask- Whoa! Whoa! Ok!" he yelled, causing us to jerk apart in surprise, and when I looked up at him he had his eyes covered with his hand in the doorway. "Ok. Uh... Hmm. Ok. Well, I guess it can wait 'til later," he said loudly and practically ran from the room.

We looked back at each other and the only thing we could do was laugh.

A couple of nights later we lay in bed. We had gotten so much more comfortable with each other, with touching, just being together, in each other's space. He would kiss me sometimes instead of waiting for me to, but most were tame, sweet and almost chaste, careful.

He was especially affectionate tonight, placing little peck kisses on my neck and shoulders. I turned to face him and he kissed me before I could say anything. A good thorough full body, hands-lips-legs-arms kiss that made your toes curl. We hadn't had one of these since the first kiss, the first night we slept in the same bed together.

He handled himself better than he did back then, controlled himself better. Don't get me wrong, he got worked up, but nothing we couldn't handle. I could almost always feel his heart beating fast against my chest.

Gah, I loved it when he framed my face with his hands, when he moved his fingers through my hair. It was the most protected and cared about I'd ever felt. He responded, too, and seemed to like it when I nibbled his lip an awful lot, more than liked it actually, which was incredibly cute to see a big strong man get so taken in by such a little thing as a nibble. And he murmured candy sweet things against my lips.

"I adore you. Do you know have any idea what you're doing to me?" he whispered one night. Then another night he said, "This can't be real. You can't be real." And tonight, as he leaned over me on his elbows and wrapped my hair around his fingers he said, "You are so beautiful, you know that?"

"It's dark in here," I said playing with him, knowing he could see me in the dark.

"Doesn't matter. You look beautiful even in the dark where no one can see you but me."

After we settled down a little bit I resumed my favorite position, sprawled out on his chest and waited for sleep. I felt his hand slide from my back to the bed when he finally fell out.

It wasn't often these days that I lay awake after Merrick fell asleep, too much contemplating tonight I guess. Too much gorgeous guy beside me, too much recovering, too much worrying over everything.

Tap, tap, tap.

I eased out of Merrick's grasp and peeked slightly out the drapes and window and gasped. Standing in the driveway was Bobby.

He was alone and staring directly at my face through the dirty window pane.

I realized the noise I heard was him throwing small gravel stones to get my attention and suddenly he was there, at the window in a flash, almost too fast to be humanly possible, almost touching the glass with his face, startling me. He looked like him but not.

I stumbled back immediately and scrambled up to the bed to wake up Merrick. Shaking him, he grabbed my arms gently, instantly aware, setting me aside.

For some reason, I didn't even have to explain, he jumped up and ran out the room door. I saw Jeff as well, flashing down the hall. I ran after them and a few others were awake, peeking out their rooms.

When I reached the motel hall outside door, Bobby was standing there, our Keepers in between me and him. Merrick yelled for Danny to stay back out of sight. Jeff reiterated that all Specials stay out of sight, in the hall.

Out of nowhere Bobby grabbed Ryan by his shoulders, throwing him into the side of the van with inhuman force. Ryan slammed into the side of the van, leaving a dent, and then crashed down hard to the pebbles and dirt gravel.

Merrick and Jeff reacted automatically. Jeff struggled with Bobby while Merrick ran to Ryan. I couldn't sit by and do nothing so I ran around the brawl to help Merrick.

"Sherry, go back inside. I'll handle this," he says calmly, contradicting the situation.

"Merrick, let me help. It's fine. I'm fine. What can I do?" I said already crouching down beside him, cradling Ryan's head in my lap.

At first, he seemed almost peeved at my disobedience of his direct order. "You shouldn't be out here. Bobby shouldn't see you. Go back inside."

"Bobby's a little busy right now. It's fine. I can help."

Grunting, clearly not happy but seeing I wasn't leaving he pulled his shirt off over his head and handed it to me wadded up. I tried to focus on our patient and not the broad tan chest in front of me.

"Put this under his head, hold pressure on it." Then he grabbed my chin gently so I'll look at him. "And stay here. I mean it, Sherry. Stay right here...and don't watch," he said with a stern look.

I was a little surprised actually, at his slight harshness. I mean, I understood, he was worried, trying to keep me safe, almost lost me once already, I got it. He'd just never spoken to me with a tone anywhere in the same ballpark as that before. It was surprising to me because even in this stressful situation it was... incredibly hot.

I nodded and intended to obey and when I looked down at Ryan, I saw his head behind his ear was bleeding, already coating the gravel beneath us and my sleep pants with a warm sticky red.

He was awake and looked up at me.

"I'm fine, Sherry, just a bump. Help me up? Let's get you back inside," he said quickly but his voice was quiet and strained.

"Mmmm...Ryan. I don't know. Merrick will not be pleased with me for disobeying orders," I teased him knowing he heard Merrick order me to stay put. "If you think it's safe..."

"Safer than it is out here. Let's go," he ordered and grunted already lifting himself.

I put Ryan's arm around my shoulder as we begin to hobble inside. I saw Jeff's leg swinging low to clip Bobby's knee, making it buckle and he twisted and fell to the ground while Merrick grabbed his hands behind his back. They brought him to his feet.

At once Bobby's face turns in a pained expression. Jeff and Merrick grabbed him and brought him wiggling and yelling in the door. Kay closed it after us and locked it, pulling the shade closed. We followed them to the kitchen, where they laid him down on the table and I put Ryan in a chair in the corner.

When I removed Merrick's shirt from his head to inspect, it had mostly stopped bleeding. He grunted and winced when I grabbed his shoulder to lean for a better look. I carefully unbuttoned and removed his shirt, despite his protest and yelps and to see his shoulder looked to be dislocated. I grunted in frustration.

"Ugh, Ryan," I moaned. "That's not good. I'll have to get one of the big boys to help me with that one. Just sit here, ok?"

As soon as I turned to survey the scene I saw Bobby. He was thrashing and yelled a piercing scream, his eyes looked at me and he focused on my face twisting his head to the side. My arm began to throb and then the needle pricks were over my shoulder again. I gasped in pain and Jeff, who was closest, reached for me to keep me from falling.

Merrick placed himself, with inhuman speed, in between us to block Bobby's gaze and the pain stopped just as he yelled to me.

Sherry, don't look! Don't look at him!

So that's why Merrick didn't want Bobby to see me outside. He knew it would hurt me.

Merrick pulled up Bobby's shirt and I couldn't help but see a red circle of some sort attached to Bobby's skin above his ribs. It looked like the outer rim of a bulls eye.

Jeff set me aside and I quickly turned away from them. He exhaled loudly and went to Bobby's side.

"I'm sorry, Bobby," he said sadly.

When Jeff touched the mark to remove it he jerked back in an agonizing scream. Merrick yelled my name in my mind and I turned to him from behind, placing my hands on his back.

Sherry, don't look in his eyes, but I need you to pull the patch off, quickly. It won't hurt you, I promise, baby, just don't look at his eyes.

I trusted Merrick completely and followed his instructions, coming around his back to the table to stand in front of him. I felt Merrick leaning over my shoulder, watching and he whispered something, an encouragement I thought, but I couldn't hear him. The circle was squishy and solid, like skin or a vein, velvety and smooth. It seemed attached and didn't want to come off easily.

I finally got an edge up and ripped as hard as I could. Bobby's howling was the only sound for long seconds. Agonizing. The strange circle burned up in a bright flash of light and fire then ash as I threw it on the table, then it was gone.

I reached down to help Jeff up off the floor. His hand was raised and red where he touched the 'patch' as Merrick called it. Bobby was completely still.

Jeff leaned over Bobby. I heard him mutter something about wasted life, and sorrys. Merrick turned, hugging me, turning me, pushing me from the room, and telling the others to go as well.

I didn't want to leave, I wanted to talk to Bobby. How could he betray us like that? Was he leading them here? What was that thing on his stomach? Why did it hurt to look at him?

"No, Merrick, I want to talk to him. He needs to tell us how he found us. What he's doing here. He owes an expl-."

"He's gone, Sherry." Everyone stopped to listen in the door way. "Once a patch is removed, the body dies. He was dead before this... I'm sorry."

I heard Celeste gasp and Danny put his arm around her.

"Oh."

But why was Jeff still here? His Special was gone, for good. Shouldn't he be leaving, going home?

Jeff came up behind us speaking to Merrick.

"Sorry, Merrick. That was stupid. I haven't had to deal with one in so long, I panicked about Bobby and forgot I couldn't touch it."

Ryan! I remembered Ryan in the other room.

"Merrick. Ryan," I said as I quickly headed back towards the room, but Merrick grabbed my arm, stopping me.

"Sherry, no, don't go in there. I'll get Ryan," he said as he turned.

"Careful. His shoulder is dislocated," I called to him.

We brought him into the game room and placed him on the table. The same table where they burned me. I hadn't been back in this room since. I swallowed before heading over to hold Ryan's hand. He didn't have any idea the pain that was

147

coming.

"Do you know what to do, Merrick? Jeff?"

"Mmmm..." Jeff mumbled.

"I'll take that as a no. You have to pull as hard and as fast as you can so it goes quick. This is gonna hurt. You have to make it as fast as possible. Merrick can pull his arm at the wrist while Jeff holds his chest and shoulder down. I'm sorry Ryan. This is *really* gonna hurt," I said as Ryan looked up at me.

"It's ok, just do it. Fast. We have got to get out of here." He squinted, feeling them get into position.

I grabbed Merrick's arm.

"Quick and fast," I reiterated and he nodded and counted to three as I took Ryan's other hand tighter.

Ryan grunted and yelped once, his face turning red and then sheet white as we all heard the pop as his arm settled back into socket.

They got it the first try, thank goodness.

Everyone released their hands and Jeff ran to the hall. Merrick and I helped Ryan up from the table as I murmured my sorrys.

"It's all right. We've got to leave," Ryan's breathed heavily, still no color in his face.

"What? Why?" I asked.

"I told you Lighters can search minds," Merrick explained as we set Ryan down in the hall chair. "When they possess someone, they mark them like they did him, then they can see through those eyes as well. Double their efforts."

"That's what you were looking for on me? That first day, and then Jeff in the van," I realized and he nodded. "So they put that patch on him to control him, knowing he would die once it was removed? They made him take it?"

Merrick and Ryan looked at each other. I looked around sensing I wasn't going to like this answer. Calvin wasn't here. Good. Merrick, began again.

"Lighters persuade. You don't have to be dead to take the mark, the patch. They can't physically hold you down and make you take it, but they can persuade you to want to. If you take it willingly, you give your life. You're alive only until it's removed. If it's not removed, you show the Lighters everything you see. That's why I told you about them. They will do anything to turn us against each other. You can't ever let them speak to you. Cover your ears." He was speaking to everyone now, louder. "Hum, yell, whatever it takes, but don't let them speak to you. Once you listen, you'll not be able to stop listening."

"Did he see?" Jeff asked Merrick.

"I don't think so. I blocked him, but he looked at her for a few seconds before I noticed," Merrick said, his hands going to my waist to look at my face directly. "Sherry, did you see anything when Bobby was looking at you?"

"No," I answered quickly, but I realized that wasn't true. A glimpse. "Wait. I saw a flash of the highway in front of the motel."

Merrick's scowl meant that was not a good thing.

"Was it day or night?" Jeff asked from behind Merrick.

"Night."

Their faces turned whiter than they already were.

"Ok, listen up. We are leaving now. Go to your rooms, grab things you literally can not live without. We are pulling out of here in five minutes."

A murmur began, questions and gasps. Jeff and Merrick both stiffened in frustration.

"Hey!" Merrick, yelled. "Life or death. We can all talk about it later. Get moving, five minutes."

That got them going. Merrick didn't get upset. He was kind of scary looking that way, reminding me of the previous owner to that face, but it had to be done.

He grabbed my hand and dragged me to our room.

We got our things together fast, changing our clothes quickly, him hurrying me along gently. We were in the car and only waiting on Celeste and Danny as he helped her lug her suitcase into the van then scrambled to jump in the back with us.

Once underway, Merrick started explaining, without me even asking as he led the way for our convoy.

"He was looking at you because you were marked, until it heals completely, if they're close enough, they can see you, sense you. Not just what you're thinking about like normal, but the other thoughts, too. Where we're going, where we've been, our plan, thank goodness we didn't have one yet. If you go into the coma that the poison makes, it's like a beacon. They can find you anywhere and in no time at all."

"What was the vision I had?"

"When they take thoughts from you, some of theirs get crossed over as well. Whatever they are thinking at the time. You saw this street, which meant they were coming here. He led the way, to make sure we were here before they came for us."

"Why couldn't Jeff touch the patch?"

"It's just like the Marker. We can't touch them, and they can't touch us. That's why the Marker wouldn't attack us. We are opposites of each other. The pain is like trying to fit something in a place it doesn't belong. Square peg, round hole," he winced as he spoke.

No doubt reliving the memory with me when he had felt just that.

"Why is Jeff still here? If Bobby's gone..."

"The rules are different now. This is a global thing. None of us will go home, until the big task, the Lighters have been dealt with."

"How did the Marker find us?"

"He didn't, they're mindless. They are set loose like hunting dogs. It was just bad timing. Wrong place, wrong time." He squinted at the memory still.

"What was he doing to you?" Danny asked me, leaning in between the seats.

"It felt like it did before, after the Marker scratched me. Like needle pricks. The pain from the poison..." I shuddered and Danny rubbed my good shoulder while Merrick's hand came over to settle on my knee.

"Where can we go?" I asked, changing the subject back to the crisis at hand.

"We'll do like the last time, drive until we find something. It's going to start getting rough from now on," Merrick said, sounding too worried.

We drove, Danny slept. I couldn't, even though the warmth from Merrick's chest was begging me to close my eyes, I sat and thought. I wondered if Merrick could be hurt worse than a red spot by these things. Lighters, Markers.

If they couldn't touch him for fear of pain, then surely they couldn't kill him right? One less thing to worry about. It must have been so against the grain for him to run and jump on the Marker knowing the excruciating pain that was coming.

I couldn't think about him hurt, it sent pain through my chest and I shook away the thought.

I thought about the word 'love' this week, too. It amazed me how I could know someone so little and yet feel so strongly. I dated Matt for months and not a hint of love, not even a smidge. Merrick had to know though right? I mean, we spend so much time together. He had to know how I felt.

We pulled off for gas, anxiety setting in as we pulled in under the bright lights out of the cover of darkness. We let Danny sleep, Merrick pumped.

We had all pooled our bank and credit cards together and designated a 'pay person' to handle this kind of stuff, hopefully, all of our money together would be enough to last for while. These old stations didn't have pay at the pump.

Tonight the pay person was Margo.

Merrick flashed her a quick glance and smiled to steady her nerves as she moved between the pumps and crossed the parking lot. She was freaking out, I could tell, wringing her hands as she marched stiffly. I watched her, while trying to look like I wasn't watching.

The attendant came over the intercom and asked if the lady inside was authorized to use the card for both vehicles. Merrick said yes and we heard the click of him turning off the intercom.

I folded my legs up in the seat under me, twirling a curl of hair when I saw Margo exit and head back swiftly towards the van. I felt Merrick staring at me. I wondered how long as I'd been watching Margo. When I caught him he smiled sheepishly. I shook my head in disbelief.

How could he still look at me like that? That look of awe and wonderment. Gashes and bruises, not a stitch of makeup or mousse for days...ugh.

Danny's snore startled us both, and I giggled. Merrick replaced the gas cap and climbed in, waiting for the vans huge gas tank to fill up.

"Feeling all right?" he asked me, reaching for my hand, intertwining our fingers.

His thumb rubbed little circles on the inside of my wrist.

"Mmhmm. You?"

"Yeah, I'm ok. I'll be better when you two are safe somewhere. I don't like being out at night, especially now." He let out a frustrated sigh.

"I don't like it either, but we'll find something."

"Well, we'd better find something fast. Come daylight, it's going to be a lot harder to blend all these people in somewhere, let alone find a place to hide."

"It'll work out, Merrick. It has to."

"So optimistic," he crooned smiling. "It's one of the things I've always loved about you."

I was having trouble concentrating because I realized he just said the 'L' word again.

"Well if you *could* get in my head you'd see the internal argument is usually quite different."

"I'm sure. I'd still love to see it," he said still smiling.

I smiled too and then it faded as I saw the attendant coming to the car.

Merrick turned to look and I felt his hand tense. I was thinking, if it was one of them, he'd notice my mark if he came any closer. I wondered if he was thinking that, too.

"Hey! The woman left the card on the counter," the man said in his slight southern accent, holding it out for Merrick to take.

Lies. Oh, no.

"Thanks," Merrick said as he reached for it, not looking at the name on it. I tightened my grip on his hand several times to warn him. "I'll make sure she gets it."

"Say? What happened to your arm?" he asked looking at me.

"Accident," I mumbled quietly but loud enough for him to hear.

He could clearly see the bandage on my shoulder with my tank top on. The jacket I had wrapped around the front of me had slipped down to my elbow. I pulled it back up.

"What kind of accident?"

I didn't know what to say? He was obviously trying to bait me.

"Bird. A freakishly big bird clawed me. Weird, right?"

Knowing I wasn't so good with the lies I figured I'd tip toe around the truth. He eyed me wearily. Merrick continued to assess things but didn't give any indications yet.

"Huh. That is weird. What kind of bird?" the man asked, taking a small step forward.

"I'm sorry. We're kind of in a hurry?" I smiled to soften the blow. "Is there something else you need from us? Gotta put the kiddies in bed." I motioned to Danny sleeping the back and rolled my eyes.

"Nope, that's it. Y'all be safe. Guard you in all your ways, brother."

That stopped Merrick's heart and I looked to make sure he was ok. He stared at the man and slowly released my hand to get out of his now open door. The man stepped back but didn't show any emotion. When I thought about it, I'd heard that said before.

"And you as well...brother," Merrick said but he didn't seem convinced.

"It's ok. I had to make sure first," the attendant said. "There are more of us, a couple more. There's a cellar under the store." He waited with that, gauging Merrick's reaction.

To my surprise Merrick looked at me questioningly. "Is that the truth, Sherry?"

"Yes," I said, beaming inside. He trusted me.

"Who are you?" Merrick asked the man.

"I'm the son. My mom's the Special, her Keeper's name is Max."

That did it. Merrick loosened and reached for the man's outstretched hand. "You scared me, there," Merrick said, blowing out a breath of relief.

"Sorry. Max told me to say that to people I suspected were on the run. That only a Keeper would know what it meant. Look, they are downstairs. If you want, even if you don't stay, could you just come down for a minute? We've been here a long time. You're the first ones with a Keeper with you."

"How did you know?"

"Well. That poor lady that came in was scared out of her mind and can't act one lick so I pulled out my binoculars. I saw all those people loaded in the van, and then your arm and face," he pointed at me. "I assumed you'd all been fighting with something, everybody looks so scared, so I decided I'd give it a try. I was beginning to think that Keeper was out of his mind with all those crazy stories about Lighters or whatever their called."

"You have no idea," I said as I slid out of the seat and stood up next to Merrick. I extended my hand. "I'm Sherry, the sister. This is Danny, the Special, if that's what you want to call him. And this is Merrick, the Keeper."

Merrick's protective arm was already around me out of habit and I saw our new friend's questioning eyes dart to the hand on my waist and then back up to us.

"I'm Phillip. Nice to meet you."

Jeff's face was priceless. We parked in the back in a big shed and Kay pulled the van in behind us to some old mechanics shop or something. Phillip led us through the back of the store and the storage room. Under a roll away shelf was a fall out door. He lifted it with ease and we followed him down the dark stairs.

Merrick went first, cautiously, peeking left and right as we descended. Phillip's mom's Keeper, Max, came around the corner wearily, hearing more than one set of feet.

Keepers apparently could sense each other, or maybe they just speak in the mind with each other so quickly, I don't know, but there was no more hesitation the moment he laid eyes on Merrick and Jeff. Merrick and Max joined in a brotherly embrace and then Max and Jeff. It was very heartening to see.

Even though they didn't know each other personally, they knew they were akin and that was enough. If only humans could be like that. The Special, Phillip's mom, Trudy, an older, but very attractive women came to greet us.

Phillip looked maybe a few years older than I, taller than me, of course, sandy blonde hair left a little too long, past his ears. He was slim, but muscular and he apparently thought himself attractive by his manners towards me. He hadn't stopped looking and glancing at me, smiling and tilting his head at me.

His mother on the other hand was nothing if not southern hospitality. Her completely shiny silver locks were ear length and curled in big loose curls. She was wearing a matching pant and sweater suit, loud but still tasteful, she could pull it off. Her makeup was perfect and so was her attitude.

I thought Trudy and I would be good friends. She was the friendliest person I'd ever met, no exaggeration. When she shook my hand, she called me sugar and I fell in love.

The fall out shelter was good sized, but once we all got down there it looked pretty skimpy. It seemed to run along the length of the above ground store. We followed the narrow hall into a commons room.

We all sat down, most of us sat on the floor, as we talked and shared stories. Jeff's description of the Marker attack was graphic and hard to listen to but he was clueing Max in since they thought there weren't anymore of them around. Phillip seemed very into it.

"Freakish bird?" he asked me smiling.

"I can't lie. I'm really bad at it," I explained.

"But you can sense when someone's lying? The guy asked you outside if you thought I was telling the truth."

The guy? He was sitting right next to me.

"Yeah. I always have. I don't know why or how, but I can just tell when people are lying, most of the time."

"All the time," Merrick corrected.

"Hmm. Anybody else got special powers we should know about?" Phillip said and looked around jokingly to everyone else, laughing as they did.

It was light conversation, everyone laughed and talked and joked. It was nice meeting someone new, in the same situation.

Phillip used the store as a cover. He worked the store while his mom was safe downstairs, and they had a constant supply of food from the store. They had a delivery every two weeks so they never even had to leave the store at all since all this started. I hoped we weren't messing that up.

They wanted us to stay. We could, it was cramped but we could make it work. Max started to explain that there were lots of storage closets at the ends of the short halls, this bunker was mainly for storage.

The rooms, though small, were room enough for sleeping and they have doors for privacy. I was ecstatic at that news. What more can you ask for at this point? Roof, food, company and a closed door for bedtime. Ah...

The Keepers convened and we assured them all we'd follow whatever decision they came to. I was almost certain they'd want us to stay, but I'd been surprised a lot lately.

While they talked in the other room, I walked around and checked out the place. One end of a hall was a wall of dirt.

Curious.

There were five halls all right next to each other on the other end of the commons room.

Each hall had three rooms on it. I peeked in one and there was literally only sleeping room. There was a few sleeping bags rolled up on a shelving unit by the wall and I grimaced. Looked like we'd be roughing it after all.

Trudy was fantastical. She was boisterous and clever, witty. She seemed very taken by her Keeper as well, but not in the same way as I was with mine, well not mine but...you know.

Phillip asked me about Merrick and my relationship, in a very skeptical way, like it was unbelievable or a joke or something. I didn't really know how to explain it so I just told them all "we're together" and got the usual response, wide eyes, dropped jaws, questioning eyes.

Trudy was polite about it, but I was still irked. Why were people so freaked by the idea? And was it my imagination or was Phillip giving me the once over?

He hadn't stopped staring since we got here, and now that I thought about it, he had kinda shadowed me. Why did I only attract guys at world's end? Didn't I

154

make it perfectly clear I was with Merrick?

The Keepers came around the corner and Max called Phillip and Trudy into the other room so the rest of us could talk privately. The Keepers came and stood in front of us, all together there was only nine of us left. We gathered around as Jeff explained everything to us.

"They want us to stay. It would be a good idea, for us all to stick together. They have all this security and supplies right here. We have room, but one hall could be extended if need be, it was left open for building an addition. We'll go out and look for others, maybe build as we go. They really want us to stay, but we wanted to make sure you were ok with this first. They have a television, and get the local news. They said the town has made it mandatory for everyone to be checked for the ear mark before any purchases can be made from now on. We knew this day would come. We don't have much of a choice anymore. What do y'all think?"

"Yeah."

"Sounds good."

"So we'd never leave, ever?"

"It's the best idea so far."

"What choice do we have." A statement, not a question.

After a quick unanimous vote, it was decided. We were staying.

Do You or Don't You?
Chapter 14

Our first night in the new hideout proved to be interesting. Celeste and I helped Trudy make dinner for everyone. Mashed potatoes, meatloaf and green beans. After eating pasta and canned soup for a month, it was the most delicious looking thing ever. I could barely wait to finish cooking it and then have to wait to eat it.

There was no table big enough, so we all just sat around, again, most of us on the floor.

I tried to ignore Phillip's constant stare, while cooking and now eating. It wasn't that hard to do, not with Merrick there beside me on the floor, leaning against the south wall facing one out of the two couches.

When we were done eating, we sat and watched the news. It'd been a long time for most of us. I wasn't interested myself, having done so many stories on the visitors but everyone else seemed glued.

Everyone except Celeste and Danny who were trying to be inconspicuous in the corner. They were whispering and she leaned in to speak in his ear. He had her hand in his, playing with her fingers. No point in trying to end it now. Besides, who cared?

I honestly couldn't even remember why I objected in the first place. If we were going to die soon, why not enjoy what little we could until then? I decided I was happy for them. I was happy for myself too, despite what others thought. I could care less, and as I felt Merrick's arm brushing mine, I cared even less than that.

A little later, Merrick grabbed my hand and pulled me up, without a word. He picked the room farthest into the last hall on the left. There will be no fighting this time between friends, nothing to fight over. All the rooms were equally dreary and impossibly small. We grabbed a sleeping bag and though most everyone else was still up, we turned in early, Merrick leading the way, towing me behind him.

Saying our goodnights and getting a huge 'uh huh' smile from Danny, I rolled my eyes at him and caught the disappointed look on Phillip's face as he watched us go.

I was a little confused. I must not make myself very clear around others with these things. Bobby didn't get it and now Phillip wasn't getting it. Tomorrow I would make a definite point to show him, that I was absolutely not available.

I scooted as close as humanly possible to the wall for him to lay out the sleeping bag. Flipping the light switch off, I then crawled in next to him and he immediately reached over to grab my waist, pulling me as close as I can get to him.

He kissed me differently this time. Not slow and easy, not cautious like usual, but passionately and his hands had a mind of their own.

I was euphoric!

Not wanting to push too far so he would stop, I placed my hands on his chest and forced them to stay there and not move an inch.

He hovered over me, his hand glided down my hip to my thigh, pulling my leg closer, making me gasp. He'd never done that before. I couldn't help but pull away to breathe and let the electricity fizzle out, but no, he trailed kisses down my neck and somehow it was even worse that way.

He must've sensed that, too, because he began to slow down and removed his hand from my leg, so I know this was the end. Always the gentleman. I joked to myself that if he wanted me to marry him, I would.

I'd waited, like a good girl, I saved myself, but did I really want to die a virgin? Seriously?

I must have let a slight giggle escape.

"What?" he whispered against my jaw.

"Nothing, just thinking."

"About?"

I couldn't help but giggle more at the thought.

"What?" he insisted.

"Nothing! I'm just being silly."

I have ways to get it out of you, you know.

"Oh, yeah?"

"Yeah," he breathed into my neck and began kissing across my collarbone.

I couldn't breathe yet my breathing was embarrassingly loud. When his mouth reached mine again, I felt his hand come up to my cheek. I put mine on his chin, my palm on the adorable scruffiness on his unshaved face.

Then we lay there, noses touching for a bit. Soon, I was drunk on his breath. I leaned in to touch my lips to his again and again.

"I think I may have some competition," Merrick began, through ragged breaths.

"You noticed that, too?" Then it dawned on me. "Is that why you were so eager to go to bed?"

"Yes. I'm surprised at how jealous I am about it," he muttered low making me laugh softly. "I'm sorry, I shouldn't be, but sometimes my body reacts without my permission," he admitted like it was shameful.

"I told him," I assured him.

"What did you tell him?"

"That we were...together. He asked about us."

"You did?" he said seeming genuinely surprised. "Hmm. Well, I can understand his dilemma. You are gorgeous and amazing. It's hard not to fall in love with you. I've tried."

"Oh, please," I said smiling. "I'm gonna talk to him again tomorrow. The staring is kind of freaking me out."

"Yeah, it is. If I had to sit out there and watch him watch *you* another minute..." he drifted off as he nuzzled my neck.

"Ah! And here I thought you came to bed for...another reason," I said in mock outrage.

"Well yeah, that, too."

I laughed as he tickled me and kissed my neck. I covered my mouth with my hand thinking I was being entirely too loud. Wouldn't want people to think something was going on in there, especially when it most definitely was not.

I imagined trying to go to sleep in this silent, enclosed, dark space, quiet and hot. Or maybe it was just Merrick. I wiggled out of my sweatpants and he pulled his shirt off. I couldn't see, but I could feel his bare arms in the dark. I ran my fingers along the contours of the muscles of the arm around me.

I chuckled when I felt him shiver with goose bumps. These arms never belonged to Matt anyway. He didn't know how to use them like Merrick.

He wrapped those arms that were now his around me tighter as we drifted asleep, even the silence and dark didn't bother me in those arms.

Breakfast the next morning was interrupted with unexpected bad news. The easy set up we had thought we were getting was no more. Phillip's supplier for the store sent a letter and told him they can no longer make deliveries way out here for fear for the driver's safety. There were too many Keepers running around.

I shook my head at the contradiction.

The news stations were throwing the word Keeper out at every turn. It was a curse word now to this new world, them beating it into the brains of anyone who would listen that Keepers were the trouble makers. Merrick was right, I could see their words and deceptions for the poison they were. Now we had to come up with a plan.

We knew they are checking for marks, so no Keepers could go on supply and food runs. No Specials could go either. That only left me, Margo, Phillip and

Calvin's mom, but no one was comfortable sending her out. Not only because she was deaf, making it harder for to communicate with her partner if need be, but also because Calvin was so young, if anything happened to her, what would he do?

And Margo, her nerves couldn't handle it, nor her knees. If she needed to run she would slow us down. So Phillip and I were designated as the only logical choice.

Great.

And the smile that spread across Phillip's face showed me and everyone else how thrilled he was about it. A quick glance at Merrick and I could see the tightened jaw and flat eyes. A jealous angel?

Though Merrick kept insisting he was no angel, I could think of no better word for him. Of course, wasn't that exactly what an angel would say? Alien seemed too freakish and he possessed so many angel like qualities. He had told me once, that the place where he was from was very bright and wholesome, even the air was alive.

He said words couldn't describe it but he wished I could set my eyes on it just once, just to see what he meant. It wasn't a planet. It just was what it was. They weren't angels. They just were what they were.

He may be Danny's Keeper, but to me, he was my angel.

That night while we all sat in the commons room and talked about the next day's events and what items needed to be gotten, I walked over to check on Ryan's shoulder. He hadn't complained any, but I knew it couldn't be better already.

"Sherry, I'm fine, you shouldn't worry about me," Ryan said as I tried to lift his shirt sleeve.

Ryan was young like me. Well, the body was, maybe 22 or so. That body was probably a surfer or something; blonde hair, nice build, tan. Any girl would swoon, but I already bagged myself a Keeper.

"Ryan, don't be silly. Of course I have to worry about you. Look, this isn't going to work. I've got to take your shirt off to look at it. Are you modest?" I sang with a teasing tone and a lifted eyebrow.

"No...but maybe we better go into the kitchen," he muttered as he slowly pulled himself out of the slump in the middle of the couch and I couldn't help but laugh at him.

Merrick and Jeff glanced up at us to see what we we're doing. I placed us somewhat in the doorway so I could still hear the conversation, as it did pertain to me, setting him on a chair and carefully pulling his t-shirt over his head.

"What have you been doing for it?" I asked as I began my inspection.

"Nothing. Should I be?"

159

"Ryan! You need to be taking an anti-inflammatory and putting ice on it. I'm sorry, I should have told you before. Look at it. No wonder it's still purple. I bet it still hurts too, doesn't it?"

"Not really," he lied looking over his shoulder at me, knowing I would know he was lying.

"Oooh. Liar." I smiled as I walked over to get the eucalyptus oil out of the medicine cabinet out of the hall.

I warmed a little in my hands as Danny came in to grab a glass of juice then sat at the table.

"She's awesome at that, ya know," Danny offered.

"Awesome at what?" Ryan asked puzzled.

"Massage."

"What's massage?" Ryan asked, turning in his chair to look at me with a strange look.

"It's medicinal. It's fine, Ryan," I assured, trying not to laugh, remembering Merrick and his bungee cords.

I forgot the simple things they didn't know. I placed my hands on him and he jumped a little.

"Relax. Tell me if it hurts too much," I instructed as I started to swirl my hands around the blade and shoulder.

His skin was just as warm as Jeff and Merrick's. After a few minutes, I felt him as he loosened up a little, the shoulder skin and muscles moving more fluidly. He groaned a little and I stopped.

"Too much pressure?" I asked.

"No. I've never felt anything like that before. It's amazing," he said smiling like he'd been given some kind of revelation.

"Told ya," Danny said laughing as he got up to rejoin Celeste as I resumed my hands working around the front collar bone.

"Massage is really good for things like this. You ought to let me do this every day for a few days. Your body is young and uh...healthy," I said and cleared my throat but he didn't seem to notice that I was sort of checking him out, so to speak. "Shouldn't take you too long to start feeling better. There's no reason for you to just sit and be uncomfortable, Ryan."

"Hey, you'll get no more complaints from me, like I said, that feels great," he insisted, grabbing one of my hands and turning his head to look at me. "Thanks, Sherry. I mean it."

"No problem, really. I like making people feel better, if I can."

I smiled as I resumed the massage.

I wonder if anyone had even *really* spoken to Ryan since he'd been here. Calvin hadn't seemed to take to him much and Lana, Calvin's mother, can't talk to him so, I kind of feel bad for him. Has anyone even stopped to show him anything human?

"Where did you learn how to do this?" he asked, stretching his neck to the side.

"Mmmm, nowhere, everywhere. I just kind of taught myself, practicing and looked up some things on the internet."

"The internet?"

"Never mind," I said laughing. "Some people make a career out of it, but I wasn't interested."

"People get paid to do this? That can be their job? Huh." Ryan seemed puzzled again.

"Yep. Welcome to earth. The land of the weird."

It had been a couple of days since the bad news and we prepared for our first supply run and a scope out of the land. We want to see what the world had come to, and with no Specials or Keepers to worry about, and no cover to be blown as we'd have nothing to hide, I was hoping we could devise a plan or code or something, to lead Keepers to us, and people who weren't interested in what the Lighters were selling.

I hoped we could find a van load of people and bring them back but I feared this was going to get harder and harder each day.

Too much poison was being fed to them from the Lighters minions' mouths and the news. Jeff was talking about building an army but we needed some recruits. I suddenly thought of the original members of our clan, wondering if they all found safe refuge somewhere.

Jeff went over some things with us, not wasting time. He insisted we go as soon as possible, before things got worse. Merrick was not thrilled with this idea. His dilemma, he told me, was that he had promised to protect me and not leave my side and now here he was, sending me out into the lion's den without him.

I assured him this was the only way. I realized, we hadn't been apart since he found us that day. I was a little scared too, to be away for him. I don't even know Phillip that well and to have to put up with the staring all day...Ugh.

Jeff checked my shoulder and determined that all was healed so every trace of the poison was gone. I was clear to go.

I waited for Phillip to get dressed and get things situated in the store before we left. I asked Ryan how his shoulder was doing today and he concurred it was much better after two massages.

But something I hadn't expected was Merrick, pouting. He walked me to the stairs, locking his arms behind me, pressing his forehead against mine.

Wow! He was actually pouting for me! Amazing how incredibly cute that was.

"If there was any way to keep you from going, I'd do it. I don't like the idea of you going out alone. I know you wont be *alone*, but..." He sighed harshly, pulling me even closer to him.

"I know. I don't like it either, but it's got to be done. There's no other way."

"Be careful," he demanded hard then his tone recanted to something softer. "Maybe...maybe I can ride with you and just stay it the van?" he suggested, looking hopeful.

"Merrick, what if we got stopped? I don't want to have to worry about you the whole time."

"No. Instead, I'll be here worrying about you," he rebutted gruffly, running a hand through his hair.

"Isn't that what Keepers are supposed to do? I'll be fine. I'll be extra careful. Don't. Worry," I said rubbing my knuckles over his scruffy chin.

"It feels wrong. It goes completely against the grain. I've been protecting you for years. You can't know what it feels like to let you go like this where I can't see you. You haven't been out of my sight for eighteen years. Do you understand how hard this is for me?"

He caught my fingers in his hand, kissing them and pulling them down to his chest.

"I understand, it sucks," I said softly. "I don't want to go. If there was some other way, I'd do it, but there's not. Phillip said something about a gun by the back door. I guess he's planning on bringing it, just in case we run into trouble."

"Honey, you can't stop them with guns."

"Mmmm. I really like it when you call me honey," I crooned and bit my lip for good measure.

"Really?" he asked surprised and then my favorite smile showed up, then faded into acceptance. "Well, I'll remember that for when you get back."

He pulled my face up to his and kissed my surprised, parted lips. I strained on the tip of my toes, both of us completely oblivious of the audience watching us as I wrapped my arms around his waist and let him pull me closer.

When the kiss turned serious, I heard Danny's cleared throat making us aware and I pulled away gently, recoiling into Merrick's chest for a warm hug and shelter from my blush. We were whispering but somehow I thought they still heard us, given away by all the turned heads and profiles of chuckling faces, but Merrick was oblivious and continued his plight for my safety, pulling my face up with a finger under my chin.

"I'm serious, Sherry. Don't try anything with them. If you see a Lighter. Run. If you can't run, don't listen and remember, you can't think about us here, the

Specials or this place," Merrick reiterated his last warning to me and waited for me to nod.

His thumb rubbed a couple times over my chin and then he kissed my forehead before releasing me reluctantly.

I was pleased to see Phillip seemed to be present for the kiss. The disgusted look on his face was indication of that. Merrick turned to Phillip as we make our way to the stairs.

"Watch out for her. She's...important."

"Gotcha, slick. I'm all over it."

I took that as metaphorical, not literal, from Phillip and leaned in for more one more quick peck from Merrick before heading up the steps, our fingers pulling and trailing to the ends before finally letting go.

It was entirely painful and heartbreaking to leave him. My chest felt like it was pulling me in two, but I made my way up those stairs and out the door somehow.

My annoyance level was quickly climbing as we got outside in the van and Phillip's flamboyant happiness of us being together, alone all day, was bouncing everywhere. I decided it was best to clinch my teeth and make the best of our mission.

I put my feet up in the seat under me and began a platonic and relevant line of questioning.

"Ok, so, generic response. Like, if we get asked why we're buying all this stuff, we say...?"

"You and I are married counselors and we've got a camping trip with our church youth group. That'll explain all the food- feeding teenagers," Phillip quipped.

"Huh. That's actually really good, Phillip," I admitted cheerfully and wrapped my hair around one side of my neck wishing I had a ponytail holder with me.

"Thank ya, sweetness," he said, flashing me a crooked smile.

"Phillip. Please, can we just be friends and not do this? I understand it's possibly the end of the world and it sucks being alone, but I am totally and completely, no going back, no changing my mind, in love with Merrick. So please-"

Holy Cow! I just said I was in love with Merrick and it sounded so true!

"Alright. Alright. I think it's crazy...but if that's what you want..."

"It is. And thank you."

Break the ice with small talk.

"So, have you always owned the store?"

He told me his story, how he bought the store a few years back, moving back here from where he was living in California, so he could better take care of his mom. More flexibility.

Trudy had Leukemia, adult acute lymphoblast Leukemia, and he needed to be here often for her procedures and doctor visits. This shocked me, she looked so great. So healthy, so happy. He explained she was in remission and that was why she was so fascinated with her Keeper.

She thought that whatever she had to do, her task, would have something to do with cancer, helping someone or pushing them to find a cure. She was excited about it and couldn't wait for it to come her turn to act. Wow. What an impressive lady. I was almost more shocked to hear that Phillip was twenty nine years old. He didn't look near that. His family aged gracefully apparently.

I told him I was only nineteen, figuring that might detour his affections even more, but he just smiled sideways at me and shrugged. "Age is just a number to me."

We neared town and I began to get anxious, wrenching my necklace charm back and forth down the silver chain furiously, but Phillip seemed perfectly fine and calm.

"Relax, sweetness, we'll be fine. Don't worry your pretty little face about it. I won't let anything happen to you."

The grocery store wasn't anything special or large, some local dive. It was going to be harder to buy in large quantities.

I turned to him before we got out and explained that we needed to feel this out, test people, see if anyone might be interested in joining us, but be careful not to give us away. He looked amused and I could tell he was just letting me act like I knew what I was talking about, but I let it go.

He nodded and we stepped out. No sirens, no flashing lights, no screeching half bird half human beings. No black haired, black eyed men. Must be safe.

The parking lot wasn't crowded and not too many people in the store. As expected the plump orange vested security guard checked behind my ear. I turned to wait for Phillip to be checked.

"Oh, it's fine. We only need to check one of you. I don't need to check your husband," she said and waved us through.

That got my brain thinking about future possibilities, about maybe a Keeper coming with me. A particular Keeper.

We both grabbed a cart and made our way. I was glad that Phillip didn't feel the need to split up because I didn't want to be alone, even with him, it was better than alone. Sweeping fear gripped me as I even thought about it.

My cart was full in no time so we began with Phillip's. I saw a sweet looking woman, alone, walking down our aisle.

"Whatya think?" I asked Phillip whispering and hooking my thumb her way.

"She's semi-cute," he said, eying her speculatively.

"I mean what do you think about testing her, goon." I slapped his arm playfully as he laughed at me. "I'm going to try. I need the practice anyway."

He smiled and waved his hand for me to proceed. I walked over her direction and she smiled a hello at me before I spoke.

"Hey, um, do you happen to know where the pasta is?"

She laughed and pointed behind me.

"Ah. Thanks," I said as I try to put on an embarrassed face. "Hey, have you been watching the news lately? Pretty crazy stuff the past few days, huh?" I started my line of questioning I had assembled in my mind.

"Yeah, I guess. Seems a little farfetched to me. I still want to think this is all some big hoax, like crop circles or something."

"That's been my theory, too," I said inching closer to be more intimate. "A hoax or just paranoia."

"So, business as usual for you then? Some people are going pretty nuts," she said, cocking a brow and glancing at our cart.

"Yeah. Just staying busy. Me and my husband run a youth group at our church. Teenagers, ya know."

"Oh, yes. Sounds like fun and an awful lot of stuff." She looked over to our carts again.

"Camping for a week. Eleven teenage boys," I stage whispered and raised my eyebrows.

"Well in that case I don't think you have enough."

We laughed and she told us to be safe on our trip before turning to leave. I stopped her and tried one last time for some indication that she wasn't too far gone yet.

"Can I ask you one more thing? So, besides a hoax, what do you think this is? The end of the world, maybe?"

"I don't know, but I'll tell you one thing. If it is all true, I hope those filthy Keepers get what's coming to them for doing this to us."

That answered that. We waved good bye and I returned to Phillip who looked to be holding in a laugh.

"Shut up," I muttered and he finally let his chuckle slip.

We grabbed everything on the list plus what we thought we might need and some liquid foundation and powder, in multiple shades, with a plan in mind. We finished up our cart and headed to the register to pay.

With all the bank card pin numbers memorized we joked about the 'youth camping trip' to ward off any suspicions as I swiped the card. The cashier laughed and told us she had three teenagers, and once again we get the 'are you sure you got enough?' joke.

As we left, I glanced up to the wide open windowed manager's office. There it was. I saw his dark coat and pants, his jet black hair and dark eyes and pale skin. He was looking around the store, watching people intently, with clear fascination and disdain.

I immediately panicked. What if Jeff was wrong and all the Marker poison wasn't gone. Oh no. Why was a Lighter in a grocery store anyway?

I kept walking, glancing to my cart then back to the Lighter. The last time he caught my glimpse, locking his gaze with mine and I froze. The smile he gave was nothing but fake, unadulterated evil. He nodded a hello and I faked one back and shuddered as we moved under the exit sign. Phillip noticed nothing of my distress. I couldn't help but think if Merrick had been here, he would have noticed right away.

With the van loaded down, but not near full, we drove around, but found nothing that looked different on the surface. Phillip took us past the city limits. There were a lot of abandoned buildings, but none seemed to have been messed with recently. That would be the point if someone was hiding there wouldn't it? We can't just go and investigate every empty place in town, no, we'd have to find another way for that. I groaned and slumped in my seat. This was impossible.

Then I hear a thumping, a loud thumping and banging. And then cursing. I looked over at Phillip.

"Flat tire," he said curtly.

I rolled my eyes at the timing as we pulled over to the side. He went in the back and searched frantically.

"No jack," he yelled up front to me and my heart jumped.

It was already 3:00 in the afternoon and getting darker. They'd start to wonder where we were. Phillip said he was going to walk up the road a bit and try to find someone. I got out and started walking to him, amid Phillip's protest for me to stay put.

"Un-uh." He pointed behind us. "Get your cute butt back in that van. You are *not* coming with me."

"Hey, I have legs just like you. You're not leaving me here, alone."

"I'm the man here, darling. I think I can handle it. Just stay with the van. You'll be fine, nobody will mess with you way out here."

"I don't doubt your abilities, Phillip. I doubt mine. I can't stay here by myself. It's too... It'll be dark soon." I so didn't want to reveal my silly insecurities to Phillip, of all people.

"Merrick told me to keep you safe. Now just go on back to the van," he said softer this time.

Oh! He was pulling the Merrick card, huh? No way!

"You're not leaving me out here alone," I repeated. "I'm coming. Let's go." I passed him in our walk to drive my point home.

"Fine. Fine by me, toots. You can tell your *old man* you wouldn't listen to me, if anything happens to you," he said, emphasizing 'old man' with clear disdain.

No point in waiting for someone that isn't coming to save us and I'm not being left alone. I had my sweater but it was still cold. I wrapped myself up and rub my arms as we walk.

Time passed quickly as my mind raced. Every time I looked at my watch at least fifteen minutes has passed. Adding it together, it'd been almost two hours of walking and talking. Well listening.

Phillip was good with the small talk. In the past two hours, I'd learned everything there was to know about running a convenience store, being in a hunting club, Leukemia and making your own pickles.

Odd, but to each his own.

He explained how the store used to be packed with people but then the interstate came in and took most of the business away.

He still makes enough to live off of, but nothing extravagant. I wondered to myself how many rich convenience store owners I'd ever seen anyway.

I'm glad that he dropped most of the flirting and just talked to me, like a normal person. To me he seemed like he finally understood that there would never be a him and me. I tried to fit in a question or story in, but Phillip was a talker for sure.

Did he even realize he'd talked so long non stop?

Suddenly, Phillip grabbed my arm, pulling me down abruptly, making me squint from the pain in my shoulder and drag my pant legs in the dirt as he pulls me behind a bush, none to gently. I felt some gravel in my shoe.

"There's a van parked behind that thatch of bushes," he whispered and I felt the goose bumps rise on my arms. "Sit tight. I'm going to walk over, see if anyone's in it."

He crept up slowly and began to sweep towards the van, bent low but quick. I barely saw the silhouette of the dark conversion van against the darkened purple and baby blue streaked horizon.

I could see him, he looked as if he was going to open the door, without knocking? I heard a click behind me, making me jump. I turned to see the rusty barrel of a gun, pointing right in my face.

Merrick - Fancy That
Chapter 15

As I watched her leave up the bunker steps, my heart fell. It felt like it was being pulled from this fleshy chest. It was completely wrong to let her go without me but I couldn't go and put her in danger if someone found out what I was.

I can't stop her from going either, no matter how much selfishness I could conjure, and we do need someone to get supplies, but why her? Why out of this many people the most fragile and sweet had to go out? And Phillip. I couldn't believe he had the nerve to ask me about her.

He actually asked me if we were serious. What did he think I was going to say, 'No. We're not. She's all yours'? He's about as lame as Bobby was if not more. Shameless.

I know how it is, I understand. I do.

She's amazing and irresistible and so gorgeous but she was *mine* until she decided not to be and I wouldn't trade her for anything in this or any other world. For whatever reason, she chose me.

And the second time this morning that Phillip made a point to mention to me that Sherry was 'something special' was the last straw for me. I made a very pungent point to glance over my shoulder at him before I kissed Sherry, knowing he was there watching her and gloating about getting to take her away from me for the day. Even though the room was full of people, I had to make a point. She was mine.

Sherry did not disappoint. She wrapped her arms around me, fingers gripping my shirt back, completely pliant and trusting in my arms. The way she always was with me. I hope Phillip finally got the message and let it go. I know her and she wouldn't have wanted to go with him today had she known the things Phillip said to me about her.

Mrs. Trudy was always in the kitchen. Max was there with her. She seemed to really like him. A good Keeper-Special relationship used to be really important when we made our way here. These days, I guess it doesn't matter anymore. Everyone is in danger now.

"You want a snack or something, honey? I got some homemade peanut brittle," she asked me, smiling as it seems to be the norm for her.

"I'd love some. Thanks. I've never had any before."

"Land sakes, really? How's that possible? Oh. I guess it is possible." The wholesome fluttering laugh that came next was contagious.

"Yes ma'am. Thank you."

I took a quick bite and it is good. Very good, seemed to get better the more you chew.

"So sugar, that Sherry sure is a sweet thing," she prompted.

"Yes ma'am. She is."

"My Phillip sure has taken a liking to her, but she said she was already taken."

"Yes ma'am. She is," I repeated.

"So, how's that work?"

"Still finding that out."

"Hmm. Well. In times like this, anything's possible. You know, Max is real nice, I'm really enjoying him. Phillip's gone so much with the store, Max is good company but...I have no interest whatsoever in taking it beyond that. So what happened with Sherry? What did you do that was so wonderful she couldn't resist ya?" she asked with genuine curiosity, not animosity for her son's competition.

"I'm not sure but I'm not Sherry's Keeper. I'm Danny's, her brother. Sherry was just an...unexpected surprise."

"So... It was you then." How she jumped to that conclusion must have had something to do with the look on my face. "You fell in love with her. It wasn't her chasing after you. Interesting."

"I've kind of...watched her for a while..."

Mrs. Trudy was altogether wonderful. I couldn't stop talking nor confessing. I kept saying things I shouldn't but she was so understanding and her tone of voice was so non- judgmental. I couldn't help it.

"So you watch her and come to earth to save her brother, tell her how you feel and somewhere along the way she falls in love with you, too. Well...fancy that."

I paced in the commons room. If there was carpet, I'd be wearing a hole in the shag. It'd been way too long. I knew I shouldn't have let her go.

No. She was ok. We should have set a time frame. Sherry was probably doing something stupid, like trying to drag the high school senior class down here for protection.

Oooh. She was in so much trouble. She has to know I'm worried sick about her.

But it's dark. They wouldn't intentionally stay out after dark. Sherry doesn't like the dark, let alone driving in it.

"Hey. They'll be back soon. Phillip won't let anything happen to her," Max said out loud, which was kind of nice.

Makes me feel even more human, though he was reading my mind at the time.

"I know. It's just...hard...to sit here, doing nothing and waiting and not seeing her every move."

"You act like she's your charge, Merrick. I mean, I guess she kind of is now, huh? How in the worlds did that happen?"

I wonder if people ask Sherry this question as much as I get asked.

"It's complicated. I'm sure you've seen it in my head," I ventured and quirked a knowing brow at him.

"Yes, I have. I just didn't know if you wanted to talk about it or not. She seems great, in your thoughts. I still don't quite understand it all, but who am I to judge? Stranger things have happened."

"True. Though not many," I joked but Max isn't fluid with the humor either and it just hangs in the air.

Danny, Celeste, Calvin, our entire little group had been checking the staircase, like me. Even Ryan and Jeff. Not pacing like me, but checking. Everyone trying to look like they weren't worrying.

Apparently, we don't have any liars in this bunch. It was all over their faces. Even Mrs. Trudy has come out of the kitchen to peek at the stairs a couple times.

Calvin came to sit by me on the stairs for a while. He sat one step above me so we'd be almost the same height. He didn't say much, just sat. Peeking up behind us every so often. I guess he was trying to show me he cared for her just as much as me.

It reminded me of Danny as a little boy. Always trying to cross the threshold into manhood, show they can be tough when they need to be.

I watched Max, Trudy and Jeff talk about the store, how it's run, how we'll stock it from now on, to keep up our cover. The store is just as important as feeding us. Without it, we'd soon have no income and no cover as to why people would be here. We needed the store to stay running.

I tried to busy myself and not think about Sherry and Phillip, who better be keeping his hands to himself.

I washed clothes, helped with dishes, did an incredibly hard old chipped sailboat puzzle with Calvin, talked to Jeff and Ryan and was tempted to take a nap just to make the time go faster but didn't. Couldn't.

I thought about Sherry, sitting in the passenger side of the van, looking out the window. Hoping she'd be thinking of me, but who knows. It was still such a mystery as to why she tolerated me.

I could literally see her sitting on her legs in the seat, twirling a strand of hair, rolling her eyes as Phillip kept glancing over at her, as I knew he would. His intentions were not shy when we spoke earlier.

I tried to stay calm, but I think my clenched teeth just made it worse, more exciting for him.

Oh, no. Would Phillip... No. No way, but I was sure he was taking his sweet time bringing her home though.

Humans! Uh!

Why did I let her go?

What's Your Business Here?
Chapter 16

The long, rusted shotgun barrel was inches from my face. There was a flashlight attached to the barrel, blinding me.

"Get up, thief," she said through clenched teeth to me, motioning up with the gun barrel under my chin.

"I'm not a thief. My van broke down, I promise you. I saw your van here and thought-" but she interrupted me.

"Thought you'd just take mine, is that it?" she yelled.

"No! I promise. I'm not here to hurt you or steal from you," I said loudly, hoping Phillip will hear.

"Mmmhuh. So what's your boyfriend doing in my van then?"

"Just looking for you."

She came around and poked the barrel in my back, edging me forward towards the parked vehicle. I stumbled my way over the bushes and rocks at we inched closer. I felt something hard poke through my pants leg, scraping my skin, briers were clinging to me.

Once to the open beat up conversion van door I say Phillip's name, calling him out. I heard him yell something about 'stubborn girls' then he emerged and saw the reason I disobeyed his order to stay put. The lights from inside the van were illuminating.

He hopped out swiftly and cockily, jumping all three steps and waited for her to speak.

I couldn't move, but I forced my eyes up to at least see my attacker's face before we're blown to bits. A girl, no...a woman. Couldn't be much older than me.

She was slender and wearing short cutoff jeans and a dirty yellow tank top. Her face was not sweet, pretty but determined and all business. She looked like she might have some Asian in her.

Her night black hair was blowing in the cold evening air and her dirty fingernails were a flag, a warning screaming that this girl has been through a lot.

Was she alone? Was she staying in that van? What had she been eating? Was someone here with her?

"What do you to want?" she spat out with the same harshness as with me.

"Van broke down. We just need a jack," he said coolly.

173

"Well, I got one, but why would I let you use it? You'll run back to town and tell them right where I am."

"Who?" I asked.

"Those things! The Lighters. I know you know what I'm talking about. Don't play dumb with me!" she yelled.

"I'm not. I'm not." How did you test someone for which side they were on with a gun in their hands? "Um. We aren't headed to town. We're headed home, back past the bridge," I answered, trying to look up into her face.

"What the heck you doing all the way out there?"

"Hiding. You can come with us..." I could say we were hiding from Keepers if she needed me to.

"Hiding? Hmmm. Lift your shirts."

I automatically obeyed, knowing what she was looking for, Phillip followed more reluctantly. When she was done searching and satisfied, she nodded for us to put our shirts down.

I know I saw Phillip staring at my bare stomach and bra, since this woman decided to pull my shirt up further to fully inspect.

"We aren't wearing patches," I said thinking she must know what I was talking about.

"How did you know what I was looking for?" she stopped mid search to glare at me from under her lashes, her hand still on Phillip's arm where she was looking.

"Because I had to pull one off a guy. Are you a Special or family?"

She jumped at the word but looked satisfied and settled down, leaning her gun against her shoulder.

"My Keeper is dead." She scoffed. "Shot by some idiots trying to steal the van. I've been out here, alone for weeks."

"I'm sorry. There are twelve of us. Four Keepers and three Specials."

"How's that? Why more Keepers than Specials?"

"We lost some too."

She sighed, lowering the gun to the ground now and nodded for us to get in the van. She pulled shades of sticks and branches she had stacked and staked up for a blind for the van and tossing them aside. I could only imagine living this way.

She drove us a few minutes what took us hours to walk and Phillip quickly changed the van tire. The Marker story may have been fun for him to hear, but waiting for one to come was another story.

As he finished up I tried to talk some self preservation into the woman, and invite her to go with us.

"I can take care of myself," she answered for the fifth time.

"Come with us. Please. We're in a shelter and have room. There will be

174

others coming for you, you know that. We can protect you," I pleaded just wanting to say at the end of all this I helped save at least one person.

"Well. I don't know. I..." She kicked at the dirt and rocks under us.

"What's not to know? Come with us. Please."

"I can take care of myself," she repeated.

"I can see that, but why not come with us and be with others like you. We take care of each other. Come with us."

"Yeah, come! We could use some fresh meat in there," Phillip chimed, grinning.

"Ok," she ignored Phillip and relented. "But if it gets too...weird, I'm out. I can take care of myself, like I said."

"I know. I wouldn't have made it a day out here by myself. Thank you. Follow him, I'll ride with you?"

She and Phillip nodded.

The twenty minute ride that was left wasn't quiet. The girl told me her name was Marissa and she was only nineteen too, her Keeper had been Miles. Being alone gets to you and she had plenty to say, not being able to talk to someone in so long. When we pulled into the back of the store she looked skeptical but I patted her arm to reassure her.

It had gotten really dark and late and I couldn't wait to run downstairs and calm the worried Keeper I knew would be waiting for me.

Merrick was pacing by the stairs when I finally pried the door open, not waiting for assistance from Phillip. Merrick exhaled loudly and happily, instantly grabbing me from the stairs, swinging me around in reunion, kissing and squeezing me tightly.

"What in the worlds took you so long? What happened to your clothes? I was so worried," he only breathed the last part.

"I'm sorry. Flat tire," I said against his chin. "But...we brought a gift. Marissa?"

The dirty cutoff shorts began to creep slowly down the stairs until we saw her face. She looked scared but defiant too, showing us she didn't need us and could bolt at any moment.

"Merrick, this is Marissa. Marissa, this is Merrick, one of the Keepers here. Marissa kinda saved us, gave us a jack."

There was a crowd and Jeff came to the front of the group.

"She's a Special," Jeff blurted out, a statement, not a question.

"Her Keeper died. She's been alone for a while. She helped us fix the flat. The jack was missing from the van. I told her she could come back with us and stay...only if she wants to." I fixed it when she looked at me.

175

Jeff and Merrick seem saddened, I realized why.

We heard of death so much, it didn't seem so drastic to us anymore, but to them... They lived forever and death was scarce. I felt horrible and rubbed Merrick's back with my hand.

"Well," Jeff started and cleared his throat. "Marissa, let's get you situated, shall we? Danny, Calvin, Ryan? Can I get you guys to help Phillip bring in the supplies?"

They headed off after Danny flashed me a quick welcome-home smile.

Merrick wrapped his arms around my waist for another hug, lifting me from the floor.

"I'm so glad you're back. You don't know what I've been going through. Are you ok? You can't ever do that again," Merrick said softly.

I didn't argue or tell him he was wrong because no one else could go. I hadn't realized how tough it had been. It felt like my stomach had been a knot the whole time and now released. Back with him I felt right again, all uneasiness gone.

Marissa threw me the usual questioning glance at the picture of us hugging intimately. I just smiled sheepishly as Jeff escorted her off.

I was sorely in need of a shower and took a quick one. Long shower meant longer time away from Merrick. Once done I guessed that Merrick, nowhere to be seen, was already in bed, so I practically ran to the commons room and there he was. In the hall, waiting by our room, leaning casually against the wall.

I went in first, in clear anticipation of what was to come, and once the door was shut he grabbed me, pressing me gently against the wall, splaying serious kisses over my face and lips. Just like I had wanted and predicted. I swung my arms easily around his neck, his warm hands clenched around my hips. After a long day without it, the electricity I missed all day was extra strong against my skin. It took no time at all for me to become breathless and too warm.

I pulled back just enough so our lips weren't touching so we could breath and speak.

"Hmm. I missed you," he breathed against my lips.

"I can tell. I missed you, too."

"Did Phillip behave himself?" Merrick asked, lifting his face from mine for a moment to see my face.

"Yes." I chuckled. "Surprisingly so."

"Good." I assumed he was satisfied that a beating wasn't in order and he began kissing my jaw. "Anything interesting happen?"

"I saw a Lighter," he stiffened and I began again. "It's ok..."

I pulled him down to our makeshift pallet and told him the strained day's worth of events, as I lay on his stomach, using it as a pillow while he twisted my hair in his fingers and listened anxiously. He grunted his disapproval at all the appropriate parts.

I must have fallen asleep.

I awoke in the middle of the night without remembering even falling out or how far along I'd gotten in the story. I creaked the door open, trying not to jostle Merrick. He was still asleep, looking irked and worried, even in his slumber. I stared at his face for a while, so comfortable with his warmth around me.

In all the commotion I didn't get to eat anything for lunch or dinner so I crawled out and tried to be quiet so as not to wake him.

I donned my usual night time attire, a pink camisole and short set, courtesy of Celeste and her gratitude for saving her life. She was constantly gifting me with items from her apparel. She practically brought everything she owned anyway.

It was so late I doubted anyone would be in the kitchen. This wasn't exactly '*walking around with other people*' attire, but I took my chances.

I tip toed along down the hallway and through the commons room and into the dark kitchen. I wouldn't want to turn the light on to alert anyone so I just opened the fridge and used the light from that to make a quick sandwich and glass of sweet tea. Milk would be nice but it doesn't last long around here.

The sandwich hit the spot, but as famished as I was when we got home, I was hungrier for Merrick. It took me by surprise how much I ached for him when we were apart. I never thought I'd be one of those girls. All my stereotypes and assumptions of others I'd passed judgment on over the years were beginning to melt away. Crumble. I was beginning to understand them, feel for them. You really can not know a situation until you yourself have been placed in it. And then I realized something that I'd known but just now could see clearly and put it in words.

I was hopelessly in love with him.

I laughed to myself and goose bumps raced on my arms and legs. It rocked me to my core. I was in love with him. Desperately and epically in love with him.

I leaned against the counter in my trance as I took small slow bites, eyes gazing into nowhere so I didn't see that I had company until I heard someone clearing their throat.

Phillip. Crap.

I immediately tugged at my shorts to lengthen then, though the whole idea was skimpiness and comfort.

I tried in vain. He eyed me. I could tell he knew what I was doing but I tried anyway. It felt so uncomfortable to be ogled by someone and you watch them doing it. And they see you see them doing it, and they still do it.

"Phillip," I said his name and took my index and middle finger, pointed them to my eyes. "Eyes up top, please. You promised to behave, remember?"

"Sorry, sugar, but when you got it, you got it, right?"

Did he really just say that? I was going to pretend he didn't and change the subject.

"So, interesting night."

"Yes, it was. I thought Marissa was going to blow my head off."

"I thought she was going to blow *my* head off and then blow your head off. Thank God she was out there or who knows what we would have done. I'm glad she came with us too."

"Yeah, me too, I guess. She's not really my type but we gotta get some new bodies in here. Fresh meat."

"Is everything about that with you? Have you ever even dated before?" I said but winced at the harshness of it.

I wasn't trying to insult him, but he was pretty clueless and arrogant.

"Course," he said indignantly and snorted. "Why?"

"You just don't seem to... Look, I'm not trying to hurt your feelings, I want to help. Ok? You just don't seem to know what a woman would want to hear. We don't want to be called sugar all the time, we don't want you shamelessly eyeballing us, and we don't like a constant spew of sexual innuendos."

"Really? Never had any problems before. Maybe you're conditioned to something other than a real man now?" He clucked his tongue. "Ever think of that?"

"No. I haven't." I clenched my teeth. "When I start dating someone who's not a real man, I'll let you know what I find out."

"Sure, sweetness. Sure thing."

He was smiling, laughing at me, amused by my protest. This was going nowhere.

"Ugh. Be nice to Marissa, ok. I'm going to bed. Night. Oh and uh..." I tried for civility. "Thanks for today. You handled everything really well."

"You, too, peaches. Night," he said so slow and dramatic, cocking his head to the side.

I know he was looking at my backside as I turned to go. I knew it, so I walked quickly refusing to glance back, giving him the satisfaction.

In my plight, I bumped into the couch in the dark commons room. So much for a graceful exit.

Morning.

I woke up content and surprisingly rested. I didn't shut the door all the way after my snack last night so there was a little stream of light lying right over Merrick. I rolled over to look at him, still asleep. I watched him. His unconscious mannerisms were hilariously adorable. All Merrick, nothing of Matt.

His eyebrows lifted like he was talking or thinking, but he never spoke. He smiled, he turned his head to the side. I wondered if I did these kinds of things when I slept.

I wondered if Merrick had ever watched me do them. Then I remembered and I was certain he had.

I traced the muscles on his chest with my finger, his stomach, watching the goose bumps rise. I heard him making appreciative noises and he started to shift, but didn't wake. When I moved to his belly button he groaned - almost a growl - shocking me at how much I liked it. Then he reached for me in his sleep, trying to pull me to him.

Out of nowhere, Phillip bursts through the door, without knocking and flips on the light quickly making me jump thinking something was wrong, not thinking to cover myself. Again in my skimpy sleep clothes - though he saw them last night - this time I was sprawled out on Merrick's bare chest.

He looked me up and down, then Merrick and looked frustrated, like he was expecting something else.

"Jeff wants to speak to us about the store trip," he said flatly.

"Shh! Ok. I'll be out in a minute," I whispered, but Merrick had already begun to stir and I rolled my eyes.

"Sorry," Phillip muttered as he closed the door, which I'd remember to lock the next time.

Merrick was awake so I told him of the meeting I was being summoned to.

"I'll come, too. Did you sleep well enough last night? Honey?" He smiled, seeing if I'd remember our conversation from earlier.

"I slept ok, though I had to get up a few times. And I want you to come with me to the meeting. I really missed you...babe."

"Mmmm. Sounds good, honey."

"Yes, it does sound good, babe."

"Great, honey," he growled playfully and braced himself over me on his hands.

"Fabulous, babe!"

The tickling and giggling and wrestling began, and I was thinking it was going to be near impossible to pry myself from this man again.

I grabbed a clean pair of jeans and a green tank from the pile in the corner. He pulled on some jeans and a black pocket t-shirt that made me want to stay in the room much, much longer. I pulled him to me for one more kiss and he chuckled happily before engulfing me in his arms.

We finally made out way to the commons room and no one seemed to be upset by our taking too long.

"Jeff? Done already?" I asked with humor.

"Done with what?" he asked, barely looking up from his book. The cover read 'Master and Man.' Hmm. Jeff was reading Tolstoy? I wondered if it was from Trudy's or her husband's collection.

"The meeting? You wanted to talk to us about the store trip?"

"Uh. Yeah I do. Whenever you get ready."

"You didn't send someone to fetch us?" I said tight lipped as I looked at Phillip, who was sitting, leaning on a box of records.

"No. I figured you guys were beat. Plus I thought after yesterday you and Merrick might be a little...preoccupied. Didn't want to bother you."

He couldn't contain his crooked smile and neither could the others. I heard their chuckles as they tried not to look at us. Normally I would have laughed or blushed maybe except for the fact that Phillip had barged in, without knocking and semi-lied just to get us out of our room. And he finagled it in such a way so I couldn't tell he was lying.

Scum.

It wasn't really a lie, I didn't detect one, Jeff did want to talk to me, just not right that second.

That whole act yesterday was just that. An act. I glared at him angrily and he looked so smug and unrepentant. I saw him mouth 'oops', then winked and smiled. Furious I grabbed Merrick's hand and took him to the kitchen for some breakfast.

Trudy is already cooking up a storm of pancakes. Merrick was still too dazed and groggy to notice what had happened with Phillip, or just hadn't put it together yet because he didn't say anything. In a way, I was glad. Though I'm tired of Phillip's crap, I don't want Merrick to fight. And I'm not sure how Merrick would handle Phillip, if he knew all the crap he was trying to pull at this point.

The pancakes were divine. Even Merrick seemed to enjoy them more than he had any other food we'd eaten.

"So. You enjoy our human food then?" I asked playfully.

"Yeah. There are definitely some perks to earth," he said leaning over to kiss me over the corner of the table and our empty plates.

I could taste the sweetness from the syrup on his lips still.

"What's your favorite food so far?" I asked, leaning my chin on my fist.

"Hmmm. I'd have to say these pancakes. Mrs. Trudy, those were the best things I've ever had."

I hadn't realized she was still in here with us.

"Why thank ya, darling. My mama's recipe," she answered and you could tell in the tone of her voice she appreciated getting compliments on her mama's food.

"I'd ask what your favorite food is, but I already know. Lasagna, scrambled eggs and cheesecake, in that order," he said, smiling widely, that smile that made it hard to breathe.

That was the first time I saw how truly happy he was to know absolutely everything about me. It wasn't just a useful tool anymore, he just loved knowing things about me.

"Do you like any music?" I asked.

"Fly Me To The Moon?" He smiled again.

"Ha ha. You really haven't heard any music other than me singing kiddies to bed?"

"No, not really. I wasn't paying attention to anything else but you."

I blushed at his sweet words and glanced at Mrs. Trudy. She was smiling at me over her shoulder.

"Mrs. Trudy, does that record player out there still work?" I asked, getting an idea.

"You bet your knickers it does. There's a whole mess of records in there, if you want to go dig through it, be my guest," she answered, her back to us as she poured more batter in the skillet.

"Leave the dishes, Mrs. Trudy. I'll get them in a minute, ok? Come on, Merrick. You haven't lived until you've listened to *real* music."

I dug through and found some pretty good stuff. No Frank Sinatra, which was disappointing, but there was some Chicago with and without Peter Cetera, Guns N Roses and James Taylor mixed in there. That should be a plethora of options for him to get a feel of some musical history. Nothing recent of course, but I wasn't surprised being that it was Trudy's collection.

I did miss my music and I'd probably never hear their music again. They could be under the Lighter speak for all I knew, but it was a good thing I wasn't that picky.

My MP3 player was very eclectic. If you read the artist list you'd see Mutemath, The Killers then next would be Kenny Rogers then Journey, then Phoenix then Rachal Yamagato. I just loved music, all kinds, since I didn't like the quiet, I played music everywhere I went.

Phillip eyed me quizzically as I plugged in the huge console record player and put on James Taylor. I figured we needed to ease Merrick into the Guns N Roses.

As 'You Can Close Your Eyes' blared from the old crackly speakers, the commons room was suddenly very full. Everyone piled in to listen. I hadn't thought about how long it'd been since anyone had had some entertainment.

Mrs. Trudy came out of the kitchen area and grabbed Danny from the wall. She showed him where to place his hands to dance and they started sliding back and forth.

People smiled as Danny looked like he was having fun, albeit embarrassed. Celeste looked at him with that look I knew all too well. Huge smile that reached her eyes that were wide with wonder.

Dang it, they *were* in love, a freight train that could no longer be stopped. I realized the huge smile on *my* face and that this was good news! I was happy for him, for real. These weren't just words to reassure myself anymore.

I was happy for him. Celeste was great. Genuine and sweet and she couldn't ask for a better guy, past job situation excluded, in my brother. He had grown up a lot since we'd been on the run. I wished Mom and Dad could see this, their son twirling a sweet old lady around the makeshift concrete dance floor. I sighed out loud at the wistful thought.

"Are you all right?" Merrick whispered in my ear as we sat in our usual spot on the floor.

"Yeah. It's just sweet, that's all." The song changed to 'How Sweet It Is'.

"You like the music?"

"Yeah, I do actually. It's catchy. You don't want to dance do you?" he asked with a furrowed brow.

"No!" I said a little too loud. Taking it down a notch I tried to recover. "Uh, no. I promise. I'm not exactly light on my feet."

"Hhmm...I beg to differ," he said, smiling deviously.

"Don't you dare," I spouted, again way to high an octave and he laughed.

"I would if I knew how, honey, but you're safe for now." He laughed again pulling his arm around my shoulder and kissing my temple.

We listened and sat and swayed and laughed at some of the oldies that Danny kept popping in. The Temptations, Elton John, Kiss, The Rolling Stones, The Beatles. Jeff looked more intrigued than anyone. I wondered why that was? He never seemed interested in our worldly things before. In fact, he thought Merrick was crazy for wanting anything to do with it. I smiled as I watched him on the couch, head bouncing absentmindedly to the music. First I caught him reading and now dancing?

The new Special, Marissa, was on the couch near Jeff. She'd been there the whole time and I realized I hadn't even spoken to her today. She looked tired, but seemed to be enjoying the music, but not the crowd.

Every time someone bounced too close to her or wiggled the couch she flinched back and recoiled, her knees pulled up to her chest. Like she didn't want to be touched. I again wondered what this girl had been through.

I decided maybe we should start the meeting before lunch and get everything out in the open.

"Jeff. I'm ready whenever you are," I said smiling.

"Ok. Great. Danny, you turn that down a notch please. Thanks. Ok. Now we know we have a new addition, if she so chooses. Everyone, this is Marissa, for those of you who haven't met her. She helped Sherry and Phillip yesterday." She awkwardly waved and smiled, pulling her knees up tighter. He must've been able to tell her shyness because he moved on quickly. "But we also want to know what else happened on your trip yesterday. Sherry?"

"Sherry saw a Lighter," Merrick threw out matter-of-factly before I could speak.

Everyone froze and gasped. If his intention was to call order to our meeting, he had certainly done that.

"You did? Where?" Jeff, the concerned Keeper face was back.

"You really saw one? With your own eyes, you saw one?" Danny was freaking and came over to squat in front of me, not giving me a chance to answer.

"In the grocery store, the manager's loft. The walls were all glass." I looked at Phillip realizing he hadn't seen it and I hadn't said anything then to him. "It was when we were leaving, I didn't tell you because he already looked at me, and I didn't want to draw any more of his attention."

"He looked at you?" Merrick asked swiftly.

"Guess I fell asleep before I got to that part. It was a glance really, then he smiled right-"

"What?!" Merrick, Ryan and Jeff said in unison.

"What do you mean he smiled?" Kay asked and Max stood up across the room.

"What?" I said puzzled, looking around.

"What do you mean he smiled at you?" Jeff repeated, pushing himself to the edge of his seat now.

"I mean he smiled. Ya know...pull up your lips, show teeth in a friendly gesture." I was trying to joke but no one was amused.

"Lighters don't smile, Sherry." Merrick was breathing heavy now. Oh, no.

"So what's the big deal? I made a mistake then. It wasn't a Lighter." What kind of can of worms had I opened now.

"Sherry, you're a horrible liar. That was it? He looked at you and smiled, and just kept standing there?" Merrick asked breathlessly.

"Yeah, that was it. They checked our ears at the door, though not Phillip's. She said she only needed to check one, cause surely I wouldn't be married to one of 'them'. I almost forgot about that. That means that a Keeper can go next time if

183

we need to, just make sure one of us goes first and we look cozy."

"That's not a bad idea, Sherry, but first, I gotta think. If you saw him smile, that only means one thing-" Jeff started but was cut off.

"Jeff don't," Merrick said sharply. "They don't need this right now."

"It can't be true. Can it? I mean, we just got here," Ryan argued, looking at Jeff.

"Come on brothers, be reasonable. This isn't happening now, it's too soon. He would let them do the dirty work before he showed up. There's another explanation, we're just looking at this from the wrong perspective," Max chimed in like he sincerely didn't believe what they were thinking.

"Merrick, brothers, sisters. We can't hide this, not this. I think they can handle it."

"I wasn't questioning if they can handle it or not. I just..." Merrick said, looking at the floor defeated.

"I know, brother. It's just one more thing to add to the list of things not going our way. It's time though." Jeff took a breath and started to begin again but Max cut him off.

"Jeffrey, wait. We need to make sure first. I mean, what if we tell them this and get everyone all upset and then it's not true. Maybe Sherry...I don't know." He turned to looks at me. "Are you sure he smiled at you?"

"I want to say no now but yes. I'm sure," I said wishing I knew how to lie properly. "Why?"

"All right. All right, Jeff." Max waved his hand at Jeff to continue.

"He's here, sooner and even closer than I would have ever imagined. Their leader. They call him the Taker. He's not like the others, he's much more powerful. If he's here...it's too late." Jeff scrubbed his hands over his face as Max flopped himself back down on the couch. "We won't be able to save them, the others. Ah, I thought we had more time. He's not like the Lighters. He doesn't persuade, he commands and you can not physically disobey. He can fly too, making him even more dangerous. Eventually, they all will obey him and he is not here to play games. We won't be able to save the ones influenced by the Lighter speak now. If he's here...it's already over."

You could hear the breathing, the tiny gasps, the small murmurs. Everyone was stunned and horrified, including me.

"I'm sorry I didn't say anything before. I didn't know that was important," I said, feeling guilty somehow, though my speaking up wouldn't have changed anything.

"It's fine, Sherry. You couldn't have known," Jeff said in his soothing Keeper voice.

"What now?" Trudy spoke up.

"I don't know. We can still search for others, but once he's gotten to them, there is no going back for them. They are lost and can not be saved. Look. Nobody watch the TV anymore. If he's here, he'll be on the news soon enough. He's the only one that can be seen by your media. He'll take advantage of that and start making preparations for his plans," Jeff explained.

"Why's that? Why can he be seen and not the others?" I asked.

"Because he was human."

Gasp. Gasp. What?

"What do you mean?"

"That's the reason he's so different. He was once a human, that's why he smiles, has feelings. He was consumed by a Lighter who came here to take his body, but for whatever reason, somehow fought it, though he was dead, and consumed it instead, absorbed it. He took all the hate and evil of the Lighter in himself. So he's the worst of the human and the worst of the Lighter. Every time a Taker dies, which has only happened four times in all of history, a new one comes to take his place when the time is right. They have all the original Taker's memories and thoughts. He has to absorb life to live and will continue to absorb humans and Lighters until there's-"

"Wait. He consumes the Lighters, but they still follow him?" I asked, dragging out the words in disbelief.

"To the death. He's their leader. It's like someone with a gun to your head telling you to dig your own grave. If you thought about it, you wouldn't dig because they are going to kill you anyway, right? But most people...dig."

"Why?" I seemed to be the designated questioner.

"Scared. Hopeful. Many reasons."

Merrick sat quiet by me for a long time while Jeff explained over and over, answering our questions, always patient.

"If that were possible for him to consume the others like that, would it be possible for you?" Celeste asked from the back corner.

"I've never heard of such a thing. Lighters are our opposites, so if they can do it, most likely we can't. Well, I say we get started soon. We'll go out, Merrick and I will call for others, I'm not sure how this is going to work. I've never tried to call nor listen to another Keeper without knowing what to look for, a face, a voice, something but it's worth a shot. We have enough supplies for now. We can start with a small perimeter and work our way out. In the morning?"

Jeff was waiting on Merrick's answer, but he was lost in thought. I squeezed his hand to get his attention.

"Oh, yeah. Yeah. Morning is fine," he said gruffly.

Trudy cranked the music back up for lunch, trying to lift spirits. Everyone ate their roasted turkey sandwiches and Celeste helped me with the dishes as Marissa dried, though she still seemed a little overwhelmed.

We three sat with Mrs. Trudy for awhile in the kitchen, trying to get Marissa to open up, feel welcome.

Phillip seemed to be quite taken by her, good for me, bad for her. She didn't seem to like it any more than I had. Maybe he needed a better pep talk in less creepy behavior.

Jeff seemed quite intrigued with her as well. He sat with us at the small kitchen table for a while, asking his own questions, his eyes dancing as she described life with her Keeper in the desert and woods.

Washing clothes in the big utility sinks was the only way to do it these days. No washing machine down here like the other place, and one shower and one toilet. One.

That night after dinner, dishes, clothes and showers, not in that order, some settled in for more music. Some continued the discussion with Jeff about the next day's activities. Some just sat and talked. Merrick and I sat with Danny and Celeste. I wanted us to be easy with each other, no weirdness with us two couples together, and surprisingly, there was none. It was really nice.

After a while, Merrick went to take a shower and Celeste went to go see what Calvin was up to leaving Danny and me.

He put his arm around my shoulders like he used to do when we were kids, like he was the older one and I was under his protection. I was quite smaller than him, he pulled it off, no problem.

"So, what do you think about Celeste?" he asked, finally after dallying with lame questions to throw me off.

I thought about all the things Celeste said to me about him, all the ways Danny had changed since we'd been on the run, all the faces of love and wonderment I'd seen on Celeste's face.

"She's great, Danny. Really. She's sweet and... I can tell she really likes you. Be good to her, she's really good for you."

"Yeah. She is sweet...I...really like her."

I was glad to see the affection wasn't one sided. I saw that same look on his face now.

"Mmhmm. I can see that. I'm happy for you." He smiled at me sideways. "And you and Merrick seemed to be getting along good too. Is it just a Keeper-Special thing?"

"No, I don't think so anyway. We're friends. He talks to me a lot when you're not right here. Which is hardly ever." He shoved me with his arm. "He's a great guy. I like him. He uh...he talked to me about you, you know."

186

"What about?"

"He was kind of...making sure I was ok with it all, I guess. He didn't want there to be a problem with you and me over him. He... He *really* likes you, sis. Like *really*. He doesn't understand it though, why you...like him. He asked me if I knew what happened to change your mind about him." He chuckled. "I told him his guess was as good as mine."

"He said that to you?" I asked and Danny smiled and nodded his head. "Wow."

"Anyway, I just wanted to tell you that I'm really happy for you. And mom and dad would be too. They'd most certainly approve of you dating an alien." That made us both laugh and smile, because it was true.

Hippies 'til the end.

When Merrick returned from his shower he came up behind me and placed his warm hands on my shoulders. His calloused, clean fingers ran down my arms and back up to my neck.

When I turned to him I see his close shaved face and smile and I think about the things Danny just told me. I grabbed his hand before he could sit down. I led him through the wad of people convening on the floor and along walls to our room. Without looking back to see or care what anyone thinks, I pulled him into our dark windowless room and shut the door.

"I can't believe you," I said to start.

"What?" he asked startled.

"I can't believe how incredibly...sweet you are." I laughed and hugged him around his waist.

Talking to Danny, huh? That Special and his big mouth.

I laughed as he squeezed me tighter.

"Asking permission? That's very human of you." I paused but he doesn't say anything so I went on. "You really can't see why I'd want to be with you?"

I asked the question, but in my mind it needed no answer. I pulled him to me, tiptoes as usual. The electricity was there before I even felt his lips on mine. I could smell the soap on his skin and the warmth from the hot shower was still there making his skin extremely hot.

I wrapped my arms around his neck tightly and met his lips with mine with much force. I wanted him to know I meant business. This wasn't some game or me just fooling around, biding my time for lack of something to do. I would make him see.

I loved him.

187

I traced the edge of his lip with my tongue and gently tugged on the fistfuls of his hair in my hands, I could feel him groan against my lips. He lifted me, pressing me against the wall so he could reach my lips without straining. The tingles jolted through me, making me gasp at the intensity. This was the most worked up I think I'd ever seen him, myself included. I couldn't believe how quickly I went from giddy to clawing at him in a frenzy.

He moved to kiss my neck, tracing my collarbone, jaw line, that crazy sensitive spot behind me ear. I couldn't stop my hands this time, moving in his hair, and on his back. He returned to my lips and the tingling lingered on my collarbone. I pulled up at his shirt hem in my fist as I reached around to his back, pulling him as close to me as I could.

That did it.

He let go with a sigh, pulling me back down to the floor and lies down on his back to catch his breath next to me.

"What is it, Merrick? Why do you always do that?"

"I can't, Sherry. More like...I won't."

So. My intentions were clear.

"I understand the chivalry, I appreciate it even, but I don't think the rules are the same for apocalypse."

"I'm not going to do that to you. You believe in waiting until you're married. I've heard you say it a thousand times."

No point in holding back now. "I love you, Merrick."

It was dark and I couldn't see his face, though I knew he could see mine, which made waiting for him to respond even more difficult. He already told me he loved me, so I couldn't imagine the response not being happy. But still, nothing.

"Merrick?" He was breathing faster. What did that mean? "Merrick? Please. What's the matter?"

"You...love me?" he breathed the words out, like they were really that unbelievable.

"Yes, I do. What's the matter?" I repeated with more force because he was scaring me.

"Don't say it unless you mean it, Sherry."

"I wouldn't do that!"

"I just... I'm not human."

"Yeah, and I'm not what you are, but you still love me, don't you?"

"But...how can you love me? I can't give you things, human things. I'll never be normal...I..."

"Merrick, do you not know me at all? I've been waiting for someone like you my whole life. Someone who knows me completely, but can still see past my faults and blemishes. You are exactly what I want. What I need. Don't act like you're nothing."

"You're so young. I just thought you were having fun. I never thought you would actually...could actually love me."

"Merrick, I am not like that! I wouldn't do that to you or anybody. I'm not going to kiss, sleep with, or do anything else...with someone I don't feel something for."

He sighed long and loud. "I don't know what to say, Sherry."

My heart skipped painfully.

"Why aren't you happy?" I asked and heard my voice catch.

I felt my breath getting heavy and my brain felt fuzzy. I couldn't understand it. Did he not love me anymore? Was that why he was doing this? Was he the one just having fun? He hadn't said he loved me since that first time he confessed to me. Maybe there was a reason for it.

"I just can't believe this. Are you sure you're not just reacting because of my feelings for you? Wanting to make me happy? I'm not going to push you, Sherry. I just want *you* to be happy. I'll take you anyway I can get you. You don't have to do this."

Well, maybe not. He just flat out couldn't believe that I loved him. So I dodged his question with a question of my own.

"Why are you trying so hard to talk me out of this?"

"I'm not. I've just been waiting for you to wake up...to realize this is crazy, and it's not what you want," he said desperately.

"That's not going to happen."

He was quiet for a minute, coming up with something else to say. Or another argument. Then he repeated a previous argument but I was ready this time.

"I can't give you things-"

"Weren't you watching that day? The day at the doctor's?"

"You know I was."

"Well, then you should know that you're not making me miss anything. An inhospitable womb is still just that. I can't have kids, ever, even if I am dating an angel."

"I wouldn't call myself that."

"I would."

I felt his hands on my face. Caressing my cheeks, my earlobes, my jaw.

"You promise this is what you want? I know you, Sherry Elizabeth. You can't lie to me. You *want* to be with me and not just because I want to be with you?"

"If you know that I can't lie then you should already know the answer to that. I love you."

"I love *you*," he said and sighed as he pressed his forehead to mine.

189

Defeat never sounded so good.

"I know. And I love that you love me."

"Would you say it again, please?"

"I love you. I've known for a while now. I should've told you already. I love you."

"I love you so much, sweetheart," he growled huskily.

He kissed me with a force unlike any before it. His fingers on the hand on the nape of my neck tugged and played in my hair and the other one was kneading my thigh with his fingers. I was undone, unglued with anticipation as we faced each other on our knees. He must have known that we could be together now, right?

Ecstatic, I began to pull his shirt hem up once more and he let me. I threw his balled up shirt in the corner. I kissed his neck, heard his breathing hitch, but when I reached for my shirt hem he grabbed my hands, placing them over my head on the blanket and lacing our fingers, continuing to kiss me senseless.

After some time of steady kisses, hot kisses but steady, I realized that no, I was not going to get my wish, he was just extremely excited and in the moment.

Generally he took his shirt off when we slept anyway because it was hot in the rooms so technically, I hadn't gained any ground. When I realized this fact, I wanted to tackle him in my frustration but remained, as always, my nonviolent self and let him gradually slow us down and eventually halt to a screeching stop before tucking us into bed.

I may have tried to be wily and make a few advances later than night, when he was a bit sleepier and not as alert, but who can really remember these things correctly.

One important fact remained, though I was frustrated and a little confused about how a human male body could keep refusing such invitations, what was more important was that I loved him. He knew it and I knew it.

I loved him.

I loved him.

I loved him.

And maybe most important of all, he still loved me. After watching me, living with me, eating with me, bleeding with me, sleeping with me and only sleeping.

He loved me.

Merrick - She Loves Me, She Loves Me
Chapter 17

So, she loved that I knew so much about her, huh? From my short stint with the few women I've had to take charge over, most of them would hate knowing that fact. That was why I assumed she'd be upset with me when I first told her I'd watched her. Instead, she turned it around and made it about her. About how she wasn't good enough to be watched.

And what was that with the Lighter? The Taker? I can't believe she was right there with him. I could feel bile rising to my mouth listening to her describe him and realized it makes me sick to my stomach to think of it. I'd never been sick to my human stomach before.

I saw Ryan on the couch so I walked over and plopped myself down. Sherry's in the shower, alone, without me, ugh... Why did she ever bring that round of thoughts to my mind?

"Hey, Ryan."

"Hi, Merrick. How's Sherry?"

"Fine, always fine. She's not even really that upset by it all. In the big picture yes, but not for herself."

"That sounds like Sherry."

"Yep. How's the arm?"

"Doing great. So, you guys are really serious then huh?"

"Subtle subject change, Ryan," I chuckled and shook my head at their relentlessness.

I wouldn't let them in my head so they tried to finagle answers by mouth instead.

"Well, you know..." He smiled guiltily. "I'm just curious. I still worry about you, you know. Sherry is the kindest mortal I've ever met and she seems committed to you, I just don't want this to be some human fling and then you're...but I don't know her like you do, so."

"I hope not," I joked and he laughs. Finally another Keeper was getting the humor. "Sherry and I are fine, more than fine. I think you don't need to be worried about me anymore. That's all I'm going to say about it."

"So she loves you then." He watched me closely as we talked. "A human loves you. What's that like?"

I thought about how much I loved her. I wondered how to describe it to him.

No Keeper experience came to mind. How could I explain something they'd never had a comprehension of feeling or seeing firsthand?

"Like nothing you've ever felt."

"Jeff said you told him it was better than home, better than The After."

I wondered if he was bringing up our Paradise, we call it The After, the place Keepers go when we retire with our chosen mate to go and be 'content', to make me feel reminiscent. Make me miss home. They would never understand.

"It is better. I can't explain it, Ryan. It's just like when we try to explain our home to humans. Until you've felt it, it'd just seem silly to you."

"Me? Silly? I'm a realist, but I'd like to be an optimist."

"And you will be if you stay here much longer. I love it here, even with all the problems, everything is so real here."

"I've noticed. Jeff has even toned down in the past couple weeks. Earth has done that kid good."

"Kid? His body is almost thirty."

"Yeah and mine is barely twenty, but our life is in the thousands. If I'm a kid, he's a kid."

I laughed at his logic. "I guess you're right. So, how's the arm, really?" I asked leaning back and crossing my ankles, amazed at how tired I was but Sherry did keep me up half the night, and it was so worth it.

"Feeling a lot better. That woman of yours sure knows what she's doing. She's got magic fingers, as they say."

"Coming from anyone else I'd be worried about that," I said yawning and we both laughed.

"So, the Taker. What are we going to do?" he asked, sitting up to the couch edge.

"No idea. This is all happening way faster than I ever imagined it would. I figured we'd be here fighting and dying and on our last leg before he finally decided to show up."

"Me, too. Me, too. But, hey, Calvin's finally coming around a little bit. He even asked me to do his homework with him the other night."

"I told you he just needed time. It's a lot harder on children. Calvin's really smart though. He's a good kid, he knows you're just here to help him."

"Well, I think Sherry helped me out on that one, too. All right, I'm starving. I'm glad things are working for you and Sherry. I really am, despite what the others might be thinking."

"Are thinking, Ryan. It's all right. I know what they say, but I also know what's important for me. Thanks, I appreciate it."

He nodded and as I watched him walk away, I thought about the store run that will have to be made again. I'd have to devise a plan somehow to stop Sherry from being able to do the shopping. She was so trusting and sweet. She didn't have the heart for this kind of life and the Taker could have had her, right then and there. It was only luck that she was still alive and he just wasn't craving at the time.

I don't know what I'd do without her. And Phillip. I totally misjudged him. He was so much worse than Bobby. I had to watch him with both eyes lately. He fooled everyone into thinking he was interested in Marissa but I know better.

While Sherry was in the shower, the morning after he barged in our room, he had asked to speak to me...again. I was getting pretty tired of these manly talks of his. He went on to explain again how she would have no real life with me and if I really loved her, I'd let her go.

When I refused to listen anymore and started to walk away, he grabbed my arm and yanked me to a stop. I felt my eyes bulge in shock and anger. My pulse jumped and the blood rushed through my veins. It took all I had to not punch his arrogant jaw, so instead I pushed him against the wall, letting him feel my not-quite-human strength, probably giving him one more reason to think Sherry shouldn't be with me, but I no longer cared.

It was my first experience with real human rage. It was terrifying. I felt like I could have crushed him and not thought twice.

He gasped and threw his hands up to defend himself like I was completely unprovoked.

"Hey, man! You know I'm right. You are not good for her. You're not real. I'm her own kind. She belongs with someone like me, someone who can understand things you never could."

"I'll let Sherry decide that," I said as I tried to calm down.

"And she will but will you just let her go when she does? I know it won't be you. She's too smart for that. She may be having fun, for a while, but she'll come around."

"If...if she chooses someone other than me, I'll deal with it then. Until then...keep your hands, mind and eyes off Sherry. She is *mine* until she decides not to be," I said and could hear the guttural growl of the words.

That was all I could say and walked off before I hurt my first human. Something I would regret, even if it was Phillip. Jealousy was a heinous human emotion.

Sherry. Sweet trusting Sherry didn't pay attention to Phillip. He was constantly watching her and analyzing. He was a predator, collecting data and watching for the day to make his move. He actually said he was better for her and he would have her someday, that she would choose him. If for no other reason than the fact that he was human. Maybe he was right.

And what was he thinking? Busting in our room and faking a meeting emergency. It took all I had to just keep calm and play dumb in front of him, for

Sherry's sake. No point in ruining a perfectly good morning with the smell of pancakes in the air. Wow, they were good.

After all that, she said she loved me. Her lips spoke the words. No prompting, she just blurted it out with no indication of a lie. It has to be true. She can't lie. Oh, wow. I just can't believe it. All this fighting with myself, convincing myself to enjoy it while it lasted, knowing I'd one day have to let her go to Phillip or someone else human and of her choosing, but no, she chose me.

Me.

And she was relentless when she wanted something and now...she wanted to go too far. I couldn't do that to her. I mean...I could. I wanted to, badly, and she was making it very difficult to resist, almost impossible to control myself, but I wouldn't. She was too important. I know she thought she wanted that, but if we live through this, I want her to look back with happiness, not regret. I can't. I won't.

And wow is she amazing. And persistent and sexy. I may have to go sleep with Danny if she kept this up. She knew what she was doing to me, didn't she? She had to.

She thinks I'll crumble under this human flesh. If only she knew how close I actually was, she'd push harder than ever and I wouldn't be able to stop. What is it that men do? Oh, yeah.

Football, pickle bucket, dirty dishes, television newsroom, ice cream sandwich. Not working. Not working.

Gah! She's so shamelessly sexy. She has no idea, that's why she's so dangerous. She has a weapon that she doesn't even know she has and she was using it, full force. No wonder every man she meets wants to keep her as his own.

Sherry, stop, baby. Please behave. Sleep.

Finders Keepers
Chapter 18

Though it was clear to Merrick now that I loved him, and I was certain he loved me, he did not give in last night. Oh, I tried and he struggled with himself, but eventually chivalry won out.

Maybe I wasn't as sexy as I wanted to be.

I didn't understand? What were we going to do, actually get married? Walk into the church and tell them we want to get married, but hey, don't check behind the ear. Wink, wink.

I didn't think so.

I would marry him, in a second, that was not the problem. I had no doubt that a guy that would risk everything and travel light years to be with me was worth it, I just don't see why tradition still counted in times like this. I mean I wanted to marry him, I always dreamed of marrying my guy.

Would the commitment in our heart and the knowing of our little family here not be enough in times like these when you can't reach a preacher? Are Merrick's intentions to marry me or was he just expecting our relationship to be only kisses and torture?

Once again waking before him, I lay there next to him and marveled at the arms around me.

Some would say that this was crazy. I was sure plenty of people in the bunker with me said this was crazy but what else can you do? You find someone who knows you completely, inside out, your best, your worst and he loves you anyway. More than loves you, adores you with every breath.

Could you really turn away from that for one minor detail?

That he wasn't from this world?

I couldn't, I wouldn't. Especially since this life might be almost over.

While brushing my teeth the next morning, I saw Merrick come up behind me in the mirror. "It's time."

They were leaving to go look for others, to call other Keepers.

"I'm coming," I mumbled, trying to hurry and spit.

I made this decision last night, while lying there watching him sleep, that I would go with them today. I wasn't sure how much of a fight I'd have to put up, but I was about to find out and I had a feeling, it wouldn't be easily won.

"No, you're not. Too dangerous," he said matter-of-factly.

I rinsed quickly and turned to face him as he stood all take-charge in the doorframe.

"Merrick, you said you didn't want me out of your sight, take me with you. I can be useful. Girls are least likely to be problematic looking. They don't question sweet innocent faces." I smiled a sweet smile and prayed he was considering it.

It actually looked like he was, then squashed it.

"No. I don't feel right about bringing you when you can stay here. I won't willingly put you in danger."

"I want to come. I don't want to stay here while you go and be at risk."

"I won't be at risk, we'll be fine. We're not even going into town."

"Then it won't be a risk for me either." He sighed at my rebuttal and tipped his face back to look at the ceiling. "Merrick, please."

"No, Sherry," he said with finality as he turned to walk back to the commons, me on his heels.

"Merrick." No answer. "Jeff, who all is going with you?" I said loudly across the room.

"Well, I thought just Merrick and I would go," he answered, sitting in the chair tying his shoes.

"And if you get stopped? You need one of us with you," I suggested and by us I meant not-Special humans.

"Good point," Jeff said and Merrick shot him a sharp look. Jeff shrugged. "I said good point, I didn't say it had to be Sherry. We'll take Phillip."

"Come on! You need a girl with you. Nobody ever gives me trouble. I'm too short and puny to look like a problem. Please, let me come," I begged, looking my most sullen.

"She's got a point, Merrick," Jeff said, arching an eyebrow.

"No. She doesn't. We'll be fine," Merrick said through his teeth, glancing between Jeff and me as if to say that was the end of it.

"Why are you so set against me going? We have to do these things. You can't hide me away every time, I'm not a Special," I said looking directly in his eyes, willing him to see my point of view.

"Sherry, the last time you went out..." he breathed, shaking his head, remembering the Lighter and then the flat tire and Marissa with her gun.

I was a little uncomfortable having this conversation out in front of everyone, my fault for chasing him down, so I whispered my response, walking to stand right up against him.

"Babe, that was different," I said softly, "and you weren't there with me then. I don't want to be here without you. I don't feel safe without you."

"I want you to feel safe, but..."

"Then please, let me come."

He looked down, unblinkingly into my eyes for long seconds, then sighed. "You're impossible, you know that." He rubbed my chin with his thumb and smiled that smile that made my heart jump, then turned to Jeff. "All right, let's get going."

I tried not to be one of those girls who bragged with their eyes and smile when they got their way. I wasn't entirely sure I was pulling it off, but I was trying.

As Jeff stood at the bathroom counter, I applied the liquid foundation to the symbol behind his ear with a cotton ball. It wasn't perfect but hopefully we wouldn't need to test it. This was just a precaution.

Jeff didn't seem at all fazed by my touch or my closeness as I stood between his knees. Comforting. Jeff was Jeff and that was that.

Merrick on the other hand, couldn't sit still. His breathing accelerated and his hands squeezed my hips in frustration as I leaned over him.

When I blew on his neck to dry the foundation, he lost it. He reached up from his seated position and pulled me down, kissing me fervently, wrapping his arms around me. I spilled most of the liquid in the sink in my trance as I laughed at him.

If I were honest, I was sure I was quite a bit more flirty with my application of the makeup to Merrick that with Jeff.

"So, does this mean you're not upset with me anymore?" I asked, facing him on his lap.

"I was never upset with you. I'm sorry if you thought I was, I just want you to be safe, that's all that matters. I don't know what I'd do if you weren't here anymore. You've had enough close calls to last for a while."

I couldn't argue with that.

"I know. I just want to be with you. Ok? That's where I feel the safest."

"And I want you to feel safe and be safe, but...I just don't like the idea of us getting caught and you being with us."

I rechecked his ear, again not perfect, but not so noticeable either. "So how old are you?" I asked trying to change the subject to something less stressful.

"Uh...why?"

"I just want to know."

"I don't know exactly. Really, really old." He chuckled sadly. "How old was Matt?"

"Twenty four."

"Then I'm twenty four," he said smiling.

We walked out to the commons room and it hit me that we should bring Marissa. She'd been living out there, in the open, probably knew this area better than anyone. We could take her and leave Phillip. Oh, but she was a Special. Too bad.

I saw her talking to Phillip, he had cornered her against the wall. She told him to basically get lost and pushed his hand. He did it. He walked away just like that. I wondered what she said to him. That girl has some skills that I apparently don't.

Everyone, even Calvin, who'd been scarce lately, came to see us off. I missed his hugs. We headed up the stairs and Marissa ran over to me, touching my elbow before speaking.

"Be safe. Look beyond what you see. Things are not what they seem," she said and I nodded almost robotically.

At the time her advice sounded just as that, strange advice from a strange girl, but it lingered in my mind and I couldn't be rid of a nagging sense of purpose, something I was supposed to do. Like I forgot to pay a bill or turn off the coffee pot or something.

"Shotgun!" Phillip called, and Merrick and Jeff both stopped.

"What? Where?" Jeff asked anxiously.

"What?" Phillip looked back at them and then smothered a laugh in his fist. "Nah, man. There's not a real shotgun. You call 'shotgun' when you want to sit in the front passenger seat," Phillip explained.

"Why?" Jeff continued to look completely puzzled. "Why not just call 'front passenger seat' instead?"

"Well, back in the old wagon days, they used to have a driver and then a person who held a shotgun beside him in case they were about to get robbed..." He stopped at their blank expressions. "Never mind, you probably know all about that, huh? Ok... I call front passenger seat," he said laughing and rolling his eyes.

I tried to stifle a giggle, unsuccessfully, and Jeff glared at me. He hated it when he didn't understand something us mere humans knew and not him. Merrick on the other hand was pretty used to it and sent me playful scowl before winking and smiling.

I drove again with Phillip up front while Merrick and Jeff sat in the back so they could concentrate, and also to be out of line of sight.

I started the van and backed up. As we got going down the road, Phillip's job was to keep an eye out for anything strange. My job was to make sure to follow all speeding laws and keep driving. As we drove, full of coffee and Mrs. Trudy's fried eggs, I felt something in my stomach still.

The nagging.

I looked around, almost instinctively, looking for something but having no idea what. It wasn't the food in my stomach, it was the purpose. I pushed it down, taming it. I wasn't sure what this was but I was going to sit with my mouth shut.

I didn't want Merrick to regret bringing me after I pitched such a fit to come. Calm down, Sherry. Focus and drive.

We drove for a bit longer. I kept looking back at Merrick. He looked like he was sleeping almost but I saw him drumming his thumb on his pant leg. He was just peaceful.

Jeff looked that way too. He had said before how peaceful their world was, how peaceful they were with each other. It made sense that trying to communicate with other Keepers would be a peaceful thing for them as well.

Just as I reached my turn around point I saw a little hill off to the side of a bunch of billboards. This part of the state looked a bit like an open grassy plain. A prairie. Nothing like Chicago. Again my dad's city girl remarks were playing in my head, but then something else.

Something not mine.

A strangeness overcame me; a foggy, stress-filled feeling. I was not myself and the nagging as no longer going to accept me controlling it and pushing it down and away. It was no longer just uncomfortable, it was overtaking me.

It bellowed to the surface. I felt like I was drowning in fire, the hot warmth too much to handle. It was on my skin, in my throat and nose, my stomach. My stomach worst of all. I gasped and then something else that words couldn't describe took my body and senses over completely.

I screamed. It just came out. I didn't will it and I couldn't stop it. My muscles bunched and rebelled and twitched.

There was a pain in my stomach past the burning. It was a twisting and turning in my gut. I couldn't breath. I struggled to pull the van over and press the break but there was nothing but the pain.

Phillip reached over, lifting his leg to press the brake and grabbed the wheel just in time before we ran into the ditch. I hear them mumbling, I hear them yelling. Only muffles and noise to me. My eyes were open but I could only see what my mind willed me to see.

If forced me to look, it forced me out the van, banging on the door wildly and scrambling for the handle. I felt a hand grab for my arm but I pulled away. I tripped and stumbled, scraping my palms in the dirt and dirtying my pant legs. I felt more hands on me, but I yanked free. I needed to focus but I couldn't.

I fell to my knees in the dirt and prickly dead brown and yellow grass. I laid down in a ball to make it stop, fetal position, but it willed me to roll over and sit up straight, facing away from the street.

They were around me, I could feel them but couldn't respond to their worried touches and voices. Nothing mattered but the pain and the purpose. I tried to fight it and force it down once more with all I had but it accelerated and fed it and I doubled over screaming. My face felt the scratchy grass under me. My stomach twisted and muscles pulled painfully.

No more.

I gave in.

I'd do whatever it wanted if it would just end this!

It willed me to sit up, relax my muscles and pay attention, to focus, to give it complete control. It took over, showing me the hill, and I looked at it- No I saw it, really saw it, beyond it.

I had a weird sense of Déjà vu.

It looked and felt familiar though I had no idea why. It looked out of place, the hill, bushes grown up around it. There was greener grass growing on top of it and it was awfully round and precise to be a natural occurrence. The pain lessened, loosening its grip.

A willow tree by the back of the hill caught the edge of my vision.

I hadn't seen a willow tree in years, not since my birthday. My mind involuntarily started to float to a fleeting flash of that day and then the pain jabbed me again, forcing me to scream again until I refocused.

The billboards were out of place as well. No one stacks bill boards that close together like that, and way out here, in the middle of nowhere. The grass was awfully green on top of the hill, brown and yellow everywhere else.

Look, it willed me. Commanded me. It yelled it to my brain with no words.

I saw it!

The child playing under the canopy. It was not a hill at all! It was a camouflage canopy! The child's small hidden dark silhouette would never have been seen in the dusk light had I not stopped and stared insistently at it.

One last thing it willed of me.

I raised my shaking finger to point, a hand tried to grab it and I yanked it back in frustration. I pointed again, stabbing with more emphasis and then I could see. My own eyes could see and I could hear.

I gasped a breath of relief. My rapid breathing was the loudest thing as there is no other noise.

The pain was completely gone, not even a shadow of it. Merrick held me in his lap in the dirt and grass, his arms around me, holding me tight as if I were to flee.

They are looking where my finger was still pointing and they saw it too. Merrick looked back at me, shocked to see I was back, that my eyes were clear and it was me. Sherry.

"Sherry! What the hell happened?!"

200

He cursed. He cursed for me. He never curses.

He hugged me to him so tight with more protection than relief. I wished there was some way I could show them instead of tell them what had just happened. Would they even believe me?

No one saw the Lighter but me last time and now this crazy stunt but the boy was there. Still there playing, unaware of our presence.

Merrick placed a finger under my chin to make me focus on him. He looked anxious. I steadied myself and tried to explain with as few words as possible, the least crazy that I knew how.

"I don't know. I was fine." I looked at the boy but Merrick pulled my face back around to look at him again. "And then I got this horrible pain in my stomach and... something ...made me look, there. I couldn't hear or see. I couldn't respond to anything but what it wanted me to do. The pain...I don't know what...how to explain it," I said hearing the tears in my voice.

I looked up to three faces. Phillip's utter disbelief. Jeff's anger and revelation, Merrick's urgent concern and revelation.

"What? How is this even possible?" Jeff yelled jumping to his feet and pacing, angrily.

"What is it? What was that?" I asked, begging if they knew something to tell me.

"A Muse? Who is it?" Jeff yelled but was talking to Merrick. "It could be anyone. It could be Phillip for all we know!"

Phillip looked aghast as Jeff continued on, not even looking in Phillip's direction.

"Jeff, please! If you know something, tell me!" I couldn't take it anymore, so I yelled.

It was very unlike me and it startled them both back into Keeper mode.

"A Muse. They give you *inspiration* to do a task. To see something, do something, say something. They say the words and touch you, and you have no choice but to do it, or you endure excruciating pain until you do," Jeff explained.

It dawned on me that I knew who the Muse was.

"Marissa. She told me to...look beyond what I see, and then she touched my arm before we left."

Phillip jumped forward as he yelled, pointing his finger.

"I knew it! I knew I wasn't crazy! She kept telling me to leave, go to the stairs, go sit it the kitchen, and then when she touched me, if I didn't leave, my head would hurt so bad. I thought I was going nuts."

"Marissa. Great. Now what?" Jeff asked no one.

"Well, let's just hold on a minute. Why did she lead us here? The kid is there. It might be a hideout. It looks that way to me," Phillip told Jeff, who was still fuming.

Merrick cut in before Jeff could tear Phillip's head off.

"Muses supposedly don't take sides. They help whoever they want to help, whenever they want, whatever entertains them. We haven't seen them in a long time either. I guess everyone's coming out of the woodworks. Jeff's worried because we don't know if she's helping us or hurting us right now. Once she gives you a task, you have to do it. Muses are very dangerous if you can't trust them," Merrick explained.

"Well. I'll go check it out," Phillip said. "See what's up with this place."

"Maybe I should go," I chimed.

I got a solid angry chorus of three distinct 'No's.

"I think you've been through enough. I've had a Muse's mojo on me. I know what it feels like, though from the looks of you just now, I only got a taste of it," Phillip said wincing.

"He's right. You're done. Let's go to the van and wait." Merrick pulled me to my feet as he spoke, and I felt woozy.

No pain but definite drunkenness and weakness.

"I just meant that they wouldn't hurt me before I could-" I tried, but I could barely walk straight let alone talk.

"We know what you meant, and you're done. Let's go. Phillip, you ok for this?" Merrick asked but was already walking me to the van.

"Yeah. I'll wave if it's an all clear to head in that way."

Jeff, Merrick and I went back to the van. Merrick helped me into the middle seat and climbed in next to me, pulling me back onto his lap.

"You are all about trouble, aren't you?" Merrick whispered once we were settled. He tried to laugh, but couldn't fake it.

"I'm sorry," I said weakly.

"Don't apologize, it's not your fault. You're just...a magnet for it, apparently. I'll just have to keep an eye on you more closely from now on. Two in fact."

"Four," Jeff chimed in from the back, smiling my way.

"Why do I feel so drained?" I asked and noticed how my voice seemed to drag.

"Well...if you don't fight it, the Muse's wrath, then it doesn't hurt at all. But you didn't know so, you were fighting it, I can see it clearly now. I should have realized what was happening. She should have warned you so you knew what to look for. When you fight it, it takes a lot out of you."

"You'll be ok, just not as strong as usual for a couple days," Jeff finished the analysis for Merrick.

He did that a lot lately. They made a good team.

"So, I thought you said you told me everything already," I asked jokingly.

"Honey, I can't tell you everything. It would take an eternity. I wouldn't even know what things to tell you and what not to, to be useful. There's a lot you don't know about."

Hmm, honey. How could I think about things like that at a time like this? A quick glance at Jeff and he was still watching out the window for Phillip.

"So you think everyone in the bunker is ok with her there?" I asked, as Danny was in my mind.

"Muses don't have an agenda...usually. They just entertain themselves. I'm sure they're fine."

Merrick pulled my head to his chest, rubbing my upper arm with his hand, warming me. He could always tell when I was cold.

"Why don't you ever get cold?" I asked, feeling my speech start to slur even more.

"Because, this body doesn't work like it use to. I won't ever get cold or hot," Merrick answered.

"But you feel warm to me."

"Yes, but I don't feel it."

"Do you feel me?"

"Yeah. I feel it if your skin is cold or hot, usually cold," he chuckled.

"What about weather or showers? How can you feel the water and not feel the temperature?"

"I feel the temperature on my skin, it just doesn't bother me. My body doesn't respond to my physical temperature only the temperature of what I can touch." He laughed. "What's with the twenty questions?"

"Just curious."

"Well, anything else?" he said lightly.

"Yeah. Why are they called Muses? I thought Muses were there to give inspiration."

"They are inspiration. Supposed to be. Made to be. They can see the future too, in visions and flashes. Not very predictable, but very useful. If more than one Muse is together, a human's brain nerves would fire rapidly from all the motivation with ideas. In the old days, the Muses could make or break a battle. It was when they started playing with their powers to their own uses when they became more nuisance than inspiration."

"Huh."

After a minute of sitting and warming me, Merrick started again, more quietly, in my ear.

"You've got to stop scaring me like that. This heart won't make it long with you to worry about." He put my hand over his heart, the body's heart and I could

203

feel it thump against my fingers.

He was making a joke but his face was serious.

"Aren't you glad I came now?" I said, raising my eyebrows in jest and even they were tired.

"Yes, I am. If she had done this while we were gone..." He grunted. "You were right, you're just safer with me," Merrick said, sounding angry again.

I hated that he felt like this. I hated that he worried so much, but looking back at the amount of trouble I'd gotten myself into, I guess I needed his worry.

"There he is!" Jeff yelled. "There's Phillip, and he's waving."

I was sorely regretting the tank top I had worn, thinking I was going to be in a warm van all day, instead I was freezing and tired. So very tired.

I walked with Merrick's help to the entrance where Phillip stood. No one, including me, was comfortable leaving me in the van to wait and it was already getting much darker.

"You ok? You don't look so good," Phillip asked me.

"I'm fine," I mumbled.

"It's the Muse. Where are they?" Merrick explained and asked, swiftly looking around.

"The basement door is under here. Come on."

When we entered the camouflage dome tent on the back side, there was a man inside, waiting for us. Once again, Jeff embraced him. I knew right away this was their Keeper.

He shook Merrick's hand sensing I needed him for support and muttered the name Patrick. I must have looked pretty bad from his expression.

After introductions he took us down into their bunker, really just an old, very small basement that had been covered over from a torn down house. The only sign of that was a still standing old brick chimney off the side.

There were five others waiting to meet us.

The first Keepers name was Ann, an older lady with salt and pepper hair. The second one from upstairs was Patrick. He was older too and had a white beard and mustache. The Specials were Katie, an extremely pregnant and pretty thirty something with brown hair and Laura, exactly the same but not pregnant and her hair was short instead, twin sisters. Their husbands were there as well, Paul, glasses and comb over, total banker looking and Eli, a cute athletic looking Jamaican, I could tell from his very distinct accent as he said hello to us. Eli and Laura had a son, Franklin, who was about twelve and was an in between skin shade of the two parents that would have the girls swooning one day, and the most vivid green eyes ever.

204

After a few incoherent sentences I thought I understood that Katie's was an accidental pregnancy. I couldn't imagine someone would bring a baby into this world as it was, on purpose.

There really was no point in trying to keep track of what Special belonged to what Keeper at this point. Merrick had said they were here for us all now.

The Muse had led us to the right place. I wondered what entertainment could she have gained from this. Even with the events of today, we found six people to add to our band of misfits. The day was not a waste, and I wouldn't take it back, even if I could.

So unbelievably tired, Merrick took me to the small loveseat, the only sitting furniture in the very tiny place and laid me down. It smelled like lavender.

He threw an afghan that was lying on the back over me and I felt him smooth my hair back. I could hear Jeff telling the other Keepers about the Muse and heard the anger in their voices as they looked at me and protested and conversed about it, understanding now the events that had transpired and the dead-on-my-feet appearance.

They all discussed things I could no longer hear. Mumbling turned into just white noise as I drifted off, unable to fight any longer the sleep that came for me.

When I awoke next, I was in the van again, my head in Merrick's lap in the middle seat. Phillip was driving and there were headlights behind us, I could see them in the rearview mirror. No one seemed alarmed which meant the others were joining us. I tried to sit up but Merrick held my shoulder down.

"Just rest, honey. We're almost there."

"Everything work out all right?"

"Yes, *miss worried about everybody but herself.*"

I laughed a tired laugh and I licked my lips. I touched my finger to them, asking. He smiled crookedly and bent down to kiss me, picking my back up just a little bit to reach.

His lips were extremely warm and comforting as he kissed me quickly and softly.

"I love you," I said before collapsing, laying my head back down on his lap.

"I know," Merrick said, a smile in his voice.

I fell back asleep with Merrick twirling a curl of my hair in between his fingers.

We made it back and I roused just as we entered the steps to the bunker, being carried in warm arms. Suddenly I was scared, feeling tension in the air.

Merrick's arms were tense around me and I was afraid of what he and Jeff might do to Marissa, not giving her a chance to explain. I just had a feeling she wouldn't purposely do this to me to hurt me. I could already hear the yelling as I became more coherent. I lifted my head and looked around.

Merrick saw me and tested my feet down to the floor, making sure I could stand first. Jeff and Marissa were at it and everyone was watching, worried and not knowing what this blow up was for.

"I'm sorry!" she yelled "I thought she needed to find it on her own. I haven't known I had this gift but just a few years, you know, and my Keeper died before he could really even show me much more about it. I thought that it would be easier for her this way. Usually when I tell people, they don't listen anyway, they think I'm a freak."

"She brought you here," Jeff boomed, "has been nothing but nice to you. You knew what would happen and you let it happen anyway. And Merrick. Merrick had to watch her go through that not knowing what was going on either. You are a selfish girl!" Jeff yelled and made a slow advance inching Marissa's way.

Everyone glanced at Merrick and me, still not knowing what was going on, but no one would dare interrupt Jeff at this point. I couldn't remember a time he ever looked so angry. I felt kind of proud he was defending me, but Marissa looked so innocently young and unknowing and utterly frightened by Jeff's behavior.

Maybe that was part of the Muse disguise.

"I'm sorry. Ok. I won't do it again. I just... I thought you wouldn't let me be here if you knew I was a Muse and then when y'all were leaving, I couldn't just let you go without telling you. You needed to find *them*." She pointed at the newcomers behind us, then looking at me. "Sherry, I'm sorry. I should've said something, but I was scared. I'm sorry, really sorry. This is why I was so reluctant to come here with you in the first place. Can you forgive me?"

"You don't have to answer her, Sherry. She knows I won't hurt her. I wouldn't anyway but not only is she a Muse, she's still a Special, too. We're stuck with her," Jeff said looking calmer, but still upset. He must've known how I'd react.

"It's fine. She's telling the truth and we did find them." I pointed to the newcomers. "That's what's important."

Merrick squeezed my hand and shook his head, his jaw clenched. If I could see his eyes I would bet they were rolling. He thought my understanding for others was a weakness. That I was too trusting. He was just a little biased. Besides, they were no different. The Keepers weren't violent and revengeful. Why would he expect me to be?

"I am sorry. Is there anything I can do to help tonight?" Marissa said, her head hanging down.

"You've done enough, but...yes. We have a lot of unloading to do. We have some new roommates." Jeff motioned for her to go upstairs and waved his hand for a few others, apologizing to the newcomers on his way out for yelling.

Danny came up to me and started to ask me something but I held up a hand. "Tomorrow, Danny. Please, I'm sorry...Merrick..."

I was about to collapse. I'd never been that tired before and now that the excitement was over, it overtook me again like an avalanche.

Merrick grabbed me up in one swift motion. I heard him tell Danny that I was ok, but Danny didn't sound convinced. He would be angry with the Muse, too.

The last thing I remembered was being tucked into bed, under Merrick's chin. The warmth from his body surrounded me like a blanket, making me feel safe again.

Fairweather
Chapter 19

The Taker. Why was he smiling at me? Staring? I've done what he asked. He told me to bring him Calvin, and here we are...

Wait.

Where was Calvin? Why would I do that? I would never do that! Has he gotten to me? Am I under the Lighter speak or worse, a Lighter myself? It is too late and Merrick can never be with me now. A mortal enemy, a clone, a puppet. I feel the same, but he's still smiling, smugly.

I have no shopping cart, but I'm standing in the check out line, looking at the manager's loft. They turn, they all turn, they are all Lighters. Everyone's black eyes in the store suddenly fix on me with deadly intent, and they are all dark haired, dark eyed Lighters.

The lights in the store are off, only letting the sunlight in from the windows. It's a shock to see this much black hair and pale skin. And now, they are moving.

What do I do? I'm human. Do they know something's not right, that I'm on the other side? Calvin? Where's Calvin? I'm so confused.

Wait! No!

They are moving closer, feet not touching the floor, toes gliding and dragging. They are parting the way for the Taker now. He is melting through the thick glass and floating his way down to me. He opens his mouth wide, wider, much wider than humanly possible.

The fright takes over and I'm shaking so hard my teeth rattle and then the tears come. The pleading tears.

"Please don't hurt me," I beg but don't know why I did, I'm not usually a beggar.

He closes his mouth abruptly and smiles again, that façade of a smile. He stops dead in front of me and brushes a cold finger down my cheek and watches me intently as I shiver. Then his mouth opens again and he lunges for me in one swoop as I open my mouth to scream.

I was screaming, waiting for the pain of whatever happened when a Lighter took you over. It must be painful. He grabbed my arms, shaking me. My eyes fluttered open for one last look before death but it was Merrick I saw.

"Run!" I yelled at him. "He's here."

He wasn't listening. Why were they just standing there. Danny, no! Why was

208

Danny here?

The slow fall into coherency is not fun or graceful, the embarrassment, the confusion. I soon realized that Merrick and Danny were there, in my room, kneeling over me with horror stricken faces, and I was safe in my sleeping bag, causing yet again a panic from my loved ones.

Best to start apologies now.

"Oh, gosh, I'm sorry. Bad dream," I explained.

"We could tell. We've been trying to wake you for five minutes," Danny spouted, sounding annoyed.

"Are you all right?" Merrick said softly as he wiped the tears from my face with his finger.

"Yes," I said, sitting up and wiping my face with back of my hand. "Sorry. I'm fine, I'm just a trouble maker." I elbowed Danny playfully.

He didn't seem amused.

"Is this crap 'cause of the Muse?" Danny asked Merrick, his voice dripping with aggravation.

I knew it. I bet he had been stewing all night about this. I let out an exasperated breath.

"No," he said to Danny, then turned to me. "What were you dreaming about? You told me to run."

"Yeah, I was dreaming about a Lighter. It's ok, I'm fine, really," I pleaded as Merrick helped me up, Danny got up too. "Listen, please don't be mad at Marissa. We don't know her yet. Let's not make assumptions, ok? Her reason last night was legitimate. Jeff freaked when he found out she was a Muse, she was afraid we wouldn't welcome her here. Just let it go, for now, until we learn more. Please?" I pleaded, looking at Danny first because he was the one I was mainly worried about.

"Fine. I'll let it go...for now." Danny hugged me tightly and looked into my face for a minute before sighing and leaving the room, not shutting door.

I could hear lots of voices and noise.

"I'm sorry," I said to Merrick again.

"Why do you always apologize for things that don't need one. Don't be silly, it was a dream, honey."

I nodded and took the clothes he gave me to change into, kissing my forehead quickly before heading out the door. Then he stopped.

"Do you want me to get Mrs. Trudy to help you dress?"

"No. You could help me," I said coyly and smiled.

"Um, no. Trudy?"

"No. I'm fine, unless you want to help, then I couldn't possible do it without you."

His smile was bemused and he shook his head at me before leaving.

I sighed and then blanched, beyond embarrassed. My door was open that whole time I was yelling and screaming in my dream? I could hear them which meant they could hear me.

Jeez. The damsel in distress label was definitely taken. The newcomers must have thought I was a loon.

I changed quickly and headed to find out what all the noise I somehow slept through was. I figured it was later because everyone was up. My eyes bugged when my watch said 6:00...PM!

What!?

"It's 6:00 at night? Are you kidding me?" I asked myself out loud, just before turning the hall into the commons room.

When I rounded the corner I saw at least ten smiling faces, but one not smiling. Marissa.

Celeste jumped up and hugged me like it had been days, technically, I guess it had. I hugged her back, which must've surprise her because she started to squeeze with enthusiasm.

The chest hugs with this girl were never comfortable but I tried, how could I not? The sweetest, doll face girl desperately cared for my safety and well being, not to mention that of my only brother.

"Danny has been sooo worried about you. He didn't sleep a wink last night," Celeste said and then bit her lip.

Uhoh . How would she know if he slept last night or not unless...

Celeste, realizing she said too much, quickly changed the subject. "We are adding onto the last hall. Neat, huh? Now we'll have a little bit more personal space around here. That's where most of the guys are now."

"Hmm...that'll be nice," I said as I eyed Danny, his "I'm busted" face was full on.

"Merrick's there too," she chimed.

Nice one Celeste, trying to distract me with the mention of Merrick.

I smiled big and made my way around the couch. Mrs. Trudy cried out a little when she saw me, startled. Everyone else seemed to try not to stare at me, making me more embarrassed. I hated it when people were so worked up over me.

I was absolutely starving, and Trudy must have heard my stomach growling. She grabbed my hand and started pulling to the kitchen, around the people seemingly piled everywhere. The tension was really going to build with all of us literally on top of each other but as I glanced around...

What? What was that?

I jerked from Trudy's grasp and ran to the clock mirror on the wall. I let out an anguished sigh-shriek-gasp.

Everyone turned to look, hearing my gasp. Under my eyes were huge dark circles. Huge, insanely dark circles. My skin was at least three shades whiter, which looked terrible against my features that usually were flavored by my olive beige skin. My eyes were almost golden yellow, the lightest I'd ever seen them, which made the under eye circles look that much darker.

When I looked over myself, my arms and hands, I saw my fingernails were a sick yellow and the blue and green veins were standing out drastically in my arms and hands.

"What in the...?" I asked my reflection, poking and rubbing at the eye circles like they will wipe off.

"Merrick said it's from the Mu...from yesterday. Something to do with it draining you. It should be gone by tomorrow. We hoped you'd go the rest of the day without looking in the mirror," Danny explained smiling apologetically but I noticed how he didn't accuse the Muse even though he started too.

I was grateful that he was willing to try, for me.

"Why in the world did you let me sleep until six o'clock at night?"

"You needed the rest."

"Jeez."

I knew Marissa was still in the room so I just laughed it off and continued to walk with Trudy.

Dinner, as everyone had already eaten, was reheated lasagna. Sweet, sweet Trudy had asked Merrick what my favorite food was to make for me.

Afterwards, instead of heading back into the crowded commons room, I decided to go and see what was up with the new hall.

As soon as I saw them, I could see what Celeste had been was saying. The dirt at the end was being dug out and carted and hauled up the stairs to be dumped. It looked back breaking. Merrick, Jeff, Phillip, Ryan, Patrick, Max and the husbands of the newcomers were down there, barely all fitting in the hall together as it was.

I started to turn and go but Merrick saw me and squeezed through them.

"Hey, you. Are you feeling any better? I'd hug you, but..." He motioned to his shirt and I understood, head-to-toe dirt and looking absolutely gorgeous working-man.

"It's ok. I'm fine, I just wanted to check on you." He stared with that sympathetic face I remembered and I covered my face. "Yeah. You could've warned me," I muttered, muffled through my fingers.

"Sorry. I just figured-" he started, but I cut him off.

"Yeah, Danny told me. Avoid the mirrors. So, y'all are going to extend the hall, huh?" I removed my hands, but pulled my hair around the sides of my face to help hide it.

"Yes, just keep on extending and bracing as we go along to make more rooms for newcomers as they arrive. What do you think?"

"I think you look mighty hot with a dirt mustache," I said pulling him down for a quick gritty peck before turning to leave and was satisfied to see the smirk of a smile on his face.

I left them to it, whatever *it* is, sensing there would be no more fun to be had down that hall.

The next couple of days were spent recuperating for me, trying to get my strength back. It was like having the flu without the coughing. I felt like I had run a marathon. I wasn't just tired, I was dead tired and achy.

The night I slept til 6:00, I actually went back to bed at 8:30, but not before making a point to say hello to Marissa, loud enough for everyone to hear.

Everyone else, including me, eventually started on hauling dirt and rock from the hall and carrying it out. It was backbreaking.

We wanted to get as much done as possible so we dug farther than we needed to for our present situation but leaving plenty of room for a while. No one let me work for very long without making a fuss and forcing me to take breaks and sometimes insisting I go back up for a nap or a snack.

I wasn't sure if it was the tiny frame or if I just looked breakable or if it was the unfortunate events of the past few weeks that kept everyone so up-in-arms about me but I had had enough of that treatment and decided a little playful payback was in order.

I hauled dirt with my red five gallon pickle bucket that I couldn't fill all the way to carry it. I picked up a handful of dirt out of the bucket on my way down the hall and threw it at Danny's back.

He turned, but didn't think much of it and went right back to digging. I picked up another handful and threw it at Jeff. It pelted his legs and he turned with his eyebrows furrowed. I quickly looked away to keep from laughing and him seeing me laughing.

I dumped my bucket up topside and came back for another run. I picked up handfuls and hit quite a few others, including Merrick, before I got back with my empty bucket, chuckling to myself. I made a couple more runs and then this time I was surprised.

Ambushed.

As soon as I picked up my first fistful to throw at Danny, he got me first, dropping a handful down the back of my shirt, making me squeal in mock anger.

"Ooooh, Danny! You are so going to get it now!" I yelled and that was it. That was all it took and we had an all out dirt war.

Apparently, they had discussed it while I was dumping my bucket and had decided to ambush me.

Everyone started pelting handfuls of dirt in every direction. Keepers, Specials, kids and nobodies, even Marissa was fighting back with Ryan, going at it with enthusiasm.

I had dirt everywhere. Hair, ears, clothes but I refused to give in. I threw as much as I could at anyone I saw and got as close to Danny as I could get. Then I dumped and rubbed two handfuls in his hair.

"Aho! You are so paying now, little sister!" he yelled, just like Danny used to do, call his big sister little.

Then, Merrick jumped in front of me. "Sorry, Danny. I can't let you do that," he said calmly and then plopped another handful on Danny's head.

Everyone was laughing and shouting and screaming, dirt was flying everywhere, raining down and flinging sideways. I heard Celeste squealing incessantly about her hair, but as I looked at her she was laughing hysterically as Danny grabbed her and they dumped dirt on each other.

It was the happiest everyone has been since I could remember, and it was comical that something as simple as dirt could do that.

Merrick turned to me and rubbed a dirty hand across my cheek, making me shake my head and feign disgust and rage.

"Ooh. Oooooh!" I closed my eyes and when I opened them, he was inches from my face.

"What's the matter, shorty? You can dish it out, but you can't take it?" he crooned smiling widely and speaking to me in that deep, lilting voice.

"Oh, I can take it! I just didn't expect such behavior from you! We're supposed to be a team," I shouted over the noise and laughter.

"We *are* a team, baby. We are," he said smiling, and then gave me the grittiest kiss I'd ever received while we were hit with dirt from every direction. My hand rubbed through his hair and I felt the dirt all over us. It should have been a turn off, but it wasn't. Not at all. Then mid kiss, he shoved more dirt down the front of my shirt and started bellowing a laugh so devious and hilarious that I couldn't help but laugh, too.

He had been distracting me, with kisses no less! Clever.

Before I could retaliate, we heard someone yelling behind us. Yelling *bad*, not good.

"Land sakes alive!"

We all stopped and looked up to see Mrs. Trudy standing at the hall entrance, golf club in hand and she didn't look pleased.

"What in the world is goin' on down here?" she yelled and even though I wouldn't have thought it possible, her southern drawl was even more pronounced.

"Uh.."

"Well..."

"We were just-"

"I don't care what you were *just* doing," she said mockingly. "You all need the stew beat out of you! You scared me half to death thinking the Lighters had come up from the ground or something." She grabbed her chest, steadying her breaths. "Now, what in tarnation's are ya doin'?"

"Sherry started it, Mrs. Trudy," Danny said cutting me an evil sideways smile.

"Snitch!" I yelled back at him.

Everyone laughed and started brushing themselves off. We all looked around at each other and laughed some more at our unseemly appearances. We were covered head-to-toe in dirt and smiling, showing teeth that were blindingly white against the contrast of dirty skin.

Mrs. Trudy announced that lunch was ready, but she guessed we'd all need to clean up first.

We washed our hands and ate our sandwich lunches but when it was time to go back to work, I wasn't allowed. They said I had worked hard enough already today, but I could sit and be the water girl if I wanted. Merrick, Danny and Jeff were the culprits to this idea.

Funny, they were my main targets in the dirt war.

"So, I can dirt fight, but not actually work?" I asked Merrick sarcastically.

"Yes," he said smiling and then seeing that I was going to disagree he said, "Sherry, just let me have my way. You don't need to overdo it and hauling dirt is hard work."

"I'm ok to do it."

"Don't fight me on this," he said huskily, trailing his hands down my arms, smiling that smile that sent me goose bumps.

He knew I would cave, and so did I. It didn't take much, especially with him laying on the irresistibility pretty thick.

"Fine. Fine," I said, sighing after a minute, not wanting to argue.

In truth I was feeling a little tired but didn't feel it was fair to everyone else who didn't get a break. So I was the water girl for the rest of the afternoon, getting people a cup of water from the jug when they wanted a drink. Exciting stuff.

It was very weird having people treat me this way. Even into the next week, I was still getting sweet smiles, Celeste constantly playing with my hair and spending time with me, Trudy refusing to let me help in the kitchen, insisting I needed to take it easy still. Jeff, Calvin and Ryan were always checking on me. And Danny and Merrick...don't even get me started.

A few good scares and people got antsy. As much as I appreciated it, I was ready for things to just be normal again. Well, as normal as it could be these days. We needed to start looking for others again.

The hall wasn't done but well underway and the rooms had already been dug out. Merrick was spending an insane amount of time there, along with Jeff. I checked on them frequently.

"Hey, studs," I announced as I walked into there workspace, holding two bottles of sweet tea out for two very dirty guys.

Jeff was the closest and it felt like I hadn't seen him in days. He picked me up with his dirty self and hugged me.

"Hey, you. I feel like I haven't seen you in forever," he said as he squeezed me.

"Ditto."

He placed my feet back down and looked me over.

"Look at you. You look so much better. And hey look, you can barely even see the scar on your eye anymore, but that one..." His eyes drifted to my shoulder. "I think you're stuck with that one."

"Yep, I noticed that, too." I ran my fingers over my eye. "Grateful for small favors."

"How do you feel?"

"Great, a lot better, thanks, but I think you guys are working too hard. Why don't you let someone else take over for while?"

"Danny and some of the others are already working nights on it. We need to get it done," Jeff said, graciously taking the bottle I offered to him. "Thanks."

I walked over to Merrick with his bottle. He was shirtless too and I could easily see the large red splotch still covering his left arm making me twinge with guilt and, of course, that stupid bull tattoo on his chest.

As I glanced back, I saw Jeff had his shirt off, too, but I hadn't noticed. Jeff was a very handsome black man. I mean very. As Celeste would say he was hot with a double T. His body was about twenty seven or so, he wasn't sure exactly how old his body was, as most Keepers didn't. His body was built and rugged. However, when he was next to Merrick, there was no comparison for me.

"Hey, I've been missing you," I told him, handing over the bottle.

"I know," he said apologetically, giving me the sorry face. "Me, too. Sorry. It's got to be done, though," he explained taking a few big gulps from the bottle.

"So does another shopping trip. Trudy says to tell you we're days away from empty."

He grunted with unhappiness. He knew I would probably insist on going and win because of my previous times doing it and being one of the very few non-specials here. I needed to go.

215

Plus, I couldn't stand sitting there and being told to take it easy all day. Short, fragile people with a proneness to incidents should have responsibilities too.

"Yeah. Alright, well let's stop for the night, Jeff. We gotta work up a plan. Supply runs are going to get harder the more people we have," Merrick said, downing the rest of the tea.

"I'm all for that. Let's go get some grub. I'm famished," Jeff agreed, wiping his mouth and throwing his shirt back on.

He got up and shot out of the hall in no time.

Merrick laughed at him and threw his shirt over his shoulder, grabbed my hand, linking our fingers in a slow caress as we shifted slowly down the hall. Very slowly.

I hadn't seen him in days and at night after a shower he'd slink into bed and pass out from exhaustion in mere seconds. I felt bad for him, his human body, giving him limitations he wasn't used to. Poor guy. Filthy as he was, I wanted to kiss those lips. I missed those lips.

Shortly after showers and dinner, we all sat elbow to elbow in the commons room and discussed the shopping to be done and the next trip to find others. I was happier than I'd been in days, sitting next to Merrick on the floor against the wall, his arm twined with mine, his hand on my thigh, as warm and comforting as always.

Calvin finally got a friend; the new boy, the son, Franklin. They were eating on the stairs. I was happy for him, but sad too. He hadn't asked me to play with or sing to him in a very long time. I kinda missed him.

I never told Merrick what that dream had been about, that it was about the Taker but that he had asked me to bring him Calvin. I didn't understand except that I felt protective of him, like I used to with Danny.

"Well, no Keepers should do the shopping, since Sherry saw the Taker in the store. We'll stick to the searching," Jeff started the meeting.

I wanted that job, too. Let the others do the shopping. I was interested in finding others like us.

"We'd prefer," Jeff pointed between him and Merrick. "That we take Sherry, Phillip and...Marissa, with us on search trips. The rest of you that aren't Specials or Keepers, can alternate on shopping duty. The rest can do hall duty. Is that good for everyone?"

A few nods and it was set. Merrick didn't seem to fight it this time. He must have meant what he said about me always being with him from now on, no matter what.

Someone started the record player and I felt my head start to fall and bob,

216

then Merrick got up and pulled me with both hands. Everyone else was busy or resting as he guided me to our room.

I assumed sleep was on the agenda since most of his day had been spent digging, but once inside, I saw he had a lone candle lit in the corner on a saucer. He knelt beside me and pulled me down to kneel in front of him. I didn't even remember him getting up to do all this.

The tiny room smelled of warm vanilla.

I smiled and reached for him in thanks for his romantic gesture but he was shaking. Before I could ask what was the matter, he reached up with both hands and framed my face gently. He searched my face with his gaze for a long time and I remained quiet and waited. Something was up, something important, and he was trying to sort it all out so I just waited. Then he spoke, still holding my face as he smiles at me and began.

"Sherry Elizabeth Patterson. I love you so much. If I hadn't broken the rules and watched you, falling in love with you all these years, I'd be lost. You are all that is good and right and beautiful in the world. You are the love of my eternally long life. I couldn't love anyone or anything more and no matter what you say now, I can't live without you. Please, make me the happiest...*man*...ever in the universe. Say you'll marry me."

I was completely shocked, but for once in my life but I was absolutely certain at the same time. It had been only waiting four short months for me but an eternity for him to find each other. Not to mention that was the most perfect proposal I've ever heard. For once 'universe' didn't sound cheesy, because it was true.

There was no out of body experience, no shaking with indecision. I was certain that Merrick was the one for me and that I would say yes before the words were even spoken, I knew it. I couldn't even question his sanity for wanting to be with me, not right then. All I could do was yell my answer with conviction.

"Yes! Of course I will! Yes!" I said grabbing him for an enthusiastic hug.

That was apparently more than he had hoped for, his smile was ear to ear. After he squeezed me and kissed every inch of my face, he leaned me back to sitting and opened his fist to reveal a shiny object in his hand.

"I uh...of course don't have a real ring," he said apologetically, like he could actually purchase such an item in these circumstances.

"Merrick, you know me better than that, I don't care about-" He put up a thumb over my lips to halt my speech.

"I know that. Trudy gave me this, for you. This was her one year anniversary gift from her late husband."

He pull the small, shiny thing from his palm and I heard my breath catch. It

217

was a little silver ring, with two circles connected and crossing over each other in the middle.

As he slipped it on my finger he explained, for him it meant two worlds coming together. Colliding. Making room for the other.

The tears were falling before I knew it, or felt them. It was so perfect. Ah, I loved it! He smiled gratefully at my reaction and I threw my arms around his neck and kissed him, tears still streaming. I could taste them when our lips parted and opened together.

His hands and lips were enthusiastic but gentle, this was about more than lust. I was beat, as I'm doubly sure he was and the kissing wasn't like normal, the electricity wasn't overwhelming, it was just present, like a sweet reminder. There were more important things right then than desire.

I pulled back to breathe, pressing my face into his neck. Was I dreaming again? Merrick was always present in my good dreams lately. Maybe he'd shake me awake in a minute before I got too worked up over it.

No, it was real! I couldn't believe it.

"What are we going to do?" I asked, in no way disparaging.

"I'm taking you on a search trip, alone. We are going to find the first open church and throw a fifty at the preacher who'll just marry us with the words and forget the paperwork." He sounded so confident, so collected.

"Wow. Got it all planned out, huh?" I said, not able to stop the spreading smile at his cunningness.

"Yes. And I understand if you won't want to tell anyone around here. It can be our secret. I know they are kind of on your case, about me," he said and looked down at his hands.

"Hmmm. Keep it a secret that the best guy ever asked me to marry him?"

"Sherry, I know you've gotten some flack for me not being...human. Just like I did with you for *being* human. It's all right. I understand and I don't care. I just want to marry you."

"Like I said, this is the end of the world as we know it. It shouldn't matter to anyone what I do anymore if it makes me happy. And I am happy. Very. If you're comfortable with it, I am."

"Honey, I'm the happiest man alive. There is no one I wouldn't want to tell."

He smiled, rubbing his fingers over the ring on my finger where it would stay.

I was about to cry again when he wiped my cheeks with his thumbs, kissed me softly on my eyelids and lips, then pulled me down next to him. The burgundy sleeping bag being pulled up to me by the strong hands that watch over me, would be over me forever.

When the time came to tell Danny, the next day, I felt sick. Not because I had doubts or was ashamed, but Danny was the only family I had left. He felt like he had to protect me, and even though he likes Merrick, a lot, this was different. Way different. I mean, it had only been four months, even though the world was crazy, it was still soon if you thought about it for a nineteen year old to be getting married.

However, even though I kinda sorta explained my uneasiness to tell Danny, Merrick seemed very excited about the whole thing. I had no idea he had any desires for this kind of human stuff. He assured me Danny would be fine and happy for us.

Merrick went to get breakfast, leaving me to finish dressing. When I was done, I headed for the commons room.

I saw Danny coming around the kitchen corner. I suddenly couldn't breathe. I couldn't disappoint the one person I had left in the world other than Merrick.

But that was silly! He wouldn't be mad but before I could speak Danny grabbed me in a big hug, pulling me off the floor.

"Congratulations," he whispered in my ear.

"Wha- Merrick," I realized.

"Yeah. He said you wanted to tell me, but thought I'd be angry. Why would you think that?"

"I don't know," I said as I fidgeted with my necklace charm. "I just imagined telling Mom and Dad, and seeing disappointment on Mom's face for whatever reason. Not dated long enough, not vegan enough, not independent enough, not human enough, not alien enough. Then I just couldn't tell you. I'm sorry. I know that's stupid," I said through tears that were already running down my face.

"Don't cry, shorty. I'm happy if you're happy. It doesn't matter what other people think. I know you love him, and I know he loves you. That's all that matters, right?"

Then I heard an apology in my mind.

Sorry. I saw you were worried about telling him so I thought I'd help.

Merrick was standing in the kitchen doorway with a glass of juice. Relief swept over me. I mouthed him a 'thank you', as I swiped my cheeks with my hand.

Anytime, you know that. I'm headed down to the new hall to get Jeff. Be back in a bit for us to leave. Relax. Get some coffee and don't worry so much. He winked. *I love you.*

I nod and mouth 'love you'.

"Gross," Danny joked. "Get a room."

He laughed as I punched his arm. We sat and talked for a while, Celeste joining us for a bit, and it took all my strength to grab her and calm her before she could scream when we told her about Merrick and me. I knew she'd keep our secret and she hugged me at least seven times before I could get away.

And she cried. I'd never seen her cry before and it warmed my insides to know she cared that much about us.

I explained that she couldn't tell a soul and she agreed. Danny hugged her to him with an affectionate and amused face on for her tears when I left to go find Merrick. I looked back over my shoulder and couldn't help, but think that they looked so sweet. Then it's time to leave. Our first trip out with Marissa.

I had hoped it'd prove to be useful, without the pain and visions this time.

Merrick - Da Dum Da Dum
Chapter 20

She said yes.

Yes. Yes, she will marry me. She didn't even hesitate. What did I do to deserve this girl?

Enough, just accept it already. As crazy as it was, she loves me. She loves me like I love her. Well, maybe not like that, but close. She looked happy and she was so cute fretting over telling Danny.

I knew Danny would be ok. It was always been so funny to watch them. As protective as she was over him, he was with her, too. She never saw it until now.

And Trudy was a Godsend. That ring was so perfect for Sherry, petite, beautiful and sentimental. I couldn't believe how intuitive she was. She just knew, knew I wanted to do this for Sherry.

The only person I talked to about it was with Jeff and that was a very brief and quiet conversation and all I did was tell him I was thinking about what it would be like to be married. That was all, but Trudy was a very understanding and open lady just offering it to me, no questions, no mocking, nothing. Like she had known or heard somehow. She just put it in my hand with her sweet, twangy smile, told me her husband gave it to her, winked and walked away.

How in the worlds did Phillip turn out to be such a jerk with a woman for a mother like that? Matter of fact. I'd ask Max right now.

I saw Max down the hall with Jeff going over some of the plans for the new beams.

"Hey. About ready?" I asked.

"Yep. Ready," Jeff answered.

"Hold on Jeff. Max?"

"Yeah?" Max answered, not looking up.

"Tell me about Trudy, her husband."

"Well," he said standing upright and scratching his chin. "Honestly, there isn't much to tell. He used to be good to them. The first fifteen years of their marriage were great in Trudy's eyes. Then he lost his job and they lost their first home to foreclosure. He was never the same after that. He was pretty hateful. He died eight years later. Trudy had four other sons, Phillip is the youngest. Her husband didn't set a very good example for them after he started drinking and...well, other things. I know Phillip is a jerk, and I've talked to him once already about Sherry."

"You have?"

"Yes. You can't keep me out remember?" He poked at his head and smiled. "You were worried because Sherry was upset about him...staring...a lot."

"Oh. Yeah. Well thanks, just curious."

Merrick, let's go, times-a-ticking.

"All right, let's go," I answered Jeff out loud.

It was becoming more natural to speak that way, even with the Keepers, unless I was thinking about it.

So, Trudy gave me the ring from the best part of her marriage, wishing us a well blessing. Poor lady. I guess I can't help but feel a little bad for Phillip too, though that doesn't excuse any of his behavior towards Sherry.

As we walked back I remembered earlier, asking Danny if I could have his blessing to marry Sherry.

I had walked back into the kitchen, saw Danny and Trudy talking. Trudy was strangely smiling widely, like she knew something was up. I wondered if she knew I proposed already? But how?

"Danny. Can I talk to you for a minute?" I asked him.

I was still holding my cup of coffee Trudy made for me earlier because I didn't have the heart to tell her I didn't like coffee.

"Sure man. What's up?"

"Let's go sit on the stairs." I led the way and he followed, straight-faced with his hands in his pockets.

Not suspecting anything.

"Ok. What's up?" he asked again as we sat down.

"Well, how is everything with you and Celeste?"

"We're good."

"You're not just with her because she's the only one that you can be with, are you? Because if you are, that's just-"

"Uh, no. Thanks for the vote of confidence, dude." He laughed. "Is that how you see me? Is that how I treated girls when you used to watch..." I raised my eyebrow at him. "Ok, maybe, some. Celeste is different. Yes, I admit, I liked her at first just because she was young and cute, but now, I feel like she... belongs to me. I would've went after her if I'd known her before all this."

"Ok. I just want you to be careful. Be happy."

He eyed me curiously.

"What?"

"Ryan told me about the conscience thing, the buzzing. Do you still have that with me?"

"Of course. You're still my charge."

"But I thought that because of everything going on, you know, you all just kinda watch out for everyone. I thought you weren't just...my Keeper anymore," he said shrugging.

"Well that's how I feel about it too. That we should be here for everyone but it's not that easy. My conscience doesn't buzz for everyone."

"Hmm."

"I'm...sorry? I don't want you to feel weird about it, I know it's awkward, and I've tried to tone it down, but I can't help my still being somewhat protective of you to-"

"No. No, it's fine," he assured and waved me off. "I understand you don't have any control over that, I told you, Ryan told me all about it. I just don't want you to feel like you *have* to be like that. Like with Sherry, I know you feel just as responsible for her as you do for me, but she's not your charge and you don't, uh, buzz for her." He rolled his eyes apparently at something he'd said. "But it's fine. Whatever you need to do, I'm fine with it and you don't have to worry about just Sherry and me. We're all family now."

Good jump-in point as any would have been.

"Ok, thanks. Um, speaking of family, I know I asked you about Sherry a few weeks ago. Well, I have another confession."

"Uh oh. It can't be *that* bad."

"It's not. Sherry is planning on telling you, but she was worried you would be angry. See...I asked her to...marry me last night. She said yes."

I waited for the reaction. Maybe I had read Danny wrong, but Sherry was wrong. His smile was huge and happy.

"Hey, man! That's great! Wow. I can't believe it. I have a brother in law!"

He slapped me on the back while he spoke. Typical congratulatory male manner.

"Thanks. I just want to make her happy. I know you know how great she is, but I just..." for some reason I couldn't speak.

The words I was searching for to explain to her own brother how great she was and how much I loved her and wanted to make her happy just didn't exist.

"I know how much you love her. I couldn't be happier, really. She's lucky. And so are you," he said proudly.

"Absolutely, I am." I reached for his hand to shake, but he grabbed me in one his hugs usually reserved for family and Sherry.

He confirmed my thoughts.

"Welcome to the family, man."

As we walked back to the kitchen, right before he saw Sherry and ran to her, beaming, I could've sworn I saw Phillip sitting in the hall out of the corner of my eye, but when I looked back, there were just dark shadows.

Swift Kick In The...
Chapter 21

We were getting ready to leave now, all of us, the supply run and the search party. I turned the ring on my finger, around and around. It didn't look like an engagement ring. Seemed I'd have a new piece of jewelry to fidget with.

No one would think anything of it. We decided to keep it quiet until we actually got married, of course Trudy knew, and Danny and Celeste, and all the Keepers who wouldn't stay out of Merrick's mind, so, that was about everyone anyway.

Trudy was in the kitchen and I made a break for her to thank her, but Jeff caught me first, grabbing me sideways, I didn't see him and he startled me.

He picked me up and swung me around in his big bear hug, per the usual. I guess I just looked pick up-able and swing-able.

I wondered what in the world was on his mind this time and then he spoke to me, only me and I felt like an idiot for not remembering the Keepers mind.

Congratulations! Merrick can't stop thinking about it. You'll be getting hugs all day from the rest of the Keepers.

"Thanks. I don't know why, but...I kind of thought you might be disappointed."

Never. I am beginning to rethink a lot of things lately. You are a wonderful human, Sherry. Just what he needs and wants. I've never, in my thousands of years, seen a Keeper so happy and content and alive. We may live forever, but what's the point if you don't actually live? I know you love him more than life and you'll make him happy. That's all that matters to me.

I wanted to cry. For a split second I got hung up on the 'thousands of years' remark and realized that must apply to Merrick too, but I was already crying. Thanks Jeff, appreciate it. Jeff drew attention to us with his bear hug and people were looking at us, not hearing our silent conversation.

I sometimes forgot how funny we must look when we do this. Just staring into each other's eyes like weirdos, when really I'm listening. Merrick and I did it quite often, but I never think about what it looked like to others.

Merrick rounded the corner, seeing our embrace. The big lug still hadn't put me down and now they are the ones silently conversing and Merrick smiled widely. He walked over to us and Jeff placed me easily back on my feet. Merrick had apparently heard Jeff's little speech to me and was as happy as I was about his warmth.

Merrick had seen me hug Jeff tons of times and never once looked jealous or uneasy about it, even though I seem to be the only one that he ever did that to. Jeff was still just Jeff. He was like...a favorite uncle, full of wisdom and opinions and advice but still fun to be around.

The mind reading thing between the two probably helped also, no secrets among Keepers. Jeff was so great for me to have in absence of my parents and any other relatives. He was definitely saner than Margaret and Robert Patterson.

Mrs. Trudy finally caught me on the way out and I whispered a quick 'thank you' before heading up the stairs.

Kay smiled at me from the back wall.

I'm really happy for you, Sherry.

I smiled and nodded to her. This wasn't so bad. What had I been so worried about?

Merrick, Jeff, Phillip, Marissa and I headed upstairs. We took the Jeep the newcomers brought with them, since they would need the van for shopping.

I was glad Jeff decided to bring Marissa, but a little confused as to why. She was still a Special and none of the other Specials were allowed out of the bunker, but I didn't press.

She seemed genuinely remorseful for what she did to me and still very quiet and reserved but I needed to try to stop thinking like a human girl and more like a Keeper. Merrick was right. I trusted people a little too much.

We got in the Jeep, the sun was shining. It wasn't cold at all, in fact it was blazing. Maybe that was the difference. The sun made that much of a difference these days as to affect the temperature this much.

Marissa drove and Jeff took shotgun, leaving me in a Merrick and Phillip sandwich in the back. I scooted as far left as physics would allow. Merrick seemed to understand and scooted as well, putting his arm over my shoulders as a shield. I heard Phillip snort but I didn't look over.

Merrick, however, did. "Is there a problem, Phillip?"

"Nope, just dandy. Say, sugar, what's that on your finger?"

"Trudy gave it to me. Actually..." feeling the need to reiterate to make sure that Phillip understands, "Trudy gave it to Merrick, who gave it to me."

"That was my dad's ring. She shouldn't have done that," he said bitterly. "That's too bad if you don't approve," I said flatly and cold, turning my body to face Merrick.

We had barely left the store driveway and he was already on my last nerve.

Merrick and I talked about Lighters more and some of the other creatures that could be making an entrance. Merrick wasn't worried, I was just curious. I loved hearing about all the different things. You just didn't know what was out there.

He explained that Lighters retain some of the memories of the deceased person's body they go into, unlike the Keepers. Only Takers can absorb others, Lighters can't do anything but kill. Specials, Lighters and Markers can be absorbed. Normal people can too but most just die and become Lighters if they snatch the body quick enough. That was one more reason they wanted the Specials, to feed the Taker with them and ruin any chances of whatever tasks may come out of them.

That makes me wonder if all the Lighters and Keepers were here yet. I asked. He said there would be no way to tell for sure but he doubted it. The Keepers and Lighters would be scrambling over bodies the second someone died, but there were a lot of them. He explained that Keepers couldn't concentrate on anything but their charge, because of their conscience when they were in trouble, so Keepers would have done anything to be first in a body to come here.

It was horrifyingly fascinating and he could tell, his eyes lit up like mine telling the story of when he came here before and met a Distinct, a Special but an animal. Apparently animals have purposes, too, tasks to be fulfilled. This one happened to be a dog.

They didn't have souls or speaking brains, but they were still important enough to influence and hinder people's actions, lives, and efforts. I laughed thinking how much my mom would love to hear that.

There was not much to tell him that he didn't know about me, but I talked anyway. He asked me on certain days or events, questions like 'What were you thinking when that happened' or 'What was your favorite part?' or 'Why did you do that?'.

I forgot sometimes that he couldn't see my mind, badly as he wanted to. Now I knew I was grateful for that blessing. All those embarrassing kissing and touching moments where I couldn't breathe, all the times I thought worse of him, thinking he hated me. All the things I thought about him when he wasn't around. Oh, no.

Marissa pulled off the road suddenly, slamming on the brakes and forcing us to grab on to something to stay seated. The Jeep's backend swerved in the dirt sending gravel flying.

Jeff looked puzzled. He had been trying to reach another Keeper this whole time. Nothing. Merrick would try on the way back.

"Why are we stopping?" Jeff asked coarsely.

"There." She pointed at an open field.

"Ok. Where there? What?" Jeff asked tersely.

He clearly hadn't completely forgiven her.

"I see some sort of...ditch or river? This used to be an old town out here a long time ago. Maybe it's from that, I don't know, that's just what I see."

"I've got this," Phillip chimed. "It's a little *stuffy* back here anyway," he said glancing at Merrick and me, and jumping out before anyone could say anything, running.

"What? Wait!" Jeff called, but immediately just shook his head and sat back forcefully.

We sat there for a few minutes, watching Phillip peruse the field.

Merrick had been very touchy feely with me, to my satisfaction. I wondered if it was because Phillip was there. I had stretched out in Phillip's absence, my head leaned back on Merrick's chest with my knees up in the seat. Merrick was rubbing little circles into my thigh with his thumb on my jeans.

Phillip waved to us, telling us to join him. At first I thought Merrick would insist on my staying in the Jeep, but no. He opened the door and pulled me out right behind him.

We all got out and started walking the field. The dead, yellow grass was tall and scratchy on my flip-flopped feet. The weather had already begun to change. The sun had gone down and it was getting colder already. We couldn't see what Phillip was looking at, but he was stunned, staring at the ground.

Merrick held my hand and the closer we got to where Phillip was standing, he pulled me farther and farther back behind him. I peeked around his arm to see what it was that had everyone so stunned silent.

It was a black skeleton.

A perfect set of bones laid out in order on the ground, but it wasn't human, it was a Marker. You could see the thick wings on the sides very distinctively.

At first, I didn't see the big deal. It was dead, just like they had killed the other one.

Merrick and Jeff stared at it like a puzzle for a long time. Finally the suspense was too much for me.

"Babe, what is it? What's the matter?" I asked Merrick, Phillip shooting a quick annoyed glance at my term of endearment.

"This Marker was killed by something other than a Keeper or a human. The bones are here, which means it didn't burn. That can only mean one thing. The Taker is hunting. He killed it by absorbing it like I told you before and left it here."

Yes, now I saw. Hmmm. So he hunts. This just kept getting better and better.

The sun was going down, making the air chilled. I looked out beyond the cliff that Marissa had seen on the horizon. Goose bumps crept up from looking at the bones and thinking about what being absorbed had to feel like. Merrick's arm tenses under my hand. I thought it was because he felt me shiver, but then Marissa screamed sharply. I whipped around and saw it.

A lone Lighter.

The Lighter was standing between us and the car. Still. Motionless. When he finally moved he was so quick my eyes couldn't adjust to keep up and then he slowed to a menacing pace. His black hair was curly and his black clothes baggy. His boots squeaked in the now cool, damp, dead grass.

It had begun to rain, when I wasn't paying attention. This was not the Taker I had seen, this was another Lighter.

Merrick told me to cover my ears in my mind and must have told Marissa and Phillip the same thing because they followed suit. 'Fly me to the Moon' hummed so loudly in my ears I could hear nothing else, muffled but still blocking the sound. I could see the Lighter was speaking as he inched closer to us.

Merrick was still standing in front of me, my shield. I didn't like this. Could they fight a Lighter? Why, if they could, would an outnumbered Lighter just walk up to our group and ask for it then?

The Lighters lips moved again, I hummed a little louder as he inched even closer. I couldn't take my eyes off him for some reason. He just looked so...evil. The body he was in was young and handsome. Some of the curls were coming across his forehead and came down a little past his ears in what would have been adorable before. He had a tattoo of a spider web on the side of his neck. He looked like some kinda cute Goth college kid but all that is displaced by how evil he looked now.

He danced around like he was chanting around a campfire. Then with a quick movement from Jeff he was behind the Lighter in a flash. It turned to him and Merrick, also in a flash. Merrick pulled me gently to the ground, holding a hand over me telling me to stay down in my mind.

Jeff looked for something to use, I assumed, to stab the creature like before. There was nothing, in the wide open field, just grass.

I saw Jeff changing tactics, flashing around in a circle, confusing the Lighter. His boot connected with the Lighters jaw and he fell back, feet over head.

Then the hail started.

Jeff ran over and put his foot on the Lighters hand, crushing it into the ground. They could only hurt each other by touch of the skin then, I realized.

He knocked Jeff's feet out from under him with a swift kick to his calf and got back to his feet. I glanced over at Merrick and it was hard to believe all this had happened in just a few seconds.

The Lighter eyed us three on the ground and made his way over towards us.

Merrick was moving. He ran and grabbed the Lighters jacket back, slinging him over his head and down, backwards to the ground. It must be equally as painful to Lighters to touch the Keepers because, even though the Lighter could easily reach Jeff's bare leg now, he didn't touch him. He looked...scared.

It was strange to see these human faces so full of hate and loathing and yet so afraid at the same time. But...I thought they couldn't fear? No emotion. Where Keepers have emotion, Lighters have none.

"Marissa! Phillip!" I yelled, making sure they were still ok.

She was holding her ears and couldn't hear me. Duh. Phillip was too, but his eyes were closed. I began to crawl on my elbows towards Marissa, not easy while cupping my ears. I reached her and bumped her arm with mine, she let out a yelp and looked my direction.

I wished more than any other moment that I could have the Keeper's mind talking thing, right then.

The hail falling wasn't that big but still didn't feel good pelting on our open and exposed spines and heads. I was shivering in my tank top.

I needed to rethink wearing tank tops out of the bunker. It never worked out.

The Lighter swung up and around in a twist to regain his balance and turned to us once again. I looked up and met his dark hateful gaze. He had the smallest twitch of a smile, I may have even imagined it. Then he blurred towards us and Merrick ran to jump in front of me, us. The Lighter stopped but continued to eye us and Merrick with deadly intent written all over his face.

He moved closer, more left and back a small bit, then wider left. I studied him and tried to figure out what the dance was for but when he quickly blurs to get past Merrick I saw that it was just a diversion.

I heard Phillip yell and Merrick looked back to see what was going on as did I.

When I looked back, Merrick was jumping directly in front of me as the Lighter made a swoop for my arm. He knocked the Lighter back but not before the Lighter did a roundabout sending Merrick flying through the air at the same time the Lighter flew the opposite direction. The Lighter kicked him in the chest across the field the same time that Merrick hit him in the chest. Merrick landed with a very visible thump and skid that looked extremely painful.

I lost it and screamed for him, uncovering my ears for just a second before hearing Merrick's voice in my head.

Keep your ears covered! I'm fine, honey. I'm fine.

Lies. Merrick's breakable body lay on the ground at least twenty feet from us, him barely lifting his head to look at me.

I glanced at Phillip, still shutting out the world. When I looked back, Marissa was gone that quick.

Looking up to the Lighter, I saw he had her by the throat and was hanging her up in the air by it.

"Muse..." I heard the Lighter start to speak, a growl really, and I hummed as loud as I could and tried to think of something to do to help.

Marissa's ears were uncovered, trying to keep him from choking her, attempting to swat at his face and scratch at his neck but couldn't reach. She was barely holding herself up, trying desperately to hold on to his black long sleeves and gloved hands.

Her feet make contact a few times, but it didn't seem to faze him. Merrick and Jeff both ran over and assess, trying to figure out what to do. Merrick had hobbled over, grabbing me and pulling me back behind him again. Marissa finally got a solid slap across the Lighter's face.

Then all of a sudden, the Lighter dropped Marissa on her bottom to the ground. She rolled over choking and gasping.

The Lighter took off running through the field, full speed, a black blur. We all watched as he ran towards the cliff.

In one single bound he threw himself up in the air with his arms spread wide, like a high dive, and plunged into the ravine below from the cliffs edge.

I gasped in disbelief.

Why on earth would he do that? He couldn't fly. Can he like a Marker?

Then one bright flash and thunder of lightning broke through the sky right through the ravine. What in the world was that?

I looked at Phillip and he too was stunned, having opened his eyes. Glancing at Marissa, I saw her holding her throat, rolling on the ground, coughing and gasping still. Jeff was checking on her, trying to examine her throat. Merrick was beside me, kneeling on the ground. I dropped down too.

"What was that? Lightning?"

I thought back and I hadn't seen lightning since the moon disappeared.

"Yes. It was something that would look like lightning to you. When they die, the light from within them is dispelled. "Are you ok?" he asked me, but he didn't look so good himself.

"Yes. Why did he do that?"

"Marissa," he breathed painfully.

Then it hit me why she was swatting at him, more than just trying to connect a hit to release her, she was trying to touch him to will him to jump. The Muse's wrath.

Then the hail stopped, it just sprinkled a light cold rain on my already wet and freezing body.

"Oh, wait. Are you ok?" I remembered the kick Merrick had received and immediately ran my hands over him in search of injuries.

"I'm fine."

"Liar."

Pulling up his shirt I saw the huge boot size print and red purple mark over his ribs. I sucked in a breath through my teeth in agony for him. I touched it and he winced and groaned, but quickly stopped. He was a bad actor, too.

"Oh! Merrick. Oh, no. I think he broke your ribs. Does it hurt bad?" Stupid question I asked.

"I'm fine, honey." He grabbed my face with a palm, reassuring me, but his face was not lying to me like his lips were.

I could see the unfamiliar-to-a-Keeper pain all over it. How much worse did pain feel to them, to someone who had never experienced it?

And then I remembered it was my fault.

"You did this for me, to protect me. Look at you." I ran my hand ever so slightly and softly over his bruise. "You took this for me."

"I told you I would do anything for you," he said firmly, looking right at me. "It's fine, really. Don't worry about me. Let's get you up and back in the car. You're freezing."

Glancing around I saw Phillip, still sitting. He hadn't moved, but uncovered his ears. He was looking at us in disgust, but I couldn't conjure up any annoyance right then.

Marissa was breathing a little better. Jeff was helping her up and she was standing, leaning on her knees.

"Marissa? You ok?" I asked her, but I couldn't leave Merrick's side to physically check on her.

"I'm...ok..." she said between strained breaths.

She wasn't though. You could see the bruises on her neck forming already. Those were definitely going to be purple and yellow and not pretty.

Maybe that would get her some sympathy, and maybe everyone would stop being so cross with her about what happened with me.

Merrick's breathing was strained. He tried to get up but could barely get to his knees, let alone to his feet. I realized there was no way I could lift him by myself.

Jeff was already walking back to the Jeep with Marissa, carrying her in his arms. She must've not been able to walk well. Looking at Phillip, I could tell he knew what I was about to ask. He waited, staring bemused. He was going to make me ask for his help, out loud.

"Phillip, can you help me with him please?" I asked, meeting his gaze, trying to not show the anger I felt for him.

"I guess I don't really have a choice, do I?" he said softly, surprising me when I expected sarcasm.

He came over getting on the opposite side of Merrick. We lifted and Merrick yelped. I looked and saw that Phillip was grabbing around Merrick's side to lift him.

Lifting him by his ribs.

We were standing and I was furious. This was stupid! Why intentionally hurt Merrick just because he was mad at me?

Jerk!

Buffoon!

As soon I saw Merrick was standing steadily, I released his shoulder and held his arm to steady him and shoved Phillip's shoulder as hard as I could, stunning him with my gesture more than actually moving him. Of course no real damage was done. I think I moved back even farther than he did, with my puny excuse for a body.

"You did that on purpose you jerk! Just go back to the car, Phillip! I've got him," I shouted.

"Whatever you say, sugar."

"Ah! Go!" I yelled through my clenched teeth.

I put Merrick's arm around my shoulders again and helped him as we walked. Phillip sprinted his way and sat in the back seat, watching us hobble back.

"Wow. That was so...sexy," Merrick managed to get out through his heavy breaths, he was even smiling a little.

"What?" I ask puzzled.

What is he talking about? Did I miss something?

"You trying to defend me." He chuckled but winced.

Aha. The human male in him finally made an appearance.

"Yeah, well, I wish I could have done more damage. He's such a jerk! He knew what he was doing."

"Yes, he did. He's just angry at me for winning. He thought you would pick him."

"What? What are you talking about?" I stopped him and looked up at him.

"He told me," he said matter-of-factly.

"He did? When?"

"He had a 'talk' with me, more than once actually, and he explained why you should be with him instead of me. That he would be better for you and he was going to make you see that," he said, his voice strained.

"What? That's the...dumbest thing I've ever heard."

"It was all worth it to watch you just now."

The smile on his face was that of pure elation, no mockery.

"Shut up. You're delirious," I said smiling.

I couldn't help but smile at his enjoyment of the situation.

Jeff ran back to help us, reaching to grab under Merrick's other arm, as Phillip should have, to help steady the weight.

"Is Marissa ok?" I asked him not looking so we wouldn't get off balance.

"Yeah. She will be. I'll get Phillip to drive home so you're not stuck with him in the back. What in the worlds was that about? I've never seen you hit anybody, Sherry."

"He deserved it," I said flatly.

I glanced over and saw he was looking into Merrick's mind, seeing what he wanted, he smiled and started laughing.

"I see. Well, it's nice to know that if I'm not here, at least Merrick's got a bodyguard." Jeff kept trying to stifle his laugh, but it just was not working.

"Ha ha. I can't even protect my own puny existence, let alone anyone else," I sulked.

"Worked didn't it? What is it they say? It's not the size of the fighter in the fight, it's the size of the fight in-" he started with a very mocking playful tone so I ended it.

"Don't you dare finish that sentence, Jeff! Don't you dare," I yelled playfully. He still hadn't stopped laughing. "I'm glad to see you finally got the humor thing down. Real funny."

We were all laughing out loud. It was the very first time since meeting them, we all had a laugh about something together. Though, it was at my expense, and Merrick was making it worse by trying not to laugh because of the pain, and that in turn made Jeff laugh even harder, I was more than ok with it.

Those two were my family now and families laughed at each other.

I was amazed at the love pouring out of me for them, considering the strange string of today's events. Amazed and overflowing.

Phillip was in the driver's seat, looking at us like were nuts and Marissa's face was not far from that, as we climbed in the back and headed home. Considering the events that had just transpired, I didn't blame them for thinking we were strange, but I wasn't about to explain myself to Phillip.

Marissa seemed like she didn't care much anyway. She kept holding her throat and looking out the window the whole way home. I caught Phillip's glare in the rearview mirror a couple times but looked away quickly and tried to focus on making Merrick comfortable for the ride home.

We didn't stop for anything, no one tried to call any more Keepers. No one was sure of what a lone Lighter was doing out in the field either or why the Taker would be out there hunting, leaving the Markers skeleton for us to find. The mysteries kept piling up and it seemed to me, more day by day, that this was unprecedented.

Merrick, Jeff and the rest of the Keepers seemed to be just as puzzled as the rest of us lately.

Maybe things wouldn't go like they thought, be different. Maybe things would work out, for our benefit. For now, I was going to dream that just that could be possible.

Foe's Folly
Chapter 22

The past couple of days had been spent with me tending to Merrick and his bruised and broken ribs after our fight with the Lighter in the field. Merrick made out like I was fussing over him but I could tell he loved every minute of it. And I loved doing it. I loved taking care of him.

We didn't have anything, but over-the-counter pain medicine for him, but he seemed to not be too bad off. I massaged his shoulders and neck and arms daily, trying to relax him so he'd rest and sleep better, to which he moaned and sighed appropriately over. Even he couldn't resist my massaging charms.

He was getting awfully pampered.

Between Mrs. Trudy making him peanut brittle, Jeff and everybody else checking on him constantly and my massages, which it seemed he'd grown rather fond of, he was getting entirely spoiled. I was grateful that he, even though it was pretty much forced on him, was accepting something for himself.

We spent a lot of time 'resting' in our closet of a room. Merrick said he needed the rest and I needed to be there to nurse him back to health.

I didn't mind, of course I didn't.

It was awfully hard though, trying to fit kissing embraces around his sore ribs but it made going too far impossible. Good for him because he didn't have the strength to fight off my advances.

"You're killing me, Sherry," he would say as I kissed him none too easily. I apologized emphatically, which he'd brush off, laugh and pull me closer. Or, he'd say, "Honey, I think you're seriously misunderstanding the duties of a nurse," and then we'd chuckle.

Kay and Trudy had examined him and we all determined a couple of the ribs were broken but there wasn't anything to do but wait for them to heal and rest with icepacks.

We talked about the Lighter with everyone else in a meeting and the fact that Marissa saved us. Jeff explained we were unprepared and there was nothing to be used to run the Lighter through with, as that was the only way to kill one, and was wondering what we were going to do. Some were still skeptical, saying Marissa was only saving her own skin. They were right, that was true, but I didn't buy it.

Yes, it was dangerous to have a Muse around, she could have just as easily touched any of us and made us jump off that ravine but I had to believe she wanted to be here and help us.

Jeff explained that Lighters didn't have the same brains as humans and they instantly react to a Muse's wrath. They don't fight it because they don't know how to they just do it, whatever it is, without question, without hesitation.

Thankfully, Jeff didn't feel the need to disclose everything and left my embarrassing temper tantrum with Phillip out of it.

Phillip no longer attended any of the meetings, nor sat in the commons room with us. He spent most of his time in the store, pouting. I wondered why he had been so adamant on us staying with them in the beginning.

He wasn't making any friends here and didn't seem interested in talking to anyone or trying, even with Trudy anymore.

Maybe he regretted us coming and invading all their tiny space. I kinda felt bad, thinking about it like that, but he invited us, sought us out and this was the end of the normal world, no time to be stingy with the underground bunkers.

After about a week and a half, Merrick was moving around and walking almost normally again. Sad to say that I kind of missed him bedridden, tending to him instead of him to me, per the usual. Because he was better, so were the make out sessions, though, he still was standing his ground, a stone, unmovable.

I thought it was silly, but I had to admit, it was awfully sweet, his whole bit to protect me from myself and my lack of will power. Shouldn't this situation be in reverse?

The store run had came through without a hitch, no Lighters were spotted and they had returned safely so we would continue on with that route until we no longer could, forcing our hand into another avenue. I didn't want to think about what that might be.

Sitting in the commons room on the couch, Jeff and Merrick talked some about what happened in the field that day.

"I've never seen a Marker skeleton. The only reason that that Lighter was there, was to wait for someone to come. He wouldn't have been out there alone otherwise. The Taker absorbed that Marker, so he's hunting for himself. Hmm. But why was... Hmmm," Jeff prodded himself and Merrick for a theory, while we sat on the smaller but newer couch the newbies brought with them.

With Merrick's midsection less colorful and sore, he was constantly holding me now that he could. His lap was my favorite seat in the house, especially since every other seat in the house was literally taken.

It wasn't going to be enough to expand the sleeping rooms. We were barely able to all fit in the commons room anymore together, but we couldn't split up. Safety in numbers, building an army, all that.

Calvin and Franklin were playing in the hall, by the stairs. I patted Merrick's hand to tell him I was getting up and headed over to see what they were up to, without interrupting Jeff, leaving a room full of chatter behind me.

They were playing spoons. Twelve year olds were playing card games. Times had changed. As I walked towards them I realized I'd never been behind the stairs before.

It was dark back there and I never thought much about it. Past the boys, I saw a room off to the side. Must be Phillip's. As I peeked through the half closed door I gasped. I couldn't believe what my eyes were telling me.

It was huge. It was the size of the commons room, if not more, piled wall to wall with lots of his stuff. Personal stuff that none of the rest of us had. I understood, this was his place first, but jeez, we had all been cramped and bunched in the other room, not to mention the small sleeping quarters. Twenty people could have slept comfortably in this room.

I didn't go in, just looked from the hallway. The bed was ginormous with at least eight pillows of different sizes and color stacked against the headboard. He had a small red lava lamp on the bedside stand that was left on. Posters, provocative posters at that, lined the walls. C.D.s everywhere. Huge stereo system near his desk on the opposite side of his bed.

I even saw bags of chips, candy and can drinks lined up on the bedside table. Food hoarding.

There was a tabletop fan blowing, oscillating on the floor pointed to his bed. I thought about all the times we'd sat out in the commons rooms sweating sometimes because it could be so stuffy down here. I gasped again in utter disbelief.

Just when I thought I couldn't be more disappointed in Phillip and his behavior, I was wrong again. What a selfish-.

"Hey. Snooping?" the voice behind me was Phillip.

"Just looking around. Hadn't been back here before. That's quite a room. No wonder you kept it a secret."

"What's that supposed to mean?" he said taking a step towards me.

"It means, there's tons of room in there, Phillip. And tons of people out there. We've been breaking our backs trying to make more room for people and this room is huge. Not to mention all the stuff you've been keeping to yourself. It's just...a little selfish." It came out way softer than I intended, but I was in shock.

238

"This is my place, and you're a guest. Be happy I let you stay here at all," he barked.

"You're right. I'm sorry, I didn't mean to pry. I just never imagined you being this way." I began to walk off but he grabbed my arm gently.

"We could share it you know." All traces of anger were gone and replaced with soft pleading. "You could come stay in here with me and be more...comfortable," he suggested, pulling me closer as he did so.

"Phillip," I sighed, dreading what I was going to have to do. "We talked about this, didn't we? I'm with Merrick."

"I know, but I can't give up on you. I know you can't really want to spend the rest of your life with him."

"Why not?" I asked, humoring him.

Wanting to hash this out once and for all.

"Because, the obvious. He's not human. He doesn't feel, it's fake. It's a copy of the emotions his body felt before he took it over."

"I'm sorry, Phillip, I don't agree. You don't have to like it, but you do have to respect my decision."

"You can't do this. He doesn't know what you need. He can't understand you like I can," he breathed.

He moved to caress my face. I backed into the wall to evade him but he followed. His fingers were cool, nothing like Merrick's warm ones, on my cheek.

"Phillip. Please don't."

"I want you to see that it's not just him that can give you goose bumps." As if to prove him right, gooseflesh spread rapidly down my arms. He ran his finger down my arm too. "See." He closed his eyes. "Mmm, you are even softer than I imagined," he almost moaned the words and pressed me further into the wall.

"Stop." I pushed his hand away. "Tickling will give anyone goose bumps, Phillip. It's not goose bumps I'm looking for. Please stop this. I don't want to fight with you anymore."

"I don't want to either. I just can't sit back and watch you throw everything away," he said softly.

"I'm not throwing anything away. I love him. This isn't a game to me. I want to be your friend, but you've got to stop this. It makes me uncomfortable."

"What can I do to change your mind? What? Tell me. Anything. I'd do anything for you, Sherry," he asked desperately, pulling my hand to his chest.

I felt sorry for him. I also questioned him, his feelings for me had moved rather swiftly with absolutely no help from me.

"Nothing, Phillip. There's nothing you can do to change my mind. It's not your fault, there's just nothing you can do. The heart doesn't get to just choose who it wants to be with. Please move," I pleaded with him softly.

"Stay." He grabbed my arm. "Come and let me show you my room. Maybe you'll change your mind once you've seen it."

"No thanks. A room isn't going to make me change my mind either. Like I said before, I don't think you really understand what a girl wants. I'll stick to my closet."

I jerked my arm away and removed myself from the cage of his arms swiftly, and didn't wait for his response. I walked away in a fog. A mixture of annoyance, pity and sadly- guilt. I had no idea why I should feel guilt for what he said but I did. I felt sorry for him. Sorry that he had to be so adamant and I had to say no. I hated making people feel bad. Hated it. He seemed so sincere. No lies. So soft with no sarcasm. I'd never seen him like that before.

I walked back down the hall and when I got to the very end, just before the stairs I saw a small piano. Ah! All this time that was here and I never knew it!

I immediately sat down and started playing 'The Scientist' by Coldplay. It was amazing the things you remembered. I hadn't played in years before that once in the motel but every note seemed to flow easily, just like before.

Calvin and Franklin joined me on the cramped bench seat. It made me sigh that sitting down, I was only mere inches taller than them.

I sang the first verse and chorus softly, very softly, not wanting to draw attention but just so happy I remembered how to play it.

Come up to meet you, tell you I'm sorry
You don't know how lovely you are
I had to find you to tell you I need you
To tell you I've set you apart

Tell me your secrets, ask me your questions
Oh let's go back to the start
Running in circles, coming up tails
Heads on a silence apart

Nobody said it was easy
It's such a shame for us to part
Nobody said it was easy
No one ever said it would be this hard
Oh take me back to the start.

The kids listened for a minute and then wanted to help of course. Calvin gabbed on and on to Franklin about how I used to sing to him all the time.

Exaggerating just a bit but I let him.

I showed them what keys to press in what order and we banged away at the ivories together. You could barely make out my melody with those two going at it but it was so sweet, I could care less.

It was a shame they were stuck down here like that.

I picked up Calvin's hand and put his fingers under mine. He followed my slow motions and I showed him how to play 'Twinkle Twinkle Little Star'.

He squealed with delight when we were done and then Franklin shouted it was his turn.

I felt a slight tap on my shoulder and turned, bracing myself for Phillip but it was Calvin's mom, Lana. She was smiling and signed 'thank you'. Hand to the chin then out towards me. I signed 'why', hand across the brow then out with a Y-thumb and pinkie out with all other fingers tucked in, and she motioned toward the piano.

I smiled and signed 'you're welcome', like an ok sign. I remembered a few more things over these past months, and signing with her the few times I had had jogged my memory.

I thought she would leave, as she usually did, but she pulled me up from the bench seat and hugged me, long and hard. I was so startled I could feel tears threatening.

When I turned into her I saw Merrick standing behind her at the stairs. His arms crossed over his chest, leaning back against the wall with an amused smile playing on his lips.

I wondered how long he had been standing there.

She pulled back, peeking at me one more time. She signed 'thank you' and motioned toward Calvin. I realized she wasn't just thanking me for the piano lesson, she was thanking me for being nice to Calvin, all this time. I nodded and smiled. Instead of trying to sign my ABCs to spell out each word for twenty minutes I looked at Merrick.

"Will you please tell her that Calvin is...wonderful and no trouble at all. I really enjoy spending time with him. That he's polite and sweet...and she should be very proud of him."

She smiled as she listened to the voice of my Keeper in her head.

Amazing how this worked.

She smiled at me widely, signed 'I am' and strode slowly back to the commons room.

Calvin and Franklin were still banging away at the piano when Merrick walked over to me, putting his arms around my waist.

"So how long have you been standing there?" I asked.

"Long enough. You really are a saint, you know that?"

"Absolutely not. Anyone would have done that," I insisted and he leaned in and whispered in my ear..

"Then how come no one else has."

His words stunned me a little. He was right. Why had no one else attempted to talk to Lana or buddy up with Calvin or Ryan or Kay for that matter. It was a little strange.

"You have. You played basketball with him several times and I've seen you chasing him and Franklin, fooling around."

"Hmm...not the same. I needed the exercise."

"Oh, sure. I guarantee you this body doesn't *need* exercise," I said playfully as I poked his six pack. He laughed, but winced a little.

"Oh! Sorry, forgot." I rubbed the spot where I so stupidly poked his broken ribs but he just continued to look at me. Openly and honestly, looking into me.

"Why do you do that? How can you look at me like... like you're looking at me for the first time?" I asked.

He just smiled knowingly, rubbing my necklace in between his fingers and kissed my forehead before he spoke.

"Come on. We've got to talk about the next search and store run."

"Ok. Later, Calvin. Bye, Frank." I waved over my shoulder as Merrick led me away with his arm through mine.

The crowded room was still buzzing with voices, all talking different things. Merrick, Jeff, Marissa and I huddled together. Phillip was no where to be seen. I wasn't sure if I wanted to bring up what I'd seen earlier.

Marissa looked a lot better and it seemed my thought had come true. People were nicer to her somewhat, despite their doubts about her motives. She still wanted to come on the runs with us so I took that as a good sign.

We talked about what to do and where to go next. I was thinking about how long it would take if we kept going this way. If there was only a way to mass produce a sign or flag of some sort that only Keepers would know about.

Wait. Light bulb.

"Wait. This may be stupid, and you can tell me if it is, but what about making like...a flyer. We take it to public places advertising the store but at the end of the flyer, put that thing you Keepers always say to each other on it, guard you brother, or whatever it is. That way it won't be conspicuous and only the ones we want to see it, will find what they are looking for. What do you think?"

Silence. Hmmm. It didn't quite have the same ring in my head as it did coming out of my mouth. It was stupid. I started to shake my head to tell them never mind.

"That's...that's actually really good. That's perfect. I mean, it'll be more tense around here with all the extra people coming unannounced but...Sherry, that's a great idea," Jeff said, seemingly going over it in his mind.

"Really? It's ok. You won't hurt my feelings, I promise."

"It'll work," Merrick said. "It'll be safer that way too. Going out on these runs every week are proving to be hazardous to everyone's health."

I looked to see if he was laughing but he was not. He looked contemplative.

"Ok, well it's set then. That's what our next run will be. Flyer printing and distribution. Great. No worries." Jeff seemed beyond pleased and linked his hands behind his head.

That made me feel better about it. If they thought it was good, it was.

We would wait until Monday when everything opened back up again. It was Friday afternoon and the hall was almost done, beams in place, concrete poured and rooms sealed. Those unfortunate people did not get a real door like most of us. They got a plywood board fit to cut but it was better than nothing. They even put a couple more toilets and showers down there. Nothing fancy but plumbing was plumbing.

Later that night I told Merrick about Phillip's room. About how he practically had that whole huge hall to himself. There was no telling what else was down there.

He looked puzzled for a bit but settled on the fact that Phillip was just a jerk and we already knew that. Once again, I knew it was his bunker to begin with, but still, he wasn't playing nice.

I decided to cook that night. Mrs. Trudy always insisted on cooking, it was her 'thing' she said and definitely her forte. She was a wonderful cook but this was growing to be quite a crew and it didn't seem fair for her to always be in the kitchen.

I saw her cranking up the record player from the kitchen doorway, pulling Merrick from his chair to show him how to dance.

He looked a little nervous.

I wanted to watch so badly but I couldn't leave the noodles I was prepping if I wanted to finish anytime soon. I kept glancing up and they were twirling away. Paul and a still very pregnant Katie had gotten up to join them.

As Billie Holiday sang and they danced, I took a quick peek from the kitchen doorframe after I stuck everything in the oven. The scene was so sweet looking in its normalcy it made my heart ache with gladness. How wonderful for there still to be such easiness and some amount of normal in such trying times.

Merrick and Mrs. Trudy were laughing. I actually saw her throw her head back. The newbies were laughing too, Paul was bending Katie down gently, then swinging her out and back in. He wrapped his arms around her from behind and put his hands on her belly as they swayed. So sweet.

Everyone seemed happy, for just a moment there were no problems, no heartbreak, no discussions to be had, no enemies in the field, just relaxing in a sweet moment.

Not everyone was watching though, some were wrapped up in their own sweetness. Danny for instance had found his favorite corner with Celeste. She had her head on his shoulder and they bounced a little with the music, eyes closed. I saw him kiss her forehead and she smiled without opening her eyes.

Mrs. Trudy saw me and summoned me to her by crooking her index finger. I shook my head playfully, thinking she was joking. She wasn't. She yelled for me.

"Sherry, get your pretty face over here."

"Mrs. Trudy, no, I can't dance. Besides...I'm cooking."

"Sherry," she said with a crescendo, telling me that she meant business.

I looked at her and Merrick, begging her with my eyes to please don't make me do this. Then Jeff and the others started in, urging me. I sighed and made my way out, still wearing the kitchen apron. My protest only called more attention to me.

As I reached them I tried one more time.

"Mrs. Trudy. Dinner?"

"Sugar, I know how long ziti takes to cook, you ain't fooling nobody. Now, put your hands up here." She told me where, but this was not where her hands had been.

She put my arms around Merrick's neck and his hands around my waist.

"That's it. Merrick will show you how to do the rest."

Then she grabbed Jeff from his amused perch on the edge of the couch, his face dropping and his eyes going wide.

He looked more scared than I did as she started to turn herself under his arm. Then I looked up at Merrick's face.

Everything else went away. He was so gorgeous, happy, and he was looking at nothing but *me*. I tried to forget if anyone was watching us or not. Immediately, I stepped on his toe and bumped into him while trying to get my bearings and rhythm as we jostled each other.

"Sorry, sorry... I knew I'd be bad at this."

"Don't apologize to me. You're not bad at it, we just got started. Relax." He leaned down to whisper in my ear, giving me chills as his breath hit my neck. "You don't have to be nervous. It's just me."

I smiled at his ability to always make me feel better and surrendered, followed his lead. I was surprised by how much easier it was when I stopped trying to dictate which way I was going. Merrick had actually picked it up quite well it seemed. He was an excellent lead.

"So...dancing," I said.

"This isn't so bad. This is what you were getting all worked up about that day?"

Merrick's gaze was nothing if not fixed intently on mine.

"Yeah, I'm a chicken." I pressed closer to him. "Nobody ever showed me how to dance, unless, spiritual fire chanting counts."

He laughed, as I knew he would, reliving the memory with me. My crazy parents.

"You do look awfully cute in that apron," he observed, looking me up and down.

"Oh, yeah..." I said looking down and frowning at my definite un-cuteness.

"It's time, Sherry," he said abruptly, pressing his forehead to mine. "I'm not waiting any longer. When we go out Monday, you and I are going out alone. To *cover more ground*," he said smiling, still holding me close and swaying with the music.

"Really?" I squeaked happily, knowing what this meant.

I bit my bottom lip thinking about the possibility of it. On Monday, I'd be married to the most beautiful creature in the universe.

"Would that be ok?" he asked, always second guessing how I could love him.

"That'd be better than ok!" I said loudly and then lowered my voice. "I love you."

"I love you."

"I'm so ready to be Mrs...uh...how's that going to work?"

"Well, I could take your last name since I technically don't have one."

"No. Make something up. We'll start completely new. New name, new everything."

"Hmmm... How about Finch?"

I laughed out loud at that. "Finch? Really? That's what you want? Merrick Finch?" I laughed again, and I realized I threw my head back, just like Mrs. Trudy had done.

Merrick brought out the best in us.

"You don't like it, huh?" He laughed. "You pick something."

"Um. What about...Keeperofsky?"

I was just toying with him and he knew it. We both laughed and he squeezed me with a tight hug whispering in my ear.

"Whatever you want, baby, whatever you want."

I wrapped my arms as much as I could up to his shoulders, barely reaching, so I put them around his waist instead. We stayed there, swaying with the rest of them.

Jeff looked to really be enjoying himself. Phillip stood by the stairs, brooding. He finally decided to join us, huh? As soon as I met his eyes across the room, he barged off, back to his insanely spacious room with all the amenities. He was so strange.

I couldn't even remember how many songs we danced to when I heard the oven ding. Merrick kisses the palm of my hand quickly before I headed back into the kitchen to finish up.

The huge industrial pans were something. I had trouble lifting them even without the pasta on them. I managed, how I'd never know, to bring the four huge racks of food out of the hot oven and onto the counter top. Miraculously only burning myself once.

When we all finished, I began to eye the dishes and the horrid pile was eyeing me too. I insisted that no one help me in the kitchen tonight, not even for clean up.

The guys were putting the last finishing touches on the new hall and bringing the brand new supply of cots and sleeping bags they had gotten on the last run out of the outside shed.

I'd avoided the dishes long enough so I ran the water and started the suds, pulling my hair to the side of my neck so as not to be swinging in my face. Almost immediately I felt hands on my hips, squeezing affectionately.

Merrick's warm breath teased at the back of my neck. I thought they were going to be down the hall for a while but maybe they got done sooner than they thought or maybe he snuck away, to be alone with me. Hmmm.

I tried to turn to look at him, but he wrapped his arms tight around my stomach and kissed my neck.

"That's going to get you in trouble, mister," I crooned, but he didn't speak.

I didn't think about it at first, because who else would be kissing me, but the feeling that something was off was too much to dismiss.

Horror washed over me.

My heart slammed painfully and my stomach heaved. I realized with certainty that it was definitely not Merrick. I knew what Merrick's lips felt like, what his warmth felt like. I tried to look again and he grabbed the back of my neck, pushing me up against the counter, pressing his body against mine.

He kissed me harder, moving down my shoulder and back up to my ear with me trying to turn the whole time and him shoving me forward into the counter so as not to see his face. Not Merrick. He wouldn't be rough with me like that. Oh God. Everyone was down the hall and this was...

Phillip.

Without turning I know it was him. Should I scream? No one would hear me down there with the record player going and the noise from the tools. If I made him angry, who knew what he'd do with no one here to stop him, but I couldn't just sit here and make out with him!

"Phillip...don't."

He must have known already that I had figured it out because he never even flinched at his name or my plea.

"Stop," I said and meant to be assertive, but it came out breathy and weak.

Nothing, not a word but his grip tightened a little and I winced.

"Phillip, please. You're hurting me."

Nothing. My heart pounded out of my chest and the angry and scared moisture sprung to my eyes. I searched the sink for a weapon of some sort but there was nothing but plates. Dang it. I would use them if I had to, though I certainly couldn't outrun him.

"Phillip-"

"Admit it," he interrupted me with his mouth on my ear. "That feels good on your skin...you like it, don't you? See? Merrick isn't the only one that knows how to make you happy. He isn't the only one who knows what you like."

He swung me around forcefully to face him, squeezing my arms so tight, I could feel my pulse under his fingertips.

I heard the crash as the stack of plates fell to the floor at our feet, but I couldn't look at the mess. My eyes were fearfully locked with Phillip's. He pulled me closer, pausing just before my face, still looking in my eyes.

His eyes looked excited and bright.

He grabbed my jaw none too gently with his other hand and pulled me as close to him as possible, my eyes were still open wide with waiting.

"Phillip, No! Please! Don't do this," I half yelled.

He kissed me. I tried to struggle but his grip was so tight I could barely move at all in my slightness. Why did I have to be so helpless?

I fought him as best I could, my fist pushing at his chest but to no avail. I closed my lips tight and kept hitting and pushing him but he grabbed both my arms and squeezed them around my back, pulling them back too far and I gasped in pain. He must have been trying for that outcome because he used that opportunity with my mouth open wide in pain and took it with his.

He thrust his tongue so far into my mouth like he was trying to plant something, some idea or notion to make me love him. His tongue swept back and forth and his lips were hard and punishing.

He groaned which made it even worse. He was enjoying himself. Though he was hurting me he was enjoying it! I felt the panic welling up as the truth I didn't want to see came to face me.

He was not going to stop.

The tears came and fell, spilling over to roll down my cheeks. He didn't stop or pause or really even look at me. I fought, tasting the salty tears in my mouth, knowing he could taste them too. I tried to kick him but he stood his ground.

Eventually he pulled back and by that time, my arms were aching with the release and blood rushing back into them. It was so painful but the prickles didn't distract me. He held my arms in front of me and began to explain his reasons.

I tried not to throw up.

"There. See? We can be together just as easily as you and him. You were *my* destiny. Mine! That...freak got in the way and messed up everything! You were supposed to come here and be with me. I knew you would come, I knew it.

"The minute I saw you outside the store that night I knew you were the one I'd been waiting for. You can't love that thing, that alien, that inhuman monster. I won't let you screw all this up for us. We don't need to worry about the world, we can live down here together with Mom and have our own family. Our children will be gorgeous," he whispered and caressed my cheek and lips with his fingers. "Just like you are, sweetness."

As he spoke that last sentence I couldn't contain myself any longer. I screamed, kicked and punched as hard as I could but he still held me still enough to kiss me again. His hands wrapped around my upper arms, squeezing hard.

He was trying to make me believe him. He was angry and taking it out on my unarmed and fragile body.

He pushed me hard backwards against the counter top. I bumped into the sharp edge of it with my lower back hard enough to take my breath, and I cried out into his kiss, but it only came out as a whimper. He pressed so hard on my lips I could barely take a breath and the skin on my face and neck burned from his coarse unshaved face rubbing.

He pressed his face to my neck.

"Mmm, you smell so good," he all but growled.

He took his hand, wrapped it up in my hair pulling back hard and grunting in satisfaction when I gasped as he kissed my neck roughly.

Didn't he care that he was hurting me?

Then suddenly, my silent prayer was answered. Someone pulled Phillip off and threw him across the kitchen. He landed on the table and rolled, falling to the other side on the floor with an audible thud against the wall.

Jeff.

He grabbed onto me, pulling me to him before I collapsed to the floor.

I held his shirt in my fists for leverage and grounding to help pull myself up, but he didn't need my help. He pulled me to him easily and let me bury my face in his warm shoulder, away from Phillip's gaze and I couldn't do anything but sob as

I felt Jeff's soothing hand on the back of my head.

"Phillip, you better run," Jeff growled in a voice that gave me goose bumps.

He wasn't telling him to run away for fear of his life, he was telling him his life would be in danger if he didn't run away, from him.

"Sherry!" Phillip got up and leaned on the table to plead with me. "It was supposed to be this way. Don't let him ruin it!"

"That's it," Jeff said angrily and started to take me to sit in a chair.

"Sherry, we belong together." He took a step away as he spoke. "I can love you, he can't. Come with me. Our kids would bring real people back, not these...freaks. We can be our own family. We don't need anybody else," Phillip pleaded with me as he inched closer to the kitchen door frame.

"I can't have children."

That was all I could say as I stared into Jeff's chest, fisting his shirt. Phillip and Jeff both looked at me.

"What? What do you mean?" Phillip said, even more angry, then a flash of something in his eyes. He looked surprised, off centered and quickly back pedaled. "Look... Marissa, she willed me to do it, ok? Sorry."

The first lie in the whole bunch. He actually believed everything else he had said which made it sound completely true.

He really was insane.

I couldn't be angry or worried or scared. I couldn't speak or think anymore. I just cried. Jeff didn't leave me to chase Phillip as he made a break for it.

I was glad because I would have crumpled to the floor without him holding me up. I felt my tears soaking into the front of his gray t-shirt.

He wrapped his warm Keeper arms around me and shh'ed me, telling me it was alright, that Phillip was gone, that I was safe. He calmed me just like a human would.

My arms throbbed and pulsed where Phillip had squeezed them, but that was hard to concentrate on because I could feel my pulse in my head too. Everywhere, pounding, pleading for clarity, but all I got was fog, a haze trapping me in a state of uncontrollable shaking and crying.

Apparently someone must have seen or heard and went to tell Merrick and the rest because they all ran our way through the commons room. Or Jeff called them, which was more likely.

They were an angry lynch mob, not knowing what was going on but just that someone was in trouble and they had to do something about it.

Merrick didn't know it was me who was hurt. His eyes were wide with surprise and horror as he pushed through the crowd at the door with that 'oh no, what now' face.

"Sherry?" Merrick yelled through the crowd.

The lynch mob was stunned as well. I couldn't help but think as I looked at them that I was so tired of playing the damsel role.

Jeff handed me over gently to Merrick who pulled me in and grabbed my face in his warm hands. The hands I should have recognized weren't there from the first second Phillip touched me.

"Sherry? Honey, what happened?" Merrick asked me with a very worried face, but I had no idea what to tell him so I just stayed silent and buried my face in his shirt.

"Talk to me," he said lifting my face with his finger to look at him but I still stayed silent as I struggled to maintain his gaze.

Merrick turned to Jeff and started searching his brain for what happened.

"Don't, Merrick. Just let me tell you what happened," Jeff pleaded, but must feel it as I heard him sigh exasperatingly.

Too late. Merrick had seen the gruesome scene through Jeff's eyes and made it one hundred times more painful and real than it was before. I felt the heaving of Merrick's chest as he tried to contain his anger and breathing.

I had a feeling I was about to be passed off to someone else so the manhunt could begin. Thank God Jeff didn't see and hear the rest of it. I feared he may have killed him himself.

Trudy came pushing through the line. She looked as if she already knew what happened. Jeff was gone in a blur of colors.

"Oh, sugar...he didn't," Trudy said slowly, and looked at me horrified and knowingly.

I knew she knew. I couldn't bear to face her and tell her son did this to me, so I turned and put my face in Merrick's arm around my head, the silent tears and shaking came again.

"Trudy, I'm sorry, but...I've got to..." I heard Merrick begin, but stopped, choking on his words.

"It's ok, sugar. Go. I understand," she said softly.

She reached her arms for me and I stiffened, gripping his shirt tighter, not wanting to leave Merrick. I glanced up at his face, it was tight with anger, but he didn't say anything, just nodded. I reluctantly moved towards Trudy's still outreached arms, but my fists were pried in Merrick's shirt.

He pulled my fingers away gently with a pained look on his face and ran from the room with blurred speed, before I could convince him to stay. The onlookers weren't there anymore, they were giving us space and privacy.

"Where's Danny?" I asked her, trying to stop the uncomfortable and uncontrollable heaving from my crying.

"I don't know. He wasn't with us, maybe he's with Celeste."

Good. Telling him was one thing, but just like with Merrick, seeing it with your own eyes made it so much worse. Danny would be furious, too.

I didn't want to think about that or anything else. I wanted Trudy to just put me in my room but I couldn't be in the dark alone. I couldn't.

"I'm sorry about your plates, Mrs. Trudy," was what came out when I finally tried to speak to her again.

"Honey, don't you worry your pretty little head about that... I'm the one who should be sorry." She held back a sob but barely managed to get her words out. "I figured he might try something, but I never imagined...this. He talked about you all the time, baby, but I kept telling him that you and Merrick were happy and to leave you alone. I should've said something to you. I'm so sorry."

"You can't blame yourself for this," I countered.

"Did he...succeed?"

"No. Jeff came-" I had to stop because the tears were chocking my words.

"My own flesh and blood. His father was not a nice man. He started out that way, but eventually turned into something else. He didn't raise those boys right in the way of women. I'm sorry, honey, and I'm not making excuses for him."

"Of course not. I'm sorry."

"What are you apologizing for?"

"I just wish you didn't have to deal with this either. I wish I was stronger or bigger...or something."

"Honey, you're just fragile and people take advantage of that sometimes. I'm sorry. Tell me what you need? You want to go lie down?"

"Yes...but...can I sleep with you until Merrick gets back, please?"

"Of course, sugar. Come on."

Through the doorway to the commons room, I could see a huddled mass of people trying to busy themselves and not look at us. Danny came out of the back wash room with Celeste in tow. He had no clue and one look at me would send him into a frenzy. He looked up before I could turn. He released Celeste's hand and ran to me franticly.

"What happened!?"

I had no idea what I looked like but it was probably a mess to make him run to me like that. I could not say the words to describe what almost happened to me so Trudy tried instead.

"Phillip. He..." Trudy started but was crying too. She couldn't say those words either.

"He what?" he asked the question but by his tone, he knew the answer.

He could tell by our faces and I could tell by his constricted voice, he knew.

"He tried," Trudy finally managed out.

She handed me over to him gently and then ran to her room in the back, crying loudly. I saw one of the other ladies run after her, Kay I thought.

I was getting dizzy from all the passing me off. There was enough tear soaked shirts already. Danny took me into his chest tucking me under his chin, not wanting me to see his face, but I could feel him shaking with anger.

Celeste stood off to the side, her hands covering her mouth with eyes wide. Danny looked at her.

"I'm taking her to bed," was all he said before leading me to my room, tucked under his arm protectively.

At first I thought he would leave me there and I'd have to beg him to stay but no, he just lay down with me. I shrunk into his arm, trying not to cry but not able to stop the tears from coming in wave after wave of embarrassing, painfully long sweeps.

Danny didn't say anything except to shh me and murmur something about it being over. I couldn't speak if I wanted to. I knew I shouldn't be embarrassed in front of Danny, my brother, but I was. I was the oldest. I was supposed to be the strong one. I hated to let loose and he rarely had seen me do so.

So we didn't speak. He did the best thing he could do for me. He didn't ask me questions about what happened or try to calm me with empty 'Sorry's' and 'It's ok's'. He just put his arm around me and let me cry myself to sleep in the dark.

Merrick - Manhunt
Chapter 23

It was so hard to pry her scared, shaking fingers from my shirt. I knew she needed me, but I had to go. Phillip couldn't get away with this.

I couldn't look at those eyes so I ran like a coward. Ran away before she could speak and I wouldn't be able to go and do what needed to be done.

I sped up the stairs, out the fall out hatch and the back door. It was dark outside already. That was not going to make things easy for Phillip.

I searched everywhere outside. I couldn't see anything moving so I circled the store, trying not to be too fast in case someone was there and saw me. Margo was minding the store.

"Have you seen Phillip?" I asked her just as quickly as I could get the door open.

"Yes, about five minutes ago, he ran through here, but that was it. He didn't stop or anything."

"Which way?"

"Out back, but I think he got in Sherry's car. I thought I saw it leave. What's the matter, Merrick?"

I couldn't even begin to answer her so, rudely, I left without a word letting the door slam behind me.

I ran around back and saw that, yes, Sherry's car was gone. The van was coming my way in my peripheral.

"Get in!" Jeff yelled.

I hopped in and he sped off fish tailing. This was so dangerous, especially at night, two Keepers alone, but I had to look for him. I might need to.

Could I kill a human? Not could, would. Would I kill a human with my bare hands? I was afraid of the answer. We would find out when I found Phillip.

"I'm sorry, Merrick. I should have ran after him but Sherry was..." Jeff told me gruffly.

"I know. I saw. Thank you for staying with her."

Her face in Jeff's memory when he found them like that was the most scared I've ever seen her, even watching her all these years.

My breath catches when I remember Phillip pulling her hair, pressing himself against her and kissing her violently before Jeff grabbed him and threw him across the room.

Her eyes were round and wide, red from crying and smudges underneath them. Her cheeks were pink, not in a good way. Too pink, from scratching and rubbing.

I had to close my eyes and force out Jeff's memory that I took from him. It physically hurt to see it.

"I told you not to look," Jeff snapped as he looked in my mind, seeing what I was seeing.

"I know. I also knew you wouldn't tell me the whole truth and neither would she. I needed to know. I don't even want to think about what happened before you got there."

"Don't, Merrick, just don't. She's ok, just shaken. That's what's important."

"If you hadn't left to go get the drawn plans that were on your bed. If you hadn't been-"

"Merrick, stop! Don't do this to yourself. Despite her being...tiny, she's strong. She'll be over this in no time."

"Thank you, Jeffrey. You've always been really good to her. Throwing him across the table was a nice touch. Didn't know you had it in you."

I could barely speak, let alone think, just stare into the darkness.

"You're family, so now so is she. She is one of the best humans I've ever met. Ever. She's got some Keeper qualities and watching him slam to the floor was only the tip of the iceberg of what I wanted to do. I've never thought of actually killing a human...until tonight." He shook his head in disgust. "Let's just look for him, ok. We'll stay out all night if we have to."

"Yeah. Ok," I answered but barely heard it myself.

I could feel myself slipping into a strange numb but painful unawareness. It felt messy and awkward in my head and body. Some kind of human sadness, but more.

It hurt so bad in my chest, my stomach, the opposite of what I usually feel when I think of Sherry, but this hurt. I kept quiet for a while and looked out my window for a white VW Rabbit and the dead man driving it.

We drove around all night and didn't find a trace or sign of Sherry's car nor Phillip. Jeff kept going, waiting for me to call it off. I eventually gave in and told him to go home. We were both exhausted and I knew Phillip was long gone.

"So now, we've got to worry about him turning us in, don't we?" I asked, suddenly stiff.

"I don't know. Do you think he would turn Trudy in?"

"I don't know, I hope not. We've invested too much into the bunker to lose it now."

"I know. Let's go home. You need to check on Sherry anyway."

As Jeff spoke her name the hurt in my chest and stomach returned like a punch in the gut.

Fear. It was brutal fear.

Fear that she wouldn't want my comfort, fear that she would hate me for not being there when it happened to stop it, for not protecting her, fear that she would hate me for leaving her to look for Phillip, that she wouldn't want me, fear that she wouldn't be able to forgive me.

I knew we had been gone a long time. The wall clock in the stock room read 3:30 am . Almost five hours gone. Wow. We drove around for five hours. I knew she would be asleep and maybe that was for the best. It would give her some time.

I came down the stairs to the silent bunker, everyone was asleep. Only the sound of the humming kitchen appliances could be heard. Jeff headed straight to his room and I headed to mine. Mine and Sherry's.

I peeked in, not sure if she was even there, thinking maybe she stayed with Trudy, but there she was, with Danny. Thank goodness she wasn't alone. I could see her hair was still mussed, her eyes were puffy, she had apparently been crying even more and a faint bluish dark ring banded around her upper arm which was laying over Danny's stomach.

Phillip's fingerprint bruises.

My stomach churned. I couldn't go in there anyway, there wasn't room and I didn't want to wake her, so I went to stew in anger in the living room. Phillip better hope this Keeper didn't run across him again.

Ever.

When I woke up only a few hours later on the couch, a few people had begun to stir and make their way out of their rooms. I sat up from the uncomfortable sofa silently cursing as my neck stung with a kink.

Marissa immediately sat by me.

"She's ok. Danny stayed with her last night," she offered and patted my arm quickly before jerking it back just as quickly.

"I know. I saw."

"Don't treat her like she's breakable. She's stronger than you know. She wants to have a purpose, she needs it."

"I know how strong she is but she *is* breakable, Marissa. What happened doesn't help that, it proves it."

"Physically, yes, but she doesn't want to feel weak. She doesn't want to feel like she can't take care of herself."

"She can't! It's a full time job trying to keep her out of trouble." My voice cracked as the memories of all the time I had to rescue her flooded my mind.

All those close calls. It wasn't her fault. It was just a fact that the girl was a magnet for trouble and there was nothing she could do about it.

"I know. Listen to me, I've seen it. Sherry will be fine. She won't be harmed from this and Phillip won't be back. He won't tell them our location either, but..."

"But what?"

"He will become a Lighter."

"You see that?"

"Yes. I don't know when, but it will happen. I think revenge has been served, don't you? Please don't tell Trudy. She's had a rough night. Hard to believe your own flesh could do such a thing, you know."

"Yeah, I won't. Thanks." I started to get up from the couch and paused. "Say, Marissa? Why are you helping me?" I was exhausted and couldn't wait for pauses and couth and manners like usual conversations.

"Because, she helped me. Sherry. I had a gun to her head, but she begged me to come with her. She even defended that jerk, Phillip, about why he was snooping through my van. She wouldn't let it go, wouldn't let me go, even when I resisted she kept telling me how much she wanted me to come, to protect me."

"Yeah. That sounds about right. Well, thank you."

"You're more than welcome, and I'm sorry about before, the vision. Really sorry," Marissa said and got up to walk into the kitchen.

As I watched her go, I could tell that she really meant it.

I decided instead of waking Sherry I'd go do some work for a while to keep busy. I knew deep down I was procrastinating, but I couldn't help myself. I should go in there right now and snatch her up, hug her to me and ask her if she was ok but I was still a coward. I could take anything in this world but Sherry's hate or rejection.

I did some things in the laundry room. Stacked up some boxes and baskets that others had left in there.

Our washing machine was two huge utility sinks. I started the water and poured in the lavender scented soap. I needed to just keep busy until she woke up. Maybe she wouldn't even try to find me, still too upset with me. Maybe she needed to just spend time with Danny for a while. Maybe she wouldn't want to see me at all.

I plunged my shirts into the water over and over and picked up the wad to wring and rinse but then I heard Sherry's voice. She was singing and I froze.

A Whole Lot of Loving Going On
Chapter 24

I woke up to see Danny still there with me in my room. He stayed with me all night. Sweet guy. Who knew how long he'd stayed up after I fell asleep, stewing.

I tried to get up without disturbing him and I succeeded. I slipped out the door quietly and shut it behind me.

I ran my fingers through my hair in an attempt at fixing it and prepared myself for the onslaught of sympathy and questions and stares and worst of all-attention. Even after he was gone, Phillip still got to torture me with unwanted attention.

At least, I thought he was still gone.

I glanced down at my arms and there was a purple uneven ring and circle bruise. One a little darker and wider than the other. I wished I had a different shirt with me before I had to see anyone. Me and my dang tank tops.

I didn't want any more sympathy.

When I reached the end of the short hall, I saw them, the mass of people waiting to ambush me. Trudy wasn't there, which was good, though I smelled coffee so she may have been in the kitchen.

I got a lot of quick glances but that was it. Surprisingly, Marissa came up to me first.

"Hey."

"Hey." I was a little off put by her sudden interest.

She never spoke to me first unless there was a painful vision to follow. "Are you ok today?"

"Yeah, fine. As good as I can be, I guess. Have you, uh...seen Merrick?"

"Yeah. Listen, he got home last night late. He didn't want to disturb you. He thinks you're upset with him, for not being there...with Phillip."

"That's absurd. How can he-"

"I'm just telling you what I know. He's really worried about you but he's angry at Phillip and himself, he's scared that you won't forgive him."

"That's ridiculous. Of course I'm not mad at *him*."

"It's a guy thing, and Merrick is a guy now."

I just nodded. I really needed a shower to wash away the events of the past day so I walked out past the kitchen, not looking for Trudy. I was not ready to see her heartbroken face yet.

I glanced back and saw everyone in their own world. No one was watching or staring at me. I don't know who talked to them, but I needed to thank them as they all graciously tried in vain to look busy.

I turned our homemade sign over to show the 'In Use' side as the door had no lock. I closed the door to the little green bathroom and removed my clothes. My arms ached and I could still smell Phillip on my shirt as I pulled it over my head. I immediately threw it across the room far away from me. It fell in a heap in the corner by the trash can. Fitting.

I felt a little panicky in the shower. I didn't know why. Maybe because it was so far away from everything else and I was alone and confined.

I tried to focus on relaxing, imaging the stress and everything else falling from me and going down the drain. I let the hot water rinse away the previous night and everything that happened with it.

I scrubbed with my washcloth and soap on my sore arms and jaw. I didn't want to be one of those women who wasn't able to get over an attack, always fearful. I felt for them and understood now more than ever their panic.

My heart started to pick up again so, I sang. Billie Holiday's 'The Very Thought Of You', the first song Merrick and I danced to, was the only song that came to mind.

The very thought of you
and I forget to do,
those little ordinary things,
that everyone ought to do.
I'm living in a kind of daydream,
I'm happy as a queen.
And foolish though it may seem,
To me it's everything.

Then I heard his voice in my head, saying my name, his voice stretched with strain and guilt.

My Merrick.

I peeked out and he was there, walking in and shutting the door behind him. I couldn't think to care about anything else but getting to him.

I jumped out of the shower and ran the short distance, naked, wet and probably still a little soapy. I jumped up into his arms and wrapped my legs around him.

He didn't try to stop me. He wasn't bashful with me anymore, didn't care about anything, but me. He turned us around a couple times in a whirlwind of emotion and then fell back against the door, sliding down to the floor with me still in his lap.

He held me to him in a tight embrace, keeping me there, his uneven breaths harsh against my ear. We were a heap of heaving, thankful sighs and breaths.

After a minute of just sitting in each others arms, letting him calm me like nothing else ever did, I finally speak to ease the silence. The only other sound was the still running shower making steam pour over us from the floor.

I had to speak. He couldn't feel guilty or responsible for this. I couldn't allow him to feel that.

"Merrick," I whispered but he continued to hold my head down to his chest so I couldn't see his face. "Merrick, look at me." He slowly obeyed. "I'm ok. Look at me. I'm fine, I just-"

"I'm so sorry."

"Merrick, it wasn't your fault."

"If I had been there-"

"Don't do that. Listen to me." I grabbed his face and pulled it up to see his eyes. They were tired, angry, clouded and tortured. "Merrick. Babe, I need you. I need you to be *you*. I need things to just be normal. Please?" His eyes glanced down to the dark rings on my arms and then quickly looked away. "I'm fine. I promise."

"You're not fine, Sherry. Look at what he did to you." He gently rubbed the bruises on my arms with his fingertips. "I wasn't there. For the second time in your life you really needed me, I wasn't watching and wasn't there."

I didn't contradict him, knowing he was talking about the Marker attack but he hadn't seen the first time when Matt tried to force himself on me either. I knew he was just beating himself up and there was no use in trying to take that road of reason. So I took another one instead.

"It's nothing. He didn't hurt anything that won't heal."

"It's not nothing," he snapped.

I could see I was going to get nowhere so I changed the subject.

"I need to talk to Jeff today and tell him thank you. He was very sweet to me...but you know that. You shouldn't have looked."

"I needed to know and yes, I'm very grateful to Jeff, too. I owe him everything."

"What time did you get in last night?"

"After 3:00." He shook his head. "We didn't find anything."

I tried to hide my disappointment at the news.

"Why didn't you come to me?"

"I did, but I thought you might need Danny more than me. I didn't want to wake or disturb you."

"I'll never need anyone more than you, ever again. I'm ok and I don't want you to worry about me. You can't blame yourself for someone else's actions anymore than I can blame myself." I bit my bottom lip in frustration. The words that seemed to fit just wouldn't come to me. "I love you...so much."

He put his head on my chest and cried, wrapping his arms around me tightly and protectively and I let him. Of course, I was crying, too.

I was shocked by the emotion he felt. I could almost physically feel his hurt for me, his needless shame and guilt was pulsing off of him. My Merrick, who loved me so much and would do anything for me and his constant need to keep me protected and safe was breaking, for me.

My heart stopped and broke right along with his as I felt him shake and squeeze me to him.

I would no longer refer to him as an angel or an alien or anything else. Whatever he was, he was just Merrick. He was more human than most people and that was all I needed to know. No one had ever loved me like him and no one else ever would.

"If anything had happened to you I would never have forgiven myself." He ran shaky hands down my arms and my hair, his fingers grazing my cheek and neck.

"Merrick, you can't watch over me every minute."

"I don't see how I can not," he joked, but didn't laugh. "I can't live without you, Sherry. I won't live without you."

"You won't have to. I'm not going anywhere. I just want to forget this ever happened. You are the only thing I want to think about right now. You and finding more of us out there."

"Yeah." He nodded for a while as if convincing himself. "I'm sorry. I'm done feeling sorry for myself. You need me and I'm... Are you sure you're ok? I thought you wouldn't want me to...comfort you or touch you."

"I don't want you to *stop* touching me." I grabbed his hand and put it on my cheek. "Merrick, you're my life. There is nothing, but you and me down here in this hole with the rest of the nonconformists." I smiled a little bit of a smile.

"Sherry." He grunted and closed his eyes like it was too much. His fingers roamed my lips and face, like he was memorizing me, then he opened his eyes. "I love you." He said firmly. "I promise you something like this will never happen again. I'm not ever letting you out of my sight. I promise to take care of you from now on, for the rest of our lives, always together. I'm so glad you're all right."

"I am. I love you, too. You're completely and utterly stuck with me," I joked and smiled a crooked smile, hoping he'd go with it and let the rest fall to the way side.

"I wouldn't have it any other way." He smiled slightly so my heart could beat again.

He pulled me closer to him to kiss my lips, his fitting over mine perfectly. The only lips I would ever kiss again. I couldn't imagine any more love could fit in my chest.

I wrapped my arms around his head, feeling the electric tingle on my bare back and waist where his hands were squeezing. His hot breath and tongue with warm lips were strong with possessiveness. He smelled of soap and sweet sweat but it wasn't sensual, not right then.

I mean, *it was,* but it felt like home. *He* felt like home.

I completely forget that I was stark naked, but of course my Merrick pulled me back into reality. He also pulled the towel I brought in with me from the closed toilet seat lid and wrapped it around me, gently lifting us off the floor.

I couldn't seem to let go of him. I didn't want him to leave and he either recognized that or felt the same. So I said screw the shower, I was pretty clean and I got dressed quickly while my gentleman turned his back to me and waited.

I was very thankful to this group of people. Maybe they knew me better than I thought they did because no one acted weird around me or asked me awkward questions or stared at me with their sympathetic eyes.

Let me rephrase. Everyone tried with great effort not to do those things and that was more than I could have asked for.

My little bunker family that was growing quickly and that I was so grateful for. Funny, it was the most normal family I'd ever had.

I had been right. Mrs. Trudy was in the kitchen earlier and still was. The coffee was calling my name, and Merrick's too, though he didn't listen to it like I did.

Poor Merrick looked absolutely bushed. I had it on good authority that he didn't sleep very well at all. Even I slept through most of the night.

I tried to persuade him to lay down, but he wouldn't. He wouldn't leave my side and I had no idea where he slept last night or for how long, but I was determined that no matter what happened, we would sneak a nap.

Mrs. Trudy hugged me quickly and awkwardly before slipping out. It was still too hard for her to accept and look at me, but I didn't take it personally. I couldn't imagine how hard this all was for her.

Through Merrick's wall of protection I saw Danny slowly coming to greet me in the kitchen but Celeste wasn't with him this time.

Being so tightly bound in a small space with so many other people was more than awkward, especially in times like this when I wanted to just burst into tears seeing him, his pained expression, him looking everywhere but my eyes.

Without stopping he lifted me a hug and held me there, being completely still and silent. Merrick was trying to fit a smile on behind Danny as he finally put me down slowly.

"I'm sorry I wasn't there."

"Why does everyone keep saying that?" I said, but I looked at Merrick. "It wasn't your fault, either of you. I'm fine."

"It could have been worse. It would have been if-"

"Danny, please, don't do this. I am ok. Between you and Merrick, you're not going to leave me alone for one second for the rest of my life, are you?"

"No," they both answered together firmly.

Danny released me and turned to Merrick.

"Thank you for going after him."

"No." He shook his head. "I was wrong. I should've stayed with Sherry."

"No, he shouldn't get away with this. I'm glad you went to look for him. Thank you."

He turned to go when he saw Celeste waiting for him in the doorway, squeezing my hand first.

By this time, it was almost lunch and I hadn't seen Jeff all morning. Trudy's coffee helped some but I still felt achy and tired, maybe from just looking at Merrick looking so tired.

When I finally saw Jeff coming through the commons room I took off running towards him, jostling a few bystanders.

He smiled as wide as his cheeks would allow as I jumped into his open arms. I felt the tears falling, though I could see some of the others watching us, I closed my eyes and gripped him tightly. They probably understood the need for such a reunion of two people that just saw each other yesterday. I wouldn't care if the president himself was here watching.

He spun me once or twice and Merrick smiled sadly behind us.

"Jeff! I don't know what I would have done if you hadn't come when you did. You saved me. Thank you," I whispered, crying again as he set me back down.

"You don't have to thank me. I'm just sorry I didn't come sooner. How are you doing?" he asked, wiping a tear from my cheek.

I let out a shaky sigh before speaking.

"Good. Ok, I guess. I'll be fine, I know that. I can't say the same for Merrick though."

"I know. I won't tell you about last night, just that...he loves you. I know you know, but he feels so-" he stopped and looked behind me.

I did as well. Merrick was walking closer.

"Ugh. Did you sleep at all last night?" Jeff asked him.

"Sure, some. I'm fine. Thanks again, Jeff. I owe you."

"Come on, guys, cut it out. How about we grab some grub? I'm famished!"

We laughed as he led the way. Jeff could always be counted on to be the same old Jeff.

After lunch I finally persuaded Merrick to come nap with me. Not much persuasion was needed and he fell right into our sleeping bag like it was the most comfortable down mattress instead of a padded slippery bag on a concrete floor.

It made me ache when people suffered not only *for* me, but *because* of me. I slipped in next to him, cuddling up in his warm arms protectively around me.

I was supposed to be making him feel better, not the other way around. It still took me by surprise how the warmth from his body wasn't just warm, it was like a slow burning candle. I felt like I was slowly melting and the tension and whatever else I was feeling just melted away. Everything that couldn't get washed away in my shower that morning was melting away with him now.

I thought he was finally asleep and I felt it coming myself, but then he spoke to me in my mind. His voice a rumble of sleepiness and love.

We can postpone the wedding if you want to. I know you're probably not up to it after everything that's happened...

"What? Why? Because of Phillip? That would be just giving him what he wanted. I don't want to wait."

Sherry, I'm just saying, if you want to postpone, it's ok. I understand, it's only two days away. Are you going to be ok with it?

"What's not to be ok with? I am going to be Mrs. Finch, and I can't wait."

I heard him laugh in my mind. I'd never heard that before. This laugh was so much softer and more genuine than that body could pull off. I loved it. I wished he would talk to me more often this way, with his real voice. It was so much more natural and rich, more Merrick.

Ok, if you're really sure, but we have got to come up with something other than Finch. You were right, it's just not working for me. He said and laughed in my

263

mind again.

I lifted my face to press my nose to his.

"We will, but please...sleep first." I kissed his nose and started to hum a little.

It was weird and even I started at the noise. I hadn't intended to do it, it just came out of me, very soft, like a whisper. It was me wanting to comfort him, like I had with Danny and Calvin.

"Hey, I'm supposed to be making you feel better," he said drowsily and I wanted to laugh because I had thought the same thing.

"I'll feel better when you get some sleep."

"I'll feel better and sleep when you start worrying about yourself a little bit. You are important no matter how much you try to sweep yourself under the rug."

"Ok, ok. How about you worry about me and I'll worry about you, that way we're both taken care of."

I could feel Merrick's smile against my cheek as he pulled me closer to him, kissing the side of my neck. "Deal. Keep humming. I like it."

Then he finally drifted off to sleep with my quiet humming to fill the silence.

Things were starting to be more normal the next day. It wasn't so so tense and scripted feeling. As we convened in the commons room, Katie's husband, Paul, had been telling jokes all morning as we laughed and spent some communal time together.

Katie sat rubbing her belly, now bulging more than I ever thought a belly could, with her feet in Paul's lap, him rubbing them for her.

I thought she was about to pop when I first met her but apparently she wasn't. Her due date was still 3 weeks away and everyone was a little worried.

We couldn't take her to the hospital and no one here had ever delivered a baby, though Trudy assured us she'd seen enough baby and doctor shows on TV to manage. She said when she was born, her parents delivered her themselves in their bedroom so how hard could it be? Hmm.

However, I was not one to argue with Trudy logic.

Katie didn't seem worried about it at all. She kept saying 'God put him in there and God will get him out.' I admired that. I wouldn't be so cool headed about it.

She was sure it was a boy. I asked her once how she knew and she said she wanted a girl so badly that she convinced herself it was boy. Now if it was a boy, she wouldn't be disappointed and if it was a girl that it would be a pleasant surprise. You couldn't argue with that logic either.

The day dragged on but in a good way. Merrick had been diligent in his questions about how I felt. Was I ok? Did I need to talk? Was I sure about marrying him? I kept assuring him I was completely fine so, we spent the day with our family. After lots of questions, laughs, time together and getting to know each other more, we told stories about the people we used to be.

Marissa, the newbies, everyone seemed to enjoy themselves and no one seemed focused on me and my blunders with mishap. Except Merrick, of course.

I tried to make sure I was constantly touching him because he seemed reluctant to touch me unless I instigated it. He was still waiting for me to freak out but it just wasn't coming. I felt fine, more than fine because I'd already dealt with it once before, with Matt.

To be honest, Phillip was gone. He wasn't just gone from this place, but gone from my thoughts too. Why worry about it? I felt safe with Merrick and that was all that should matter.

As I sat on Merrick's lap with his hand on my thigh, where I put it, I couldn't help but think about the clothes that needed to be washed. Merrick never finished his load yesterday and I certainly hadn't done mine the past few days. I leaned over to whisper to Merrick.

"I'm going to go wash some clothes while the wash room is free."

"I'll come with you," he said and started to get up but I pushed him back down.

It was subtle and no one saw.

"Honey, baby steps. You have got to let me do some things by myself," I whispered.

"No, I don't," he whispered back fiercely.

"Please, I need it. I almost freaked out in the shower. Baby steps for you, too. You've got to learn to let me be by myself a little now. I'll be fine, it's just laundry."

"Nuhuh. I warned you yesterday you'd have a new shadow didn't I? It's too soon." He shook his head in disagreement.

Before I could protest further, Mrs. Trudy came over quietly and whispered to us that she would come with me. I wondered how in the world she could have heard us talking, but I looked at Merrick with raised eyebrows. I knew he wouldn't refuse Mrs. Trudy.

"Ok. Since you don't want my company, fine." He laughed out loud quietly. "Thanks, Mrs. Trudy."

"Sure thing, sugar."

As I walked back through the corridor I heard him.

I'll just be out here. Waiting, bored, and waiting some more...

I heard him laugh in my mind again and I giggled into my hand so Mrs. Trudy didn't think I was nuts.

Soap, scrub, dunk and rinse. So much we took for granted before all this. I never thought I'd be washing my clothes against the grate on a huge metal sink instead of a washing machine and with homemade lavender soap. I never thought I'd be sleeping on concrete, never thought I'd have to share a bathroom with twenty people, after college of course, but even after all that had happened, we still had so much to be thankful for.

We were safe in an underground bunker, had food, a perfect cover story in the form of a convenience store, and company, still have our bodies and lives. Lots of other people in this world didn't have half of that.

This reminded me of the times we camped, which was a lot when I was a kid. My mom and dad were so 'in tune' to nature and wanted nothing more than for us to follow suit. We used to camp all the time when I was a little girl, all around the state and I hated it, absolutely loathed it. There were no sodas, no chips, no real food and the only company was our parents.

We washed our clothes in the river, yes, the river. We ate whatever fruits and berries we could find. Mom brought some necessities, I mean it was still against the law to starve your children right? Of course her reasoning for that was man ruined the earth and it was no longer plentiful with the things we needed.

I just thought it was because no one had gotten out there and planted anything, tending to the crops but hey, that was just me.

I remember seeing the sleeping bags when we first got there and remembering those camping trips. With only sleeping bags on the ground, not even a tent because it ruined the effect and blocked our stargazing view. And Dad, poor Dad. He just obeyed Mom's every whim and notion, every raised voice command, every time she verbally beat him down in front of us and anyone else who might be within earshot. The only time I ever remembered him 'defying her authority' was that one birthday.

Marriage should be a partnership; an understanding of compassion, love, submission and friendship on both parts.

I wondered what they were doing and where they were now. Maybe it was best not knowing.

Mrs. Trudy was quiet. I wasn't sure why she wanted to come back here with me, but I was hoping it was to talk, if she wanted, but silent we stayed.

Silent, silent, silent.

I was done so I took my load over to the so clever drying racks. They placed the racks over drains in the floor and under the air conditioner vents in the ceiling from the store. It wasn't terribly fast, but it was good enough.

We started to venture out into the night some, not far but at least got out and smelled real air and saw real stars, which could be seen as bright as anything with no moon in the sky.

We only all went out together at night and only behind the store. The first time we took Calvin, it had been weeks since he'd seen the outside and he took advantage of it.

Calvin and Franklin ran and chased Merrick, Ryan, Paul and Danny with flashlights. Everyone played like we were kids. We kept a watch out for danger in the sky, but we couldn't just stay cooped up. We might as well live a little while we could. We were careful by not staying out too long at a time and never ever going out in the daytime.

Jeff and Merrick had become sort of the appointed leaders of our band. The others were constantly asking them questions about what they thought about this or that. They really trusted them and looked to them for guidance.

It made me very proud of my boys.

I felt like an original member with special privileges. The other Keepers helped, too, and still kept watch over everyone, but even found themselves looking to my two for leadership.

I'm just glad we could get along, most of us anyway. With the exception of me, no one else had run-ins with anyone else so far.

Later on that evening, I decided I would try to speak to Mrs. Trudy as she was most definitely playing tight lips with me.

"Mrs. Trudy?"

"Yes, sugar."

For some reason those pet names only revolted me from Phillip's mouth. From Mrs. Trudy, it was sweet and genuine and she did it to everybody.

"How are you doing?"

"I'm doing...better. How are you doing?" she asked, placing a hand on my arm.

"I'm fine. Really, fine. I wish everyone would stop worrying about me so much."

"They just care about ya, honey. You've been through a lot lately, and you're just so sweet. It's just hard to think of someone hurting you."

"Well. I'm fine. I hate feeling so fragile and breakable. Would everybody

267

Collide - Shelly Crane

feel better if I took some karate lessons or something?"

Trudy laughed. "I don't think so, honey. You are what you are and not everybody is meant to be the protector, some of us need the protecting."

"I don't like feeling helpless. I just..."

"I know, I know. I'm sorry this all got brought down on you, sweetie."

"It's ok, Mrs. Trudy. It's not your fault and from what I hear, it wasn't really Phillip's either. Look, I'm not saying I don't care about what Phillip did but when you're in desperate times people do crazy things. I heard about his dad, too. That must have been hard on him and you."

"There is no excuse for what he tried to do to you, Sherry. None," she snapped, but then softened. "I don't care how fragile you are, you don't take advantage of people like that. I'm ashamed of him, so ashamed." She looked like she was about to cry so I moved over to hug her side.

"Ok. Ok," I reassured her. "I'm sorry this happened to you too but I'm going to get over it and so are you. Come on, let's go make some dinner for this crew," I said, trying to slightly pull her forward with me.

She nodded, happy for the distraction, and followed me out, down the hallway and to the kitchen. We made grits, fried eggs and bacon with biscuits. Mrs. Trudy was from the south, originally, a little town called Folkston in Georgia. It was a real place. I looked it up on an old Rand Mcnally.

She told me all about it as we cooked, with our colorful handmade aprons on. She brought a lot of flavor to our lives, and not just in the kitchen.

Some of the folks were a little wary of her homemade cooking creations but it was always decided in the end that it was good, especially the grits.

She also made these Swamp Cookies. Everyone loved these cookies. When I found out what was in them, I couldn't believe it. I was bowled over. You put leftovers in them.

Leftovers!

Disguise it with sugar, flour and spices and presto! Swamp Cookies. We had been eating these things for weeks and no one knew. When I found out, I laughed so hard I cried and vowed not to tell a soul.

"How else you think I keep us alive around here. Gotta eat the leftovers somehow," Mrs. Trudy had said matter-of-factly and a bit deviously.

I loved this woman!

That night, she told me all about the swamp, Okefenokee Swamp, and small town life. I had no clue myself, being a city girl, but it sounded so nice. How can you actually know everyone in the town you live in? It sounded intriguing and nice even. If we ever got out of there, that was where I was going. Small Town USA.

268

After dinner was served and cleaned up, we went and sat with Lana and Calvin. I practiced some of my sign language and Lana helped show me a few more. I forgot how much fun it was.

When I was in grade school, I had a deaf friend. We couldn't talk to each other so she showed me the American Sign Language alphabet.

I could remember her face like it was yesterday. My favorite part of the school day was recess for my sign language lesson.

Calvin signed like a pro with no thinking or hesitation. Lana was not a very social person but had begun to come out of her shell some. She signed really slowly to me so we could talk. She found it hilarious how I tried to spell out each word using all the letters individually.

It was the first time I'd ever heard Lana laugh.

Cry, Cry Baby
Chapter 25

The next morning we planned to get everything ready for our flyer distribution. Jeff had taken the heads off some golf clubs Trudy gave him, ones she had found in the back from her husband, and we brandished some weapons out of them.

He said we needed to have something, a weapon, when we went out from then on. You could only kill a Lighter by stabbing it through or burning it. Preferably stabbing as that was less hazardous.

I wondered if I'd be able to do it if it came down to it. Could I stab something knowing it would die? It gave me chills thinking about it, but if I had to… What if I had to protect Danny or Calvin? Yes, I could.

If I could reach.

It was snowing, but that was ok. It was supposed to snow now, in the winter, not in blazing June. I could deal with the cold when it was supposed to be cold. The bunker seemed to stay warm enough despite the chill outside.

What we thought would be a peaceful day turned out not to be. I could tell something wasn't right with Katie. She seemed extraordinarily tired and uncomfortable. She was even squirming on the couch with slightly labored breathing.

Paul sat on the couch with her rubbing her lower back. She said her back was killing her which didn't seem significant to me but I would see later that it was.

Marissa ran into the commons room and to all our surprise, addressed us as a group.

"Listen. Katie, you're going to have the baby. Today. Like, right now. You're about to go into labor," she said so matter-of-fact.

"What? How can you…Oh, that's right…oh, my," Katie said and seemed a little startled and took a deep breath.

Paul seemed even more scared than Katie.

"It's going to be ok, your baby will be fine, but…it's going to get a little rough. I wanted to tell you so you'd know and be prepared. I've seen the baby, it'll be ok so just, don't freak out."

I noticed Marissa didn't say 'he' or 'she' would be ok. I found I was glad that she didn't ruin the surprise for them and in their fright of the news they didn't think to ask her either.

"You're scaring me, Marissa. Why would I be worried?"

"Because it's going to take a while and we don't have medicine and…it will be a little rough," she repeated.

"Oh. Ok, I can do this. We're ready."

She began panting as if in labor already and Paul, moving out from behind her, scrambled and tried to prepare what to do and where. Really he was just turning frantic, inadequate circles in the middle of the room.

Trudy came over and grabbed his arm to stop him. "Daddy, calm down. Go get me some towels out of the wash room. Momma, come with me. Let's go get you situated and comfortable in your new room." Trudy helped Katie up and took her the opposite direction of the halls.

"Our room is that way," Katie said, pointing down the new hall.

"Not anymore. You're gonna have my room. You two can't stay in that little room with a baby. My room's not terribly bigger but it's at least three times the size as yours, with a real bed. I already had Merrick and Ryan put the baby's things you've been getting together in there. I'll take your room."

They rounded the corner and I could no longer see or hear them. Wow. There was going to be a baby in there in a couple of hours.

It wasn't long until the labor started, just as Marissa predicted.

Lana kept Calvin and Franklin in the back room to play as they didn't need to hear that and also Katie needed her sister, Laura, with her during delivery. This way she wouldn't be worried about Frank.

After her first real whimpers started, we turned on the record player but even that couldn't drown it out completely once the labor came full blast.

It started that early morning right after breakfast and stretched on until well after supper. Some of the others went to their rooms. Most of us stayed in the commons room. Everybody pretty much just munched for supper on whatever we could find.

I sat with my legs under me, wide-eyed, on the couch with Merrick. How could someone survive thirteen and a half hours of constant pain and it still wasn't over? Some people went to bed, but I was too fascinated.

I tried intently not to hear the screams. Merrick sat beside me, looking a little sickly himself. It felt strange, hearing someone scream and not feel the need to go save them.

After two more hours of screaming I saw Mrs. Trudy come around the corner by the stairs.

"Sherry. I need you," she said quickly and I froze.

"Me? Why me?"

"I just need you, come on."

"Mrs. Trudy, please..."

Her serious face was on, so I slowly got up and moved towards her. I peeked back to look at Merrick and he was smiling sympathetically.

No one said no to Mrs. Trudy, no one.

When I entered the room, I saw Katie. She looked terrible. I mean terrible in the nicest way possible. She was sweating, screaming, yelling, red faced, clenching fist and gritting teeth, hair a piled and sweeping mess and...she was spread eagle.

271

I tried to keep my eyes averted which was surprisingly easy.

I was there for at least another hour, maybe longer. I couldn't believe it took this long to have a baby. Then, Mrs. Trudy handed me a towel and told me to stand behind her there and wait. I did. I couldn't do anything else because I was frozen in fear and had no idea what I was doing in there.

Katie started to scream louder and louder. Paul looked almost as exhausted as her but urged her on, coaxing her to give it all she had. He looked so sweet pushing her hair back from her forehead, murmuring in her ear that it was almost over, they were finally going to have the baby they have been trying for for years, he loved her and she was doing great.

Then I saw it under Trudy's arm, the baby! It was coming! I saw the head of shiny black hair.

Trudy leaned back to me.

"Sherry, I'm going to hand the baby to you. I want you to take him or her over there to where they've set the warm water out and clean him up a bit. Then go for a walk around with him for a little while. She's torn so I'm going to have to sew her up and I've got no medicine to do it. Paul and her sister need to stay with her for this. I *need* you to do this. Can you do this for me...and don't freak out?"

"Yes," is all I could say.

What else was there to say, so I braced myself. I had never in my life, other than Danny, held a baby and that was a long long time ago. I *was* freaking, but I wouldn't tell Mrs. Trudy that.

I watched and waited, each time I thought this push is the one, it still wasn't. It was cruel and unusual. Oh, how did women do this? Why, when you knew this would happen, would you purposely get pregnant? I was almost thankful God spared me from this by making me sterile.

Then there it was. There *she* was. It was a girl! Katie got her girl. I was so happy tears welled up in my eyes.

Mrs. Trudy held the baby up for Paul and Katie to see for a few moments then handed her to me. She was so tiny. So very tiny compared to what I would have imagined. So pink and perfect and a little patch of black curls on top of that rounded head.

I walked over to the pallet holding her head. I remembered my own advice to my mother about baby Danny very well, 'Hold the head'.

I talked to myself since no one was around and they couldn't hear me anyway.

"You can do this, Sherry. It's perfectly natural. Back in the day, people had babies at home all the time and they didn't even have diapers. You can change a diaper."

After I got her cleaned up, I placed a teeny diaper on her. I was only guessing which way it was supposed to go on, but it stayed on when I picked her up so I went with it.

"There. See. We did it," I told the baby, but she just squinted her little eyes.

I wrapped her in the smallest yellow blanket I'd ever seen on the makeshift changing table Trudy had made out of her dresser top. I held her tight and secure and walked slowly out of the room without looking at the others for fear of seeing something gruesome.

Panic set in all around me like a fog and it wasn't even my baby, my flesh. Katie said her name was Sky, on the account that she probably wouldn't see the real sky much in her lifetime. My slow scared rocking pace was a lull and she, little precious Sky, fell right back to sleep.

As I turned the corner around the stairs I heard happy gasps and awe's of the ones who stayed up to wait for this moment. I couldn't help the smile on my face. I never imagined how warm and perfect this would feel. Marissa, Celeste and Kay were right there in a second, cooing and sweet talking, even though Sky's eyes were closed. The others slowly gathered around.

Jeff and Eli walked up, too. Jeff was in a trance in the truest sense of the word. He couldn't remove his eyes from her.

"Katie named her Sky," I said, my voice cracking.

"She's beautiful like her mamma," her uncle Eli said, tilting his head and running a finger down her cheek.

Jeff stepped even closer and looked at her intensely. I saw Eli start to make his way to the back room.

"Eli, you probably don't want to go in there yet. Trudy's sewing her up, but she's doing fine. Laura's with her still."

"Ok, I'll just wait by the door," Eli said and hurried off.

Then the baby talk commenced.

"Ah, look at her. What a sweet baby."

"She's precious, yes she is. Adorable."

"I bet she's got sky blue eyes too. She's gonna be gorgeous!"

"Wow. I've never seen a real baby before."

The baby talk could literally have gone on forever. I realized I had a tear running down my face, then another. I felt Sky's little breaths against my chest and I wanted to sob at the surreal ease of it all, but held back. I looked up trying to find Merrick. He was standing by the couch where I left him and he was looking at me with a face I couldn't decipher.

I'm so sorry, honey. I'm sorry that you can't be a mother yourself. I wish you could see what I see, right now. You are so beautiful. Baby, please don't cry.

I saw him walking to me at normal human pace, coming to stand behind me, feeling his hands on my waist. I was not crying entirely for my own reasons. I was just so happy for them. To see life come full circle with all this death was like a miracle.

I was still smiling though the tears were falling. It was such a strange sensation. I was utterly devastated yet so incandescently happy in the same moment. No, I wouldn't ever have this for myself and yes, I wanted it. She was so beautiful and fragile.

Merrick tentatively put his hand on her head. He smiled. He'd never touched a baby either.

What a wonderful father he would make. I couldn't help but let it flash before me. A new life; me, Merrick, a wedding, my pregnant belly, Merrick on a craving ice cream run, a new baby, late night feedings, Merrick teaching Jr. to ride a bike, Jr. meeting a girl... It was so perfect and yet so impossible and unreachable.

"You want to hold her?" I asked Merrick.

"Uh...no...no...that's ok," he stammered nervously.

Lies. So, I handed Sky to him, ever so gently, which he didn't protest to just like I knew he wouldn't. He held her like she was breakable, but in her case he was right.

She was breakable and beautiful and breathtaking.

She grabbed my pinky finger so tight in her sleep her little fingers turned white. I looked at Merrick's face. Just like me I could tell that he could sit there and hold her all day and be perfectly happy.

It was too bad Merrick would never have this either. He looked so perfect holding her.

He finally pried his eyes from her to look at mine. I laughed a silent laugh at his awe of her, wondering if that was how it started with me. Wonder and awe. His smile widened like he could read my thoughts and he continued to look in my eyes and hold this precious cargo.

Some of the others made their way out of their rooms to meet the new little black haired beauty that added to our growing crew. Sky got passed around a few times before Trudy finally came in and said it was all clear. The faces on those people as Sky and I walked away...

It would be so hard to let her go.

About as soon as I saw Paul's face I immediately knew how to let her go. He needed her, I could tell. It was more heartbreaking than anything I'd ever seen.

I handed her over and he immediately whispered his love to her. His face lit up so I left to give them their space to get acquainted with their new little one.

Merrick waited for me and as soon as I turned the corner he grabbed me and pulled me to him in a hug.

I'm sorry if I upset you before, by what I said.

"You didn't. I was already thinking about that before you said anything." I sighed remembering what if felt like to hold her. "She's so gorgeous."

"Yes. Yeah...she is. Wow. I had no idea," he said looking off into space in a daze.

"You looked adorable with her," I told him and he immediately looked back into my eyes.

"So did you. I'm so sorry, honey."

I felt them again, happy tears with a twing of regret. He pulled me in tighter, wrapping his arms all the way around my back and letting me soak his shirt front with useless but warranted tears. His warm hand smoothed the back of my head to soothe me.

I didn't have to explain to Merrick because he understood completely. I wondered if Trudy had known I couldn't have children if she would have found someone else to help her. I was glad she came and got me though. That was so wonderful to be a part of.

"I'm ok. Silly, but ok," I whispered finally, wiping my eyes with his sleeve but he stopped me and wiped them with his thumbs.

We turned in for the night, saying our goodnights. Seeing Merrick hold Sky was so sweet. Actually, I couldn't think of anything more sexy.

As I shut the door and flipped the switch off I felt him behind me, wrapping his arms around my waist. He kissed my neck up and down from my ear to my shoulder scar. Then he tugged me down.

As we climbed into our sleeping bag I reached over to kiss him. He kissed me back eagerly. I wondered if he was thinking the same thing I had been.

I hovered over him which he never allowed. I kissed him with all the wiles of the seductress I was, which I had to admit to myself weren't very much.

His hands were on my waist just under the hem of my shirt on my skin, tight and tingling. I pulled upward at his shirt hem and pulled it over his head. He grabbed me as soon as he was free of it and kissed me harder, pulling me under him and then we rolled back to me on top.

For a moment I thought he was finally giving in, but no. He slowed his enthusiasm and lips but I didn't want to and I tried to pull him to me tighter. He grabbed my face between his hands so gently and pulled it away just a bit, looking into me.

275

"Sherry. Baby, you've got to stop. One more night. Please... behave," he breathed, pleading with me.

I laughed a frustrated chuckle and he gently lifted me off him with incredible ease, folding me into his chest under his chin. I couldn't argue with one more night and a perfect warm embrace to last me until then.

Oh, how I loved it when he said 'behave', like I was capable of misbehaving. Like I was tough, rugged and maybe not so fragile and breakable. I calmed my thoughts. If I was actually going to behave I'd better just enjoy the warmth and go to sleep. Immediately.

The next morning, my eyes burst open as soon as I woke. I was wide open, coherent and eager. I knew exactly what today was before I could think of anything else. I turned to see Merrick's wide awake face too, just as happy and anticipatory as mine.

"So I guess we're getting married today then?" he asked and it still drove me crazy the way he acted like I was going to change my mind and give him up.

"You have to ask?" I yelled and kissed him, but he pulled away.

"Listen. I love you, but I just want to make sure this is what you want."

"Are we back to this? If this wasn't what I wanted, then I wouldn't be here right now, with you."

"I just...seeing you with Sky yesterday and knowing you're giving up a lot being with me makes me wonder if you might have reconsidered."

"I'd say the same for you."

"That's different."

"How? I can't have kids. That's not going to change no matter who I end up with. You could still go on to your paradise, The After. Jeff told me all about it."

"He did?" He seemed disappointed.

My heart clenched violently with guilt. I hoped that look on his face wasn't because I chose to marry him anyway, taking his chances of it away from him knowingly. Then I suddenly felt overwhelmed with regret at disappointing him.

"Yes and I thought so long and hard about it. I just didn't see how we'd make it through all this so why not live while we're alive?"

"Honey-"

"I know that sounds morbid, but if I thought - really and truly believed - that this would all be over soon and the Keepers would be going home, I wouldn't be marrying you. I wouldn't have even gotten involved in the first place. I couldn't have done that to you, not knowing what I was taking from you. I'm sorry, I feel terrible about it now, but I just...couldn't not be with you." I looked down as I spoke, feeling red shame creep over my face.

"Sherry." He lifted my face with a finger under my chin. "Is that what you think? That you're taking something from me? What is a life if there is nothing in it? What good is paradise if you don't have the one you want to share it with? Who wants to live forever all by their self?"

"Piper was pretty eager to help you out with that," I said and was a little surprised that I could still feel jealous over her.

"Keepers don't love each other the same way humans do, Sherry. It wasn't like that."

"The jealousy looked the same to me."

"Huh... Wow." He smiled a huge cocky grin which surprised me considering the conversation we were having. "How incredibly cute that is."

"What?"

"You're jealous," he whispered, amused.

"No. No, I'm not. I just noticed how she...I mean she was... Look, I just talked to Jeff about it and he told me she was interested."

"Yeah...well like I said, it's not the same. I promise you, she didn't feel for me the way you do," he said, still smiling smugly.

"Good. I wasn't jealous."

"Uhuh. Welcome to my world. I am constantly fighting off suitor assaults everywhere we go. First Bobby, then Phillip, who's next? I know another one is coming along soon. You're too irresistible for your own good." He looked me up and down slowly.

"Shut up!" I yelled playfully, pushing his chest but not moving him an inch. "Guys just freak cause they think the world is ending. It's not really me they are attracted to, just the thought of... procreation."

"Really. Hmmm, I disagree." He leaned forward, nuzzling his way into my neck. "Men notice how amazing you are. Everyone notices, just not you."

"Ok, ok," I said, hoping to stop this Sherry-fest. "So are you going to marry me or not?" I smiled widely and hoped he would accept my subject change.

He pulled back to look at me. "If you'll have me."

"I wouldn't have it without you."

He placed his hand on my cheek and closed his eyes, like he was checking to make sure he was awake or that I was real. His eyes opened and they were bright and alive.

He pushed his mouth to mine, easily and sweetly. He pulled back just a bit and sighed a long, wonderful, intoxicating-me-with-his-happy-breath sigh. Then he gave the order I'd been waiting for.

"All right, you. Get dressed."

Collide - Shelly Crane

Two Become One
Chapter 26

Merrick couldn't hide what we were doing from Jeff or the other Keepers. I thought he just completely stopped trying to block them out all together, but as far as everyone else was concerned, we were keeping a tight lip.

I got lots of sideways looks and smiles from Kay and an enthusiastic hug in the kitchen from Ryan who told me how happy he was for me and he had no further objections to mine and Merrick's union. Jeff was so ecstatic, in true favorite uncle spirit, but tried not to show it so no one would suspect anything.

Eli made the flyer on Phillip's old computer in his room. A lot of that stuff would come in handy.

We decided to make Phillip's old room a second commons room pushing one of the couches in there. We just needed places to put the people when they weren't in their rooms sleeping. His bed we kept in there for sitting and napping purposes and Calvin and Franklin had already made a fort out of the sheet and the light fixture from the wall.

Taking Keepers into town to put up business flyers would be risky and tricky. We had originally said no Keepers in town, but this was our search operation now.

Katie and the rest of the newbies were busy with the new baby and Phillip was no longer here. Specials were still considered 'Special' and therefore forbidden to leave since the Lighters could sense them. There were only so many of us left who were able to do these missions.

We took our headless golf clubs with us, laughing at the thought of carrying them around, stabbing dark haired men like vampires through the heart.

Merrick was apprehensive about the day's events, knowing that I would be the one, heading into the print shop by myself, then for all the pit stops for flyer distribution, going in by myself. He seemed a little too preoccupied with the wedding to be too upset though and it made me happy that he was so...well, happy.

If I could be some slight sliver in the happiness pie of others, that just added to my own feeling of purpose. I was making him happy. Me. Short, boring brown hair, no job, no home, nothing special not even a Special, just me made him happy.

I twisted my ring around my finger the whole drive. The old Jeep hadn't been driven in a while and it spat and sputtered for a minute but eventually evened out. Merrick handled the gear shifting like a pro in no time.

He extended his hand over to rest on my leg when he wasn't shifting.

Aerosmith was playing on the radio and he seemed to like it, indicated by the slight head bob. He looked so handsome and happy, his hair blowing in swirls from the wind from the top down. He seemed so human and completely normal.

Once we got our flyers printed, and I got hit on by the Kinko's copy guy, we made our rounds to the places we all thought would be good business advertisement. So hotel lobbies, truck stops, restaurants. No grocery store though as neither of us was comfortable with that after the Taker being there.

We started towards the church and it was already starting to darken in the skies. Hopefully the other crew had as much luck with the flyers as we did.

Last on the agenda for today was matrimony.

The first church we came upon was called Heaven's Gate Baptist Church. It sounded perfect to me. I took Merrick's shaking hand after we slid out of the Jeep. I knew why he was shaking, we were in the lion's den as he once called it. Anyone could call him out as a Keeper here and that would be that. It would all be over. He would be gone and I'd become a Lighter or worse, a mark carrier, trying to be myself but working for the enemy. I realized the risk he was taking for me, for my dream.

I squeezed his hand and bit my bottom lip with a half smile. He smiled too and slowly towed me inside behind him.

The cover up job done early this morning to Merrick's mark had kept it really good and hidden. It stopped snowing yesterday so we would be ok, at least until we got done with one small task.

I couldn't believe how giddy I was.

I tried to steady myself as we approached the pastor sitting in his office at the end of the long hall.

"Excuse me? The door was open, I hope that's all right," Merrick began.

The pastor was sitting there at an ancient computer on his desk. He was writing in an old brown leather binder with multiple scribbles all over the page. The desk sign said 'Pastor Robert Berns'. His gray hair was plastered across his forehead and when he saw us he swiped it with his palm and pushed his glasses back up on his nose.

"Of course. You are always welcome in God's house. Come in, please. How can I help you today?"

"We want to get married. Right now."

"Oh, I see," he said and flinched with surprise. Then he cleared his throat and continued. "Ok. No witnesses? Did you take your blood tests yet? Got your marriage license?"

"We just want the ceremony. We know it won't be official or on the books. We just want to hear and say the words."

"Ok." A long pause. "Well, I guess I can do that. I'm not sure what you think you could gain from it, but alright. You know you can't claim 'say and hear the words' on your taxes right?"

He was joking and Merrick laughed before I did. I was so proud of my human.

"Yes, sir. It's just something...sentimental and important we need to do. Nothing to gain, just us," he said and looked at me with that smile that made me heart jump.

The preacher looked pleasantly surprised and smiled, too. "Sounds like the best reason I've heard in ages. Why don't you follow me?"

We followed him back down the hall as he peeked his head in at the plump secretary and mumbled something I couldn't hear, then he motioned for us to continue to follow him.

The sanctuary was beautiful. It was an old original 1800's church restored as he explained. It was so simple with clean lines and curves in the architecture. Huge stained glass windows with no pictures of shining suns or angels, just colorful glass pieces fit together to make something beautiful and let just the right amount of light in.

It was perfect. I sighed as I glanced around and Merrick looked over to eye me curiously. While the pastor looked for something, I pulled Merrick down and whispered in his ear.

"If you could read my mind right now, Keeper, you'd see that I think this is perfect. This place is what I would've dreamed about for my wedding day, had I ever thought to do so."

"I'm glad you like it. I'm sorry you can't have the big to-do," Merrick said, wrapping my hand in the crook of his elbow.

"This is all the to-do I want."

He knew I was telling the truth and smiled.

"Aha! Found it," the pastor yelled, "my Pastor's manual. You would think after all these years I could remember the words to marry someone, but this mind doesn't work like it used to."

He stepped forward as he laughed and motioned for us to stand in front of him by the altar right near the piano. The secretary was playing something softly. I didn't know the tune and it didn't really sound like a song, just slow melodious playing. It was very sweet and timely.

The pastor went through the whole spill and I wanted to just yell at him to get to it already. I just wanted to hear the words 'I now pronounce you'.

When he got to our names he said to just fill in the blank, so we did. Merrick started with 'Sherry Elizabeth Patterson', then it was my turn to copy the pastor's line of vows. I started with 'Merrick...Finch'. We both laughed and he looked at us like we were nuts, but went on once we settled. Then I heard the sweetest words in my whole existence.

"Merrick and Sherry, it is my pleasure to pronounce you husband and wife in the eyes of our Lord. You may kiss your beautiful bride."

And he did, a good and long and perfect kiss. My hands fisted his shirt front as his framed my face in complete control. The intensity of his kiss made me feel guilty being in church and all. When we were done the pastor clapped Merrick on the back and started to walk off but Merrick stopped him.

"Um, sir. Here, take this, thank you. We really appreciate it," he said, handing him a folded up paper bill. A fifty.

"Son, you don't have to give me anything. I wanted to do it, so I did. I'm just happy to see two people that can still find each other in all this...mess."

"Are you sure?"

"Yes, I'm sure. Besides," he paused thoughtfully, "the news says I'm not allowed to take business from a Keeper."

Merrick squeezed my hand in his and we looked at each other. I was sure his fingers were hurting from my intense squeeze. Well maybe not, but we were more than stunned.

"Excuse me?" Merrick tried to keep his voice even.

"It's ok, son, I understand. You just didn't do a very good cover up job and when you turned sideways to look at her, I had to pretty much stare right at your mark the whole time. Listen, you'll get no trouble from me but I don't want any trouble from you either."

"No, sir, we would never. We just wanted to get married, that was all."

"Kind of a weird predicament you got yourselves into, huh? A Keeper and a human?" he said easily.

He was puzzled but not being condescending.

"Predicament, no. Unforeseeable turn of events, yes."

"Well, I wish you the best. You ought to be more careful. The next time you might get someone who actually believes those vultures on the news, pardon my crassness. I just don't like all this business."

"Sir, don't watch the news anymore, ok? Keepers aren't the bad guys, we just want to help. Be careful and thank you for you time."

"Oh, sonny? We don't *want* to be involved, but if you ever really *need* help, well, you two know where to find us. I say people, human or not, who would risk this much to get married, to be together, must be something special in my book."

He walked over to the lady playing the piano, the secretary, and put his arm around her kissing her temple. How sweet, they were married and ran the church together.

I waved a thank you and we shot out the side door, the same way we came in. As soon as we were clear it was as if we were both thinking the same thing.

We turned and grabbed each other in a grateful embrace. He lifted me up and I wrapped my legs around his waist as we laughed and twirled, completely wrapped around each other in happiness.

I kissed him with all the tenderness reserved for such an occasion. I kissed my husband.

Once home, I had one thing on my mind. I hoped that Merrick did as well but he surprised me and seemed reluctant to my silent and not so silent pleas to turn in for the night as we sat together on the couch.

I smiled at him sweetly, bit my lip and looked at him playfully, I even nudged his arm once when he refused to look my way. I came to the conclusion that I was not a very good seductress or he was too worried about tonight to even try; probably both.

My face fell. I was disappointed. I wanted him to enjoy our wedding night, not freak out about it. Maybe he wasn't even interested in that aspect of marriage. That thought had never crossed my mind before.

He saw my expression and pulled my chin up with his finger. He looked deep into my eyes and smiled a sweet understanding but wry smile. He let go of my chin and grabbed my hand, pulling me from the couch and led me to our room. I still wasn't convinced. Maybe he was just taking me to more a private place to talk it over, though not that many people were still awake and even out of their rooms.

Once inside our room, he was more gentle and loving as I'd ever seen him. He pulled me to sit on our knees and caressed my face and neck slowly and tenderly. He kissed the scar on my shoulder from the Marker, back and forth, up and down my arm and neck. He kissed my lips easily and then framed my face with his warm hands. Then he spoke to me in the way only my Keeper could.

I'm sorry, I was worried. I just don't want to hurt you. I'd never do it on purpose, but my inhuman strength comes out sometimes and I don't... I'm still a little anxious, but I'm trying not to be. I have no idea what I'm doing, but I'm not going to ruin tonight for you. If I do something...you don't like or if I hurt you in any way, even a little bit, you tell me. If there is anything you want me to do that I'm not doing, you tell me. Promise me, Sherry.

"I promise as long as you do, too. I love you."

I love you, too, wife.

He brought his mouth to mine, parting our lips together. Our breath mingled and I felt the thrill of it all. I grasped the nape of his neck and tugged his hair gently. He groaned against my throat as he kissed my collarbone and I figured that he must have realized the same thing as me.

It was freedom.

The tingling was a full force assault. Electricity was everywhere and I felt it all the way to my toes and back. He let go of all inhibitions and so did I. There was no holding back, no sparing the other with our cautiousness and no guilt. We were set free and ready for the next chapter in our lives, together.

He placed a finger under the strap of my tank top, sliding it down my arm to kiss my bare shoulder and my breath came out in harsh bursts. Then he removed my shirt completely for the very first time, gently pulling it over my head and gazing down at me with awe and love.

"You are really beautiful," he said and ran his fingers down my cheek and neck.

I smiled and bit my lip in a moment of silly self-consciousness. I had no doubt that Merrick enjoyed the view, but I couldn't help it. I'd never been naked in front of anyone before. It was nothing like what I thought it would be like. I thought I'd be hyperventilating with embarrassment, covering myself with shaking hands, but no. I felt the little twinge, but as I saw the look he was giving me I felt grateful beyond words that I saved myself for this moment. That I saved myself for this man.

I pulled up to remove his shirt and he let me do it without his help.

"I'm so glad I waited for you," I said with conviction.

"Me, too," he chuckled huskily. "I adore you for it."

His breath caught when I reached for his jean snap. My heart pounded loudly and out of sync, my breathing was out of control. He placed me down against the pillow and twined his fingers with mine on our pallet over my head.

For someone who claimed to not know what he was doing he seemed to know *exactly* what he was doing. I'd never been so wonderfully frustrated in all my life. He knew me so entirely and was exactly where I needed him to be with just the right amount of teasing affection and attention.

He practically *was* reading my mind and he seemed to rather enjoy himself as well. His lips softly kissed my ribs and I could only hope those doors were as sound proof as I wanted them to be. I heard a moan and gasped as I realized I was making that noise. Merrick echoed me with his own.

We finally fell asleep last night completely exhausted and wonderfully satisfied. It was morning and Merrick had started keeping a candle in the corner for me since I couldn't see in the dark like him. I looked up to his face from where I lay on his chest and saw the most handsome, incandescent, rested husband. There was no awkwardness or shyness, just happiness.

"Morning, you," I said.

"Good morning," he greeted huskily.

I couldn't think as I enjoyed the warm glow and thrill of what was going on between us. Merrick had been so right. Everything was perfect last night because we did things the right way, our way. I loved him even more for that. It was worth every minute of the wait.

Then. Oh, no!

I was dragged kicking and screaming from my peaceful thought by another one. The Keepers would see this in Merrick's mind. Oh no! They would all see. Embarrassing! Why had I not thought of this before? It wasn't like it really mattered or would have changed anything, but still, it would be strange. Maybe he can block them for...oh say, forever?

Well, I just wouldn't be embarrassed. They shouldn't be in his head anymore anyway. It was their own fault and they would get a peep show assault in their mind when we walked out of here and I would wear a smug smile. I couldn't help but ask though.

"Merrick, what about the other Keepers?"

He knew what I meant right away.

"I talked to them already. They agreed that we would all try to stay out of each other's heads from now on unless it's an emergency. Don't worry about it."

"Mmmm," I crooned, satisfied with the answer and Merrick's thoughtfulness. "I'm not worried. I'm not worried about anything right now." I sighed and snuggled closer. "Thank you."

"I can't guarantee that they won't ever see, but I'll try my best. I really think most of them would really rather not see that anyway. We don't have anything to worry about." He chuckled slightly but then turned serious. "By the way, last night was...amazing."

"It was perfect. Thank you. I couldn't imagine it being any other way than that. You were so..."

"No...you...you were so..." We both laughed out loud at our inability to form coherent speech. "I didn't hurt you did I? I was trying to be..." he said bashfully and wrinkled his nose, making me giggle at his frustration.

"No, you couldn't hurt me, Merrick. I loved it."

He kissed me softly and pulled me tighter into his arms. I felt his breath on my face as he traced circles into the small of my back with his thumb. I didn't want to move. I'd starve first and I just might.

I could already hear my body betraying me with its incessant need for things, food in particular. Forcing me to leave this perfect moment. I felt if I got up that this would all go away some how. It was too good to be true. The growling continued and I heard Merrick's soft laughter.

"Honey, we're married now. You are absolutely stuck with me, so, we can get up and go eat so we don't starve and I'll still be here. Always together. I promise."

"I thought you couldn't read my mind, Mr. Finch."

"I can't, but I'm beginning to not have to."

Merrick - Heaven's Gates
Chapter 28

I remembered wishing she'd hurry up in there. Trying to think about other things so that I wouldn't freak out. Think about things like Danny. My conscience had been buzzing slightly lately. It wasn't as strong on earth but I could still feel it. When I asked Danny if anything was wrong yesterday he said it was nothing, he was just a little down in the dumps. I didn't really believe himm but I'd been so wrapped up in Sherry lately to really focus on anything else.

We had a brief Keeper meeting yesterday because it seemed mine wasn't the only conscience that was buzzing. Our Specials seemed to be fine, if not a little tired and withdrawn. That went along with what Danny told me. Maybe everyone was just tired of being cooped up. We concluded that was the cause and left it at that since none of our Specials said anything different.

Sherry was in there, handing out flyers and posting them. I thought something was wrong. Maybe someone was harassing her about the flyers but no, she was fine. I just couldn't stand sitting out there waiting helplessly. She was doing well though. No problems all day and we made good time.

I needed to make sure I told her that. She thought I thought she was weak, but I didn't. I knew how strong she was.

I didn't doubt her bravery, I doubted her right hook.

"You may kiss your beautiful bride."

I'm married, kissing her as my wife. The perfect girl. Most guys would be sweating bullets but Sherry was not like most girls.

She wasn't argumentative unless it was really important to her and then you could just forget about winning. She didn't nag me, she doesn't raise her voice, she was a helpmate without complaint and not because of duty but because she wanted to be. She was so giving and unselfish. She was sexy but modest. She was gorgeous yet not arrogant. She was fragile yet strong...in spirit.

It didn't seem fair that I should get such a girl. I'd seen some hideous things in my Keeper time. Some women were vicious and uncaring, nagging, spiteful creatures wrapped in pretty packages. Men were too. I'd seen that first hand with this body in fact, but it just seemed so against a woman's nature to be so vicious.

She actually went through with it and said the words that she would marry me. Somehow, I still thought there was a chance she'd wake up and see that she was better than me. All that worry was for nothing.

Look at her, eyeing me, wanting me. I always looked away at these parts of the human life to give them privacy, though they never knew I was there to begin with.

How do you make love? I knew the technicalities, but that wasn't what I wanted for her. I wanted it to be the best night ever for her. But how can I if...

I knew she was getting upset. I could see it on her face. She thought I was stalling and I was. She'd never understand why. She'd think I was stupid.

It wasn't just my insecurities but also my inhuman strength. I'd never had a problem with it unless I get angry but what if I did get out of control? Would I hurt her?

I couldn't ruin it for her though. I promised her we'd wait until now and now had come. If I wanted to be a man, then I needed to act like one.

I looked into her, pulling her face up with my finger under her chin. I wanted her to see that I was ready and was done being a coward. I picked up her hand in mine and gently tugged her, leading her to our honeymoon suite of a closet.

I tried to be attentive. I just wouldn't stop moving. I kissed her lips, her neck, that hideous scar on her shoulder though she pulled it off and made it look gorgeously fierce somehow. I nipped and kissed at her throat and ear lobes, trying fervently to remember any notions of human affection I'd caught a glimpse of over the years. I tried to playback all the things I'd ever done to her to make her breath catch and give her shivers.

Her hands tugged at my hair and oh...wow. It was a good thing I didn't know it would feel like this before because there was no way I could have stopped her.

I hoped I was doing everything right. I hoped she wasn't just playing it up for my satisfaction and ego. She would tell me if I was doing something wrong or hurting her, wouldn't she?

Fool, just let go! She married me, she loves me, so I should just give in and be with her. That beautiful woman wanted me. Me! No longer would I tell her to behave, instead I would beg her to misbehave from then on.

I kissed her belly and ribs and she arched her back. It would seem that she was putty in my hands. I felt a sprig of self satisfaction as I must have been doing it right. I heard her appreciative moans and couldn't help it myself as I gave in completely over to this beautiful, sexy, dangerous little woman.

My wife.

In the morning I woke up and glanced over. There she was. It hadn't been a dream after all. She was laying on my chest asleep with her arm across my stomach and her brown curls splayed out across her arm and back. I swore I could even see a smile on those perfect pink pouted lips.

I moved her hair out of her face with my fingers. She was so soft and warm. Last night...ahhh...she was so amazing. How could someone so small and cute be so sexy?

I was glad that I thought to tell the others to stay out of my head. I hoped they listened to me. I knew they would. Well, they better.

Sleeping On The Job
Chapter 28

Breakfast started out quiet. I was trying to keep my mind from running wild wondering what people were thinking. Of course the ones who knew about the elopement knew exactly what we were doing last night but the fact that they could literally see it in Merrick's head anytime they wanted was making me nervous.

I tried to push that aside and focus on the scrambled eggs I was cooking for everyone. Jeff had been by twice to check on the eggs and flash a huge I-know-what-you-did grin at me.

The more I looked at Kay, Ryan, Max, Jeff and Merrick around the kitchen table, the more I saw how much they were beginning to enjoy human food. Most of them were only here for a few hours at a time before with their trips here to salvage a Special in trouble. For the most part they never even ate food until now.

I tried to keep that in mind when it was my turn to cook. I wanted to cook things for them that they would love and want more of. I wanted them to think 'how did I survive without this'. Like cheesecake, which I was making for dessert tonight. On the last run they heeded my request for the ingredients.

Trudy, Marissa, and I began a cooking rotation last week with the other ladies who were not fond of cooking. They would do a dish rotation. Perfect setup for me because dishes weren't fun to begin with, but in this kitchen the memory of dishes gave me chills.

It was a good thing I loved to cook. Trudy had been a little down lately and less perky and active. I wondered if her Leukemia was to blame or the heartbreak. Either way there was nothing to do for her but let her rest. The Leukemia was past the chemo stage and what could you do for a broken heart?

After Merrick filled up on three plates full of scrambled eggs, I cut him off. He wrapped his arms around my waist from behind while I stirred the eggs and whispered a joke in my ear about needing his strength for later. I giggled and we got the usual grinning glances, but nothing out of the ordinary. He left to go take a shower.

We pulled it off. We eloped and got away with it. Wow. I was married.

Jeff and Ryan finished a couple plates each and were suffering.

"Sherry, those were the best eggs I've ever had. I've only had eggs once before but I'm being serious, they were great," Ryan told me, placing his plate in the sink, then returning to his chair.

"Thanks, Ryan. It was my mom's eco friendly version."

He raised his eyebrow in question and I just laughed.

"Well, whatever it was, they were awesome. Thank you."

"You're welcome. I can't believe we've been down here this long and I haven't cooked scrambled eggs for everyone yet. Merrick is the only one I've ever cooked them for."

"Well, Merrick gets a lot of special treatment around here."

Ryan could barely finish before he was laughing, which made Jeff laugh, too.

"Hey!" I swatted him with the dish towel on his arm as I tried not to laugh. "Watch it."

They both burst out laughing again as I finished up the last pan of eggs for myself and Trudy.

Celeste came into the kitchen.

"What's all the commotion about?" she chimed, honestly hoping for some drama to be going on.

She was so bored lately.

"Nothing, just some Keepers being silly."

I mock glared at them and they chuckled under their breath. Jeff's eyes were laughing over the rim of his coffee cup.

"Dang. I need something to do up in here people! Something to talk about. I'm dying here! I'm even out of nail polish," she whined.

I chuckled and turned so she wouldn't see me laughing. She dramatically plopped down at the table with Ryan and Jeff, throwing her arms on the table and laying her head down on them. I could hear her continue to sulk in a muffle.

"Bored. Bored. Bored. Why does it have to be the end of the world, huh? I'm too young to be so depressed and sullen."

"Well, you could learn to knit from Trudy. She'd probably love the distraction," Ryan told her.

She even surprised me with her answer and following enthusiasm.

"Really! Wow. I'd never thought I'd ever be excited about something like *knitting*. I'm going to go talk to her right now!"

Just like that she ran off to find Trudy. I wondered what Danny was doing for Celeste to be so bored. Come to think of it, Celeste seemed to be the only Special up and running around lately. Even Calvin seemed pretty mellow. Hmmm.

I ate my eggs quickly standing at the counter, putting a lid over the leftovers for Trudy and the rest of the lazy bones who weren't up yet.

I wiped my hands on the towel hanging by the fridge and playfully pushed Jeff's shoulder as I walked by. I heard them laughing as I walked out, making my way to the bathroom. I was just about to shut the door when Celeste held it open with her hand.

"Hold it. Let me grab my- Sherry! What's that on your neck? Oh my-" She lunged for me, pulling back the strap of my tank top and swiping at my hair. "Sherry! Is that a hickey? Oh. My. Goodness."

She just stood there staring at it so I pushed her fingers off and turned to look in the mirror. When I shifted the tank top strap and my hair around to the back there were quite a few hickeys and raspberries around my neck and collarbone, in fact.

I felt the blush coming but then I realized I was a married woman and had no reason to be ashamed but...she didn't know we went through with it yet, so I turned back and smiled sheepishly while shrugging.

"Ah! Bad!" she said winking and laughing like we were in some secret club together now.

I hoped we were not in the same club. I fervently blocked that thought as she walked out giggling loudly. I fixed my hair to hang around my shoulders to hide the marks and then took care of business. Then I decided to go see Danny.

In the commons room, Marissa and Jeff were on the couch with lots of space between them but they were turned toward each other. Marissa was laughing and they looked pretty cozy in their conversation. Hmm. I cocked my head. It would be nice to not be the minority on alien courtship around here.

I knocked on Danny's door and peeked in a little when I didn't hear him say anything. He was asleep still which was not unusual for him.

I sat next to him and shook his arm. He woke right up, even looking around alert. That wasn't like Danny. Danny was the king of grump in the morning.

"Hey. You ok?" I asked startled by his actions.

"Yeah, why? Something happen?" he said, rubbing his palms into his eyes.

"No, I just wanted to check on you. You've been sleeping a lot. Is everything ok?"

"You wouldn't believe me if I told you," he muttered and slumped back down in his sleeping bag, turning away from me.

That sent a shiver down my spine. Danny always told me everything. Whatever was on his mind, it couldn't be good.

"Yes, I would. What is it?"

"Sis, something's going on with me. Something's not right."

"Ok, Danny. Please, you're scaring me. What are you talking about? I won't laugh."

"I don't think you'll laugh. I think you'll think I'm crazy."

292

"I won't. Please," I pleaded as he turned back over to look at me, hesitation on his face.

"I can...make other people think things or do things. I can control them with my mind."

"What?" I tried to sound the least threatening as possible.

"I can make people think things, like Merrick, but instead of them hearing my thoughts they actually think what I want them to. They even say it out loud or do it."

"Danny...I..."

Then I got what he meant.

The next thing out of my mouth was my voice but not my words. It was a strange feeling, like my mouth had a brain of its own. I felt it moving, but in my brain it was perfectly still.

"Danny is wonderful. Danny is the best brother ever. Danny is a skilled basketball player," he made me say and I gasped and covered my mouth with my hand.

"See... What's wrong with me, Sherry? What's going on?"

I had no explanations to tell him. We'd seen some pretty weird things lately. As shocking as this was it should be believable against Markers and Lighters.

"Does Celeste know?" I asked, swallowing.

"No. I couldn't tell her. She thinks I'm sick or something. It's been doing this for a week. Well, that's as long as I know of it. I tried to tell Celeste something and when she answered, she said what I wanted her to say instead. Then I did it again and I've been doing to people for days now. It seems they don't even realize it, really."

"Hold on. Stay right there," I said, patting his arm and headed back out his door.

What? Danny has some kind of power now?

For just a minute I buried my face in my hands in the hall outside his room and had a mini panic attack. Why Danny? Things couldn't just be normal around here for any length of time! There was constantly some kind of drama.

Ok. Back to business.

I ran to the commons room yelling for Jeff and Merrick. Jeff ran in first in a flash, grabbing my arm to make sure I was ok.

"I'm ok, it's not me. Where's Merrick?"

He must've been calling him in his mind. Merrick flashed down the stairs and ran to us with inhuman speed. I spoke before he could to stop him from freaking out.

"Danny. He's... Come on. See for yourself."

I took them to Danny's room with Merrick looking extremely worried.

293

When we went in, Danny was sitting there shirtless like before, wrapped in his sheet on the floor in the fetal position.

"Danny, tell them," I commanded. He looked at me like he couldn't believe I brought them, like I betrayed him. "I had to. Something is happening to you and they need to know. Tell them!" I shouted because I could no longer take the suspense of knowing what was wrong with my only brother.

"I can...do something. I can make people think things, thoughts."

He looked up at them from under his eyelashes.

"What do you mean?" Merrick bent down on his haunches to survey Danny. "Show me what you mean?"

Merrick looked straight ahead and began to speak the words to the song 'Crazy Train.'

"Mental wounds still screaming, driving me insane, I'm going off the rails on a crazy train." After Merrick spoke he shook his head and his eyes went wide with shock.

"See? What does that mean? What's wrong with me?" Danny pleaded, looking back and forth from Merrick to Jeff.

They looked at each other and I could tell they were talking in their minds. I reached out and grabbed both of their forearms gently and spoke softly.

"Please tell us what you're saying. We can handle it."

"We don't know. I mean, the only supernatural powers I've ever seen on a human are the Muses and the Taker. I've never heard of other humans developing abilities. I guess we shouldn't be that surprised with everything else so strange going on. I...we don't know what to tell you," Merrick said, looking flabbergasted and winded.

"Ok. Well, is that all you can do? Have you tried anything else?" Jeff asked.

"Isn't that enough?" Danny said hastily then blew out a breath to calm himself. "No I haven't tried anything else and from the way I see it, they only know I've done it to them when I tell them about it beforehand. Sherry and you knew but Celeste, Ryan, and Paul didn't. They just acted like...nothing happened afterwards, like they didn't even know they had spoken or done anything."

I believed, but at the same time I feel dismayed and unsettled. What was going on? What did this mean? Was Danny the only one and why did Merrick and Jeff not know about all this? Why did I feel like I wanted to punch something? Why couldn't we get a break?

"Look, let's keep this between us until we figure out what's going on here, ok? The other Keepers shouldn't find out either, as we are already staying out of each others head. That shouldn't be too hard," Jeff explained.

"Why are you staying out of each others heads?" Danny asked quizzically.

Crap. I hadn't even realized Jeff's slip up until Danny did.

"Uh. We are just...giving each other a break," Jeff explained but Danny didn't look convinced, given away by his squint.

"Sis? You can't lie to me, what's going on? Are there others? Someone else having problems like me? It's bad isn't it! Oh no. What's going to..." Danny was beginning to freak so I spilled all the beans.

"We got married, Danny. Merrick and I got married yesterday. The Keepers are just giving us some privacy."

He looked more shocked about that than he did about his new abilities. His jaw flew open and his eyebrows pulled together in a scowl.

"You got married without me!" Danny yelled, furious.

That definitely was not what I expected.

"Danny, we didn't want to cause a scene or whatever. We just wanted to get married first then tell people eventually. You already knew about it, it's not like we could make a big production about it, right? We went by ourselves. I was going to tell you-"

"Didn't you think I would want to be there?" Danny looked so much like dad when he spoke like that.

Soft and interrupting me with his stern yet hurt voice. Like the time I ran away from home and dad caught me sneaking in after only being gone fifteen minutes.

"Yes, I did, but you couldn't go, Danny. You're a Special. Remember?" I reminded him softly but still felt like I was whipping a puppy.

"Well...I still wish you had told me. All the Keepers knew and I didn't."

"I'm sorry. I thought it would be better if-"

I didn't even finish and Danny was reaching over to hug me.

"I can't believe you're married. My little sister is someone's wife. I never thought I'd get the chance to be a brother-in-law, no offense."

"None taken. I'm sorry."

"Don't be. I understand, it just sucks is all. I mean, I could've walked you down the aisle since dad isn't here. I would've loved that," he whispered the last part, like it was a secret that he was letting me in on.

I just smiled and held him, trying not to cry. I understood. If he had eloped I would have wrung his neck but desperate times called for desperate measures.

A quick glance over at Merrick and Jeff and I saw two smiles.

"You two are so human, I hope you know that," I told them through a comical tear strained voice and Jeff stifled a short laugh unsuccessfully.

"Danny, I'm sorry," Merrick, still bent down, reached over to shake his hand as he spoke.

"It's cool. I may not be thrilled but I understand why you had to do it that way. I would say you better be good to her, but I already know you will be," Danny

295

said with a conviction, which made me want to cry even more.

"Thanks. I appreciate that and I will."

"Ok," Danny breathed and rubbed his hand over his face. "So back to the fact that I'm a freak. What do we do other than keep quiet?"

"We'll figure it all out. Do you feel ok physically?" Jeff asked bending back down to examine him more closely.

"Um, I guess so. Just really tired lately. I've got to tell Celeste. She's not going to buy the 'I'm sick' story forever, especially with her checking on me once an hour."

"That's ok, just tell her to keep quiet about it until we find out something. Merrick and I will discuss what we need to do and let you know."

We all stood up except Danny. He did look tired even though he had slept all night and then some. His eyes were pale and glazed like he was fighting an infection. That must have had something to do with this new ability. The Muses wrath drained my strength so it made sense to assume that all the supernatural stuff would follow the same rules.

Please, let him be ok.

Katie was holding Sky in the rocker in the commons room when I walked back through. She hadn't really left her room since the baby was born.

I tried to give them their privacy and hadn't gone to see them. Not only that but I was scared about the same feelings coming back making me want a baby of my own. Not to mention the fact that we'd been kinda busy around there. I wished I had gone to see her now.

"Hey, Katie. Hey, Sky." My voice went automatically to baby talk mode when I said her name. "Wow. She is still just as gorgeous," I said looking down at them both.

"Yeah, she is. So, Aunt Sherry, you want to hold her again? We haven't seen you in a while," Katie said with a small crooked smile.

Aunt Sherry. With Danny as a brother, I assumed I'd never hear those words.

"Yes, of course I do." I reached down to cuddle the sweet baby in the crook of my arm with Katie's help. "Sorry, things have been kinda crazy lately."

"It's ok. I never said thank you for helping out the day she was born."

"It was my pleasure," I said and I meant it.

She smiled at me as if she understood, but I knew there was no way she really could. I no longer care, though, with the baby trance taking me over again even more potent than before.

Sky was sweet smelling like lavender and her straight, pitch-black hair was soft against my arm, though there wasn't much of it. I sighed rocking her back and forth as I began to circulate the room with her.

After a couple minutes I looked over to see that poor Katie had already passed out in the rocker with exhaustion. I grabbed a blanket from the couch and pulled it over her, impressively with one arm.

I swayed with little content Sky in my arms and left her mommy to doze for a minute. Merrick and Jeff were discussing things silently in the kitchen leaning against the counters. Somehow I could always tell when they were silently conversing. Because they just got this look on their face.

Merrick saw me coming as I made my way down the hall and I saw that familiar smile creep up his square jaw. I smiled at him as I passed and decided to walk down to see Calvin. I hadn't seen him or Lana in a while and I wanted to check on them.

When I walked in they were both still in bed. I quietly tiptoed out and decided to visit Trudy who also hadn't been seen in a while. I swayed back and forth while walking at an incredibly slow pace but not minding. I wanted to keep the baby soothed and happy.

With triple the time it would normally take, I peeked in Trudy's room. She was asleep too. What was going on? It was eleven o'clock in the morning. Why was everyone still sleeping? Trudy never slept past the crack of dawn. Ever.

The realization hit me and I could only shake my head. Oh great. Now we had a bunker full of Specials and everybody was sleeping their days away because they were all developing these powers like Danny. Jeez. Could we ever get a break? Peace was like glazed donuts down here; didn't last long.

I slowly peeked at Katie and saw she was still sleeping. She had good reason to. I went to the kitchen and with one look at me they knew something was wrong.

"What is it, Sherry?" Merrick asked, coming to meet me in the doorway while Jeff took a chair in front of us.

"I think we have a problem. Where is everyone?" I asked, but didn't give them time to answer. "They are all sleeping. Like Danny."

They must've seen it, too. Jeff leaned his head on his chair back and closed his eyes tightly in frustration. Merrick let out a long sigh.

"Alright," Jeff said, pinching the bridge of his nose. "After lunch we've got to call a meeting. We need to see what's going on with everybody. Maybe some of the others, like Danny, have noticed something but were too scared to say anything. I can't believe this. None of them trusted us enough to tell us? We're their guardians!" He blew out a frustrated breath. "Maybe this could be a good thing. Let's just talk to everyone first."

I walked the baby into Katie and Paul's room. Paul was sprawled out asleep on the bed. I placed Sky in her crib, her closed eyes twitched with dreams and she made little grunts and stretches then she rested peacefully still.

Merrick seemed completely at a loss, staring at a spot on the wall blankly when I came back into the kitchen. He was sitting at the table so I came up behind him and massaged his shoulders trying my best to comfort him.

"Babe, it's ok. We'll handle this. Maybe I jumped to the wrong conclusion," I reasoned.

"No, you didn't. You're right and you know it. I just don't know what all this could mean. I don't like not knowing. How can I keep you and Danny safe when I don't even know what's going on in the next room?"

"We'll figure it out, we always do."

I came around his chair and sat down facing him in his lap. Jeff was gone so he must've went somewhere to think.

I held Merrick's face in my hands and pushed my lips to his, making him tighten his grip on my waist. I pulled back just a little, still feeling his breath on my face as I tried again to soothe him.

"Don't worry so much, Keeper. We'll be alright."

"Maybe you could take my mind off of it?" His voice was deep as he ran his fingers down my arm.

"Hmmm... How would I do that?" I said in a teasing tone, but I had goose bumps already.

"I can think of a few ways."

He pulled my face to his with a hand on the back of my neck and his lips took over mine hard. His tongue turned circles around mine and his fingers bit into my flesh.

I forgot for just a second that we were in the kitchen and then I was brought back to reality with the sound of shuffling footsteps. I pulled back and positioned myself in a more respectable manner on Merrick's lap. It was Danny.

"Morning again Mr. and Mrs...uh...what are you going be called?" he asked, looking at us suspiciously.

"Afternoon actually and don't ask." I laughed glancing at Merrick.

"So, should I ask what's going on? Jeff is freaking out down the hall."

"We don't think it's just you. The others are showing signs of it too. We're going to have a meeting about it once we can get everyone to wake up. Danny, I need you to tell everyone what's going on with you," Merrick answered, back to his glum thinking.

"What? You mean others might have these...powers too? Whoa."

"We'll see."

The Powers That Be
Chapter 29

With the meeting regarding the Specials and their powers called to order and everyone present and accounted for, Merrick and Jeff seemed to already know the answers before asking them. Something was happening and changing. The rules were no longer the same for either of our worlds.

Anxiously, the conversation began. I was prepared for an overkill of gasps and outbursts, but I was surprised once again. Mostly people just looked pensive, thoughtful and scared. Oh, no.

They *did* notice something different in themselves.

I reached over and rubbed my hand on Danny's back as he slumped over on the couch edge, elbows on his knees still looking exhausted.

Celeste wasn't sitting by him nor was she looking his way. She didn't seem too worried about him earlier either. Hmmm. I continued to look at her and noticed that she too looked tired and worried.

She refused to meet my eyes or look anywhere in our general direction. Margo sat on the couch next to her and she was more surprised than anyone by the news. Kay, who knew what was going on from the other Keeper's minds, was sitting on Celeste's other side looking like a death sentence was about to be carried out.

What was going on here? If people knew something weird was happening to them, why would they not say anything? Surely Celeste would have mentioned something to her clearly astonished mother. Why did Danny wait for me to check on him and force it out of him?

Jeff finished up and asked people to please speak up if they had noticed any changes. No one said an word. He then spoke for Danny to break the ice.

"Danny already advised us this morning of his change."

That got Celeste's attention. Her face jerked up in panic, her eyebrows arched up in surprise and mouth opened wide.

"What is it?" Celeste almost yelled, looking right at Danny. Then she quieted her tone and met his eyes with nothing but concern. "Danny, what is it?"

"I can...I can put thoughts into other's heads, tell them what to do. I did it to you and you didn't even notice."

Danny seemed sad and remorseful by his admission, like he had done something wrong.

Celeste got up and walked over to him to sit on his lap as he outstretched his arms for her. They had apparently been avoiding each other and trying to hide their new developments. She pressed her forehead to his and confessed.

"Mine is seeing. I can see anybody at any time if I just think about them. I can see what they are doing or saying and who's with them."

This turned a few heads and got me thinking.

Trudy stood next. She was sullen with eyes red and dark, eerie bags under them like she'd been crying. She didn't look at all like someone who had been sleeping nonstop for days.

"I...can hear things. I can hear things I'm not supposed to from far away. You guys talking in your rooms or anywhere in the bunker really, I can hear you. That's why I've been spending so much time in my room. I felt guilty for listening, but I don't know how to turn it off. I just bury my head in my pillow. I'm so sorry I didn't say anything sooner."

She put her face in her hands and started crying again. I was closest, so I stood grabbed her for a hug. She wrapped her arms around my shoulders and squeezed me so tight. I felt her shaking and it wasn't until then that I realized how scared she was.

"Trudy, it's ok. I don't think this is a bad thing," I said, reassuring her, but myself as well. "This could be just what we need. Think about it, this is more of an upper hand that we'll have on them when it comes down to having to fight them."

She jerked her head up.

"You think we'll have to fight? I just...I just assumed we'd stay down here forever...I see now that's stupid and naive. Of course we have to fight. I hope you're right, Sherry. I hope you are. Thank you, honey."

Then she leaned down and whispered in my ear.

"Don't worry, your secret's safe with me."

I gasped then smiled at her crookedly, understanding what she meant. She knew we were married as she knew everything.

Trudy let me go from our almost excruciatingly tight embrace and sat back down on one of the few couches. Merrick handed her a tissue then looked up at me.

You are the sweetest woman I've ever seen. Everyone here thinks so not just me so don't start saying I'm biased. I'm so proud of you. I love you, wife.

I rolled my eyes and smiled at him sheepishly.

After a long silence, it looked like no one else was ready to fess up so Jeff began to try to ease their minds.

"So, it looks like all the gifts are of the mind, nothing physical so far, just enhanced senses. Is there anyone else who would like to share?" Jeff looked around at the confused and drained faces.

No one came forward, but that may just be because there was no one else with powers. Maybe I would have reacted the same if it had happened to me. You never knew how you'd react until you were in the situation yourself but it still stung that they didn't trust us to know.

That night we headed out into the pitch black yard for some fresh air and exercise. It was breathtaking still after all this time seeing the stars so bright in the moonless sky.

Merrick, who lived somewhere out there in the stars, of course knew every constellation and had been slowly showing me their positions over our few night outings.

To me it was a mystery. I wanted to see them, I really did. I saw the obvious ones; Orion, the Big and Little Dipper but nothing else beyond grade school mystification.

It's like one of those 3-D pictures, a stereogram or stereograph, where you stare at the center and another picture comes into focus out of the gibberish.

Not once in my life had I gotten one of those to work for me, but I tried still. Merrick loved talking about it and I loved listening as we lay with our heads touching, side by side on a pallet in the sand.

"So there's Draco Dragon. See the long tail that curves around the Little Dipper?" he asked, willing me to see it and pointing.

"Hmmm. I want to say yes, I do, but I still really enjoy you telling me about it." I smiled at him and shrugged my shoulders, looking innocent.

He laughed and I felt him shake his head in mock disappointment before continuing.

"Ok, here's an easy one. Only six stars make up this one. Camelopardalis Giraffe. There, see it?"

"Yeah! Yeah I see it!" I yelled.

"Really?" He jumped up with excitement.

"No. No, not really." I laughed and I assumed he was scowling at me in the dark. "I'm sorry, I couldn't resist. Some of us can't be perfect know-it-alls like others can."

"Oh, yeah?"

He reached over me on our blanket where we were laying and pinned my wrists down, straddling me in his jeans. He pushed himself against me in the pitch dark and kissed me good and hard, interlacing our fingers.

The sand moved under the blanket beneath my shoulders and head giving it the feel of a bean bag. It was surprisingly comfortable and relaxing for someone being pressed into the ground.

I didn't mind, of course. Every kiss was deeper than the one before it, sweeter than the one before it. Ah, he was so good at it. How was he so good at it? He always knew just what to do to drive me the right amount of crazy.

He released my hands and moved his into my hair and neck, holding the sides of my face in his palms. He rubbed his nose back and forth against mine as he spoke.

"Mmm, you feel so good and real. Everything about you is better than I could have ever imagined. You know, I never told you this but...I used to dream about what your hair would smell like...and what your skin would feel like." He ran his hand down from my face down my neck. "And what color your eyes were up close."

"And? What's the conclusion?" I asked trying to keep the lightness of the mood up as we are in the public eye and I was one step away from ravaging the man.

"Well, your hair smells like vanilla and is always soft. I love the way the curls wrap around my fingers and how it lays across your shoulder at night. Your skin is..." he ran his fingers down my neck again giving me goose bumps and making me shiver, "soft and cool to the touch. It feels tingly when I touch you, like static or electricity."

I gasped, barely. Wow! He felt that, too?

"Your brown eyes are gorgeous and inviting. You always look people in the eye when they talk to you and when you look at me, I get completely lost in those eyes if I'm not paying attention," he whispered.

It took me a second to get my bearings back. How had he come to all those conclusions? That didn't sound like me at all. He left out a few things, like the bad stuff.

Ah, but him. He was the perfect one and he loved me.

"Wow, Merrick."

That was all I could say after a long pause of shock.

"Does that upset you? That I used to dream about you?"

"No! No. I just...it's not fair. You got to see me all those years and you know everything about me. Everything. I haven't even begun to scratch the surface of you."

"Honey, there's not much to know. I don't have any family. All my earthly experiences I've told you about. Well, the ones worth mentioning. We've even pondered favorite foods..." He smiled against my cheek.

"Yeah, I guess you're right. I love things about you too, but we don't have time to list them all," I said smiling for him to see in the dark. Trying desperately to stop the tears that were begging to be released. "Thank you, Merrick, for telling me that. I love that you...love things like that about me."

"I do. I always have."

I brought him to me for another kiss, wrapping my legs around his waist and my arms around his neck. It was a sweltering, tongue melding kiss. His sweet true words were searing through my restraint like a knife. Most everyone had gone back inside...

Wait! I was thinking like some crazed teenager! I was still so thankful I hadn't gone through that phase. The phase of making out with boys, sometimes random boys, in random places, being completely overwhelmed and helplessly in 'love'. More like in 'like'.

No wonder there was so many teen pregnancies and such. How could any sane person have some gorgeous guy over you, spouting his love and devotion while you kiss and not want to go further? I was glad I had the sense not to put myself in this position until now.

Soon I realized I may not need my restraint as I saw a flashlight beam creeping its way across the lawn.

With a quick sobering thought I realized that we were the only ones of our group left outside. I didn't hear anyone else talking or moving, only this lone light approaching us. Merrick noticed too and shh'ed me, quietly placing his fingers on my lips. The light was coming from around the front of the building not where we go, for fear of being seen.

We didn't move. They couldn't hear or see us. It wasn't one of ours or they wouldn't be so quiet and sneaky. Suddenly the beam came up from their path in the dirt and pointed straight to us. I gasped and heard Merrick's grunt in disapproval as he began to remove himself from our embrace.

I felt my blush growing redder and redder. Even if it was the enemy, I couldn't help myself. Whoever this was wasn't saying a word and they caught us laying on each other, on a blanket, under the stars, in the dark.

A clothed embrace, but an embarrassing one nonetheless, and they were just standing there, looking. Then the flashlight went out and I heard running and muffled noises and shuffling. Merrick leapt off me and I heard him grunt.

"Merrick, what? What's going on?"

"Don't worry, miss. We've got him," a strange man's deep voice assured me in the dark.

"What? Merrick? Let him go!" I yelled.

The flashlight beam returned, pointed directly in my eyes, blinding me and I threw my hand up to shield my face.

"Miss? Are you ok?" a young, scruffy voice asked.

"Yes, I'm all right, except for the fact that it sounded like you were hitting my husband."

They pointed the light on Merrick and there were three of them who had him on his knees, holding his arms back with a wad of cloth in his mouth. How in the world did they manage all of that so quickly? I gasped in anger.

"Ah! Let him go right now! What's the matter with you?"

I sprinted to him, took the cloth out of his mouth and he choked and coughed. His lip and nose were bleeding, too. I was fuming and it took everything I had to keep my composure and not slap someone right there.

I ran my hands over him to inspect, stopping on his face, using the cloth they had him gagged with to wipe away some of the blood. I turned back to the men who barged in half cocked and half brained. Nobody hurts Merrick, he was mine

"What the hell is wrong with you? Who are you? Answer me!" I yelled and cursed which I never do that, but I could not stop myself in my sudden anger.

The same voice, the first one, answered me. "We came because of the flyer. And we thought he was hurting you, miss."

"Why would you think that?" I asked but heard only silence. "Why?" I repeated louder.

"Well...he's a Keeper and you...aren't. We assumed... We have a..."

Serious problem. This guy couldn't think anymore because he was trying to get his lies straight.

"Wait, you said you came because of the flyer? For the store?" I asked suddenly intrigued.

"Yep." That young scruffy voice was back. "Our Keeper told us about it, so we decided to come on out and see what was up. Our own, uh, hideout wasn't working out that well anymore so..."

Something more important than that springs back to my memory.

"Merrick? Are you ok?" I asked, turning, remembering him in my arms and hating that fact that I couldn't see a thing since they pointed the flashlight away.

"Yeah, I'm fine. Let's take them downstairs. We can get better...acquainted." He sounded peeved and I didn't blame him. I was, too. Who just started beating up on total strangers? "Come on, if you'll let me hold that flashlight, I'll lead the way," he finished through clenched teeth.

Suddenly we heard a screeching from above. A very familiar screeching to me. I froze remembering the pain as if it was happening right then, every tear and scratch, every kick through the dirt with its hideous claws. I remembered Merrick's face after rescuing me, twisted in pain and the days of recovery and nightmares. The Marker.

Wait- it was happening then, the pain, just like before. It wasn't just a memory as I fell down in the dirt grabbing my shoulder and gasping. Merrick grabbed my arms and pulled me up and held me up against him. I could hear other screams and shuffling, but couldn't see the source. I could only hope the Marker hadn't gotten someone, even though I was still furious with them for attacking Merrick.

Merrick didn't ask me what was wrong, he just understood. When you encountered a Marker, just like with Bobby when he was marked with the badge, the pain returned.

I was starting to understand these things more without Merrick's explanation. Pretty much, if they could come back to get you for more when you thought they were done with you, they would.

I stumbled and tripped, falling to my knees. Merrick scooped me up into his arms and carried me against him as he ran still guiding the rest of them in with us.

The bouncing flashlight beam headed towards the open door to the back of the store. I felt Merrick shaking as we make our way through the door. The others follow us into the store room as well. Slamming the door we could still hear the Marker outside, but it soon faded and a few grateful sighs were let loose.

Once inside, he put me down and reached over, tugging my arm up easily to look at the scar. When I glanced down I did a double take. The scar was almost glowing red. Not like a light, but like a serious shade of embarrassment red was all around my entire shoulder and the mark itself was bright and angry.

Merrick gave me that pained, knowing face. I heard a low gasp from across the room making me look over. One of the men had seen my mark and didn't look thrilled about it. I assumed he was the Keeper and knew what it was he was looking at.

"Are you ok?" Merrick asked me, framing my face easily in both hands in front of what my quick head count took in as five strangers.

"Yeah. It hurt like...with Bobby looking at me," I said, trying to catch my breath.

"Yeah, I know."

"Will the Marker just stay out there all night?"

"They're mindless, remember? It'll leave if it's not gone already. Don't worry about it. Come on."

He put his protective arm around my waist and began towing me again through the group of our new...uh...friends over to the trap door.

Moving the shelf he pulled it up and slowly went down the steps.

Once at the bottom he stopped and didn't let them come any further. I grabbed a tissue from the top of the piano and handed it to Merrick for his nose. Then he spoke to them.

"Sister? I'm not sure why you attacked me out there, but...I'm sure there's a good reason."

The Keeper came out and greeted Merrick before speaking. I was wrong.

The woman was the Keeper.

"Brother. Yes, I am sorry about these trigger happy males. We've had a pretty hard couple of days." She looked grim and looked around at her charges.

"Why did you attack me?" Merrick asked the man standing in front.

"We thought you were hurting her. Racine saw you in the dark and said you were a Keeper but...you were kissing her...I've never heard of that. I assumed the worst thing, I'm sorry."

"Ok. So Keepers won't kiss girls, but we'll rape them? Hmmm...that's some shaky logic."

Merrick was trying to remain calm, but the Marker had shaken him up and the bloody nose didn't help.

"I am sorry," the man said and then looked at me, almost for help it looked like. I snorted. I didn't want to save him. Merrick's nose was still bleeding. "We thought we were helping you. We came all the way from Tulsa and saw your flyer the second day we were here. Perfect timing." He smiled at me apologetically and I finally obliged by smiling back and nodding.

"Ok," Merrick started as Jeff and some of the others came around the corner to the stairs, wide eyed. "Well, I'm Merrick, a Keeper, and this is Sherry, my wife." I beamed because he said it with no hesitation whatsoever.

I heard gasps from behind us from the ones who didn't know. I squinted and turned to see Trudy, Katie, Celeste and Paul. Katie jumped over to me throwing her arms around me.

"Oh, Sherry! I'm so happy for you! Why didn't you say anything?"

"Yeah. Seriously!" Celeste boob hugged me and released me. "I mean, we're practically sisters and you didn't tell me!"

She winked at me when she finished to let me know she had kept our secret.

Then Trudy, who also knew but was now allowed to know, hugged me. Trudy's hugs were intense and tight. She rocked me back and forth as I tried to squeeze out an answer for Katie and Celeste.

"I really can't even remember why we didn't tell you. We just...didn't want any drama I guess. I'm sorry. We should've said something."

I immediately remembered something else. I knew the new Keeper would be just as awed as the others and start searching Merrick's mind for answers.

"Hey you." I pointed at her playfully, bashfully turning red. "I'm warning you if go looking in his head for answers, you're going to find...more than that." The red burned in my cheeks and I bit my lower lip. "Just stay out of his head, ok," I said as I turned back to Merrick to inspect his nose and lip, trying to hide my smile of embarrassment.

Everyone chuckled but the new group was still wary looking. I was too tired and excited about the newbies to be irked anymore. It was just common knowledge that people freaked out about the concept of a Keeper and a human in a relationship. I guessed that was what happened when you were one of a kind.

"Ok, will do," Racine said as she came around to hug Jeff who had come up behind us, but she still continued to talk to Merrick, looking at the hand around my waist. "I, of course, am curious about this Merrick. How can this be? I mean...I'm sorry. Forget I asked. It's really great to meet you Sherry and all of you. We've traveled far and haven't had very much luck on the way. The Markers are becoming more problematic. More of them appear every night it seems. We started out in Tulsa with thirteen, us five are all that's left."

Wow. It just didn't seem right. They must've been on the move the whole time. From the looks on their faces the wounds were still fresh. One of the young men who looked about nineteen or twenty years old even turned his head away from us, but not before I saw the tears he was trying to hide on his cheek. It broke my heart and my constant need to comfort took over.

We'd had such a big group for so long it just seemed fallible to think about actually losing people. I stepped forward over to him and put my hand on his arm.

"I'm really sorry," I told him but before I could say anything else he wrapped his arms around my waist and cried silently into my neck.

I was shocked at first but eventually rubbed his back to comfort him and held him while the others started to converse around us. I could only imagine what this group had been through. When I looked them up and down I saw the battle scars, scrapes, bruises and old healed wounds.

Then I saw a big gash on one of the many legs. Three long gashes were next to each other and they were glowing red. I gasped quietly and looked up to meet the face. He saw me looking at it and understood my surprise. He was the one who saw Merrick looking at my Mark earlier. He nodded an 'I know' gesture and smiled a little pained smile.

I closed my eyes and shook my head back and forth trying to force out the memory of my attack and the painful burning. I'd definitely have to talk to him later.

The guy clutching me told me about his family dying as we eventually moved to sit on the steps together. I kept my arm around him as he just seemed to need the contact. He was all that was left of his family.

After a while, we all convened in the commons room and I got drinks for everyone and sandwiches for the newbies which they practically inhaled and even had seconds. Jeff and Merrick introduced our group and Racine introduced theirs. She was the only female in her bunch.

First was Josh, a Special, the young blonde jock looking guy who so needed a hug from me. He started out with his mother, father, and younger brother in Tulsa. He was all that was left, losing them all within three weeks of each other, the last one being a few days ago. No wonder he was so upset. Poor guy.

Racine was his Keeper and his gift was that he could see through walls and objects. He was the only one of the newbies to have a gift.

Next was my older, scruffy, balding rescuer, Aaron. He lost his wife, a Special, almost a year ago. Then Michael or Mike, a Special who hadn't lost anyone because he didn't have any family and never married. Thank God for small favors in times like this but he did lose his Keeper.

Last was Miguel who lost his wife somewhere along the way. He was the one with the Marker scar and I made a mental note to speak to him immediately. He wasn't a Special nor had his wife been. They just banded with the group to escape. He spoke with an Australian accent which was a refreshing change from the northern accent of most of the people stuck down here, with the exception of Trudy and her lovely 'Paula Deen' speak, as I called it.

Their story was that they didn't have a set hideout because there wasn't anywhere to go really. They looked and looked for something more permanent but nothing ever panned out with that many people all together. Splitting up wasn't an option. The more they moved the more people they lost, their numbers dwindling.

They came this way because they were told by the news reports that the Markers weren't as significant as over in the middle West part of the country. Little did they know they came right into the Taker's territory. All in all they lost three Keepers. The rest were family, a couple Specials and some were just people they had found that hadn't been affected by the Lighters lies yet.

The mood was somber and reflective even though we were all glad they were here and could finally be safe. Now they needed to just wait for relief to set in. I was happy that my idea worked. Now we knew that it would work and others would probably start making their way to us.

We'd have to start working on a new hall soon. Jeff had an idea about going deeper down instead of extending the hall further. Whatever the outcome, we'd had to make room. An army we would soon have and need.

Welcome To The Family
Chapter 30

So it would be common knowledge that no one would be venturing out at night any longer. Unfortunately, that was when most of the people seeking refuge with us would travel to keep prying eyes off the place. At least I would hope they would know to be discreet.

The newbies got settled into some of the new rooms and I'd never seen a group more grateful for a closet living space. After sleeping in the dirt or whatever you could find, you'd be pretty grateful for anything.

We tried to get better acquainted with them which wasn't hard because they were all very talkative and thankful to us. And they had plenty of stories which most were not so pleasant and I was glad that our crew knew what tactful questions to ask and what not to.

These five had seen more action, pain, loss, and trickery than all the rest of us put together. I had a feeling that every person that walked through our trap door would have a similar experience and story. It made me feel sad and guilty for being relatively safe this whole time.

A cold week passed. The guys started work on the hall again, putting in the bathrooms and stringing up lights. There was still no air duct down there but it was winter so that project could wait. There weren't too many luxuries being added, only two toilets and showers. They wouldn't even have mirrors or shelves, just bare necessities.

Once again I was stuck going to bed by myself and trying to keep busy, with Merrick working down the hall all day without me.

The Specials who had started gaining powers were feeling better and not sleeping so much. They even looked better and more energized. I spent my days with them, as did a lot of us, showing them the ropes of living in the bunker like how to perform the chores and tell them where everything was and went.

We enjoyed talking to them. There were all very down to earth and not one of them came on to me, so I was thrilled about that although Josh had definitely taken to me. It was a sister kind of way even though he was a year older than me. I could tell there was absolutely no attraction there, the guy just needed someone because he'd lost everyone else.

I didn't mind. He was a lean and muscular jock type and it was off in my mind for him to be so meek. Danny even seemed to get a little jealous which I thought was hilarious and ludicrous. I mean, he didn't get upset about Ryan or Jeff. The poor guy just lost everything and everyone before his life had even gotten started. At least Danny still had me and I had him.

I liked them, especially Miguel. He was a lean, wiry, tan, black haired man. He had been attacked by the Marker one night not long after me. He was the first in their group to be attacked by one, but not the last. There was another one after him but he didn't make it.

He said he had actually been picked up and carried away before being scratched and let go to fall to the ground. From his description his recovery had been much worse than mine because they had no meds to make him sleep. It hurt me to even think about it, but Miguel just laughed and said 'you can't hang on to the past and you certainly can't throw a wobbly every time something happens that you don't like'. Once I found out what a wobbly was, a fit, I agreed with him. Especially in times like this when our future was so uncertain.

They brought some stuff and skills with them. A car for one. Somehow they had all managed to cram into an old pea soup colored Gremlin. One of them had a portable DVD player with about five discs to his collection and another one had a medicine cabinet in his backpack with every kind of antibiotic and painkiller you could think of.

Apparently, they had gone overboard since Miguel's run in with the Marker and refused to let that happen again so they raided a walk-in clinic. That would come in handy I knew.

Miguel was a martial arts instructor with his own studio in California, which was where he met his wife. He could show us all some basic training moves. We were going to need it.

Mike was a construction contract worker, building basements for new construction homes. What were the odds of that? He would be very useful in our hall expansion.

I did explain to them about mine and Merrick's relationship. I told them that I loved him and he loved me and that was all they needed to know and we had eloped. Racine seemed the most interested in it, but respected my tight lip decision. Knowing Jeff, he'd probably fill her in eventually and I knew she wouldn't stay out of Merrick's head forever.

And Jeff. Jeff was spending even more time with Marissa. You would think he'd want to be talking with the new Keepers and being his normal Keeper self, but no. I even saw them once locked in one of those stare gazes with the slow spreading grins that followed.

Hey, I was all for it. As I stated before, it would be nice not to be the only freak show down here.

And Jeff was so good natured and kind that any human girl would be lucky to have him. I guessed he had worked out his problems with Marissa and her being a Muse and maybe even his disagreeable thoughts about human interactions.

Marissa seemed to be different that when she first came. She fixed her hair now which she really didn't worry about before. I'd seen her tucking her hair behind her ears and smiling while she talked to him.

I refused to acknowledge it any further or even encourage the development. The minute they got a whiff of my suspicion they'd both back off and that would be that.

The purpose of that was that Jeff did not want to hear crap off Merrick for his obvious distaste of our relationship in the beginning and the scrutiny that came from our fellow cave dwellers for such an act. I'd just keep my eyes and ears off and let them figure it out in their own.

The Keepers thought it would be prudent for the Specials to start practicing their new powers and learning to be comfortable and more controlling of them. So some of the Keepers started holding 'classes' which were really just sessions where they all sat around together and practiced on each other.

It was apparent, though none of us would voice it, that there was a reason for these gifts. That we'd need them one day, which meant things were going to get worse before they got better and we'd have to fight.

Miguel was going to teach all us humans basic karate and self defense and we'd already had one lesson. It was amazing. I couldn't wait until I could chop wood in half and pretend it was a Lighters arm. Not really, but I couldn't wait to not be helpless anymore.

Trudy, the recluse, started coming out more often and Calvin and his mom were interacting with everyone else more. Calvin was growing up before our eyes.

When they were young it was amazing to watch them literally have a growth spurt and be inches taller in a couple weeks. I could see Calvin's shirts were starting to be a little snug and short on him.

I continued with my sign language with Lana as did I still teach Calvin some piano every now and then. The hall was coming along nicely and quickly with more hands available. The men worked hard while the rest of us stayed and practiced our boredom.

There were only so many times you could play spoons before enough was enough. I couldn't wait to have my husband back. *My Husband.*

311

After two weeks with our new comrades and no new visitors showing up I figured we needed to go back out and replace our flyers at all the locations.

We decided to use the same game plan as before. Divide and conquer and quickly. Three teams, one flyer, many locations to litter, and it was less conspicuous when there was only two people as opposed to six or more. There needed to be another food run as well so it was settled.

Merrick refused to let me return to the grocery store since the Lighter or Taker or whatever it was had seen my face. Though I didn't see why that mattered, I didn't argue because I didn't want to see the Taker anyway.

Miguel and Jeff decided to be the food run mates, as Miguel put it. We all started out that morning after a hardy Trudy breakfast.

She made them a mile long grocery list and went back with the other Specials to practice while we are gone. Josh hugged me and told me to be careful as did Danny who squeezed me with over exaggerated emphasis. I couldn't help but laugh watching Merrick's eyebrow quirk and a confused face on.

After all the 'be careful's and 'goodbye's we went topside. We decided to take the Jeep letting someone else take Phillip's El Camino he'd left behind. I was definitely not ready to ride in his car.

I leaned against the Jeep waiting for Merrick to come back out. We forgot to get the most important thing before we left. The flyer. As I waited I rested my forehead on the passenger window and thought about all the things that had transpired these past months. It was unbelievable. Would life ever have a sense of normalcy again?

Then I heard Phillip. Yes, Phillip.

"Hello, Sherry."

I gasped but when I turned I saw nothing or no one. I looked all around, peeking under the Jeep and the other side, spinning and breathing heavy in fright. Nothing. Alright, Sherry, calm down. I realized this is the first time I'd been alone since the attack except for my brief shower that next day. That was why I was freaking out. Ok. Ok. Calm down.

"Sherry. I've missed you."

Oh, God, no!

"What? Phillip?"

"Sherry, I need you to come to me. Come to us."

I heard him but couldn't see him. It was like he was in my head instead of me hearing him out loud. What the heck! How could he do that?

"Where are you?"

"I'm where I'm supposed to be, where we're supposed to be. Come to me,

Sherry. All you have to do is follow me. You can find me."

Phillip was cryptic and pissing me off.

"Listen, Phillip. Get out of my head. I don't know what you're trying to do, but I'm not interested."

"I can give you things beyond your wildest dreams. I'm special now. More special than your pathetic excuse for Specials. I'm a God."

"Hmmm. Somehow, I doubt the real God would appreciate that remark. Leave me alone," I barked out the order though my voice was shaking.

"We're coming for you."

"What?" I yelled.

"Sherry?" Merrick asked coming around the Jeep looking quizzical.

"Merrick," I breathed in relief, hand flying to my chest, wondering if I should bring up my schitzo encounter with Phillip. "How long have you been standing there? You scared me."

"Long enough to hear you. Who are you talking to...and why do you look like you don't want to tell me?"

"Phillip." Deep breath. "Phillip was here, well, in my head. He was talking to me in my head."

"Phillip was talking to you?"

"He was saying...he's coming for me," I said as scared tears strained my voice making it shake even more.

Merrick crossed the distance between us and pulled me to him. I wrapped my arms around his neck like there was safety there as he lifted my feet from the ground in a safe embrace. Safety from the feelings flooding back to me and the thought that I didn't have control of what went on in my own head anymore.

"How could he do that, Merrick? How could he be in my head? He wasn't a Special."

"I don't know, baby. I don't know." He let me down and took my face in his hands. "We'll talk to Jeff when we come back, ok? I promise we'll figure it out. Apparently there aren't rules for *anyone* anymore. Don't worry, I will keep you safe."

He kissed me with the soft reassurance of his promise, but it wasn't good enough for me. I pulled him closer to me with his collar, wanting to be engulfed in him and completely devoid of anything Phillip.

The ride was quiet. I could tell the wheels in Merrick's mind were turning. He was freaked but didn't want me to know. How could a human speak to someone's mind when he wasn't a Special. He shouldn't be able to have a gift. I pushed it aside to focus on our task.

I reached over and peeked behind Merrick's ear at the cover up job I'd done.

It was much better this time. He shivered and I giggled at how I could still drive him crazy. I leaned over to rest on his shoulder and enjoyed the remainder of the silent ride. Silence wasn't my favorite thing, but if Phillip wasn't in my head, it was golden.

The same young guy was behind the counter at the print shop. He took the flyer to make my two thousand copies and I boasted about how I'd gotten married since the last time I was there but that didn't seem to interest him in the least.

Retrieving the copies and paying for them I wondered when our money was going to run out. And then what would we do? Yet another thing that was inevitable yet no one wanted to discuss it.

When we pulled into the coffee shop parking lot, I grabbed some flyers from the huge stack and start to open my car door.

Merrick stopped me with a hand on my arm. He took the flyers from me and laid them on the dash.

"Are you ok, honey?" he asked me, his face full of concern.

"Yeah. Why?"

"Well, you're so quiet. I thought that you might be upset about Phillip."

"Well, I'm not thrilled...but what am I going to do about it?"

"Most women would crumple under what you've been through lately."

"I want to sometimes," I admitted softly, "but I'm afraid I don't get to have that luxury. What with the world under invasion and all." I smiled at him to let him see my light mood.

"Ok, but just remember that I'm here. You don't have to be a stone all the time, not with me." He refused to leave his gaze from mine until I understood and nodded.

He reached over to run his fingers through my curls.

"Thanks, babe. I'm fine, I promise. As long as he doesn't do it again, and we can figure this all out."

"I promise you that I won't stop until I do. Remember, don't think about home or Danny. Love you and hurry."

"Ok. Love you, too, Finch," I said as I grabbed the stack of flyers from the dash, kissed him quickly and exited the car, his quiet laughter following me from the open window.

The usual places were pretty packed; the truck stop, the gym, the coffee shop, diner. I tried to pay attention while I was in there, walking among all of them, trying to feel out who could possible be on our side.

In every establishment the television was on and the news cast was spewing the Lighters lies. People weren't really even engaging in conversation that much, just glued to the tube.

How weird that these people didn't think it strange that they all wanted to sit around and watch the news all day, even the older kids. What in the world could the news be talking about for 24 hours a day anyway? I didn't listen though because Merrick told me not to.

Though I was so curious and thought it could be helpful, I had learned it was best to always listen to Merrick.

"Hi, there. Can I leave some of these flyers here on the counter for your customers. I'm advertising my store out off the interstate," I asked the young, very nice looking non-threatening guy behind the counter.

He had a small, silver lip ring through his bottom lip and a tattoo on his arm, some military thing that I couldn't see full on, and a brown leather band around his wrist.

"Why bother when Crandle is starting up the need warehouses soon?"

"I'm sorry, who? What?"

"Crandle? The guy who's going to save us from all this mess. Where have you been lady? Under a rock?" He smiled, but I could tell he was suspicious.

"Kind of. What's a need warehouse?"

"Well, we aren't going to have grocery stores and places like this anymore. He's starting warehouses where we can go and get whatever we need for free. Pretty great, huh?"

"Yeah, great." I tried to keep my face straight, but all I was thinking was that this would be my misfit clan's demise. "So, how long before that happens?"

"Why don't you go sit over there and watch the news and see for yourself?" he suggested and toyed with his lip ring with his tongue.

"Well...uh, I'm kind of in a hurry. I've got some more errands to run." I started to slowly back away.

"Why won't you watch?" he whispered to me, grabbing my wrist gently and leaning towards me across the counter.

I tried not to panic or cause a scene, tried to be nonchalant and easygoing. Looking from side to side I saw no one was even paying us any attention.

"I'm just in a hurry right now. I'm sure you can understand that," I said smiling the sweetest smile I could plaster on my face.

"I think you should come with me. Right now," he whispered harshly and gripping my wrist tighter.

All the blood drained from my face and I knew there was no way out. Oh, God, I was taking too long and Merrick would come in looking for me and then we'd have even bigger problems.

I couldn't jerk away and run. There were too many of them. What should I do? So I decided to follow him as he guided my shaking wrist in his hand down the length of the counter to the opening.

He then pulled me closer to him placing me in front and pushed me with his hands on my back to the back room and through the door to the stock room.

Once inside he closed the door and pushed me against the wall. He grabbed my hands and pulled them over my head as Merrick had done the first day we met. He started searching my body with his free hand for a badge.

"You're not going to find one," I whispered, too scared to do anything else as his hand slid over my upper thigh a little too slowly for my married taste.

He stopped moving, not removing his hand, and looked me in the eyes, cocking his head. He was so close, if I breathed too heavy our faces would touch.

"Oh, yeah? What is it that I'm looking for?" he asked condescendingly.

"I'm not marked by them. That's what you're looking for isn't it? A badge. Well, I don't have one and I'd appreciate it if you'd remove your hand from my thigh," I said trying not to show too much emotion, but my breathlessness was betraying me.

He slowly slid his hand away but kept me held against the wall.

"What are you in here snooping for?" he asked without removing his gaze, even without blinking.

"Why would I be snooping? I was just handing out flyers for my store."

He banged his free fist on the wall by my head loud and forcefully. His light brown hair was very short and I wondered what with his tattoo and all if he'd been in the military because he certainly acted like he had authority.

"Don't lie to me. Everyone and their mother has heard of the need warehouses. You would know that your flyers are useless...if...you watched TV or came to town very often." His eyes changed to something else as he spoke, not suspicion but recognition.

"I don't like TV and I get by fine with my store. I don't *need* anything else. What exactly is it that you think I'm trying to do? I'm...not one of *them*," I over emphasized the word 'them' trying to get him to see what I meant.

"I'm...I hope you're telling me the truth, lady," he whispered and then blew out a long breath. "I'm not one of them either. I'm part of the...resistance, as corny as that sounds." He rolled his eyes. "I live with a couple others like me and also with a...Keeper." He waited to see how I'd react to that word, which I did by gasping slightly and unintentionally, eyes going wide.

He was telling me the truth and must have seen that my intentions weren't hostile because he continued.

"We live in a cabin back in the hills not very far from here but few people go up there because it's so steep and windy. Now, tell me who the heck *you* are?"

Before I could speak, someone came through the door, pushing the guy into me further...and then he was kissing me.

At first I thought he just got knocked into me by accident, but then I realized it was not an accident. Tongue usually wasn't involved in accidental kissings.

I tried to struggle but he just pressed harder into me and brought my hands down to hold them in between us. He was warm, but not as warm as Merrick and he tasted sweet like cinnamon rolls. I could tell he'd kissed and been kissed quite a bit from his obvious skill. His body was hard and muscular and I instantly felt regret for making all these conclusions within the few seconds he'd been kissing me.

I heard the intruder speak.

"Woops. Sorry, Cain."

And then he was gone and 'Cain' released me slightly, pulling back far enough to see my face, which I was sure was anything but pleased. I struggled for breath with the sudden kiss and proximity of my attacker but his blue green eyes were bright and his breathing was crazy too. If my hands were free, I wasn't sure what I would have done. Touch my lips in awkward awe or slap him.

"Sorry," he said breathlessly and relieved. "It was all I could think of at the moment." He smiled and looked a mixture of embarrassed and cocky and I had no idea what to think. "They can't know you're here."

"Kissing me? That's all you could think of?" I blew out an exasperated breath as he shrugged sheepishly. "So, you're really not one of them, huh?" I said but I knew the truth, that he wasn't one of them and that he also believed that his kissing me was his only option for the situation.

"If I were, honey, you'd be dead."

"No one gets to call me honey but my husband," I said despairingly, once again trying to extract myself from his grasp.

"Dang. All the good resistance girls are taken."

He smiled trying to lighten the tense mood with a joke, but I was still flustered, even as he let me go and stepped back.

"Look, my husband is outside right now. He'll come in any minute if I don't get back to him soon and that'll blow everything."

"He would blend in just like you did, for a few minutes anyway. It'll be ok but let's go. I want to show my family. You go first and I'll follow you out to him. I'd love nothing more than to meet more of us."

He was sincere and I knew how he felt. Though I was extremely upset with him, and flustered about the kiss, I was still ecstatic at the idea of others still to meet like us.

"Ok. I'm Sherry by the way."

"Cain. Nice to meet you, Sherry," he said reaching out a hand to shake and smiling brightly.

"Yeah, I got that." I laughed as did he, finally giving him some semblance of the forgiveness he was looking for. "Follow me."

"Hey." He grabbed my arm gently as he spoke. "Don't run, ok? I...*we* need you. We all need to stick together."

"I wouldn't run," I said as I caught his sea green gaze to let him see that I was serious.

I turned and made my way out. The possibilities of there being even more people out there and I was about to meet them was overwhelming. Questions of this new kissing stranger were circling too. How was he able to be around the TV's and not be bothered by it? How did he work and no one notice that he wasn't affected? Why had he kissed me and been so convincing about it?

I led him to the car where hopefully my husband was still there waiting patiently for me.

THE END FOR A WHILE.

Thank you to my God and my family for supporting me through my endeavors of writing. It was a whim one day that has turned into this thing that I love. Thank you all who have helped me and to the ones who purchase my books, I hope you enjoy reading it as much as I enjoyed writing it.
Thank you!

the sequels in the collide series, uprising, catalyst, and revolution.

Please feel free to Contact Shelly at the following avenues.

www.facebook.com/shellycranefanpage
www.twitter.com/authshellycrane
www.shellycrane.blogspot.com

Shelly is a bestselling YA author from a small town in Georgia and loves everything about the south. She is wife to a fantastical husband and stay at home mom to two boisterous and mischievous boys who keep her on her toes. They currently reside in everywhere USA as they happily travel all over with her husband's job. She loves to spend time with her family, binge on candy corn, go out to eat at new restaurants, buy paperbacks at little bookstores, site see in the new areas they travel to, listen to music everywhere and also LOVES to read.

Her own books happen by accident and she revels in the writing and imagination process. She doesn't go anywhere without her notepad for fear of an idea creeping up and not being able to write it down immediately, even in the middle of the night, where her best ideas are born.

Shelly's website:
www.shellycrane.blogspot.com

Shelly's other series

Significance Series

Devour Series

Stealing Grace Series

Wide Awake

Smash Into You

Collide - Shelly Crane

5137225R00173

Made in the USA
San Bernardino, CA
24 October 2013